BLOOD ROSES

By Chelsea Quinn Yarbro from Tom Doherty Associates

BLOOD ROSES

A NOVEL OF SAINT-GERMAIN

Chelsea Quinn Yarbro

TOR®

A TOM DOHERTY ASSOCIATES BOOK
NEW YORK

BLOOD ROSES

This book is printed on acid-free paper.

A Tor Book
Published by Tom Doherty Associates, Inc.
175 Fifth Avenue
New York, NY 10010

Tor Books on the World Wide Web:
http://www.tor.com

Tor® is a registered trademark of Tom Doherty Associates, Inc.

Library of Congress Cataloging-in-Publication Data

Yarbro, Chelsea Quinn.
    Blood roses / Chelsea Quinn Yarbro.—1st ed.
       p.   cm.
    "A Tom Doherty Associates book."
    ISBN 0-312-86529-5 (alk paper)
    I. Title.
    PS3575.A7B58   1998
    813'.54—dc21   98-23671
                                    CIP

First Edition: October 1998

Printed in the United States of America

0 9 8 7 6 5 4 3 2 1

for

Gahan Wilson

affectionately
and
on behalf of the Count

"... these Swellings be ... Tokens of the Black Plague the which the French do sometime call Blood Roses. ..."

Anonymous fifteenth-century English broadsheet

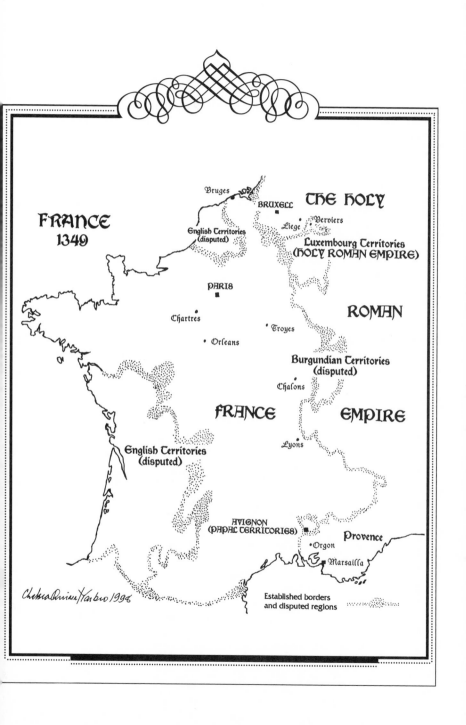

FRANCE
1349

THE HOLY

ROMAN

EMPIRE

Bruges

BRUXELL

English Territories
(disputed)

Liege

Verviers

Luxembourg Territories
(HOLY ROMAN EMPIRE)

PARIS

Chartres

Troyes

Orleans

Burgundian Territories
(disputed)

Chalons

FRANCE

English Territories
(disputed)

Lyons

AVIGNON
(PAPAL TERRITORIES)

Provence

Orgon

Marsailla

Chelsea Quinn Yarbro 1998

Established borders
and disputed regions

Author's Notes

At the height of the Medieval period in Europe, the feudal system perpetuated a social order that assumed continuing stability in spite of wars and religious turmoil, and for a long time, it worked fairly well. But in the middle of the fourteenth century, a catastrophe hit Europe. Its magnitude was far beyond any social provisions to accommodate, and in the space of four years, the apparently unchangeable order was almost destroyed; in a very real sense, the first stirrings of the Renaissance began as a direct result of the devastation of the epidemics of the late Middle Ages. Beginning in 1348, Bubonic Plague ravaged Europe, starting in Sicily, Sardinia, and Corsica and moving north from the port of Marseilles in France, and spreading throughout Italy from Rome and Florence. In three years, it went through France, Switzerland, the Lowlands, Germany, and into Britain. The loss of life was staggering. In the three epidemics between 1347 and 1383, approximately 33 percent of the population died. The first epidemic was by far the most severe, with death tolls higher than any at that time resulting from war. And there was a war going on. France and England were locked in what is called the Hundred Years War (because it lasted 116 years). The Plague brought it to a temporary halt while it spread through the regions where the fighting had been the most concentrated.

Medieval culture was not equipped to deal with such comprehensive calamity: the social system, based on the immutability of social "place" could not withstand the erosion of the population and was left in shambles. Political and civil institutions thought to be indestructible as religious institutions came to pieces and economies underwent upheavals of an unparalleled nature. Commerce was almost entirely redefined in the four years of the Black Plague. Travel had always been dangerous what with poor communications, unmaintained roads, bandits, and regional fighting, but with the coming of the Plague, travel took on an additional risk—that of bringing the miasma of disease. Merchants and other traditional travelers—with the exceptions of players, troubadours, and religious—found themselves thrown into prison or worse if a region was sufficiently alarmed.

The newly powerful Hanseatic League, an association of the central merchants' towns in northern Germany but trading as far away as the Mediterranean and Russia, was all but crippled for two crucial years due to fear of Plague in the very ports where the League was gaining a foothold.

At the end of the first epidemic, the Hanseatic League was able to resume activities without any real organized competition and as a result assumed a preeminent position in northern European maritime trade; the Hanseatic League became one of the most remarkable mercantile empires in the Medieval world.

Merchants were not the only ones at risk. Scholars, while not regarded with the same suspicions as merchants, could be the target of savage acts if the populace was frightened enough. Persons with any knowledge of medicine—such as that was in the fourteenth century—were all but worshiped unless their treatments failed. Then they were vilified if they were lucky and were killed if they were not. Physicians usually recommended treatment and left town, and not for the sole purpose of avoiding the Plague; they did not want to deal with dissatisfied patients. Religious persons—pilgrims, monks, and such—were considered good omens and were encouraged in their travels. The other group of habitual travelers who were not subjected to such arbitrary ferocity was entertainers; players, jongleurs, and troubadours continued their travels from town to castle to village almost unimpeded.

As increasingly large numbers of travelers made their ways along the roads and lanes of Europe, they became a problem in their own right. Displaced persons and refugees were everywhere after 1349, creating a compelled disruption of the population that was not to be equaled until World War One. With cities devastated and towns depopulated, the rare survivors usually had no choice but to leave the ruin behind them or face certain starvation. Serfs and peasants were dead and the land was unworked; those few who were spared were unwilling to transport food into Plague regions. Most of Europe at that time was a jumble of fiefdoms, principalities, duchies, counties, vidamies, and other semi-autonomous states; each one developed its own ways of dealing with the Plague and those escaping the Plague, most of which were arbitrary and severe. Once Plague approached a region, all semblance of vassalage obligations ended. Dread of Plague overruled all other considerations.

Survivors often profited; estates once divided among half a dozen or more heirs now ended up in the hands of far fewer. Cadet branches of great families rose to primary positions as the Plague claimed their relatives. Among peasants, land began to consolidate into significant holdings as those entitled to it died. For the next twenty years after the first Plague epidemic, relatives—or those claiming to be relatives—of merchants, landholders, and minor nobles continued to take into possession inheritances swollen in value by the dearth of surviving heirs.

Depleted and displaced populations were not the only challenge to the status quo. Social uprisings occurred in many parts of Europe, caused directly or indirectly by the Plague and the resultant social disruption. Sicily, the areas around Barcelona, the Central Massif of France, the region to the north of Paris, and Flanders were particularly hard-hit by major disruptions at this time. Penitential movements sprang up, many of them not only anti–civil authority, but anti-clerical as well. Towns, convents, castles, and monasteries were razed by penitential mobs, accomplishing what the Plague had not done: laying waste to the country.

The Church might have been able to provide some continuity during these turbulent years, but the Church was fatally divided, with the Holy Roman Emperor holding sway in Italy, whose principal followers were in Germany, northern Italy, England, the Venetian Empire, Scandinavia, and Portugal; and the Pope, Clement VI, in Avignon, whose followers were concentrated in France, the Low Countries, Sicily, Sardinia, southern Italy, and Spain. When Gregory XI returned the papacy to Rome in 1377, the situation worsened; two papacies were established and the rivalry between them continued for four decades. Any chance of providing united assistance or extending sanctuary to refugees was ignored as the two courts, Papal and Imperial, continued their rivalry, each insisting the Plague was brought about by the other. By the time the enormity of the tragedy was recognized, it was far too late for any program to be established to provide succor for those left homeless and desperate; too much of the social structure was in disarray to adapt to the new demands the epidemic imposed. The intensely political agendas of the Church became enmeshed with the social catastrophe that had overtaken Europe.

Matters were not helped by what passed for public health measures of the period. The standard quarantine precautions in cities were rudimentary and inadequate: anytime one member of a household showed symptoms of Plague, everyone in the house was boarded up inside the house, which served to increase the death rate significantly. The usual explanations of the cause of the Plague were 1) the wells were poisoned; 2) the miasma had brought the disease; and 3) it was the result of demonic visitation, a sure sign of God's displeasure and a possible prelude to the end of the world. In places where wells were thought to be poisoned, or a miasma present, the usual method used to address the problem was to burn suspected outsiders—Jews, gypsies, foreigners, the handicapped, the insane—as a way of punishing them for bringing Plague, and, less readily admitted, as an offering to God in the hope that the sacrifice of these undesirables would save those more worthy of God's good opinion. When demonic visitation was the preferred diagnosis, then all those suffering from Plague were considered contaminated and no efforts to ease their suffering was tolerated. In Nuremberg, when the first epidemic struck, the leaders of the city, typically of the period, recognized the disease as demonic in origin and prepared to address it with the methods of religion. To rid the city of all demonic familiars, all the cats—known to be agents of demons and malign forces—were rounded up and burned. The Plague promptly got worse, for there were no cats to kill the rats carrying the fleas which brought the Plague. When this worsening was realized, the city leaders expanded their efforts and began to burn heretics and the mad; the Plague got worse. These events were not unusual: they were repeated in various forms throughout Europe.

Most of the characters in this book are wholly fictional: historical figures are mentioned in passing or appear in letters. The rest of the people of this horrific period are composites, drawn from accounts of actual persons who lived at the time in that part of the world; this means I have, perforce, given preferential attention to the literate, they being the only ones with surviving accounts. Within that necessary bias, I have made every effort to remain true to their understanding of their experiences and the nature of the epoch, and to show how they lived on their own terms as much as possible. The song lyrics quoted are from the period and in regional vernaculars that are unlike the French, English, and Italian we know today.

A word about the Vidames—this title and rank was given by the Church to men of good birth with military backgrounds charged with serving the Church as a vassal served a lord, and was approximately equal to that of Count or Margrave: the grant of title carried with it the obligation to defend by force of arms the property of the Church and the religious persons and institutions that were part of the property. Vidames answered to the Church and had the option of refusing royal orders if they were not in accord with those of the Church. Vidames were awarded the title of the property they protected; unlike other, royally granted property-related titles referential to patron saints, the Vidames had no hyphen between the Saint and the Saint's name: thus Percevall de Saunt Joachim, being a Vidame, does not have the more usual hyphen in his title, as, for example, Saint-Germain does.

The small but crucial Dukedom of Verviers in the western corner of what was then Hainaut and Brabant and is now Belgium and the Netherlands, had, in fact, disappeared by the time of this story; it ceased to exist three centuries before the period of this novel, forcibly annexed to the County of Hainaut, for the purposes of protection it fulfilled so admirably as a Dukedom. However, its location and its strategic importance suited my fictional purposes so well, I have taken the liberty of resurrecting it, with apologies for the lapse in historicity.

Medieval French, as all Medieval languages (English included) had few structural rules and was written phonetically, which is why the same word may have two or three different spellings in the same document; all are pronounced the same way. Therefore a word such as *savoir*—sah-VWOH(R) in modern French thanks to Burgundian influences—was rendered phonetically in Medieval French—sah-vo-IR. Basically, if the letter is there, pronounce it. François at that time in southern France is pronounced Fran-tso-IS. Rogres is pronounced RO-gres, with a hard *g* as in grey. Hue is pronounced WHAY. Jenfra is pronounced ZHEN-frah. Heugenet is pronounced You-jen-ET. In Italian, the diphthongs were stronger than in modern Italian, particularly in the northern dialects. Because of the phonetic structure of all the writing of the time, regional pronunciations were built into the written language: in the south where the Latinate influence was strong, vowels were broader—thus *saint* was often spelled *saunt,* rhyming with *daunt,* reflecting the nature of the dialect. In the north of France, where flatter vowels prevailed, it became *saint* or *sant,* the *a* pronounced like the *a* in *that.* All three usages are in this story. Many cities had different names than they do now, and I have used the forms of the period for them. The city known to the Romans as Massilia and to us as Marseille was called Marsailla (Mahr-SAHEE-lah) in the four-teenth century, and you will find it in that version in the text. Rome and Roma were used indiscriminately in France, and the text also reflects this. These irregularities may drive the copy editor up a wall, but it is accurate to the period of the novel.

In regard to the baker/baxter, brewer/brewster usages, I have used the English forms of the period instead of the French because baxter and brewster—and webster, for that matter—indicate that the person doing the baking, brewing, and weaving is female; after the first epidemic of Black Plague many trades which previously rarely admitted women to their ranks, were left by default in the hands of wives, sisters, and daugh-ters. Using these forms of the occupational words reflects these shifts and alerts the reader to the tremendous social change the Black Plague brought about as a result of its ravages.

As always, there are some people who deserve thanks for their help. For research sources, I would like to thank C. D. Hall for his knowledge of Me-dieval France and the French, and the French language; to Gina Roselli for the same in Medieval Italian; to Donna Lincoln for her extensive in-formation on the history of epidemic diseases; to Maude Hracany for her vast knowledge of the history of Medieval Europe and the politics of the Holy Roman Empire; to Harold Lewis for access to his photographic col-lection of historical buildings in Europe; to R. J. Reyes for information on the events leading to the Rome-Avignon Schism; to E. F. Jennings for in-formation on the merchants' roads and market towns in Medieval Europe; to Louise Fletcher for information on horticulture in Medieval Europe, and the little Ice Age of that period insofar as it impacted the Holy Roman Empire and the Kingdom of France.

On the other end of the process, I would like to thank my manuscript readers, Lona Mock, Eric Rielander, and Sharon Smith, who read the manuscript for clarity; D. H. Rosemont and Alan Todd, who read it for ac-curacy; and to Maureen Kelly, Sharon Russell, and Stephanie Moss, who read it just because. Any errors or omissions are mine, not theirs. Also I would like to thank my agent, Donald Maass, for his hard work; to the staff at Tor who have borne their labor in patience; to my attorney, Robin Dub-ner, who protects the Count's interests; to Lindig Hall Harris for her newsletter *Yclept Yarbro* (inquiries: 103 Edgewood, Asheville, NC 28814; e-mail—lindig@mindspring.com); to Lou Puopolo for a decade of faith; to Wiley Saichek in Texas for all those hours on the Internet; to Tyrrell Morris, my computer maven who keeps the machines humming; to Libba and Spencer Campbell for the time-out; to Mark for giving a damn after thirty-eight years, to Alz and/for the Morgans; to the wonderful participants in the Dracula '97 Conference for obvious reasons; and to my readers who have continued to support the Count no matter how hard he may be to find, along with the book dealers who stock the books—your perseverance and persistence are much appreciated.

Chelsea Quinn Yarbro
Berkeley, California
June 1997

PART I

FRANCOIS DE SAINT-GERMAIN, SIEUR RAGOCZY

Text of court records for the village of Orgon, near Avignon, submitted on 18 October 1345.

Upon my soul and in the name of the Father, Son and Holy Spirit, this is a fair and accurate copy of the proceedings of the court at the village of Orgon in the County of Provence, being part of the Holy Roman Empire, prepared at the behest of the Papal Court of His Holiness Pope Clement VI, reigning at Avignon.

The proceedings of the peasant farmer Simon Haspordis, it has been determined that his claim on the payment to his cousin Johannes Haspordis cannot be sustained, for it is known that at no time did said Simon Haspordis provide any more or less inspiration for said Johannes Haspordis' songs than any other peasant farmer could have done, and ties of family notwithstanding, the said Simon Haspordis is not entitled to any monies his cousin is not prepared to provide of his own inclination.

In the proceedings of the clergy and congregation of Saunte-Barbara against the termites that destroyed the choir of the church, their claim is upheld, and the judgment made against the said termites, which have been exterminated with sulphur fumes and tar traps, for no other recompense may be obtained.

In the matter of Loys Moullin in his claim of breach of promise against Gabriella d'Epreuve, the lady has shown to the satisfaction of the magistrates and the Bishop that she never pledged herself to the said Loys Moullin, for although, being fifteen, she is of the age of consent, she is not inclined to enter the married state and has intended since her Confirma-

tion, to enter the convent at Saunt-Piere-le-Apostre. She opines that said Loys Moullin wants the money in her dowry, for as the daughter of a goldsmith, she has some considerable amount coming to her, and which she intends to be her bride-price upon entering her novitiate. Said Loys Moullin, as the baker's third son, according to witnesses, must be eager to find a wife with means, since he can expect little from his inheritance. Several witnesses attested to said Loys Moullin's often-stated intention to wed well by any means he had to use to achieve his ends. Said Loys Moullin has twice before attempted to press into marriage young women with monies coming to them, or already left for their maintenance. Said Gabriella d'Epreuve has been given leave to undertake her vocation at the Nativity.

In the matter of Francois de Saint-Germain, Sieur Ragoczy, living at Clair dela Luna on the road to Avignon, the claim of the merchant Giraut Doul that said Sieur Ragoczy cheated him of monies, the said Sieur has shown to the satisfaction of the magistrates and the Bishop that he paid the full amount promised the said Giraut Doul, and that no further claims may be made by the said Giraut Doul against the fortunes of the said Sieur Ragoczy. The testimony of many merchants reveal that the said Sieur Ragoczy has never been known to cheat, nor has he withheld payments without due cause, whereas it is also known by many witnesses that the said Giraut Doul often increases the price on goods once they are in the hands of the buyer. On no account does any of this proceeding compromise the standing of the said Sieur Ragoczy, whose foreignness is not to be held against him.

In the matter of the foundling children: fourteen infants and five babies, thirteen females, six males, were left for the charity of good Christians. Five of them have been bought by those seeking servants, three have been claimed by families seeking to show their piety by raising foundlings, two have been given into the hands of travelers willing to raise them. The remaining nine are in the care of the parish and will remain so until other dispositions may be made. The monks at Sacra Familia have taken these children into their care and the sum of three martlets d'or paid for their care from the funds of the town.

In the matter of the Widow Vigny, as her portion has been taken to pay for the profligacies of her late husband and her son has said he cannot afford to keep her, having no inheritance to pay for her maintenance, she is ordered to accept the marriage offer made by Leonell Braccer; refusal is not acceptable for any of the reasons held to be sufficient grounds, for the man is of sound mind and good health and has no charges of heresy or felony against him. Said Widow Vigny not being past her grand climecterate, may well produce an heir for said Leonell Braccer, who will settle ten golden crowns on her, and will increase the amount by five for every male child she gives him. Should said Widow Vigny continue to refuse this reasonable offer, she will be denied the support of the parish, which must be reserved for those truly in need.

In the matter of the players who performed tales of unpunished sins, the said players have been fined nine golden bees and sent on their way, with warning not to perform in Orgon until their works have been made in accord with the teachings of the Church in regard to sin.

In the matter of the repair of the bridge, the merchants' tax has been revoked: Sieur Ragoczy has undertaken to pay for the whole of it, on the condition that said tax be rescinded. The magistrate and the Bishop have accepted the full amount from said Sieur Ragoczy and have had it proclaimed in the market that the merchants are no longer liable for the tax.

In the matter of the sow who devoured her piglets, she was found guilty of infanticide and hanged on the public gibbet as an example to all. The serf Ambrogie who raised the animal paid a fine of five silver sceptres to the Church as recompense for the sins of said sow.

This is the full account of the sittings of the court at Orgon for the period from the first of August until this day, given in the order in which they were presented to the court. May my salvation be forfeit if I report fallaciously.

> Pare Norbert, Premostratensian
> Magisterial and Episcopal scribe

By my own hand at Organ on the Feast of Saunt Luc in the 1345th Year of Grace.
Witnessed by Eudoin Tissant, acting tax collector.

> *Amen*

1

Out in the fields the men worked under the declining sun to bring in the last of the harvest; in the vineyards grapes were being taken from the vines for making frost-wine. From his vantage-point in the gate-tower window, Francois de Saint-Germain, Sieur Ragoczy watched these labors while his athanor slowly heated. He saw the men were eager to finish their work and be done. He glanced over his shoulder as his manservant entered the six-sided room, and then turned away from the window.

"Has the Estin boy left yet?" Rogres asked his master.

"Yes." Saint-Germain did not quite sigh. "He is inquisitive, which in another time or another place would serve him in good stead. But here? now?"

"You said there would be risks when you first agreed to teach him," Rogres reminded Saint-Germain in a carefully neutral tone.

"And there are." He gave a single, tiny shake of his head.

Rogres posed a question that had troubled him for the last year. "If that is the case, why tutor him? What can it gain him, or you, to—" He stopped himself and waited for an answer.

"He does not want to be ignorant," said Saint-Germain quietly. "And he wants to travel. His father, merchant that he is, wants profit and encourages the boy. He dreams of jewels and spices. The boy dreams of distant lands and ancient wisdom. If he spoke of this to his Confessor, his liberty could be forfeit."

"But why should you—" Rogres broke off again. "Your liberty could also be forfeit."

"So it could. Fortunately the priests in Orgon dismiss me as a foreigner who has fought the enemies of the Church, which affords me some protection that the boy does not have." He tapped the surface of his trestle table. "If he wants to study, who else is there? Everyone around him knows the stars are the celestial river flowing from Heaven to earth as God wills it. They know that the Devil stalks the earth personally seeking out souls to corrupt. They know that anyone foolish enough to sail west or south will fall off the earth into outer darkness." He lifted his hand in a gesture of despair. "What else could I do, old friend?"

"You could think of your own safety," said Rogres, no rebuke in his manner.

"I have only agreed to tutor this one boy before he goes to sea," Saint-

Germain reminded him. "And Gaspard is not going to tell tales to his Confessor." He turned back to the window and watched awhile in silence.

"The men should be paid today, now that all but the end of the harvest is over," Rogres said without any sign of a change of subject beyond a nod. "If you are planning to do it yourself—" He made a gesture to the window. "They will want to leave before sundown."

"Yes; you are right to remind me," said Saint-Germain. "It would be wise to pay them myself. They might have doubts about me if I do not." His smile was fleeting, filled with ironic humor. "It would surely be imprudent to be any more remote than I already seem to them."

Rogres nodded, a faint amusement in his dignified features. "They do speculate about you."

Saint-Germain chuckled. "Of course they do. I am a foreigner, and therefore the object of curiosity. I am wealthy, and that makes me enviable. My land is productive, which is the most reprehensible of all. Neighbors may be disliked, even loathed, but neighbors are familiar. Foreigners are unknown quantities, despised for nothing more than foreignness. As we have seen many times before." He shook out the long, knotted sleeves in his Burgundian cotehardie of black Antioch silk; the black cote of fine wool beneath was Roman in style, the hem reaching his ankles and decorated with red embroidery displaying his eclipse device. The high collar of the cote was slightly stiffened so that it did not hang limply around his neck but instead curled elegantly, just as his fashionably cropped, wavy dark hair did, and his neat, short beard. "Well, I will be with you shortly, old friend. I have a few things I still must attend to here."

"You are making scent?" Rogres asked, cocking his head in the direction of the athanor. Now that they were no longer discussing Saint-Germain's student, he was once more neat and reserved, his manner was a meticulous blend of respect and affection. His cote was shorter than Saint-Germain's, and made of dark blue-grey wool instead of silk, but he had a better appearance than most of the domestic servants outside the Papal Court at Avignon.

"No, not this time. Today I work with moldy bread," said Saint-Germain.

"The sovereign remedy," said Rogres knowingly. "I did not realize your stores were low."

"They aren't," Saint-Germain replied. "But winter is coming, and with it comes illness. I thought it wise to be prepared. Even in this mild climate, putrid lungs are not unknown."

"Even in midsummer," Rogres reminded him.

Saint-Germain thought a moment. "True enough." He looked back toward the window. "At least in this part of the world they bathe twice a month." When Rogres did not say anything, he went on, "Tell the men I will come directly."

"Very good, my master," Rogres said, and bowed slightly. "There will be taxes on the harvest soon."

"Yes; yes. I realize that," Saint-Germain assured him. "And, being foreign, we will have a higher assessment than those who were born on their lands." He shrugged, dismissing the melancholy that threatened to take hold of him. "When has that not been the case. Even my native earth is taxed as if I were a foreigner, I have been away so long." His people who had claimed the land had left it more than two thousand years before, long after he had gone from it.

Rogres sensed Saint-Germain's unspoken ruefulness; he left Saint-Germain alone in the tower room with his alchemical equipment.

By the time the sun had dropped to the edge of the crested western horizon, Saint-Germain came down to the courtyard at the rear of his villa, a large sack of coins in one hand, a ledger in the other. Rogres had set up a small table with an ink-cake with a trimmed quill on it, and put a chair behind it for Saint-Germain's use; he took his seat and opened the ledger as the workmen gathered in the courtyard. None was younger than ten or older than thirty; all wore cottelles and breeks tucked into brodequins and held their caped hoods in their hands. They kept their distance until their names were called, and accepted their payment without comment. Each man was given a small bonus for his labors. Their participation in the harvest festival a few days ago had seemed more truly the end of the season than this last flurry of work, and the extra money nothing more than an appropriate gift for their continuing labor. When all the men had received their money, Saint-Germain addressed them.

"I will pay your masters for the loan of your labor. They will have no cause to make claim against you. If there is any attempt to tax a portion of your hire, inform my manservant and the matter will be settled by me. I thank you for the work you have done and I pray God will favor you and your families." He crossed himself and watched as the workmen did the same. "God willing and a good planting in the spring, I will employ you all again at this time next year."

"Right. What about the spring planting, then?" one of the men called out, faint resentment making the question sharper than their relative positions required.

Saint-Germain showed no sign of being offended. "You know well that I hire others in the spring; I have done so for the last ten years and more. That way no one group of workmen is favored above any others, and no landholder is left without gain. All of you, landholder and serf alike, share in my good fortune." He had learned centuries ago that as long as farmers and laborers belonged to the landowner, it was sensible to be certain they all profited from his employment; showing preference for any laborer or landholder brought acrimony and strife along with the scrutiny Saint-Germain sought to avoid. "I will be glad to see all of you in the autumn next year."

"And we will be glad to come," said another after scowling at his obstreperous fellow-serf. This assertion was seconded by a number of the men in the courtyard; none wanted to lose the two golden bees he gave when their labor was done. For most it was the handsomest pay they would see all year long.

"Well, then," said Saint-Germain, rising from his place. "May the Good Angels see you home and watch over you." It would be dark before long and these men did not feel safe abroad after nightfall. "My servants will light your way to the main road."

The men crossed themselves again, and the first few began to straggle toward the laborers' gate in the stone wall surrounding Clair dela Luna. Torches were being lit for them although the sun still gave sufficient light in the luminous afterglow of sunset.

When they were alone, Rogres came up to Saint-Germain. "What troubles you, my master?" His centuries-long service to Saint-Germain had taught him to read his master's state of mind with uncanny accuracy. He spoke the Latin of Imperial Rome.

Saint-Germain shook his head. "I do not know," he answered in the same language.

Rogres frowned. "Then what—"

"I said I do not know," Saint-Germain cut him off.

This curt response was unlike Saint-Germain and for that reason alone it alarmed Rogres more than it offended him. "My master, I—" He stopped as he saw Saint-Germain's face clearly in the torchlight. "You have heard something."

"No," he said quietly.

"But . . . a message, perhaps?" Rogres suggested.

"No, not precisely," he answered carefully. "It is what I have *not* heard that troubles me." He strode across the courtyard with restless steps, the heels of his thick-soled boots ringing on the dusty flagstones. "It is probably nothing more than the hazards of travel, but I had expected to have word from my factor in Trebizond by now, and no word has come. His report is usually in my hands at the end of August, yet we are well into October and . . . nothing." He made an impatient sign of dismissal. "I know; I know. There are a thousand reasons the report has not arrived, and none of them are sufficient to give me this unease." His sardonic smile faded as quickly as it came. "I have told myself that the silence means nothing, but the apprehension will not lessen."

"Do you think it is time to leave this place?" Rogres asked as he busied himself putting the ink-cake back in its box.

"I cannot tell, and that is the most troubling part of it, the doubt. If I could be certain—" He stopped pacing and looked up into the night, at the thin veil of clouds drifting between the earth and the stars.

"If the players told you nothing, then it may be you are permitting apprehension to rule you," Rogres suggested. "They hear things, players do."

"The players said nothing," Saint-Germain told him. His dark eyes grew distant. "The rains will come soon."

"It is fortunate they have held off for so long. We might have lost part of the harvest if they had come sooner." He kept his voice carefully neutral as he picked up the ledger. "When you decide what is to be done, you will tell me, I trust."

Saint-Germain shook his head, his attractive, irregular features losing some of their forbidding aspect. "You need not coddle me, old friend. We have known each other long enough that you may speak candidly—you often do. I am aware that what I am saying is not sensible. I have tried to set aside my anxiety. But it wears on me, this feeling. I do not know what is best to do." He rubbed at his chin through his beard. "And it will probably come to nothing."

"Are you certain?" asked Rogres, looking toward the door into the villa. "I think we are being overheard."

"Unless their Latin is better than I suppose it is, let them listen," said Saint-Germain with a suggestion of a bow in the direction of the terrace doors. "I doubt they would learn anything to trouble them. Whether or not they understand, what can they learn? That I am worried for no reason. That I am unable to resolve doubts regarding . . . what? Only a Dominican or an Austin would be bothered by such an admission. Or one of the monks at Saunt-Joachim might wonder about my faith, but no merchant would, or servant, or serf." He switched back to the French of Provence. "Let's get the table and chair indoors. They should not be left out all night."

"I'll send for one of the servants," said Rogres at once.

"No need," Saint-Germain told him as he lifted the table with one hand and the chair with the other in a remarkable display of strength, for both pieces of furniture were substantial and solidly made. "If you take the rest, the ledger and the ink, we need bother no more about it." He followed Rogres into the villa, and gave no sign that he heard the sudden scuff of retreating footsteps as he crossed the threshold.

"Will you return to the tower tonight, my master?" Rogres asked as he closed the door behind them.

"Later tonight, I think," said Saint-Germain. He put the table under the narrow window and set the chair behind it. "I have something to do before then."

Rogres nodded. "You have made arrangements?" It was an innocent question to anyone listening, but Saint-Germain knew what his manservant was asking.

"Sufficient," he answered.

"Orgon?" Rogres put the box with the ink-cake on the table and held out the ledger to Saint-Germain.

"Near enough," was Saint-Germain's oblique reply.

"Does she know?" Rogres spoke with a quick glance toward the door.

Saint-Germain gave a minute shake of his head. "She dreams."

Rogres frowned. "Nothing more?"

"I think more would be . . . unwise." There was something in his expression that kept Rogres from pressing further. Taking the ledger, Saint-Germain went off to his private apartment above the reception room. In his library he chained the ledger to a high desk, then passing through to his bedchamber, he removed his cotehardie and chose a garnache of heavy black Damascus silk shot with silver from the chest at the foot of his narrow, austere bed. He swung the garnache around his shoulders and closed the two tabs over his chest, making himself a patch of darkness, his eyes darker than all the rest. He smoothed the front of the long garnache and admired the swing of the flared, marten-edged hem, thinking how little the garment had changed since the Romans. He did not miss having a mirror, for he had no reflection. Satisfied that he was ready, he turned on his heel and left his apartments through his treasured library.

The evening had turned chill and the wind was keen, but neither of these things troubled Saint-Germain. He made his way along the entry lane to Clair dela Luna toward the broad merchants' road that wound through the groves of trees, leading to Avignon in the north and to Aix and Marsailla in the south. It was better-maintained than most roads because the merchants paid well to keep it in good order, and charged a toll to use it. Saint-Germain walked tirelessly and silently until he came to the first enclosure of serfs' dwellings. He stopped and lay down at the edge of the trees, closed his eyes and was quickly in a strange attentive doze; his fine brows pulled together as he searched out the dogs that guarded the enclosure and deepened their sleep so that they would not give the alarm at his presence. Only when he was certain the dogs would sleep the night through did he open his eyes, get to his feet and resume his walk toward the stockaded huts. The rough logs were easy to climb and he was over the wall without effort. He avoided the midden where it steamed in the cool air.

A donkey gave a half-bray as Saint-Germain went past his pen, but when no other disturbance came, the donkey went back to chewing on the end of his leadrope that had been left looped over the fence.

Saint-Germain paused in the overhang of the roof of the nearest hut. He listened, his senses preternaturally tuned to his surroundings; he knew five people slept in the hut behind him, and that they had eaten pork and bread for their supper. He could hear the animals, smell them, as they waited through the night. When he was certain he was unobserved, he made his way to the small cabin set apart from the rest; slowly he swung the rickety door open. The place was there for the use of travelers, but just at present it was occupied by Deonis Vigny, who was eking out an existence in this place in defiance of the order of the court that she marry. Widowed at twenty-nine, she had promised herself she would not be wife again, and so far had been able to retain her precarious independence in defiance of the magistrate and the Bishop in Orgon.

She was asleep, as Saint-Germain had intended. He stood in the doorway of the tiny room and watched her, learning the rhythm of her sleep. Then he went in, closed the door, and spoke, so softly that the sound was hardly louder than her breathing. "There is nothing to fear, nothing. Dream sweetly, Deonis. In dreams nothing is forbidden. What you seek you may have for the taking. You may have all that you want in your dream; no one will forbid you to seek what gives you satisfaction." He came a step nearer to her. "Let your dreams carry you to realms of pleasure you have longed for all your life. Find the sweetest delights and have them happily. Be sustained by rapture. Be radiant with bliss. Deny yourself nothing that would give you elation."

In her sleep, Deonis Vigny sighed and lay back more comfortably under her single, rough blanket, her head pillowed in a husk-stuffed sack that rustled as she moved. Her brown hair was confined, even in sleep, under a lace widow's cap. Saint-Germain knew her eyes were a hazel shade that was sometimes green, sometimes brown; he did not want to see them that night, and risk discovery and detestation.

"Let your dreams bear you away from your unhappiness and open the door to your joys," he murmured as he finally reached her side. He dared not touch her yet for fear of waking her and terrifying her; she had already eluded two attempted abductions and would be certain he had the same purpose if she became aware of his presence. "Nothing will harm you, nothing will put you in danger, nothing will make you unhappy," he went on, his words were like soft music, lulling her and arousing her at once.

She sighed audibly and one hand moved restlessly. She was more deeply asleep than when he had come through the door, but not as deeply asleep as he would have wished. Only when he knew she was lost in her dreams would he continue. "You are free of all unpleasantness, you are as God made you, you are filled with the delight known by those who are true to God's Will. Your whole being is consecrated to your joy. Your heart answers the music of your veins. You will achieve all you have been promised of Heavenly rewards." He wondered how much she understood of this doctrine that she had been taught since infancy. How much did she truly believe that she was as God made her and only God or the Devil could change her? Nothing in her blood revealed doubt, but nothing there showed comprehension beyond a rote grasp of the idea. His touch remained light and evocative, knowing and responsive to every movement, every breath, every nuance of expression.

When finally he bent over her, Deonis Vigny was engulfed in an exultation that seemed to be the very gift of Heaven as the priests described it, but visited on her flesh. In her dreams she rushed to have his kisses, her unfettered passion as vast as the distant sea. She reveled in the voluptuous images that swam in her mind and made her body thrill. Her needs were as fully awake as her mind was wrapped in sleep, and she surrendered to the opulence of her senses and the fervor of her flesh. When she reached the culmination of her desires, she was distantly aware of the soft brush of lips on her neck, but this seemed nothing more than the fading fulfillment of her dream.

As was too often the case with these unknowing encounters, it was over quickly and the illusion of connection could not be sustained beyond the glorious delirium of her release; he had long ago ceased to try.

Saint-Germain withdrew from her cabin, his whole being filled with the cherished reality of Deonis Vigny, his senses heightened by hers, his gratification as intense and ephemeral as her dream had been. The kinship he felt with her at that moment was as comprehensive as any he had known; he was aware that she had no similar response and that his own would dissipate because of her lack of comprehension. Over time he had come to accept this fleeting unity without grief, although he continued to search for knowing lovers; acceptance of his nature was rare and could not be imposed or demanded or cajoled. He knew the value of intimacy and revered it. Through the centuries he had sought love without reservation which continued to elude him. He closed the door with care and slipped away through the cluster of huts. How much ardor there was in Deonis Vigny, and how little she knew of it. The tenuous link of their dream-bond began to vanish as she shook off her elation; he felt her stir and smile as he went up the road toward Clair dela Luna.

By midnight he was once again in his tower with his athanor, preparing more of the soverign remedy that he made from moldy bread. As he poured out the first beaker of the opalescent liquid, he had to shake off the disquiet that had taken hold of him once again, reminding himself that he had chosen this quiet life, that he had wanted to be at peace in the troubled world. Somehow that peace had evaded his attempts to secure it: he had achieved tranquility without serenity, and increasingly the tranquility escaped him. He had to resist the lure of melancholy as he continued his work into the pale dawn.

Text of a letter from Atta Olivia Clemens in Rome to Francois de Saint-Germain, Sieur Ragoczy; written in the Latin of Imperial Rome and delivered 2 February 1345.

To my dearest, oldest friend, the greetings of the Nativity, or perhaps the Resurrection, given the exigencies of travel;

Since the Church—or more to the point, the Pope—has gone to Avignon there is no occasion quite so vexing as the Mass of Christ in Roma. You cannot imagine how hollow the bells sound. The churches try to make it seem that all the pomp is still here, but is it not, and there are those in the Church who are no longer willing to pretend. It is rumored that the Pope must return to Roma or the Church is doomed. As much as I claim to doubt these rumors, I fear they may contain more truth than anyone in this city would like to think. If the Pope is afraid of the Holy Roman Em-

peror, let them come to an understanding rather than have the Pope hide away in France.

You are close enough to Avignon to have the festivities of the season all around you. Does that please you, I wonder? Or do you fret to have so many religious around you, with their demons and dreads? To me, few things are so Roman as the midwinter celebrations, be they the Christ Mass or the Saturnalia. You told me long ago that you were born at the dark of the year, so it may be you can regard these rites as those of your birth. What a very heretical notion! I trust you will not repeat it to any cleric.

I have made up my mind to return to Trieste with the spring, and take up residence in the city itself for a change. Living here in Roma has become difficult once again, and I can see the wisdom of taking a decade or so to let the speculation about me fade. I should have remained away longer, but I thought with the Pope gone intrigue would go with him. You need not tell me that I should know better; I have said that to myself often. Niklos has been urging me to leave in March for some weeks now. I am going to allow him to persuade me so that he will have the satisfaction of bringing it all about.

No doubt you have had reports of trouble in the East. I was recently told by a Greek monk come to Roma on some errand, that there have been travelers warning that a plague is loose in the East and that it may well spread. It is not certain which plague this is, or if it is anything more than a tale. If it is a plague, it may have already reached the Moghul cities; trade from those distant places has fallen off in the last months, and merchants are delaying going to those places until it is known if there is plague or if something else has occurred. Plague and war are not the only disasters the East has known. Flood, famine, eruptions and convulsions of the earth have all taken their toll. Not that I would wish for any of these catastrophes, not even those that cannot touch us; for while you and I have nothing to fear from the plague, the terror of the people stricken is another matter. And you need not remind me of your centuries in the Temple of Imhotep, or whatever that Egyptian god called himself. You should know better than I that when plagues come, no one is safe. So I urge you to consider travel yourself, in a year or so. You have those holdings in the north, and they may well be beyond the reach of the disease, if disease comes.

I thank you again for those two Andalusian stallions. They are superb; you must have trained them yourself for them to be so willing and well-mannered. You never beat your horses into submission, as so many others do, and it makes them finer mounts than all the drubbing others do. I have kept them busy and their get will certainly be sought-after if they keep true to their sires' color. Silver coats and golden manes. No wonder every minor king in Spain wants a stableful of these fine horses. I have six mares in foal now, and they will drop in the spring. I will take the stallions with me when I go back to Trieste and leave the mares and their babies here. When I return to Roma again, I expect my stables will be the envy of Italy.

The players arrived four days ago, and they are as accomplished as you told me they would be. I will have fine entertainment here until Epiphany. How could the magistrate and Bishop of Orgon be so blind as to think they were immoral in their amusements? They showed human frailty, to be sure, but so does every parish priest in Christendom, and the priests are not faulted. I predict they will be the delight of all those churchmen remaining in Roma, for they show the absurdity of sin while causing laughter, and where is the harm in that? No, I do not intend you to answer that question. I know what the response must be. But a jest or two about gluttony will not turn one to a heretic, no matter what the monks say.

How much I have missed you these last few years. As I write this, I long to have your company, so that I may laugh with impunity, since I cannot weep. I wish you would relent and visit me for a time. It need not be long, just enough to make me feel less alone in the world. Sometimes I feel I am a leaf on a fast-moving river. Other leaves fall into the water only to be left on the shore while I am swept along. With you for company, the river does not seem quite so kindless a place. How do you endure it? This isolation that those of your blood experience must be greater for you. And doubtless I do you no service by reminding you of our plight. If plight it is. For when I am thrown into this state, I have only to remember that I would have died the true death during Vespasianus' reign but for you. So weigh my complaint against the gift you gave me and count me a discontented matron out of sorts with the world.

So I will venture out to Mass and pretend that it has nothing to do with the Saturnalia, and I will watch the monks dance through the streets while the people sing for them, and I will visit a handsome young Bishop in his dreams so he will have something wonderful to confess, if he remembers. And then I will begin to choose what I will take to Trieste. Write to me there, and deliver the letter yourself if you want to best please me.

By my own hand and with my undying love,
Olivia

At Sanza Pari, the eve of the Mass of Christ, 1345 Church years.

2

"I could have used this at dawn before we set out. The roads are dreadful," Hue d'Ormonde complained genially as he accepted a tankard of hot wine from his host. Since he had shed his long hooded cloak and shaken the rain out of his hair he had become increasingly jovial and now his ready grin was offered without reservation. "Every winter some new trouble makes them worse. Last year it was the shoring on the low meadows that rotted away. This time the stones supporting the road along the side of Saunt Mattias' Hill have washed away. Everyone will complain of the cost but everyone will want the road repaired." He sighed and drank. "Delicious."

Saint-Germain smiled at his guest. "Thank you. I am glad you and your company made it this far if the roads are as bad as you say, and with the storm." He had known Hue d'Ormonde for seven years and had reached a comfortable understanding with the merchant. "I trust you were not in very great danger?"

"Well, my daughter thought it was a fine entertainment to wallow in ruts and slide on slopes, but at her age so much is," d'Ormonde confessed without hiding his approval of the child. "You are very good to order the bath for her and her maid. Most households would consign her to the children's room."

"That youngster you brought with you?" Saint-Germain inquired, glancing toward the corridor down which the girl's nursemaid had taken her. "Well, then I must be honored by her high regard." His amusement was tempered with kindness. "But I have no children's room."

D'Ormonde ignored the last. "She is not easily daunted. She laughed at every stumble and slip. A pity she wasn't a boy; with such spirits she will be hard to marry. No one likes a headstrong wife." He drank more of the hot wine. "Still, she's young. In a few years she may come to her senses. If we could marry her off now she could be taught by her husband's family how to please him."

Saint-Germain nodded, knowing to keep his opinion regarding headstrong women and child-marriages to himself. "Will you be going on to Avignon? Or are you going to give me the pleasure of entertaining you for a while? And your daughter as well, of course."

"We'll be on our way in a day or so. As soon as the rain stops. I must not linger." He shrugged to show he was helpless to do otherwise. "I will stay longer on my way back to Marsailla if you will have me. And my daughter as well. But you see, I have given my word to deliver my goods before Lent begins, or I would be tempted to remain here until the Paschal Mass. I am expected, so . . ."

"I understand," said Saint-Germain. "I would do the same."

"Yes, I think you would," said d'Ormonde, going on with broad humor. "Which is why I am here, despite your foreignness. And for the wine, of course. It comes from your vineyards, does it not?" He cocked his bearded chin in the direction of the terrace beyond the windows. Although it was almost noon, the sky was dark with clouds and the oil-lamps burning in the reception hall were needed to banish the gloom, giving all the shadows a purple cast. The world beyond was faded and grey, promising a chilly night and a muddy road in the morning.

"Yes. It was harvested six years ago." There were jars in the cellar with dates more than a century old, but Saint-Germain did not mention them.

"I will take some with me to Avignon, if you like. I have two mules that I can use for the load; they're low on their packs—they've been carrying food. So twenty bottles would be what I could take. Think about the opportunity, Saint-Germain. At this time of year, good wine will fetch a handsome price." He winked and accepted the second serving Saint-Germain offered him. "We can discuss this further in the evening, if you would not object."

"Very well," said Saint-Germain; he already knew he would send wine to market with d'Ormonde; he was right about the market, and it would remind the authorities in Avignon that he was not a dangerous person or one deserving suspicion. "But what about your return? I would be delighted to have your company for a week or more," said Saint-Germain as d'Ormonde drank again. "If you are able, we will arrange our business then, so you will not consider the respite without benefit."

"A good notion," said d'Ormonde. "And one I shall consider. And you, my friend, should think about coming to Marsailla again. Yeselta misses you." He smirked at the mention of the famous courtesan.

"I am . . . flattered," said Saint-Germain, his wry humor taking any condemnation from his remark: Yeselta had asked no questions in regard to his lovemaking and had thanked him for giving her the height of pleasure. He had not told her that his fulfillment came from hers. He could not completely conceal his sadness at the recollection of the two nights he had spent in her company, enjoying her expert but counterfeit desires. She was more knowing but less fulfilling than Deonis, and that alone made him dejected as he thought of her.

"As well you might be; she does not often speak well of those who visit her," said d'Ormonde, misreading Saint-Germain's thoughtful silence. "She does not bestow her commendation easily; few courtesans do." Again he frowned. "She will not like it when I marry once more; she honors her mother's memory as only a daughter can and she is used to being the lady in my household. She and I have grown used to our arrangements."

"Then you have not told her?" Saint-Germain watched his friend more closely than he knew for his answer.

D'Ormonde shook his head. "No. Not yet." He sighed, a short, hard explosion of air. "But soon I will have to." He made a motion with his hand to show how quickly things were moving. "She will have to know soon. I would not be surprised if she suspects something may be happening; not that she has said anything. She is an observant child."

"Have the negotiations gone so far that you are certain of the marriage?" Saint-Germain asked, relieved to have a shift in subject from Yeselta to d'Ormonde's forthcoming nuptials, yet a bit startled to hear that the arrangements had advanced so quickly. "You have settled on the contracts?"

"Most of them. Her brother, Josue Roebertis, is reviewing them now. He is a mercer and his judgment is sound. He has accepted my terms and has offered a dowry that, for a widow, is quite respectable. He will sign over half her inheritance to me and keep the rest for her children." He drained the tankard again and helped himself to more.

"Oh?" Saint-Germain said to encourage d'Ormonde to elaborate on his announcement. "How many children are there?"

"She has two—sons. One is being raised by her husband's brother, who will take him into his business when he is of age. That was in place while the father, Vitale Pleissan, was alive; the man was a notary, and the boy did not want to enter that profession; he lacked talent for it. His father indulged him, thinking he would train the younger one in time." He coughed once. "But he was struck down two years ago, and so his hope was lost. The family has been anxious to find a husband for her, as you might suppose they would. The widow, Benoita, the woman I have offered for, has been in her brother's care since her husband died; her father brought them here from France when they were only children, and her brother continues as the father began. It was thought best to put the older son in his uncle's family as soon as the Will was received by the courts. The widow did not protest this decision. The second son remains with her. He is five years old. The older boy is nine."

"What will this mean to your daughter?" asked Saint-Germain quietly. There were two high-backed chairs with cushions on the seats; he sat in one and motioned to d'Ormonde to choose another, or the X-shaped chair.

"She claims she is pleased," said d'Ormonde carefully.

"You are not certain this is so?" Saint-Germain prompted, knowing he could easily offend his guest with his probing.

"No; I am not." He tugged at his beard. "I know she fears her stepmother will put her son above her, though he is younger. Because he is a son, not a daughter. Well, we have seen that happen often enough. That is one of the reasons I have allowed her to travel with me—to reassure her and give her a wider sense of the world. And to show her the opportunities that she might make the most of. I have been called a fool for indulging her, but she is all I have from my wife, and if I cannot indulge her for the sake of her mother—"

Saint-Germain wanted to probe further but stopped himself from posing any more questions; he had already gone to the limits of what a host could require of a guest. He nodded in the direction of the hearth where a vigorous fire blazed. "Draw up, if you like," he suggested.

D'Ormonde dragged one of the high-backed chairs close to the fireplace and dropped down into it; leaning back as far as he could, he raised the skirts of his cotehardie as far as his knees and sighed as the heat struck his exposed legs. "I must say, Sieur Ragoczy, you are a fine host. I wish the places I will stay in Avignon will receive me half so handsomely as you have done."

"I trust you will not say so to them," said Saint-Germain in what he hoped was mock-horror.

"It will be tempting, but if I want to be paid well for my goods, I must praise their hospitality to the skies. You, being a supplier, I can abuse without fear. As you are a foreigner, you do not know what you are due from me." He swung around in the chair in order to show Saint-Germain his grin, so that Saint-Germain would realize he was not in earnest.

"Prudence and tact are part of business," said Saint-Germain with an understanding expression in his dark eyes.

D'Ormonde made a sign of agreement that almost spilled the last of his hot wine. "And inevitably those I would take the keenest joy in belaboring are the ones who demand I show them courtesy worthy of the Sieurs of France; they are more demanding than any man of rank in the Emperor's domains. I shouldn't wonder if they didn't want me to bend the knee." He faltered. "Not that you . . ."

"I comprehend your meaning," said Saint-Germain and called out for Monceau, his major domo. "My guest will want more wine and something to eat."

"There will be supper before sundown," said Monceau with a stiffness that betrayed his opinion of such expansive hospitality.

"That is some time yet; d'Ormonde has been on the road in all this rain and he is hungry. Must I make a second request in my own house?" Although his tone and manner were unfailingly polite and there was no hint of threat in his words, the major domo suddenly went crimson and bowed deeply to Saint-Germain.

"No. Whatever you order," Monceau said hastily and went away again at a rapid pace.

"I can wait, you know," said d'Ormonde as Monceau retreated. He was not apologetic but there was a quality of speculation in his offer.

"If you are not hungry, your daughter is," said Saint-Germain. "And she will be out of the bath shortly. You do not want her to go hungry until just before prayers, no matter what the priests tell you." He glanced toward the corridor down which the girl and her nursemaid had gone. "I hope you have dry clothing for her. I am sorry but I have nothing for girl-children in this villa."

D'Ormonde coughed to conceal his embarrassment. "Most certainly I do. She will be delighted to get to wear her good clothes before we reach Avignon. She has a love of finery that will not delight her husband unless she marries a very rich man. If she were two years older, she would be thought immodest, but at her age . . . She will preen for you, Saint-Germain. Be prepared."

"Oh, I think I can resist her," said Saint-Germain with a chuckle and a motion of his hand to show he had spoken in goodwill.

"But will she resist you?" her father wondered aloud. "That is more to the point."

Saint-Germain decided to put d'Ormonde at ease once more. "In her eyes, I must surely be ancient."

"That will not necessarily persuade my daughter. Jenfra is an unusual child; I've warned you," he said with a admonitory wag of his finger.

"I will keep that in mind," said Saint-Germain, turning his head as the wind buffeted the windows overlooking the terrace. The designer of the villa had wisely placed the terrace on the sheltered side of the house, in the Roman style; but this storm had blown in from the southeast and drove right at the fragile windows with sufficient force to cause Saint-Germain some apprehension as the gale strengthened.

"No shutters?" asked d'Ormonde, watching Saint-Germain with mild curiosity.

"I had them taken down last week. It was a trifle premature," he said, his expression unperturbed as he turned back to his guest. "But I think the glass will hold. Unless a branch or a roof-slate should strike one of the panes." This last was spoken without obvious concern.

"You have greater faith in glass than I have," said d'Ormonde, adding, "Not that it is my concern."

"But I thank you for it, nonetheless," said Saint-Germain; he did not mention that all the glass in his villa had been treated with a preparation that combined smelted Arabian black fire-tar and egg whites with powdered alabaster which strengthened it far beyond what was thought possible. Since his alchemical skills were regarded with emotions running from distrust to awe, he had learned to mention them as little as possible. "In any case, I doubt the storm will last through the night."

"Pray God your windows do," said d'Ormonde, bending down to rub his shins through his thick leggings. "The price of so much glass is no small matter."

"Then I join you in your prayer that the glass will not break," said Saint-Germain, his dark eyes showing ironic amusement; as long as he had base metal and an athanor, he could create all the gold he required. With slightly rare ingredients, he could produce gems of highest quality. Replacing glass was no hardship for him, either in regard to cost or availability, for he had learned to make glass while the Pharaohs ruled in Egypt, when it was valued more highly than gold and precious stones together. "As you say, it is not easily replaced."

"Well, at least you are not a profligate spender. There are those who waste gold and goods as if God would furnish them with velvet and roast meats every day of the week, and for nothing more than a *Pater Noster*." His scowl revealed that d'Ormonde had someone specific in mind when he issued this general condemnation.

"Prosperity and the opportunity to enjoy them are treasures in themselves," said Saint-Germain with feeling, recalling the many times in his long, long life when neither had been accessible to him; he valued these respites from strife more and more as he grew older. The last decade in this beautiful place had been one of the most peaceful he had ever known; he would not be able to remain much longer, but he wanted to postpone his leaving as long as he could.

"You sound as if you've had a taste of the other," said d'Ormonde. "As what merchant has not?" He made himself comfortable and was about to launch into a long recitation of his fluctuating fortunes when Monceau returned with a platter of cheeses, breads, and cold meats which he set on the trestle table. "Now that is a fine presentation," he approved, inclining his head in Saint-Germain's direction. "I will have to be circumspect or I will not make a good supper."

"Thank you, Monceau. And will you add to your excellent service by bringing a cup of warm milk for the child when she comes?" Saint-Germain's voice was low and courteous, but Monceau almost jumped as he heard the request.

"Of course, mon Sieur." He bowed properly and went quickly out of the room.

"How often do you beat him?" d'Ormonde asked as he got up to make a selection from the platter. He was not listening closely to Saint-Germain's answer, and was all the more startled when it came.

"I don't," said Saint-Germain curtly.

"No wonder he tries to take liberties, then," said d'Ormonde as he piled cold pork on a slice of cheese. He bit out a mouthful and began to chew. "He brings good fare, I'll say that for him. Not that it excuses his surliness."

"So I have been told; that the food is good," Saint-Germain said. He rose from his chair and walked to the window. "I fear that the table is all the entertainment I can offer you, d'Ormonde. There were to be players coming here today or tomorrow. But I doubt they will arrive until the day after."

"If they are on the road, they will not travel today," said d'Ormonde distantly, still eating. "You receive players here without festivities?"

"Certainly," said Saint-Germain. "They need to rest while traveling, as do all men. And they need to rehearse. I enjoy watching them work. So all of us are pleased with the arrangements."

"Foreigners," said d'Ormonde, then laughed. "Not that I have not enjoyed the players I saw here at harvest time. Very good they were."

"So I thought. Which is why I will be glad of their company," said Saint-Germain, whose thoughts were far away. He recalled the last time the players had been at Clair dela Luna, performing the stories of Noah and Saunt Eligius as well as farces of their own devising. The few weeks they would remain with him would go too quickly; the company of the players always heartened him, and he looked forward to their visits more than he liked to admit.

"I must confess that I am relieved they are not here yet," said d'Ormonde as he selected more food. "I fear my daughter would be taken with them, and she is handful enough already."

Whatever Saint-Germain might have responded was lost as a child in a white linen cotteron came running into the reception hall; her dark hair was shiny, hanging in damp ringlets around her elfin face. "Papa! Papa!" she cried out. "Ancella has got all wet washing me! It's so funny. You should see her!"

"Poor Ancella," said her father, paying no attention to the wet patch her embrace left on his surcote. "Where have you left her?"

"In the kitchen. She has to get dry." D'Ormonde's daughter giggled merrily and broke away from her father. She ran around the end of the trestle table, and apparently only then noticed Saint-Germain. She stopped and stared at him. "Papa?"

"This is your host, my girl," said d'Ormonde, his ruddy face growing darker. "Forgive her, Sieur Ragoczy," he went on, using Saint-Germain's title to impress the girl. "She has forgotten herself."

"Your father tells me you are a madcap," said Saint-Germain as if he saw girls in their underclothes every day of his life. He came a few steps nearer.

"Jenfra, ask pardon," said d'Ormonde, his sternness modified by indulgence, as if Jenfra were a much younger child.

"Pardon me?" Jenfra said to Saint-Germain, her teasing smile showing she did not expect any reprimand. "I didn't know anyone would be with Papa. I would not have behaved so improperly if I had been warned." She did her best to give the impression of the childhood which was now almost behind her.

Before Saint-Germain could reply, d'Ormonde rebuked her. "Who else should be here? We are his *guests*, Jenfra. He is a foreigner, but he is not an oaf. He deserves better of us than what you show him." He came up to her. "Go cover yourself decently, at once, and do not come again until you are correctly dressed. Tell Ancella that she will have to dry off later."

Jenfra gave a mischievous look to Saint-Germain. "Must I?"

"Your father says you must," said Saint-Germain, recognizing the ploy for what it was. He went back toward the windows, looking out into the expanse of orchards beyond the terrace of his villa.

"But you are host," she persisted, coming after him. "You can make him change his mind."

"It is not my place," said Saint-Germain firmly. He knew better than to be dragged into a dispute between father and daughter.

"But—" Jenfra wheedled.

"No," said d'Ormonde. "No more. You will go and dress at once, and when you are presentable, come again. You may apologize then, when you may make some effort at sincerity." He kept up his sternness until Jenfra was out of the reception hall. "She . . . she is impulsive. Her Confessor says it may lead her into sin."

"You did not offend me," said Saint-Germain, hoping to forestall long explanations. "And she made her point, as she intended to do."

There was an uncomfortable silence between them. Finally d'Ormonde spoke. "Was she so obvious?"

Saint-Germain nodded. "If she were two years younger I might have been persuaded," he said, and went on before d'Ormonde could say anything. "I have no reason to think you instigated her . . . display."

"I did not," said d'Ormonde with feeling. "And I ought to beat her, as her Confessor tells me I must. But she is so much like her mother, I cannot bring myself to lay a hand on her. You see how spirited she is. How can I break her to my will?" This admission was made with difficulty; he put his food aside and went back to the fireplace as if his appetite had deserted him. "She will be tamed soon enough, when she has children of her own."

For several long breaths there was silence again. Then Saint-Germain came away from the window. "She is your daughter, d'Ormonde. It is not for me to tell you how to raise her."

"You are very kind, mon Sieur," said d'Ormonde, finding his dignity once again.

"Hardly that," said Saint-Germain. He changed the subject again. "Are you going to go into Italia this year?"

"I may. It was worth the travel last year," said d'Ormonde. "Not the coast. A merchant like me cannot compete with ships and barges." He opened his hands to show he was at the mercy of seas and rivers. "Mules and wagons traveling overland have their uses."

"You're probably very wise," said Saint-Germain.

D'Ormonde went back to his abandoned food. "I may go north next year," he said with elaborate nonchalance.

"North?" said Saint-Germain, who had holdings in the Low Countries and Denmark.

"To make common cause with the Hansa merchants," said d'Ormonde as if discussing a truce or military triumph. "They are looking for merchants like myself who can deliver goods without running them around Castile, Portugal, and Granada to Aragon."

"It is quite a distance to cover," Saint-Germain pointed out.

"But the rewards are great enough to make it worth my while. Even your players would say the same thing. They trudge all the way to Ghent and Eu every year, and come back through Brittany and Poitou, and Rodez in Toulouse. If they can make such a journey, playing along the way, I should be able to reach the Hansa towns and come back in ten months. I would not have to stop at every town and fair for three or four days to earn my bread." He stopped, glancing at Saint-Germain. "Not that you should find this so remarkable, if half of what you have told me is true."

Saint-Germain smiled distantly. "Ah. But I am older than you, d'Ormonde. I have the years to spare." He did not permit d'Ormonde to question him; he added, "And I have neither child nor promised bride to keep me at home."

At this reminder, d'Ormonde was silenced. Finally he said, "I take your meaning."

"If you want to be one with the Hansa merchants, perhaps we might arrange things to our mutual benefits," Saint-Germain went on, taking care to make his tone of voice calm and reassuring. "I have had some dealings with the Hansa towns in the past. With your reputation and my acquaintance, we might be able to strike terms that would bring both of us profit."

The dejection that had been about to claim d'Ormonde vanished in an explosive sigh. "God made you subtle, Sieur Ragoczy, and I am a fool to forget it. I will strive not to be taken unaware again. Yes," he went on as he paced the reception hall. "That would bring us both the things we seek. Truly. I should have known you would know the way of it."

"I will dispatch messengers as soon as we agree on our contract," said Saint-Germain, glad he would have an excuse to travel when he needed one; it was an unanticipated opportunity and he resolved to make the most of it, for leaving a place without reason tended to bring the kinds of suspicions he wanted most to avoid. "We have this evening to begin our negotiations."

"My clerk is not with me," d'Ormonde said, his enthusiasm fading once again.

"I can read and write well enough for an agreement," he said, knowing that literacy in those not in Holy Orders was often regarded with suspicion. "I will make you a fair copy and you may take it to your clerk." It was a generous offer, and Saint-Germain was aware of how d'Ormonde would regard it.

"That's right," he exclaimed. "You are as lettered as an Abbe. It may be just as well that I leave the contract to you, for you know the law as well as my clerk does. You will give me your Word that your copy is accurate and I will be satisfied; if I am satisfied, my clerk can have no reason to cavil." He halted suddenly as Jenfra came back into the room. She was properly dressed, her sorquenie modestly laced; the fabric was cut velvet, more suited to a grown woman than a child, but it was obvious she was pleased with her appearance in spite of her downcast eyes. "Jenfra," her father said, trying to give her a warning with her name.

It was to no avail. Jenfra looked up at Saint-Germain and beamed at him. "I am more grown up than you thought, aren't I?"

"You seem very young to a man of my years," Saint-Germain said candidly.

"But I will be grown soon, and you will be glad of a young wife," she said, cocking her head flirtatiously.

"Jenfra, think what you are saying," d'Ormonde admonished her before Saint-Germain could reply. "He is our host."

"Then it would be rude of him to speak ill of me, wouldn't it, Papa?" she asked, her eyes twinkling with something that was more than mischief; she gazed up through her lashes, hoping to waken a response. When none came, she regarded Saint-Germain speculatively, making no attempt to hide her dawning infatuation.

Saint-Germain was spared the necessity of responding as Monceau came into the reception hall to announce that the players had arrived and wanted to know where to house them. Concealing his relief at this interruption, Saint-Germain made his excuses to d'Ormonde and left to install the players in the gate-house while Hue d'Ormonde made another fruitless attempt to correct his daughter without beating her.

Text of a letter from Jehan Nemout, wine merchant in Avignon, to Francois de Saint-Germain, Sieur Ragoczy, near Orgon.

Good Sieur Ragoczy,

The barrels of your superior vintages have just arrived and this will inform you that all are in good condition; my clerks have inventoried them for bottles and you will find their reckoning appended to this letter. I have paid the full amount to Hue d'Ormonde, who will be returning through Orgon on his way back to Marsailla. This second visit from him is most unusual, but as the wine he is bringing is of such quality as yours is, I would be delighted to see him once a month if he should continue to bring such barrels as these.

Should such an arrangement be acceptable to you, my muleteers are prepared to come to your villa to carry away such quantities of wine as you will entrust to them. The merchant arranging the transaction shall, correctly, receive the commission to which he is entitled for arranging the purchase.

In that regard, I am informed that you have more barrels you would be willing to sell. If they are of the same character as these, let me be the first to express interest in their purchase. I am willing to pay an extra silver sceptre beyond the amount paid to d'Ormonde for each bottle I acquire without competition.

You will want to know that Cardinal Montantica has already ordered six bottles for his table on the strength of what he tasted in March. He has vowed to have a dozen more if I can supply them to him at once. I pray God you will accommodate the request, for the Cardinal is not one to brook disappointment well. For this reason, I am instructing my messenger to remain at your service in order to bring me your response. He has my order to have your response in hand upon his return.

My prayers for your vineyards are as heartfelt as those for our continued mutual prosperity.

> With respect and at your service, Sieur Ragoczy,
> Jehan Nemout (his mark)
> by the hand of the clerk Remi-Clodis

On the 9th day of April, in the 1346th Year of Grace.

3

Blustery winds swatted the buds in the orchards and smacked at the young shoots of grain in the fields, wrecking playful ruin on the new crops. Towering white clouds like gigantic teeth nibbled at the edge of the cerulean sky. Saint-Germain, mounted on a frisky grey mare, was riding out to inspect the damage the spring storm had done. Unlike most nobles, he rode without spurs. He was elegant in his silver-embroidered black cotehardie with deep cuts in front and back to accommodate the saddle, his short-trimmed dark hair disarranged by the wind into unruly waves; the men working in the fields stopped to show him respect as he went past.

Beside him rode Eudoin Tissant, the newly promoted tax collector of Orgon. He was a plump, sour-faced, self-important man with large protruding ears and a bulbous nose who had never discovered how to be pleasant, for God had given him a dour disposition and he had no wish to challenge God's Will. "You will not be forgiven your taxes because of the storm, mon Sieur; do not ask it." His cotehardie was woolen, not silk like Saint-Germain's; it was one of the many things about the foreigner that rankled Tissant's sense of order.

"I had not intended to," said Saint-Germain calmly. "I had hoped you would make note of the extent of the trouble so that the men I hire for harvesting will not be accused of keeping back food for themselves. They would not do such a thing, I know. You may speak to my major domo in this, or any other, regard. He is known as an honest man, and will confirm what I tell you. And so long as you have a record of this, none of my servants will be wrongly accused." He knew that had he made such a claim for himself, Tissant would have refused to record it. As it was, the tax collector took his wax tablet from his box-cut sleeve and wrote a memorandum to himself with the stylus.

"If you are willing to believe the harvesters will not cheat you, what is it to me?" Tissant spat, then swung around in his high saddle to look directly at Saint-Germain. "You are planning to leave one of your fields fallow?" It was more an order than a question, and he rapped it out as if expecting a dispute.

"As I have in years past: one field in three is fallow each year. I have the fallow field tathed and plowed once in the summer. It is done thus in my homeland." This last was not quite accurate, but it kept Tissant from arguing with him on what he might deem extravagance.

Tissant's eyes narrowed. "You said you still have holdings in your native land?"

Saint-Germain had expected this question for the last two years and was ready with his answer. "Yes. I have extensive holdings of my native earth." His smile was quick, mercurial, as he thought that this statement, unlike his answer regarding his farming methods, was accurate in more ways than one.

"So you are not wholly dependent on the bounty of this land?" His mouth was small and pinched and his eyes accused Saint-Germain. "Your homeland still provides for you?"

This was easy to answer truthfully. "Yes, my native earth sustains me. You know that this is so from the records of my taxes, which I am sure you have read. This estate is not the source of my position in the world. I would not retain my title if this were the case. My honor would not permit me to own it and the Emperor would forbid it." Saint-Germain did not let his patience fail him; he kept his tone crisp and his attitude tolerant. He had had other encounters with Tissant before and did not want to give the tax collector any more reason for greedy caprice than he already had. He saw the avarice in Tissant's eyes and knew some satisfaction of it would be required.

"So he would. And the Pope would in Avignon." Tissant looked disappointed. "You told me the lands were east of here?"

Saint-Germain sighed. "In mountains called the Carpathians, east of La Serenissima." This reference to the Venetian Empire brought a look of distaste to Tissant's countenance. "The land is now disputed by Hungary and Wallachia; if the Lithuanian hold on Moldavia increases, they may also try to take it." His expression revealed nothing of his emotions; his manner was unfailingly courteous.

"At which point, you may lose your claim," said Tissant with sly satisfaction. "For once your house is gone and the land granted to another, Saint-Germain Ragoczy will be no more. If you will not fight for it, you will have no native land."

"Oh, it knows my blood; I have not lost it yet," said Saint-Germain, whose connection to his native land stretched back more than three thousand years.

"Then God must will it," said Tissent as if disappointed in God's decision.

"It is possible," said Saint-Germain. They had reached the end of Saint-Germain's fields; they turned north along the boundary, past the orchards with their clusters of beehives, and beyond to the plots of squashes and melons. Here the damage was less apparent and the women tending the plants were laughing as Saint-Germain approached. They had tied their skirts up so they could work more easily, and their legs and feet beneath were bare.

"If you would have slaves instead of paid servants in your household, your taxes would be less," Tissant reminded him, as if offering a prize.

"True enough, but I will not keep slaves," Saint-Germain replied, and waited for Tissant's next sally.

This came quickly. "It is said you pay your workers well," said Tissant, scowling at the women.

"I pay their masters what is demanded, and I give them something so that they will not be wholly without means for the time they have labored for me." Saint-Germain knew that Tissant had been informed of the arrangement; he supposed Tissant had wondered if he would tell the truth.

"That is not required. If their master is willing to let you have them, the price you pay him is sufficient," said Tissant stiffly.

"Their masters do not do the work; they do. The laborers are entitled to more than what their masters allow them; I am as much aware of this as the men are. And these women are the women of my household servants, whom I employ. None of them should be punished for working for me." He spoke carefully, making certain that Tissant understood him.

"So," said Tissant, shaking his head at Saint-Germain's foolishness. "I will see the Bishop as well as the magistrate has a part of this record."

"Thank you," said Saint-Germain without any trace of sarcasm, though Tissant listened closely for it. He was almost to his stables when he pointed out the sheepfolds and pigsties near the midden. "You will have to ask the shepherd and the herder how many young we have at present. I can tell you there are five new foals in the paddocks—two fillies and three colts." He cocked his head. "What is the value of them?"

"Two silver sceptres apiece," said Tissant promptly.

Saint-Germain was well-aware that the landholders in the district were usually assessed half that amount for their foals, but made no mention of it. "You know the custom of Orgon; present me with the sum, and I will pay you before you leave." He was able to give the man an affable smile.

"The amount must be paid in full, mind," said Tissant, disappointed that this foreigner with the unlikely sounding name had not been more upset by his visit.

They had reached the stableyard, and Saint-Germain swung out of the saddle with a grace that made Tissant want to slap his face, and would have been tempted to had they been of equal rank. As it was, he clambered down from his horse and fussily straightened his clothes, and took out his displeasure on the servants. "Do not be tugging on his reins so. He will bite if you fuss at him." With a glare he said to Saint-Germain, "Be sure your grooms keep my gelding ready for me. I do not want to have to wait for him when I am finished here." He made sure he had his wallet secured to his belt and his wax tablet was safe in his sleeve. Then he bowed slightly to Saint-Germain. "I will inspect your house now."

"As you wish," said Saint-Germain smoothly, permitting Tissant to walk ahead of him through the kitchen yard into the pantry corridor. The heels of his thick-soled solers rapped out crisply on the stones as he went, making Tissant feel he was being pursued.

"You are in a hurry," he said sharply, not turning around to look at Saint-Germain as if the foreign did not deserve such attention.

"Not at all," Saint-Germain said, shortening the length and speed of his pace at once. Although he and Tissant were much the same height, Saint-Germain's long, clean stride far outdistanced Tissant's mincing steps.

This remarkable display of deference did nothing to mollify Tissant, who was certain he detected a slight in this gesture. In the remaining dozen steps to the kitchen, he convinced himself that Saint-Germain was trying to influence him, which infuriated him. He fumed as the wonderful aromas of roasting goose and pork enveloped him. "You keep good board at this villa," he said, more as a complaint than a compliment.

"I am told so," said Saint-Germain, and saw Tissant's shoulders stiffen. "If you are hungry—" He raised his hands and clapped them. "A trencher, cheese, and wine for the worthy tax collector," he ordered, and was rewarded with a flurried increase in activity. "Bring his food to the reception hall. And send one of the pages to assist him with his notes when he has eaten." He led the way out of the kitchen, remarking amiably, "I understand that Gerralle is losing his sight."

The mention of his predecessor brought out the worst in Tissant. "He can no longer read what is written, his eyes are so weakened," he snapped, then did his best to make an effort to show concern for Gerralle. "But he is an old man—forty-four: a good age to achieve. It is more than time for him to give over his post to another."

"As ancient as that," Saint-Germain marveled. "Forty-four."

"You may make jest of it, but you will see forty-four one day," Tissant reminded him. "You are not a young man."

"No," Saint-Germain said, but whether to the first or the second of Tissant's observations, he did not explain.

The reception hall was warm; the sunlight from the windows coming through in bars yellow as new butter. The simple furnishings had been recently rubbed with beeswax; they were glossy with care. The cushions that served as upholstery for the high-backed chairs had been recovered in the last month, imparting a greater sense of newness than Tissant had expected. He knew from previous records that this furniture could not be taxed, having been declared the personal property of a man of noble birth. As he looked around the room, Tissant thought it unjust that such laws should apply to foreigners as well as those born in Provence. Taking stock of the reception hall, he noticed an Italian mandola with twelve strings resting on the trestle table. He considered the instrument. "Is this yours?"

"Yes," said Saint-Germain from behind him. "I was in Italy some years ago and had it built there."

"In Roma?" demanded Tissant, hoping to find some reason to confiscate the mandola.

"No; in Toscana, in a little village where many instruments are made. My manservant will vouch for me, if you require it," Saint-Germain offered as if wholly unaffected by the tax collector's petty spite. "I have bought instruments there before."

"You play it?" Tissant challenged.

"Of course," said Saint-Germain. "Why else would I have it?" The obviousness of his question took Tissant aback; Saint-Germain watched him.

"You might have it for a mistress," he said with a glance filled with innuendo.

"I have no mistress here," said Saint-Germain with complete candor. He knew his lack of one had resulted in gossip in Orgon; surely Tissant was aware of it.

"You cannot tell me you live like a cloistered monk," he cried out, rounding on Saint-Germain and pointing at his face. "This villa is hardly a cloister."

Saint-Germain did not allow himself to be offended by this rude behavior. "No, Tissant, I will not tell you that."

"Then you must go to the courtesans and debauched women," Tissant exclaimed.

"Whom I see, or when, or if, is no concern of the tax collector." Saint-Germain's voice was quiet but it carried with it an authority that made Tissant take a step back; though Saint-Germain made no move toward him, the compelling force of those dark, dark eyes propelled Tissant as surely as a blow. "I have no one living in this house under my protection as my leman, not woman or boy." His tone was deceptively mild. "Unless you have some reason to doubt me, the matter is closed."

Tissant was well-aware that he had overstepped the power of his position. "They say you tutor a youth from Orgon. Is that true?" It was a flimsy attempt to justify what he had done. "You will not deny it."

"Most certainly I tutor the Estin boy. His father requested it," Saint-Germain remarked, wondering where this was leading.

"And you tell him about what? Why should his father want a foreigner to instruct his heir? What can you teach him that the priests and monks cannot? Is he going into Orders, or to the universities in the north to be a scholar? No, he is not: he is to fill his father's shoes, in the way of eldest sons. Then what do you know that he ought to learn it?" To Tissant's surprise, Saint-Germain laughed softly. "You dare—?"

"Give it up, little man," said Saint-Germain with an amused shake of his head. "There is nothing here your predecessor did not record, and you can discover no scandal that would stain my honor. Look as you will, you will find nothing." He saw that Tissant was trying to speak, and he fell silent to give him the opportunity.

"You . . . you are not . . . are not," Tissant stumbled, his state of mind in turmoil.

"I am not from Provence," said Saint-Germain so calmly that Tissant became angry all over again. "That is surely not a crime. If the Bishop at Orgon has accepted me, then what complaint can you have?"

"You have no right to question me," said Tissant, his voice raising half an octave.

There was a sound at the far end of the room. Both Saint-Germain and Tissant turned to see Monceau waiting with the food, his serious demeanor showing he had overheard most of what was said. "I have brought the food, as you ordered." He gave a long, hard look at his master. "Shall I ask Rogres to come?"

"No," said Saint-Germain, knowing that the presence of his manservant would only infuriate the tax collector. "But you may remain, if you wish," he added, watching the somber expression on Tissant's face stiffen.

"You have no reason to make this request," said Tissant, his cheeks flushing to a mottled purple. He wanted to find some way to lessen his embarrassment; having the major domo with them would reduce him to a servant as well.

"I have made it for your sake, so that you may have a witness to all you say to me," Saint-Germain replied. He indicated the food. "Eat. Please."

Tissant cleared his throat; his temples were aching and the light hurt his eyes, but he could not bring himself to admit any of these things. He lowered his head in an effort to be polite, to minimize any offense he might have given. "That was courteous of you, mon Sieur," he managed to say without choking.

"Please," Saint-Germain repeated, indicating the meal on the tray. "Monceau, draw a chair to the table for the tax collector."

Monceau did as he had been told, all the while keeping narrow watch on Tissant. When the chair was in place, he stepped back to the corridor entrance where he remained.

"Now, good Tissant, I ask you to accept my hospitality while you finish reckoning the taxes I must pay. You will find the pork particularly good, or so I am told." Saint-Germain noticed the brilliant sunlight, even through the thick windows, was becoming uncomfortable; he would have to change his native earth in this thick-soled solers tonight or he would be in pain when he stepped into sunlight tomorrow.

Tissant sat down as if he expected some elaborate jest. He used the knife provided to hack at the thick bread of the trencher, and carried the sauce-soaked portion of bread to his mouth, tasting it with care, prepared to spit it out without apology if it was unwholesome. To his astonishment it was "Delicious, mon Sieur."

"I understand my cooks are very good," said Saint-Germain with a faint smile. He knew that the food served here was superior; he insisted upon it.

"You take pride in their accomplishments?" Tissant was not through with his attacks, though the taste of the food was superb.

"As a host takes pride in the quality of his hospitality, which is no more than any man of honor could want to do," said Saint-Germain, refusing to be caught in so evident a trap. "Do not remind me that pride is the greatest sin of all. I have it for the skills and work of others, not my own; I am humbled by their abilities."

Tissant had a mouthful of pork and could not speak clearly. He reached for the tankard of wine and drank half of it to get the meat down, then he cleared his throat before saying, "You speak with the qualification of an advocate."

Although Saint-Germain knew the remark was intended as an insult, he bowed slightly and said, "A great accomplishment, if it is true." He was wearying of Tissant and wished he had a reason to leave the man alone with his food; without justification, any failure to attend him could give the tax collector more cause for complaint, and retribution.

"The wine is very good," said Tissant, now taking the time to savor it.

"My vineyard has been kind to me," said Saint-Germain. How many officious, petty men he had dealt with in his long life, and how tired he was of accommodating their demands. From Khem—now called Egypt—to Rome, to India and China, he had always found men of Tissant's cut, and he had spent what must now be decades of his life dealing with them. Over the centuries he had spent a fortune to assuage the pettiness of minor officials; such exigencies were inescapable: he resigned himself to losing another half-day to bureaucratic whim.

"And your taxes have been lenient, if this is the quality of the wines you produce. I will have to raise the assessment." His smile was rimmed with meat-sauce, which made his gloating more obvious. "If you haven't enough to pay in coin, you may pay in kind."

"I have gold enough for your taxes, good Tissant." Saint-Germain saw the disappointment in Tissant's eyes and wondered how much of the payment in kind he had been seeking would have been diverted to his own cellars.

"That is good," said Tissant, covering his thwarted desires with a belch. He wiped the cuff of his box-cut sleeve over his mouth and looked carefully at Saint-Germain. "You have medicament here, or so I am told."

Saint-Germain concealed his exasperation and answered flatly, "I have some experience in treating the sick and the injured. I make my own medicinal preparations here. The substances contained in them have already been taxed and I offer them in charity, as the Church admonishes us to do."

"Laudable," said Tissant in blatant insincerity. "If it is learned that you have used your supposed charity to conceal—"

"Please," Saint-Germain interrupted him. "Worthy tax collector, do me the courtesy of believing that although I am foreign, I am not a fool. I have no wish to cheat the place that has given me haven. I know my obligation to this town and Provence, and I will not shirk it. Believe this." His dark eyes fixed on a distant point.

"As you say," Tissant muttered, ducking his head to make it seem he had not intended to be deliberately insulting.

"I know the penalties I would face if I abused the laws of Provence, or those of the Emperor," said Saint-Germain, who was keenly aware that the laws were enforced arbitrarily and severely. "In Avignon, the laws of the French King prevail where God does not."

"The Holy Roman Empire is not less godly," said Tissant, his tone a reprimand.

"Of that I am well-aware," said Saint-Germain, his meaning lost on Tissant. He walked down the reception room, knowing it was folly to provoke the man, but wanting to tweak his paltry importance. He motioned Monceau to refill the tankard for the tax collector.

"You do not drink with me," Tissant complained as he accepted the wine.

"You must pardon me," said Saint-Germain. "I do not drink wine."

Tissant glanced at Monceau. "Does he?"

"I have never seen him, nor does he have wine carried to his private rooms." There was a quality of amazement in Monceau's assertion that was more convincing than a more certain statement would have been.

"Well, well," said Tissant as he pronged another portion of pork on his knife. "How very austere."

"Those of my blood do not," Saint-Germain offered as an explanation.

"Some vow, no doubt," said Tissant, knowing that the oaths of foreigners were often baffling.

Saint-Germain nodded. "Given long ago to the priest who served my father." He did not add that the priest had not been Christian, or that the pledge was over three thousand years old, given at the dark of the year in the sacred grove at midnight and sealed by drinking blood from the pierced palms of the priest who was also a god.

"Then you do well to honor it," said Tissant grudgingly. He had more of the wine, and unaware that it was going to his head, he said, "I would like a bottle or two to take with me."

"Certainly," said Saint-Germain, signaling to Monceau to fetch the bottles. "See they are wrapped in straw and secured to Tissant's saddle."

Monceau turned and left them alone.

"A gracious offer, mon Sieur," said Tissant, smug in the knowledge he would not have to report this gift. "It has been a stormy spring, and many of the vineyards are damaged." He was sounding more affable now that he had drunk the second tankard of wine.

"All the holdings have been harmed; mine are not the only fields and orchards to be marred," said Saint-Germain as he went to the table and poured a third tankard of wine for the tax collector, emptying the bottle. "The harvest will be lean in this region."

"Good reason to demand full taxes now so that there will be money and grain when the year wanes. And a good time to buy slaves; you would save money on your taxes on a poor harvest." He put a greasy hand to his chest. "It is prudent to be strict in taxes when harvests will be meager. We will have many requiring charity in the winter."

"Have I protested any tax levied against me? Have I ever refused to pay?" Saint-Germain inquired as if asking about the pleasant weather.

Tissant shook his head repeatedly. "No," he admitted.

"And in Orgon's records is there anything stating that I failed to pay the full amount upon demand?" Saint-Germain continued, his air of cordiality unaltered. "Have I ever paid any sum in false coin, or questioned the justice of the tax?"

"No," Tissant repeated.

"Then," said Saint-Germain with an expansive bow, "believe that my character has not changed simply because Orgon has changed tax collectors." He paused. "And believe I will not buy slaves, no matter what the enticement."

"More subtlety," murmured Tissant, who was beginning to have trouble holding on to ideas.

"Your faith teaches you that only God and the Devil can change the character of a man, does it not? How can you doubt it?" His dark eyes glowed, his musical voice became persuasive. "You have no reason to think I will cheat you, Tissant. You have no cause to threaten me. You may rely on me to give you whatever sum you ask. I have said I am amenable to your taxes because I am."

Tissant blinked; he wondered thickly what had happened. "Yes. I understand you." He tried to pull himself together. "My calculations are . . . not complete yet. I will present you the reckoning . . . shortly." He stumbled over the last word, and peered up at Saint-Germain. "Would that others were as cooperative as you are, mon Sieur."

Saint-Germain stepped back and put the empty wine bottle on the end of the trestle table. "Finish your meal and your sums, Tissant. Send for my manservant when you are ready to present your total. He will bring you to me."

"But—" Tissant protested; he was not steady enough to rise and he would never restrain a man of Saint-Germain's rank by force.

"You have seen for yourself how much there is to do on this estate. If I am to salvage as much of the harvest as I can, I must return to the fields. Rogres has keys to my treasury. He is authorized to pay you." The word *treasury* seemed a bit too grand for the narrow chamber where Saint-Germain kept his money, spices, and jewels, but it served to impress Tissant.

"You are being most circumspect, mon Sieur," said Tissant, striving to maintain his dignity.

"Any foreigner in Provence who is unwilling to bear his obligations should go otherwise." Saint-Germain was near the far end of the reception hall and was about to step into the corridor beyond when Tissant shouted after him.

"Sieur Ragoczy!" As Saint-Germain halted, Tissant managed to get to his feet by holding on to the back of his chair. He swayed a bit, working to recapture his thoughts.

"Yes?" Saint-Germain asked, for he had heard a note of genuine concern in Tissant's voice.

"The Bishop burned two men for sodomy last year. He said he would do the same to all other such sinners." The warning was clumsy and for that reason, Saint-Germain listened. "Their families were driven out of the town."

With an ironic smile Saint-Germain said, "I am grateful to you, good Tissant. But in this instance you have no reason to fear for me." His air of equanimity masked a first twinge of genuine apprehension; perhaps this was the cause of his inner restlessness. Had there been suspicions about his true nature? Had one of the dreams he had given been reported to a Confessor as a vision? Over the centuries he had come to realize that most people reserved their greatest ferocity for sexual expression. The tolerance of the Romans was now called decadence and they were condemned in the eyes of the world for the license they had countenanced. Some of the practices he had seen in India would be cause for worse than burning in this part of the world. He knew his own predilections would meet the same fate as the unfortunate men whose act was numbered among the Seven Deadly Sins.

Tissant clung to his intentions with the determination of intoxication. "You have no mistress. The Bishop—"

"He will find no complaint against me." His appearance of composure was convincing to Tissant, but not long after when Rogres encountered Saint-Germain on the stairs leading up to his private rooms, he saw at once that his master was troubled.

"The taxes?" he asked, wondering why they should bother Saint-Germain.

"They're no worse than usual," Saint-Germain answered waving the question away. "More of the same caprice and greed, I expect. We have seen it before, and this man will not be the last to insist that others accommodate his authority. Well. We will know by the end of the afternoon, when he is sober again and remembers what his purpose is." He knew his sardonic humor would not deceive Rogres, nor did it.

"Then what?" Rogres would not be put off.

Saint-Germain raised his fine brows, then relented. "They've burned sodomites in Orgon. Tissant told me."

"I remember something about that," said Rogres. "It was the village scandal."

"The Church condemned them for abominations, as I recall," Saint-Germain said. "They did not want to mention the specific sin."

Rogres shook his head in exasperation. "Their generals bugger their pages and everyone knows it. Monks are reputed for futtering. Courtiers have favorites and use them as mistresses. None of them are burned. These men were no different."

"No. But they were in a village," Saint-Germain said. "They were not military men, clergy, or nobility. The Church could condemn them with impunity."

"As it could a foreign noble," said Rogres.

"So I assume," said Saint-Germain as he passed Rogres and continued upward.

Text of a letter from Hue d'Ormonde in Marsailla to François de Saint-Germain, Sieur Ragoczy, at Clair dela Luna near Orgon in Provence.

Greetings to the gracious Sieur Ragoczy, with prayers for his health and prosperity;

I write to tell you that the wedding is arranged and it will take place on the Feast of the Blessed Virgin. Our contract will be signed on the first day of August so that when the priest joins us we will be able to begin our married life at once, immediately following the Mass.

As it is now June you will have time enough to arrange your affairs so that you will be able to attend the Mass if not the signing of the contract. I am hopeful that you will be willing to give me a fortnight of your time. Your lands will not yet be ready for harvest so you will not have to supervise the men in the fields; your absence will not cause you any disadvantage, I am certain of it, and your presence here will lend dignity to the occasion for which I will be grateful. Your Monceau will look after your villa for the month and you may appoint a supervisor for other duties.

If you will extend your goodwill to the extent of providing a tun of your fine wine, the joy of the event will be assured. It will please the bride's brother as much as it will please me. The priest will accept any donation of the wine that is left over, which makes it all much more satisfactory for us all. You may command a place in my house for the month, or you may hire other lodgings, as you like. Your manservant may easily be housed with mine; if this is not satisfactory, he, too, will find that no one will refuse him lodging, not in this city. The people of Marsailla are not so chary of foreigners as is the case in many other places, and you need not expect to be scrutinized as you might be in other towns away from the sea.

My daughter Jenfra has not stopped talking of you since we stayed at Clair dela Luna. By now she has invested you with every virtue and all manifestations of perfection of body and soul. I have said she must not pester you, but I must warn you, I doubt she has paid attention to a word I have spoken. Any warning I make is seen as an assault on your elevated character and she flies to your defense, incensed that I could think you capable of any transgression. The priest wants me to beat this enthusiasm out of her but I cannot raise a staff to the child, much as I know my reluctance may imperil her soul. So you may want to consider Jenfra when you make your plans to attend the wedding. She is such a madcap, impulsive child that she continues to enchant me in spite of her many faults; if you do not want her constant attentions, you might be more comfortable elsewhere.

You must not disappoint me, mon Sieur. This marriage is a triumph for my family and a benefit for hers. All our relations must rejoice for us. To have you with us must surely set the seal on our union, for to have one of your rank and fine repute among our guests will demonstrate to the world that the joining of our families is welcome to the world at large; you, being of noble birth, have the power to give solemnity to the wedding that all the merchants of Marsailla cannot. I will also admit that her brother will be impressed if our celebration is graced by the presence of a man of your station, for although your title is not of this region, it is more than any of his acquaintance can boast. It may not be suitable for the nobility of Provence to attend our wedding, but you are not so rigorously constrained.

I have sent this to you by courier and he will remain to bring me your acceptance, for I will not endure a refusal. I hope you will find the rest of the company to your liking. I must advise you to bring clothing for hot weather. Marsailla in August can be sweltering. No velvets or furs will be needed; you, as an exile, need not observe the rules of the Emperor's court. I have provided my bride with a bolt of silk for her wedding clothes and I have engaged a tailor to make a houppelande for me in fine damask. You know what display is expected for this occasion better than I do. You will doubtless present the appearance courtesy requires to honor the celebration.

May God speed and guard you as you journey to Marsailla, and may your favor to me bring you many blessings.

> *With respect and regard,*
> *Hue d'Ormonde*
> *(by the hand of the clerk Frer Beneguet)*

On the 19th day of June at Marsailla in the 1346th Year of Grace.

4

Before moonrise the villagers of Orgon had gathered in the fields on this, the shortest night of the year. For once the weather was lovely, the winds mild and coming from the south with thyme and roses to sweeten it, taking away the drowsy daytime heat. The stars shone like dew on the heavens and not even the bonfire could dim them. Farmers and serfs from the lands around Orgon had come to join the festivities, swelling the gathering to over a thousand. For such a grand occasion all of the countryside was drawn to what was usually the livestock market of Orgon; it took up too much room for the market square in the center of the village, and had spilled into the fields as well. Three barrels of new beer had been rolled out from Saunt-Joaquim and another two of wine from Sacra Familia, the monks joining in the celebration with songs and an occasional moment of silence to show they regarded this as a religious occasion.

"Which it is," Saint-Germain said quietly to Rogres in Byzantine Greek as they approached the noisy confusion. "The Christians may have subsumed it, as they have so many of the old festivals, but that changes nothing." He was in a short-skirted houppelande of silver-and-black silk, the large outer sleeves dagged in deep scallops. His leggings were Persian fashion, with a pattern in red against black, and his boots were Roman with thick soles and square heels. His mixed styles were a reminder of his foreignness as much as his elusive accent. He carried his mandola over his shoulder, holding on to the neck just below the pegbox. His only weapon was a short dagger thrust through his belt, which all men wore; the sword he was entitled by rank to carry he had left at Clair dela Luna. Their horses were tethered with others, as well as mules, donkeys, and ox-carts at the end of the festival area, each with an armful of oat-hay to eat, and watched over by orphans from Sacra Familia.

"Best say it is the birth of Jehan lo Baptiste this honors," Rogres reminded him. He was more conservatively dressed, in a linen cotehardie of a monkish grey. He walked next to his master instead of behind him, which the villagers thought impudent.

"They killed a yearling calf for the feast," Saint-Germain observed, the odor of roasting beef heavy as the smoke from the fire. His hand flexed on the neck of his mandola.

"And there will be other meats, too," said Rogres, who had brought a young goat to the Orgon market for this occasion; Saint-Germain was adamant about keeping to the local customs.

"I hope it will not be awkward if we do not eat with them," Saint-Germain said quietly.

"It has not been in the past," Rogres said, attributing these misgivings to the uneasiness that was working on his master.

"No; in the past it has not." Saint-Germain said and raised his hand to return the greetings of those whose rank allowed them to make such a gesture before Saint-Germain did. "I see the magistrate has brought his wife this time; why he should ask this of her, I would not like to think," he remarked to Rogres.

"Poor woman," said Rogres. "To lose four children in a single year. And to be pox-marked."

"Yes," said Saint-Germain, his dark eyes distant; how often he thought of those long-vanished centuries in the Temple of Imhotep, where the sick and injured were brought for treatment. "Two children lost to the pox and two to tainted meat." He shook his head to rid himself of these melancholy thoughts; when the Great Pox had come to Orgon, it had left its stamp on

the village in the faces of its people and on the headstones in the ceme-
teries. "If she had sent for me . . ."

"You offered your help; she decided not to take it," Rogres said.

"Or the magistrate did," Saint-Germain added. "Only one child left." He
had never had children of his own; those of his blood lost the ability to create new life. He had seen enough children die over the centuries that he
knew the anguish of the bereft parents as if it were his. He bowed to the
magistrate's wife, and saw her wan attempt at a smile answer it.

They had almost reached the bonfire when Saint-Germain saw Eudoin
Tissant, the tax collector, hunched over a pot of green-lentil porridge, a
bowl of beer and a round of bread beside him. He had spread his cloak on
the ground sitting upon it tailor-fashion, the pot in his lap. He was preoccupied with his meal and so did not notice as Saint-Germain approached
him, his hand lifted. "The blessing of Saunt Jehan lo Baptiste upon you."

Tissant looked up abruptly, as if he expected to have his food snatched
from his hands. "Oh," he said as he recognized the speaker. "Sieur
Ragoczy." His demeanor was so abashed he was almost comical. "The
blessing of Saunt Jehan upon you as well." He struggled to rise until Saint-
Germain gestured his permission to remain where he was.

In a swift, fluid motion, Saint-Germain went to his knees beside Tissant,
his mandola still over his shoulder. "I have your message that there is to be
an extra tax before the harvest," he said as if this were an expected event.

"Yes," Tissant said defensively. Had he been standing he would have
looked belligerent; seated on the ground he merely seemed sullen. "For
the poor, against winter."

"Of course," said Saint-Germain. "Those of us with crops to bring in
should do our part toward easing the want of the unfortunate; I have told
you I am ready to do mine."

Tissant glanced at him as if trying to discover some hidden meaning in
Saint-Germain's remark. "It is Christian duty."

"Yes, it is," Saint-Germain agreed, going on without any trace of condemnation, "But do all the landholders around Orgon approve this tax?"

There was a long silence while the sounds of celebration seemed to
grow louder. Finally Tissant swallowed hard and said, "It is levied against
only those with orchards and fields."

Saint-Germain did not bother to say the lie was clumsy. "Ah." With a
single nod, he said, "I see," and rose to his feet. "Well, you had best come
to Clair dela Luna soon to collect it. I will be going to Marasilla in August
to attend a wedding. I suppose you need the money before then."

Tissant bobbed his head repeatedly, and wished he had not come to the
midsummer bonfire. He reached for his spoon and attacked the green
lentils as if they had embarrassed him.

"We are being favored with another tax," Saint-Germain said to Rogres
when he found him a short while later near where the goats and sheep

were being roasted on spits turned over banked fires. All had been stuffed
with apples, onions, and garlic, and those pungent smells, mixed with that
of cooking meat, made the air feel edible.

"A general tax?" Rogres asked, knowing the answer already.

"No. I presume it is limited to foreigners with means and without alliances to protect them," he replied, his words sardonically sweet. He was
interrupted by a sound of bagpipes and drums; glancing around he saw a
group of musicians moving purposefully through the crowd. "They are
going to dance; give them room," he said, motioning to Rogres to move
back from where the villagers were gathering as the instruments continued
to squeal.

Rogres sidestepped a passel of children running ahead of the musicians
and dancers, at the same time avoiding the roasting meats. Saint-Germain
managed a single chuckle at these antics, and Rogres felt relief go through
him like a rush of water; his master was not yet wholly caught up in whatever bedeviled him. Melancholy could take a chilling hold on Saint-
Germain, and after more than a thousand years in his company, Rogres
knew the signs. It had been more than a century since Saint-Germain had
suffered such apprehension as he did now: then they had been fleeing
China ahead of the warriors of Jenghiz Khan. At that time Saint-Germain
had been haunted by the death of T'en Chi-Yu as well as by the destruction wrought by the Mongols. "Will you play with them?" Rogres asked,
nodding toward the pipers.

"No," Saint-Germain answered after a moment of silence. "It would
not be fitting."

"Then why—?" He indicated the mandola.

"Perhaps later," said Saint-Germain, his voice suddenly remote as he
watched Deonis Vigny on the far side of the crowd, Leonell Braccer next
to her; they would be married within the week and Saint-Germain wished
her well, for jealousy was not in his nature.

Rogres saw what had caught Saint-Germain's attention and his qualms
returned. Loss of her dreaming passion was one more blow to Saint-
Germain, and his concern prompted him to say, "She does not know?
You've said nothing?"

"What can I say?" Saint-Germain countered. "She knows only her
dreams." He looked away from her. "She would not welcome what I am
awake."

The pipers finally agreed upon a drone pitch, turning cacophony to
music, and began one of the circular melodies sung in the region; lively and
sinuous, it spiraled for as long as the pipers were willing to play it. The people gathered welcomed it like an old friend as the dancers began the first
spritely steps.

Women tending the spits shouted their disapproval as the dancers got
near to them and for a moment it seemed as though the festivities would
turn into a melee; elbows were out and the gaiety took on a more aggres-

sive edge as a few of the dancers shoved at those around the turning spits. Shouts went up as a cup of beer was thrown at one of the cooks who swore and struck out with a ladle. Then someone laughed loudly and goodwill was restored. One of the drummers moved a short distance so that the dancers had a reason not to be so near the food.

"That is a clever man," Saint-Germain approved quietly to Rogres. "He has great presence of mind."

"There will be fighting before the night is over," Rogres reminded him.

"Yes, but it is just as well to delay that as long as possible," was Saint-Germain's response as he made his way along the edge of the crowd, his manner politely aloof as he returned the greeting of Pare Herriot. "He's ambitious," he remarked to Rogres.

"Beyond Bishop, I should think," Rogres said with a nod.

"Oh, yes," Saint-Germain said, so quietly that the sound of the crowd almost drowned him out.

One of those with Pare Herriot pointed to Saint-Germain's mandola. "Turning troubador, are you, Sieur Ragoczy?"

"Not just at present," Saint-Germain replied cordially enough but with an underlying authority that reminded the fellow he had overstepped himself.

"They will wonder why you don't play," Rogres warned. "It is remarkable for you to bring the mandola."

"Perhaps I will play later," Saint-Germain said. "Shortly before we leave."

There were more dancers now, and the monks were ladling out their drink to eager celebrants, shouting a blessing with each cup they filled. At this end of the gathering, the sharp smell of beer mixed with the aroma of cooking food. A few of the more important landowners stood with the Bishop a little apart from the rest of the revelers, watching the dancing; one of them saw Saint-Germain and called out to him, "A fine festival for Saunt Jehan, is it not, Sieur Ragoczy?"

"Wonderful; an honor to Saunt Jehan," Saint-Germain replied. He bowed to the gathering, but did not linger, continuing on around the throng.

"Are you looking for someone?" Rogres asked when they had gone a little farther.

"Gaspard Estin," said Saint-Germain. "He is due to leave for Genova in a few days. I would like to wish him success."

"And exchanging words at this festival raises fewer questions than a visit, which would be noticed," Rogres said.

"The boy has had enough trouble because he has been my pupil; that he longs for learning would cause him trouble with the Church. I would do him no service to remind the village of it." Saint-Germain turned suddenly as a young man in servant's livery came up to him and bowed respectfully. "Yes?"

"The compliments of Percevall, Vidame Saint Joachim, and his invitation to join him." Again the messenger bowed. "He is in the pavilion and would be pleased if you would accompany me to him."

Saint-Germain knew better than to refuse such a charge; for no matter how courteously delivered, the invitation was a command. He inclined his head to the messenger, and then nodded to Rogres. "I will find you later, old friend." He gave his attention to the servant once more. "I am at the Vidame's service."

The servant said nothing more as he led the way through the crowd to a light-colored pavilion set up in the fallow field next to the celebration area; it was large, ornamented with tassels and embroidery and had clearly never seen more battle than tournaments provided. Four men-at-arms in half-armor guarded the entrance to the elaborate tent, one of them holding a raised sword. Saint-Germain did not speak to the men, for that would make them suspicious of him. He went into the pavilion behind the messenger.

Inside the pavilion braziers and lamps provided light. Four chairs were drawn up around a low table, but no one occupied them. On the other side of the pavilion was a low dais, and on it was an impressive chair in which the Vidame Saint Joachim sat, using an Oriental fan to keep cool, for the pavilion was quite warm. He was not quite middle-aged, perhaps thirty-two; his eyes were puffy and his skin mottled, looking chapped where it was not slick with sweat. His breathing was fast for a man sitting down. He was dressed in a Burgundian houppelande of dark yellow, the huge triangular sleeves lined in a brilliant red, the tight inner sleeves the color of butter, or so they appeared in the low, golden light; it might have been the lamplight reflecting on all this saffron hue that gave his face a jaundiced cast. He regarded Saint-Germain with a mixture of curiosity and apprehension. "You are Sieur Ragoczy?" He sounded disappointed.

"I have that honor," said Saint-Germain quietly, his manner a nice combination of respect, deference, and hauteur; if the Vidame did not know that Saint-Germain was of equal rank, Saint-Germain did. He waited to be told why the Vidame wanted to see him, his stance easy, his demeanor composed.

The Vidame frowned but held back whatever disparaging remark he had been about to make. "My page said he would find you. He has."

The young man who had escorted Saint-Germain to the pavilion almost smirked. "I have seen him before, Vidame," he reminded his master. "In this gathering, it was no hard task to find him."

"Certainly; certainly," said the Vidame. He coughed once, and wiped his hand on the glowing fabric of his houppelande. "The wheelwright of Orgon—you know him?"

"Savill? Yes, I know him," Saint-Germain replied, more perplexed than ever at this odd question.

Again the Vidame coughed. "They say that . . . that you came to his aid when he was . . . ill?" Doubt made his statement an inquiry.

Saint-Germain considered his answer with care. "I was able to offer him some relief, yes. He has an antipathy to the stings of insects."

"I was told so," agreed the Vidame, shuddering.

When the Vidame did not go on, Saint-Germain ventured, "Have you suffered a sting?" It would fit his color and breathing to have sustained such an injury. "What has hurt you, Vidame?" The man was visibly shaking, but whether from his hurt or from fear, Saint-Germain could not discern.

"I cannot tell. I have been beset with— Something has plagued me, and . . ." His words straggled into silence and he was pale around the mouth as if admitting so much exposed him to unthinkable danger. "I have been in pain and offered it up, but—" He put his hand to his shoulder and did his best not to wince.

"There is an injury?" Saint-Germain asked, now putting his mandola aside on the table and coming to the foot of the dais. "What is the trouble, good Vidame?"

"The monks at Saunt Joachim have given me a tincture and have prayed for me," the Vidame said, his trembling continuing. "It is no better and now they tell me it is the Devil's work, beyond remedy." For a man with a Church-granted title, the thought of the Devil working on him was terrifying.

Saint-Germain could smell infection now, and his concern increased. "When did you notice you had been stung?" He could not make himself sound aghast no matter how much the Vidame expected it. "How long has there been pain?"

The Vidame's eyes shone with fear. "For nine days," he whispered.

"Nine days. And when did it fill with pus?" He came up the dais without waiting for permission, ignoring the shocked exclamation of the messenger.

"Five, six days since," said the Vidame, crossing himself at this admission, for it was known that pus present in a wound for seven days was fatal. He stared up at Saint-Germain. "What am I to do?"

"Let me see the sting," said Saint-Germain, no sign of alarm in his features. "You will want me to know what the nature of the bite is before I recommend anything, do you not?"

Shuddering, the Vidame began to unlace his houppelande and then to untie the chamisa beneath, shrugging out of them gingerly and with a grimace. Then he leaned forward with care, holding on to the arms of his chair while Saint-Germain came to the side of it. "I have done all the monks recommended, but—"

The bite was on the Vidame's back, high on his right shoulder blade. Without removing the filthy rag tied over the welt, Saint-Germain could see the swelling under the linen discolored by sweat and discharge from the bite. Since washing was considered vanity by the monks, the injury had not been cleaned. The smell was appalling, a mix of rancid and metallic, augmented with sweat. Saint-Germain sighed as he peeled back the bandage and looked at the injury: the swelling was discolored around two punctures divided only by a hair-fine line of inflamed skin; the ulceration of the bites had progressed to the stage where the actual wounds looked like raw meat flecked with tallow-colored fat, and the exposed flesh pushed outward. "I think you were bitten by a spider," he said as he examined the infected punctures. He had seen stings and bites over the centuries and had come to know their origins by their appearance. "The pus should be purged from the bite so that the . . ." He faltered, trying to think of an explanation that the Vidame would accept. "The spider has left behind some of its venom to poison you, as an enemy might. If you will allow me to purge the venom from you, the healing of the monks can work at last."

"But the monks told me—" the Vidame began, then stopped himself. "Very well," he said with the courage of desperation. "If that is what must be done, then you must do it."

"I will have to ask my manservant to fetch a few things from my villa, if you will permit?" Saint-Germain spoke without any indication that he felt distressed by what he saw. "Your messenger: will he fetch him for me?"

"Cordell is my page," said the Vidame. "He will find your man for you. Won't you?" His question was an order.

"Is he the man who was with you?" Cordell asked. "Older, sandy hair?"

"Yes," said Saint-Germain. "Ask him to come with you."

The page bowed once and left the pavilion.

"You think he is old to be a page, and you are right," said the Vidame as soon as the youth was gone. "The monks had him for four years but he is too . . . worldly for them. He is too curious and they fear he may spread heresy if he remains with them. They sent him to me, as their Vidame, to train him. One day he will be a good clerk, I hope." He was speaking quickly, more so that he could forget his injury than to tell Saint-Germain about the young man. With a groan he tried to make himself comfortable in the chair. "What are you going to do?"

"Purge the bite, as I told you. Then I have a remedy that will strengthen your flesh. I was taught how to make it in Egypt." It was true enough; he said nothing about how long ago he had learned. "When the wound is cleaned of pus, then I recommend you have garlic hung around your bed and put under the sheets."

"Garlic?" The Vidame tried to swing around in his chair to look at Saint-Germain directly. "Then you think the cause is malign? You suspect the presence of hungry ghosts—"

"No," said Saint-Germain trying not to sound exasperated. "Nothing of the sort."

"Then why should I have garlic hung?" The Vidame was frightened

enough for his voice to shoot up four notes. "Garlic is a remedy against ma-
lignant spirits and witchcraft."

"It may be," Saint-Germain responded, doing his best to remain calm.
"You may be wise to maintain the practice for that purpose. But I know it
will keep away insects of many kinds, as well as some spiders, and you will
be less likely to suffer another bite like this if you will take such precautions."

The Vidame nodded, his manner satisfied. "You show admirable reserve, mon Sieur; it is as they have said: you have real skills, for which I
thank God for my delivery in this hour." He paused. "Very well. We will say
nothing of the origins of this injury and we will allow all to think it *was* a
spider and that the garlic will keep spiders and insects away." Uncomfortable as he was, he did his best to laugh once, to show he understood the
cause for the deception. "It would not be fitting for the world to know that
agents of the Devil are attacking a Vidame. The Church would be dis-
mayed if they learned of it."

Saint-Germain did his best not to argue; the Vidame was convinced
that the Devil had sent a demon in the form of a spider to attack him, and
nothing Saint-Germain could tell him now would shake his conviction.
"Be diligent with the garlic," he said, wanting to press home the small advantage the Vidame's beliefs gave him. He regretted that he would not be
able to persuade his patient to bathe more frequently, for as a noble of the
Church, the Vidame would not consent to such a display of vanity as fre-
quent bathing represented.

"Why should the Devil single me out?" the Vidame mused aloud. "Unless it is Cordell, and his faithlessness has brought the Devil to my villa."
He began to ponder that possibility.

A moment later, Cordell returned with Rogres, and bowed in good
form. "I have found him, mon Sieur."

"So you have," said Saint-Germain, and noticed that the Vidame shot
him a look of consternation.

"You have need of me, my master?" Rogres asked with a show of deference that the Vidame thought fitting.

"Yes, old friend. I do." He indicated the Vidame's bared shoulder. "This
is a badly infected spider bite. I will need my poultices and my sovereign
remedy to treat it properly, and for that I must ask you to return to Clair
dela Luna to fetch them for me." He paused, then said, "I would like you
to ride at once."

"At once," said Rogres with another bow. "I will go as quickly as I can.
With a full moon, it is safe to trot the horse."

The Vidame spoke up. "Take one of my men-at-arms with you. There
are robbers on the road and a night like this brings them out in force."

"You are most kind," said Saint-Germain, adding to Rogres, "See that
the soldier is fed for his trouble. Monceau is still at the villa, and one of the
under-cooks; he will attend to the soldier while you gather the things I

need. The drawing poultice, and the sovereign remedy. Oh, and remember to include a soporific. The Vidame will have to sleep deeply if he is to speed his recovery." It would also serve to dull the pain while Saint-Germain purged the bite.

"I will," said Rogres, turning to go. He paused in the door of the pavilion. "Pardon, my master, but should I bring anything else with me?"

"I think those things will be sufficient," Saint-Germain said, making a sign to his manservant that he knew Rogres would recognize. "I will do what I can until you return."

The Vidame called out, "Jaques, go with him." This was answered by a sharp reply of consent; the Vidame looked at Saint-Germain. "There. You need not fear thieves now, mon Sieur."

Saint-Germain said, "That is one less worry." Then he signaled to the page Cordell. "Can you bring me a pan of water just off the boil, a few clean rags, and a basin?"

Cordell glanced at the Vidame for permission. "In this gathering I should be able to." He was about to saunter off when a thought occurred to him. "You say water just off the boil—should it be heated here?"

"If a fire can be lit, it would be useful," said Saint-Germain; he was bending over now, giving the bite close scrutiny.

"And you say clean rags," Cordell persisted. "How clean must they be? Will the men-at-arms' saddle rags do, or should they be cleaner?"

"Cleaner if possible," said Saint-Germain, adding by way of explaining his odd request, "To be rid of the whole of the malign presence, clean rags are more effective, for they do not carry other humors that the evil may seize upon. If the rags have been washed—in holy water if possible—they will carry no harm." He hoped this would be enough to persuade the Vidame.

The page nodded. "I will see if the baker has any." With that, he was gone.

"It was not fitting for him to question you," the Vidame remarked when Cordell was out of earshot. "You should not have answered him."

"I would speak to a toad if it would mean it could aid your recovery," said Saint-Germain matter-of-factly, hoping he would not alarm the Vidame too much.

"A toad. You might as well address spiders also," said the Vidame, trying to make light of so scandalous a notion. Then he deliberately changed the subject, asking Saint-Germain how his crops were coming in, and continuing on such ordinary subjects until Cordell returned with a basin and a handful of linen scraps.

"I had them from the innkeeper," he said, showing them to Saint-Germain. "And I got the pan from him. The men-at-arms are building a fire to heat water for you." His expression became eager. "May I watch what you do? The monks let me help with the bleeding, so I will not faint."

"If the Vidame permits," Saint-Germain said, and then noticed how forbidding the Vidame's face was. "Let him watch; he will be able to tend your hurts when I am not by." It was a risk to say this, for it challenged the Vidame's authority, but it seemed worth the possible rebuke.

"Is that true?" the Vidame demanded, trying to turn far enough to confront Saint-Germain without hurting himself.

"You will need someone to tend to the dressing and to keep the humors from . . . contamination," said Saint-Germain.

The Vidame crossed himself. "Is there a miasma?"

Saint-Germain had long since ceased to think illness was caused by invisible clouds laden with disease, but he was the exception, and his doubts were heretical, so he said, "It is possible. If you will permit Cordell to treat you, only he will be likely to take the taint."

Cordell shot Saint-Germain a look, but said steadfastly, "I will do as you tell me, mon Sieur."

"The monks will be grateful that he has done some good," said the Vidame. "Make him your slave in this, Sieur Ragoczy."

Saint-Germain motioned to Cordell to approach. "To begin, we must have a hot, wet rag."

"Why must it be hot and wet?" Cordell asked, his attention already centered on the infected bite. "The hurt is hot and wet already."

Knowing he would have to explain in terms Cordell and the Vidame would accept, Saint-Germain said, "The Devil is lured by heat. By placing something hotter than the wound upon it, the malign presence can be drawn out. In this case, the presence is well-established and it will take some pulling to have it all. But we may begin with hot compresses." He touched the Vidame on the other shoulder. "I fear it will cause you some pain."

"If it casts the Devil out, the suffering can be offered up," said the Vidame, trying to sound brave as he clenched his teeth.

"When the water is boiling, soak a rag in it and then wrap it in another and bring it to me." Saint-Germain saw the fascination in Cordell's eyes. "Then I will show you how to bring the poisons out."

Cordell nodded, his very ordinary face shining with purpose. "God bless you for this service, mon Sieur," he said with feeling. "You will save him, won't you?"

Knowing the required response, Saint-Germain said, "God willing and the Devil routed."

The Vidame echoed these sentiments and steeled himself for what was to come.

On the table, Saint-Germain's Italian mandola lay forgotten as the treatment of the Vidame went on into the night.

Text of a letter from Jacapone Norello of Genova to Hue d'Ormonde of Marsailla, delivered on August 8, 1346.

Greetings and prosperity to my old friend Hue d'Ormonde from Jacapone Norello.

Your proposal to carry goods north overland to Hansa ports does indeed interest me, and I am more than willing to undertake such a venture next year, as you propose. I can provide linen and silks, which you can, as well. But I am certain that the qualities of our merchandise can allow for more than one kind of each. No doubt the Hansa merchants will be glad of all they can obtain, and neither of us need fear profiting at the expense of the other.

As the time grows nearer, we will make such arrangements as suits both our purposes and to our mutual advantage, and in terms framed to our present needs and expectations. You have shown yourself a worthy man in business; with so fine a reputation we should be received well in the north, where the Hansa merchants are most powerfully situated.

I am somewhat worried about the prevalence of robbery on the roads. Without men-at-arms, I could not hazard my merchandise on the roads through France. We are not pilgrims or players, to pass unharmed through the doors of Hell, and so we must provide for our safety.

The three barrels of wine you shipped to me are as superior as you promised they were. I know they will all fetch a good price at market, and I would be glad of more of the same. The foreigner whose vines produce it must have unusual skills to produce such wine. If I can procure more than two or three barrels, I will offer a fair price. You say that he also makes perfumes. I will take a keg of whatever he is prepared to offer—judging by his wines, the perfume should be excellent.

Your wedding is about to take place, as I recall. I wish you good years together, good health, and fine sons to inherit your fortune. May God smile on your union and on all your enterprises.

> *With high respect, I sign myself,*
> *Jacapone Norello*
> *Merchant of Genova*

On this 22nd day of July, in the Lord's Year 1346.

5

For six days Marsailla had simmered under the relentless August sun, and the heat was so vast and encompassing that all the windows of Hue d'Ormonde's house were flung open so that the wedding guests might have the dubious benefit of the listless breeze off the sea; the lozenge-shaped panes, so rare and costly, winked like jewels in the side of the house. In celebration of d'Ormonde's marriage, bowls of now-wilted flowers had been set on tables, chests, and cases throughout the house, and the doorways decorated with wreaths and bows of evergreens. In the central courtyard a number of tables had been set up; food and drink were laid out for the wedding feast. Ordinarily this would be served in the reception hall, but the heat made such common courtesy unbearable, or so the servants and slaves insisted when they asked to move the tables. D'Ormonde had agreed; he had no wish to have anyone collapsing from the heat at this fine occasion, for it would set an ill-omen on the marriage. So the guests gathered in the courtyard, determined to use their celebration to forget the heat, or if that were impossible, to become sufficiently intoxicated not to care.

Hue d'Ormonde did his best to ignore the sweat soaking into his marriage finery as he showed his new wife around the house, accompanied by her brother and sons, with Jenfra lagging behind, her gorgeous new garments limp and her demeanor lethargic. Her expression was dissatisfied; no one noticed but Francois de Saint-Germain, Sieur Ragoczy, who stood somewhat apart from those clamoring for food and drink. In honor of the wedding he had forsaken his usual black garments for an Italian lucco of a deep red silk, the color and shine of good wine. A silver-and-jeweled pectoral depended from a massive, ruby-studded silver chain and a neat, narrow coronet encircled his brow.

"Do you want to see the kitchens now?" d'Ormonde asked his bride as they emerged from the reception hall into the courtyard once again. His face was glistening and his hair hung in damp strands, but his smile was cordial and slightly smug.

Before she could answer, her brother said, "It will be worse than an oven."

"Yes," said Benoita, but whether on her own account or to please her brother no one could tell. "If it is hot here, the kitchens will be terrible."

"Then is there any other part of the house you want to be shown now?" d'Ormonde asked, knowing it was his duty to offer, but hoping to postpone the moment until the cool of the evening.

"We have seen as much as we need, for now," her brother said.

D'Ormonde nodded, clearly relieved, and led his new wife to the main table, enjoying the way the guests parted for them. "This is your home now, Benoita, and for your children. At last my daughter will have someone to occupy her time beyond the sewing her maid teaches her." His smile was more hopeful than confident; Abram had the intense, inward stare of one who was not right in the head.

"Your daughter is fortunate indeed," said Benoita's brother, his false smile as transparent as the expensive glass in the windows. Josue Roebertis was still congratulating himself on finding so suitable a match for Benoita and the family. "No doubt Abram will provide her with practice for her own family. And your daughter and Hilaire are much of an age and will be able to entertain one another when he comes to visit." It had been agreed that Hilaire would remain with his uncle as his ward; the boy, just turned eleven, moved a few steps closer to Josue.

From the curl of Jenfra's lip, entertaining Hilaire was the last thing she intended to do; nor did she plan to be Abram's nurse. Her dissatisfaction was evident from every aspect of her demeanor; no one paid any heed to her, and her feelings went unnoticed. She did not bother to try to smile.

"Yes; that would be nice," said Benoita, her shoulders squared but her head drooping. She looked from her husband to her brother. "I am so thirsty."

At once Josue moved to fetch her some wine, but now d'Ormonde intercepted him. "I think," he said cordially, "that it is now my turn."

Josue looked startled and slightly offended, but he knew it would be incorrect to challenge d'Ormonde's right in his own house. "Certainly. It has been my custom for so long that I did not think."

"No matter," said d'Ormonde, and went to bring cups of wine for Benoita and himself.

Jenfra was pouting now, looking at her new relations with loathing. How could her father have ruined their family? Why was he not content to visit Yeselta as he had done regularly since his first wife died? Twice she started to speak and twice she changed her mind, as if words were too difficult to voice on this sultry afternoon. Finally she pulled the short church veil off her hair and muttered she was too hot. No one heard her but Saint-Germain.

The groomsman, an advocate of formidable reputation, finally rose to offer a prayer for the marriage which ended with the command that all seal their amen with happy communion. He raised his tankard and drank deeply; the rest of the wedding party did the same. "The Church had their first pledge. We in the world have their second," he concluded to general laughter.

"The brother of the bride thanks Hue d'Ormonde for his goodness to our family," said Josue Roebertis, raising his tankard; it was a graceless statement, but a fine excuse to drink again.

As the various pledges continued, Jenfra, knowing the celebration had no meaning for her, put her cup aside and wandered off into the house. She ended up in her father's anteroom, among his account-books. She sat down at the clerk's desk, wadded some of her cotehardie's skirt in both hands, and gave herself over to the tears that had threatened to overtake her all day. Muffling her sobs with her skirt, she let out all the misery and rage of the last month, finally screaming into the makeshift gag. Eventually the cries gave way to sniffles and hiccups; she sat up, feeling slightly foolish and a bit annoyed that she had forgot herself. Making an effort to smooth out her skirt, she halted in her attempts as she heard a crisp footfall in the door. She looked up sharply, keenly aware that her face was red and her eyes swollen.

"Your father wondered where you had gone," said Saint-Germain as he crossed the threshold. If he noticed her appearance, he said nothing about it.

"Did he notice?" She spat the words out without apology or thought. "Was he able to tear himself away from *her* and her family long enough?"

"Yes," Saint-Germain said gently. "And he is not the only one."

She was not willing to be angry with Saint-Germain, so she did her best to answer without sharpness. "I . . . I had to get away. It was so hot . . ." The excuse trailed off and she felt treacherous tears welling in her eyes again.

"It is very hot," said Saint-Germain, coming into the room. "Your father was afraid you were ill."

She laughed harshly. "How did he know I was gone?"

"He saw you leave, little though you may think so," said Saint-Germain, coming to the far side of the clerk's desk. "He asked me to find out where you had disappeared to."

"And now you have found me," she said, at last letting her resentment give force to her voice.

"It is his wedding day, Jenfra. You know he has things he must do. He told you what today would be like, and you said you understood." His musical voice was soothing, which made it more difficult for her to resist a second bout of tears.

"Oh, I understand. He has two sons now. Why should it matter to him what becomes of me?" She lowered her head and wiped her eyes, hating him for seeing her do it.

"You are his daughter. His. He will not put Hilaire or Abram above you." Saint-Germain hoped what he said was true, for it was not unusual for stepsons to supplant daughters.

"No, not above Hilaire. Josue Roebertis has him. And Abram is touched in his wits. He will inherit nothing but a token for the Frer who will care for him." She made a sound that was not quite laughter and not a cough. "But Papa and his wife have a new son. Then I will be only a daughter."

"You are assuming things that have not happened," said Saint-Germain, watching her more closely than she realized. "They have not made a child yet, nor delivered one, male or female."

"It is what they want, what they *all* want," Jenfra declared. "Even that Josue Roebertis. He has it planned. This marriage is his doing. He began the negotiations. And he knows what he wants from it: there will be a child in a year or so, a son, and he will find a way to make our family fortune tied to the son, so that they will all be enriched. The child will be d'Ormonde in name only: he will be Roebertis in all things that matter. The Roebertises will have claim to Papa through the son, since I am a daughter. So they will have their son, and that Josue Roebertis will make sure that the boy gets all. And when Papa dies, I will have nothing. *Nothing!* They will force me to marry Hilaire so that not one copper crown will get away from them. If I refuse they will turn me out to beg or compel me to take up the life of a servant or a whore or force me into a convent or send me to distant cousins who will confine me as surely as any prison would." Her voice had risen; she put a hand to her mouth. "It will happen. It's what that Josue wants."

"Has he told you this?" Saint-Germain asked gently; when she shook her head indecisively, he pressed on. "Has your father told you any of this?"

"No. He would say nothing to me. But I can see it in how he talks to my father. And my father listens to him." She glared down at the floor, embarrassed to speak against Hue d'Ormonde. "He will be persuaded, eventually, and I will have to do as they wish."

Saint-Germain studied her, knowing that Jenfra had some reason to feel the way she did; in the last millennium, females had gone from positions of strength in Caesars' Rome to near-property in the last five centuries; Saint-Germain could offer Jenfra no practical consolation for her situation. He tried to suggest another approach. "If I tell him about your fears and he assures me that nothing of the sort will happen, will you believe me?"

Jenfra stared at the desktop. "He will not tell you what he has discussed with Josue Roebertis. That would shame him, for he would have to admit that he will only do what they want. He does not care what happens to me." She knotted her hands together and thrust them into her lap. "I am the most wretched female on earth."

How young she was, Saint-Germain thought, and how unequivocal. It would serve no purpose to remind her of the misfortunes of others, for he knew at this time the ordeals of others meant nothing to her and she would resent being told about them. He saw the challenge in her eyes and did not respond as she expected he would. Instead he leaned over her, one hand held out to her. "Do not give them the satisfaction of knowing it," he recommended. "Let me take you downstairs."

She would not take his hand. "I won't let them see me like this," she said flatly. "Not that they would notice."

"Then let me take you to your maid. She will set you to rights and you may return without anyone knowing of your unhappiness." He remained still, his hand extended.

"I'm not ready," she said after a short silence. "If I must watch them feast and play, then I will need to master myself, for God made me volatile and without the help of Notra Dama, I will not be able to present a tranquil countenance." She sat straighter, doing her best to regain her expected air of decorum as the occasion demanded of her. "I am not ready to leave this room. I am too distraught." She was pleased at how grown-up she sounded.

"I will wait," said Saint-Germain, and folded his arms. He wondered what would happen to this willful girl; she would be expected to accept the husband of her father's choosing. She was fortunate that Hue d'Ormonde doted on her, for her wishes might be consulted when the time came to find a spouse, and her temperament weighed in the choice of a man for her. From the observations Hue d'Ormonde had made in the past, Saint-Germain recognized the regard Jenfra enjoyed. At least her father understood that she would not be a submissive bride and would require a wise man to wed her. If her stepmother could be brought to the same understanding, then Jenfra might have as pleasant a life as any woman in Provence could hope to have.

A short while later, Jenfra got to her feet and smoothed the front of her clothes. "I'm ready now. My maid will take care of me."

"Then I will take you to her, if you will permit." He held out his hand again, and this time Jenfra laid her own on it. "Well done," he approved.

"Your hands are not much bigger than mine," she exclaimed as she started toward the door. "Look. Mine almost cover them."

"They are small," he agreed.

She paused in the door and looked up at him. "You're not sweating, are you?"

"Those of my blood do not," he said, and did not add that those of his blood did not weep, either; he led her along the passage to the private chambers. His expression did not encourage any other observations.

At the door to her rooms, Jenfra took hold of Saint-Germain's hand. "Tell my father I will be with him directly."

"It will be my pleasure," Saint-Germain said approvingly.

With a forlorn sigh, Jenfra released him. "At least you knew I was gone," she said as she opened the door.

Saint-Germain waited a short time to be certain she did not leave her rooms again, then went down the narrow stairs to the reception hall where he found Hue d'Ormonde with Benoita and Josue seated at the octagonal table from Syria, their conversation conducted in low voices. Knowing it was proper to warn them of his presence, Saint-Germain cleared his throat before approaching the three. "She is in the hands of her maid," he said, inclining his head to d'Ormonde.

"She— Oh, Jenfra," he said, recalling the errand he had given to Saint-Germain. "Good." He half rose from his chair. "I am grateful to you, mon Sieur."

"It is nothing," Saint-Germain told him. He noticed that the heat had taken a toll on d'Ormonde, who looked a trifle pasty under the slick film of sweat on his face; the excitement of this occasion did not account for his appearance. "Have you taken time to eat yet, d'Ormonde? You have spent all the morning on your feet; surely you feel it?" He asked it neutrally enough. "Your guests will devour all if you do not take this opportunity to dine with them."

D'Ormonde chuckled. "Why should you remark on this, of all men? I have never seen you touch any food, not in all the time I have known you, though your hospitality has ever been generous." He saw the alarm in the eyes of Josue Roebertis and Benoita, and hurried on in an attempt to repair any damage his light comments might have inflicted on Saint-Germain. "You have said the customs of your people do not permit you to eat with more than one guest. It is an odd tradition, but it is right that you honor it."

Josue managed to smile automatically. "What people have such a custom?" he asked in an under-voice.

Saint-Germain answered him as if the question had been directed at him. "The people of the Carpathians, where the Hungarians have their farthest borders." He bowed to Josue. "My people have observed this tradition since before Caesar reigned in Roma."

"Or so you claim," said Josue Roebertis, determined to be unimpressed with the foreigner, as much to cast doubts on Hue d'Ormonde's position as to accuse Saint-Germain of perpetuating a fraud.

"Because it is true." Saint-Germain's stance did not change, nor did his expression alter, but there was something in the tone of his voice that did not encourage any greater challenge. "I am grateful to d'Ormonde for having me among his guests at this occasion. My ways are not the ways of Provence, and many another would have disdained such company as I must be." He gave his attention to d'Ormonde again. "I think you should have some food; you look hungry."

"I fear I have lost my appetite," said d'Ormonde. "The celebration has been demanding, and I do not think I will soon—"

Saint-Germain held up his hand. "This excitement convinces me that you have allowed yourself to become overtired." He was far more concerned at the wan color of d'Ormonde's face. "You have fish roe and good wine. A little of each should restore you."

"Fish roe and wine." D'Ormonde got to his feet. "Very well. I will eat, if my new wife will join me." He held out his hand to her. "The courtyard will be cooler."

She looked at her brother, saw him nod, and put her hand on d'Ormonde's. "You are kind to me, my husband," she said, and allowed him to lead her from the reception room going toward the courtyard where the wedding guests were beginning to turn the afternoon into a grand revel.

Now only Saint-Germain and Josue Roebertis remained. "If you have anything to tell me, you might have said it while my sister's husband was by." Josue's voice was harsh and lazy at once, and he stared at Saint-Germain with an expression bordering on contempt.

"What?" Saint-Germain looked at him in some surprise. "How do you mean?"

"You could have spoken to me without contriving to get d'Ormonde out of the room," said Josue with impatience.

"You mistake me, good merchant," said Saint-Germain. "I saw that our host was lacking salt, which in this heat made him pale. You would not want him to faint before he has taken your sister to bed, would you? It would be a bad omen for the marriage." He bowed slightly more deeply than courtesy required and was about to leave the reception chamber when Josue stopped him.

"You think to persuade my new brother into dealings with the north. But I assure you, it will not be. He has my sister and her children to care for now, and the wild ventures of the past will not be approved by Benoita." He met Saint-Germain's gaze with presumptuousness. "D'Ormonde may rejoice in your business, but I know my sister will not."

"Because you tell her so," Saint-Germain finished for him.

"She listens to me," Josue admitted with pride. "She is more Roebertis than she was Pleissan, or is now d'Ormonde."

"The law requires that protection of you," said Saint-Germain, his poor impression of the man growing worse. "It is as well that you did not shirk the requirements of the magistrates and the Church."

Josue Roebertis turned a darker shade of plum than the heat had made him. "You cannot dissemble with me, mon Sieur. You may be worthy in Hungary, but this is Provence, and your state is not held in high esteem here."

"I was not aware that my place in the world was important just now," Saint-Germain responded, no indication that his cordiality was forced.

"D'Ormonde wishes to show how high-born his associates are," said Josue bluntly. "I am not readily fooled by such sham."

"Why should you think me a sham, or d'Ormonde, for that matter?" The question made no accusation, yet the steadiness of Saint-Germain's gaze was enough to unnerve Josue.

"Foreign titles are easy to claim. You could be anyone." He made a fussy gesture of disgust.

"Given that this is a great occasion, Josue Roebertis," Saint-Germain told him, his words precise, "I will not answer your churlishness. You are the guest of my friend, and I have no wish to dishonor his kindness; God send you good fortune." He bowed and was about to leave Josue to his own company when one last insult was flung.

"If you are what you claim to be, what reason have you to be in this company? Why should a well-born man like you come to this wedding but to make a mistress of my sister?" As soon as he said it, Josue Roebertis became stiff, knowing he had impugned not only Saint-Germain but Benoita as well.

"Your regard for your sister is astonishing." Saint-Germain would not be roused by such a petulant display.

"I have faith in my sister; you, mon Sieur, are another matter." He was almost rigid, and his stare was filled with fury.

A thousand years ago Saint-Germain might have indulged in obloquy, casting aspersions on the intentions of this man. Time had taught him that such attacks rarely gained more than the poor opinion of those he wished most to protect, so all he said was, "I am sure she is grateful to you."

"And I will guard her from you if her husband will not." He raised his hand defiantly.

"Then she surely will have nothing to fear," said Saint-Germain as he left the reception room. He was more troubled than he was willing to show; if Josue Roebertis' opinion was shared by others, it would not do d'Ormonde any good to remain here while the wedding celebration continued. Rumors of infidelity were potentially more damaging than the act itself, for the laws of the County of Provence required that such rumors be prosecuted in order to maintain public morality. As he reached the courtyard, Saint-Germain knew he must not linger at the wedding.

"There you are. Good. I was hoping you would spare me a moment or two before the party becomes too merry," d'Ormonde said as Saint-Germain came up to him. "It is an inconvenient time, but you will be leaving Marsailla soon, and business presses; I must discuss the Hansa matter with you. I have a few terms we need to review before our final contracts are prepared. You're still willing to sign, aren't you?"

Saint-Germain managed a quick smile. "Doubtless; but this is not the best time, is it? As you said yourself." He indicated the guests in the courtyard. "You have other things to occupy your thoughts, and a new wife who is waiting for you."

"It will not take long," said d'Ormonde, glancing toward the door leading into the house. "It could be settled swiftly."

"Certainly," said Saint-Germain, guessing what Josue would make of such a discussion; by nightfall everyone would know that an agreement had been struck between d'Ormonde and Saint-Germain in regard not to the Hanseatic League, but d'Ormonde's wife. "And for that reason, we may as easily tend to it tomorrow. I will call upon you before I go to the docks to receive my most recent shipments. You will have more leisure then to go over our terms." He did not allow d'Ormonde to interrupt. "I hope you will spend some time with Jenfra. She is afraid that you will no longer care for her as you have done before."

"She is too pert for her own good," said d'Ormonde with a short sigh. "She has been allowed to have her own way. I know it is a fault in me, and I own it for what it is; Jenfra will have to come to terms with the changes in our lives, little though she may want to. I have cosseted her too long. She has not yet accepted how her life will be in years ahead. She has not the demeanor that makes for a pleasant wife; she will have to learn something of it before she is much older. But that is not for tonight." He put his hand to his face as if to make himself stop speaking of his daughter. "You were right about the fish roe. I had not realized how enervated I had become."

"Heat robs the body of salt," said Saint-Germain in an even voice. "In such weather, you will do well to take more of it than you do in winter."

D'Ormonde winked. "And tell the tax collectors what? That I am instructed by an alchemist to defy the laws of Marsailla?" As he shrugged, he conceded, "Perhaps tomorrow will be better for business. I will not demand that you come aside with me now. Tomorrow will be time enough."

"Thank you," said Saint-Germain. "I will not remain much longer; you may look for me at midmorning tomorrow." He saw Josue emerge from the interior of the house, and decided to make his departure more noticeable than he had first intended.

"Yeselta?" D'Ormonde spoke the name with a touch of envy. "You are going to visit her tonight?"

"Possibly," Saint-Germain answered deliberately evasively. "In such heat, it may not be—"

"Love does not thrive in such weather," d'Ormonde agreed at once. "But the evening will be cooler." He cocked his head in the direction of his new bride. "Tonight I pray for a breeze."

"So must your wife," said Saint-Germain, then added, "Tomorrow we will have time to talk, and not only about the Hansa towns."

D'Ormonde looked curious, saying, "I will continue to sell your wines, if that is what you mean."

Saint-Germain did not enlarge on his remark; instead he lifted his hand in a kind of benediction. "I wish you both a joyous night."

"And many sons," d'Ormonde amended, finishing the customary wish for his guest. "Tell Yeselta that I miss her."

This time Saint-Germain bowed his acknowledgment. "Until tomorrow."

"Midmorning," d'Ormonde agreed, and gave his attention to his other guests.

The narrow streets of Marsailla were nearly empty; only a few men trudged along the winding street toward the market in front of the docks where ships were secured, riding listlessly on the ebb-tide. Activity aboard most of them was minor, the heat having driven all but the most pressed of the crews below decks or out of the vessels entirely. A high, humming sound, barely audible, permeated the dense air, as if the heat had discovered a voice for itself; the faltering wind had lost its strength and the sails of the ships beyond the docks did little more than flap in a desultory way when there was any movement in the atmosphere.

One of the ships, of Egyptian design, had arrived the day before and was being inspected by the customs officers. The double-masted, lateen-rigged vessel was out of place among the hulks and naos of the Marsailla merchants, its low lines contrasting with the bulkier European craft; its furled sails were new and white, like tethered clouds. Three sailors were on deck, two of them in the flowing white robes of Egypt, the third in Greek clothing; all were weathered to walnut-brown and had deep creases around their eyes from hours of watching the shining sea. They lingered near the gangplank as their Captain presented his records to the officers; the process was a slow one, requiring two translators and a monk to sort out all the orders-of-lading.

Saint-Germain decided that since he would be in Marsailla for three

more days, he would wait until the next day to claim his property. At this
moment he mildly regretted having left his mandola at Clair dela Luna; he
would have liked to pass the time playing. He turned his back on the harbor and went along to Yeselta's tall, private house where the woman herself would accommodate him, and where he could forget for a short while
the disquiet in his ancient soul.

Text of a dispatch from Percevall, Vidame Saunt Joachim, to twelve Vidames in the County and Margraviate of Provence, Dauphiny, the County
of Flores, the County of Savoy, and the Duchy and County of Burgundy.
Carried by military courier and delivered one-to-four weeks after being
written.

*The Kiss of Peace to all of you, whether allied to Rome or Avignon, or the
King of France or the Holy Roman Emperor, and the Grace of God upon
you all.*

*To all my peers, in reverent regard for our unique position in this per-
ilous time, and with our current worldly disputes caught up in the difficulties of the Church, I appeal to you all to stand by the religion that
provides us our titles and not permit yourselves or your men-at-arms to be
engaged in the arguments of Kings, nor in the disputes of Princes. Many of
us live in regions that have alternately been claimed by the French and the
Holy Roman Emperor, and if God wills it, we may change worldly alliances many times before Christ comes at Judgment Day. You may be
tempted to engage in many disputes, but unless they are the battles of the
Church, we must remain true to the Church and put our men into the
field only in that cause that defends the Church.*

*I also admonish you to make peace among yourselves, for if strife is the
rule, we will beget strife and misfortune. We are thus admonished by the
Evangelists, and their words are as fitting today as the hour they were ut-
tered. God did not make me war-like, as He made many of you, but I pray
you will beseech your Saunts to intercede on your behalf so that you may
more truly perform God's Will on Earth. If you will but ask God to improve
what He has made, you will be inclined through His Mercy to a character
more clement than what you now possess.*

*Many of you have been told by clergy in Roma that the Church will fail
if it is not centered in that city. But it was on the inspiration of the Holy
Spirit that the Pope brought the Church to Avignon, and here it will remain
until God once again moves His Servant to establish it in another place. We
must defend the Pope before all cries of Kings. The Kings have their
Princes, Ducs, Comtes, Margraves and Sieurs to defend them. It is left to
us to remain true to the Pope in the face of the rule of Kings.*

*Through the venom of a demon-familiar in the form of a spider I have
recently endured a great trial: I was delivered by Grace from the very
mouth of death, and I have learned that such deliverance brings with it re-*

newed thanks to God. I have been animated with purpose through the Mercy of God, who sent a foreign magician to save me when all the work of the monks of Saunt-Joachim could not save me. In this I saw God's Will, and I have prayed for the salvation of that magician from the time he ministered to my ills. I knew the magician was God's Tool, for he is an exiled nobleman whose lands have fallen to his enemies; thus he reminds me of how fleeting are the alliances of Princes. His care of me was as fine as any that could be given. This Sieur Ragoczy has been God's instrument in this, as I pray to be His instrument in turning you from the promises of rulers on earth for the surety of glory in Heaven. God has made us and given us our place in the world to do the bidding of His Pope. If we fail in this, it matters little what rewards we garner on earth, for we will be damned for our treason.

I pray each of you may meet your own Sieur Ragoczy in the Holy Season to come, to help you to remain true to your Maker, as I have been helped. In the name of the Pope we serve, I am faithfully,

Percevall, Vidame Saunt Joachim
by the hand of Frer Alexander, Cluniac

On the 22nd day of October in the County of Provence in the Holy Roman Empire in the 1346th Year of Grace.

6

Long after midnight Rogres found his master still in his alchemical laboratory in the tower of Clair dela Luna. He had climbed the stairs quietly, but was not surprised when Saint-Germain spoke his name without turning. "It is late, my master," he said in the Latin of Imperial Rome.

"So it is; the night soothes me." Saint-Germain set aside his massive, leather-bound book and swung around on his stool, the box-sleeves of his black-red Flemish houppelande swinging with his movement. "You are right; I have been avoiding the villa." He waited for a reply, then went on, "What has brought you to me at this hour, and in such weather, old friend? I would have thought you would remain in the main house." He indicated the storm beyond the shuttered windows; the winds had come up the night before and had been increasing in strength all through the intervening hours until now they howled and hooted as if possessed by the spirits of the damned, which the priests in Orgon declared they were.

"I would have done, but the stable has lost some of its roof," said Rogres bluntly. "It will need to be repaired as soon as the storm passes."

This claimed Saint-Germain's attention at once. "How extensive is the damage? Are the horses and mules safe?"

"They are, for the time being. Half a dozen of the beams are exposed, and a part of the tack room. The hay in the loft is ruined. I have assigned the shepherd to watch the stable, with orders to lead the animals to the cow byre if the stable is more severely mauled by the wind. There is room enough for half the horses in with the cattle, at least until the storm abates." Rogres came farther into the room. "Your tower will have to be—"

"Examined for damage too; yes, I know," Saint-Germain said shortly, then relented. "Do not be offended, Rogerian. I mean no slight to you."

"Your restlessness is worse," said Rogres with the familiarity of centuries. "I have been observing it for months now. Do you still think it comes from your reluctance to leave this place?"

"I wish I knew; I cannot fathom it," said Saint-Germain in self-exasperation. Then he did his best to smile. "At least the harvest is in. Had this storm struck in October, we would have lost half of it." He rubbed at his chin through the short beard. "I will have to arrange a hunt soon with one of the other landholders. Boar and deer, I should think."

"You have only to tell me to carry the message, my master, and your neighbors will know of it," said Rogres, undeceived by this sudden practicality, but willing to go along with it. "Monceau says that pine martens have been getting at the ducks again. Shall I tell him to kill them?"

Saint-Germain sighed. "It is what he will want to do. And if I fed on ducks, I might do the same." He looked down at his hands. "Who am I to condemn him, after all."

"He will want to be permitted to sell the skins," Rogres said.

"If he does the killing himself, he may have the profit from it, otherwise he must share with whomever he chooses to kill for him." Saint-Germain made a gesture of distaste. "I am doubtless a fool to worry so about these things. What is one pine marten, or a dozen, more or less?"

Rogres regarded Saint-Germain steadily. "It is not the pine martens, is it?"

Saint-Germain gave a quick, quirky smile. "No," he admitted ruefully. "Or only a small part of it." He put his hand on the book he had set aside. "When I was young, before I died, all the world was barbaric; even the Chinese had not yet brought themselves out of regional disputes to the state they have made, and Egypt had hardly begun its first, uncertain steps away from clan warfare. I thought then that our rule was benign, when I considered the matter at all—which I rarely did; none of us questioned how our lives were ordained, not then. Of late I have been thinking of those vanished times. And what I see around me now is not so different from what was done while I lived, more than three thousand years ago. At least then we did not think the camel was an earthly metaphor for piety because it kneels down to be mounted, or that roses were the sign of chastity because their flowers are protected by thorns. How have we come so far to be at no better place than this?" He folded his arms. "Forgive me: I am beginning to sound like Olivia."

"You say you believe she has cause to miss the Roma of her youth," Rogres said by way of comfort.

"And so she does," Saint-Germain responded at once, his morose turn of mind concealed in sardonic amusement. "It is easier for me to bear these sentiments when she expresses them; when I say them, I want to chide myself for indulgence."

Rogres had no easy answer to offer and so remained silent. His faded-blue eyes revealed his concern for Saint-Germain as his impassive features did not.

"You may tell me how fatiguing my self-indulgence is; you cannot think so more than I do myself. By all the lost gods, Rogres, I am heartily—" Whatever he was going to say was lost in a sudden clamor of the gate-bell. "What on earth?"

"The storm," Rogres suggested, going to the window to peer out into the blowing, wet night.

"Perhaps," Saint-Germain conceded. "But possibly not," he went on as the ringing was renewed with greater urgency and determination.

"Who would be here at this hour?" Rogres asked, his question colored with alarm.

"Well, we will not find the answer by remaining here," Saint-Germain said, and saw reticence in Rogres' demeanor. "I have not known robbers to announce themselves, and I doubt we are being summoned by familiars of the Holy Office, not with so little display; and there are no men-at-arms demanding hospitality: this is probably some hapless traveler bound for Orgon who needs shelter for the night, and we, in charity, are required to provide it," he said with a slight, ironic bow in the direction of the stairs. "Bring a sword if you like."

"You will not go armed, then?" Rogres asked, reaching for one of the weapons hung on the wall. "Is it not wiser to—"

"I think not," said Saint-Germain, leaving the light of his laboratory and plunging into the dark of the stairwell, relieved to have some activity that would not permit him to keep dwelling on his discontent.

Rogres hesitated and took a long dagger from the wall before following his master down the stairs and out into the storm.

The bell was still clanging as Saint-Germain rushed up to the gate, water splashing around his thick-soled solers; he could feel the slightly queasy sensation that he inevitably experienced when crossing water in motion, be it a stream or the broad sea. He steadied himself before he drew back the heavy iron bolt that held the gate shut.

"My master," Rogres called out as he came up behind Saint-Germain, his dagger held at the ready as the gate swung open on protesting hinges.

Darkness did not hamper Saint-Germain's vision as it did for most men; he shaded his eyes only to protect them from the relentless rain. As he made out the bedraggled figures waiting, he took an involuntary step forward, a half-spoken oath in his long-extinct native tongue revealing his shock.

A white Spanish donkey, ears drooping and head down in patient exhaustion, stood facing the gate, a habited and hooded figure on her back; both looked worn out and seriously chilled. The rider spoke with a cough. "I had to run away. I forgot how far it was."

"Jenfra," said Saint-Germain, recognizing Hue d'Ormonde's daughter with some astonishment, going at once to take the donkey's bridle and lift the girl from the donkey's saddle; he felt Jenfra's arm go to his shoulder as he cradled her easily in his arms. He paid no attention to her sodden clothes, for his were now soaked as well. "Rogres," he called out, "this animal needs food and water at once. Make sure she is given some heated bran when she is warmed enough." As he glanced down at Jenfra again, he saw her eyes close in utter fatigue.

Rogres had slipped the dagger through his belt; he hastened to do as Saint-Germain told him, but he faltered as he took the reins. "The stable-roof is—"

Saint-Germain nodded, impatient with himself for not remembering. "Indeed. Then put her in the . . . in the woodshed by the bakehouse. That should be warm still, and have room enough for a donkey. It will do for a day or two." He looked down at Jenfra in his arms. "This is going to be more difficult." He shifted his hold on her so that he could close and secure his gate once more, shoving the bolt into place without visible effort.

"Why is she here?" Rogres asked, and at once added, "You will find out when she tells you."

Saint-Germain managed a quick, one-sided smile. "You know me too well, old friend." He frowned. "I do not want to distress you, but I will need you to wake the cook's wife. She will have to come to the villa to tend to Jenfra for as long as she is here."

"I suppose I should not ask how long that will be," Rogres remarked as he tugged the donkey forward through the gate, dragging on the reins to make her move.

"Since I have no idea, I have no answer for you," Saint-Germain said wryly. "I will take her to the villa and try to get some food into her. If she will wake up long enough to eat."

Rogres said, "I will get the cook's wife as soon as the donkey is secure." This time his tug on the reins brought better results, as if the animal knew her journey was finally about to end.

"I will summon Monceau. His presence will be better than nothing." Saint-Germain ducked his head and began to run across the wide court toward the entrance of his villa; his burden did not weigh him down, and his speed, had anyone seen him, was greater than most men could achieve. Once inside the house, he took Jenfra along toward the kitchen, which was surely the warmest room in the stone building.

As he set her down on a scullion's stool, she woke enough to murmur, "Where . . . ?"

"Clair dela Luna," said Saint-Germain as he found a clean rag to dry her hair. "It is very late at night."

She managed a wan smile. "I thought . . . I was lost." Without warning she yawned hugely, then shivered as she touched the sleeve of his houppelande. "You're all wet."

"So are you," he pointed out, and went on working to dry her hair. Satisfied he had done the most he could for the moment, he tossed the rag away and tried to decide how to deal with Jenfra, who was almost asleep again. As she leaned against the chopping table, he left her long enough to go to the servants' quarters at the rear of the villa; he knocked forcefully on Monceau's door, hoping he would not have to shout to be heard over the tattoo of the rain and the roar of the wind.

"Mon Sieur," Monceau exclaimed as he opened the door to his room enough to see who was in the corridor. "What is it? Is there some trouble? Has the storm—"

"The villa is safe, have no fear," Saint-Germain was quick to assure him. "But the storm has brought us a traveler, who is even now dozing in the kitchen. The circumstances are . . . unusual. I need you to come to tend to her." He knew this request would shock his major domo, and was not disappointed.

"A woman has come here tonight? A woman alone?" He straightened up, prepared to refuse his assistance.

"Not a woman, a girl, alone," said Saint-Germain, as if this would make the circumstances better. "I fear she has been separated from her father's pack-train. We cannot turn such a child from the door." He knew he could make Monceau obey him, but preferred to have his servant agree without compulsion.

Monceau was more curious than mollified; he shrugged and said, "I will need a moment, mon Sieur."

"As you must, but hurry." Saint-Germain was not about to argue with the man.

"It would be better if you had a woman," Monceau observed before he closed the door.

"Rogres will summon the cook's wife," Saint-Germain said, hoping Monceau heard him.

By the time Monceau emerged from his room, Saint-Germain heard Rogres approaching with the complaining cook's wife. "Come, man," Saint-Germain urged his major domo. "The honor of my friend Hue d'Ormonde is at stake."

"A worthy merchant," said Monceau, more puzzled than before.

"That he is, and so it is fitting that we do nothing to bring any ill-report on him, or on his family." He paused. "His daughter has come here to find shelter. I must suppose she was in the company of her father as she has been before and became separated from him in the storm." He hoped the repetition of this acceptable mendacity would keep Monceau from asking too many questions. They were almost to the kitchen; Saint-Germain slowed his rapid pace. "She is very tired and cold."

"Um," said Monceau, still looking troubled. "But why should she come here?"

"She knows the place and it was probably the first shelter she could find." As he spoke, he wondered if Jenfra would be so foolish as to betray herself with incautious words while the servants could hear.

"And why should her father look for her here?" asked Monceau, still suspicious of her presence without escort. "Would he not go to the convent instead?"

"Perhaps," said Saint-Germain as he stepped into the kitchen just ahead of his major domo. "You see how she is."

Jenfra was as he had left her, her head cradled in her arms on the chopping table, her clothing draining to a puddle of water at the foot of the stool. She was as limp as if she had fallen unconscious; she looked more childlike than Saint-Germain had seen her appear in the last three years. Her face was pale but for dark circles around her eyes. She did not move as Monceau approached her.

"She needs our help," Saint-Germain said firmly as Rogres brought the cook's wife into the kitchen; both of them were wet and the cook's wife looked annoyed for this intrusion on her rest. "You come promptly; my thanks for it."

"What a foolish girl, to go abroad on such a night," the cook's wife scolded the sleeping Jenfra. "It would serve her well if the Devil were to send his demons to drag her down to Hell."

"But he did not," said Saint-Germain in a tone that put an end to all protest. "So, in Christian charity, we must tend to her, in her father's name."

The cook's wife ducked her head to show she would obey.

"The donkey is in the shed as you ordered," Rogres informed Saint-Germain so that the others would know Jenfra had not arrived on foot, which would be more objectionable than riding to the gate.

"See to his feed, if you will, Rogres," Saint-Germain recommended, then said to Monceau, "If you will, make one of the rooms ready for our guest. I will return to my tower tonight, and Rogres will accompany me when he has completed his duties. That way no ill may be spoken of this unfortunate child." He went on to the cook's wife, "You will remove those wet clothes and remain with her until morning. I will give her father no reason to complain of me when he comes to fetch her." For Jenfra's sake, if not his own, he hoped that moment would come soon; any prolonged stay at Clair dela Luna would damage her reputation no matter what care Saint-Germain took to preserve it. As soon as Jenfra wakened he would have to find out why she had fled her home, and why, of all places in

Provence, she had come here. "Monceau, you will make up a tray of food for her and bring it to her directly."

"I cannot carry her on my own," the cook's wife said flatly. "If she will not wake up, she must remain here."

"I will carry her to whatever chamber Monceau selects," said Saint-Germain.

Monceau rubbed his chin. "The room at the end of the corridor above is the most private, but it has windows on two sides." He pondered the situation a short while, then said, "It is still the most suitable, if you, Mère Esmerauda, will keep her from the windows."

"I will do what I can," the cook's wife said grudgingly. "If she will behave like a strumpet, I will not be accountable."

"She is the daughter of a respectable merchant," Monceau informed Mère Esmerauda, enforcing Saint-Germain's authority as a way of strengthening his own. "She will not want to compromise her family."

"Not if she intends to return to them," said Mère Esmerauda with canny insight. "She may not desire to."

"And why should she not?" Monceau inquired haughtily.

"That is something we must find out," said Saint-Germain, forestalling any more speculation on Mère Esmerauda's part. "And we will learn nothing useful tonight in any case." He bent and picked up the sleeping Jenfra, carrying her as easily as if she were an infant. "Lead the way, Mère Esmerauda. I will follow. Monceau, come up when the tray is ready."

The cook's wife shook her head. "This is a bad business, mon Sieur. Anything driven by the storm brings trouble." She went ahead of him toward the stairs. "This child is a danger for you," she warned him as she started up the stairs.

"She certainly will be if she is left to die of putrid lungs," Saint-Germain said with asperity.

Mère Esmerauda nodded heavily. "I take your meaning. And at least her father is not noble, or you would have to answer for her to all his kin."

"Just so," Saint-Germain agreed as Jenfra stirred in his arms. "Rest, rest," he said to her. "You will soon be warm."

"What? Where am I?" Jenfra whispered.

"At Clair dela Luna. You were separated from your father's train. You made your way here." He hoped she was awake enough to keep this in mind and repeat it in the morning.

"Then I am safe," she said muzzily as she snuggled closer to him.

"So you may think," scoffed Mère Esmerauda, who had overheard her. "You haven't won free yet, my girl, and you may not contrive it at all."

The room Monceau had selected was at the far end of the corridor, and exposed on two sides, so it was quite cold when Mère Esmerauda opened the door to admit them; the light from the brazier in the hall provided the only illumination. The sound of the wind was enormous, like a ravening beast worrying the villa. "Send someone to build up the fire," the cook's wife exclaimed, flinging up her hands in dismay. "It is as bad as a ship at sea. We must have heat before she is put to bed. I will manage the lamps. The fire is more urgent than light."

Saint-Germain put Jenfra into the single chair in the room. "I will fetch the wood for you." There were two large stacks next to the pantry, which would save him having to go out into the storm again to get fuel for the fire.

"Best bring a kindled log from the kitchen with the rest. It will be dawn before this chamber is heated else." Mère Esmerauda bustled to the bed and threw back the hangings. "At least there are no mice here. She has something to be thankful for."

Jenfra sighed and slumped into the most comfortable position she could find in the high-backed chair; she showed no other signs of waking.

"Tell me, mon Sieur," said Mère Esmerauda as she plumped the chaff-and-feather-filled pillows, "have you considered what you will say to her father? He will surely question you in regard to her care and well-being."

"To which I depend upon you to attest," said Saint-Germain as if this were of minor importance.

"As well you should," said Mère Esmerauda, and apparently satisfied with the response, said, "Then bring the wood for the fire. I will look after her."

Saint-Germain inclined his head, his expression carefully neutral. As he left the chamber, he heard Mère Esmerauda muttering about ill-omened guests. He hurried to get the wood, and retrieved a smoldering log from the banked kitchen fire; this he put into a bucket, and wrapping the curved handle in a thick pad of rags, went back up the stairs and along the corridor. For once he was grateful for the noise of the storm, since it covered much of the activity in the villa and would keep most of the household from investigating these late-night incursions. Entering the chamber assigned to Jenfra, he saw Monceau setting out a tankard of warm cider and slices of chicken as well as pastry-shells filled with stewed onions; Mère Esmerauda was shaking Jenfra's shoulder to waken her. Two lamps had been lit so that the room was no longer a dark cavern. Going to the grate, Saint-Germain upended the bucket, letting the slow-burning log shower sparks as he prepared to put the rest of the logs on the fire. "How is she?" he asked without turning from his task.

"With the aid of her good angel, she will not take ill from this night. Although she would deserve nothing better," said Mère Esmerauda, who had pulled a nurse's smock from the chest in the corner; the garment was old but clean and it was now set out for Jenfra's use.

"You must not think so," said Monceau, "or you may bring it on yourself as well as on her." His stern rebuke did not change Mère Esmerauda's opinion.

"That's as pleases God," she said, unintimidated. "But you will not thank her, nor will any of us."

"Stop such carping, woman," Monceau said sharply. "Tend to the girl and keep such jobations to yourself."

"Pray, do not bicker: there isn't time for it," Saint-Germain said from where he knelt by the fire, coaxing it into life. His clothes were clammy against his skin; if he was uncomfortable he was sure Jenfra was miserable. "Your first duty is to the comfort of my guest."

"Yes, mon Sieur," said Monceau, his glower daring Mère Esmerauda to speak.

The first uncertain ribbons of flame were rising through the wood, and the smell of burning became very strong. Saint-Germain stood up, satisfied that the wood would soon be fully afire. "I will leave you. Convey my welcome to the girl when she wakes, and send word to me."

"Yes, mon Sieur," said Monceau and Mère Esmerauda together as Saint-Germain departed, going down the corridor, down the stairs, and back out into the night, his thoughts in as much turmoil as the weather.

It was nearly midday when Mère Esmerauda sent word to Saint-Germain that his guest was awake and awaiting him in the reception hall; the servant who brought the message was clearly curious about Jenfra's presence at the villa, but said nothing beyond relaying what Mère Esmerauda had told him.

Now that the worst of the storm had passed, it was raining steadily but without the wind to drive it; the sound of its falling was a purr. The morning light, muted by the rain, revealed the world in shades of grey and sepia.

"I thank you for your service," said Saint-Germain, giving the man a silver bee. He had changed into a Castilian pellotes of red-and-black Arabian brocade worked in his eclipse sigil; his box-sleeved houppelande was hung on a peg to dry. If being up the whole night had tired him, he gave no indication of it. "Tell Mère Esmerauda I will join her and her charge directly."

Much as the servant wanted to find out more, he tugged the hair over his forehead and left the tower, splashing across the courtyard to the house at a run, as if the greater speed would keep him dryer.

A short while later, Saint-Germain followed his servant; he had donned a balandras of black wool to protect him and he wore the hood up; he went out into the rain and moved quickly through it in order to avoid the mild discomfort running water gave him. He had taken the precaution of wearing his brodequins with their thick soles lined with his native earth instead of the lighter solers that were more customary for household footwear, minimizing the impact of the water. As he walked, his heels sent up splashes.

Rogres met him at the door and took the balandras from him. "I will leave for Avignon this afternoon," he said in Byzantine Greek.

"You anticipate me, old friend," Saint-Germain replied in the same language. "Be sure you speak to Hue d'Ormonde privately. I have written an account of last night for you to take to him."

"Are you certain that is wise?" Rogres asked. "If it should come into the wrong hands, it could have serious repercussions."

"I realize that," said Saint-Germain. "But in courtesy to d'Ormonde, I must." He held up his hand. "I know my rank protects me, but I like the man and our business together has been profitable for both of us."

Rogres' features remained calm but his tone of voice was skeptical. "Are you certain he will accept your report? What if his daughter tells another story?"

"She is not Pentacoste, or Csimenae. She will say nothing to discredit me or herself." He hoped as he spoke that this would prove true.

"She is also a willful child," Rogres reminded him. "She could say things that she did not intend to harm you that would nonetheless do so."

"You assume she would be listened to," Saint-Germain said, shrugging slightly to indicate he doubted that could happen.

"Can you assume she would not be?" Rogres countered. He made a short gesture of aggravation. "If the people in Orgon can hang a sow for eating her piglets, or burn men for taking pleasure with men, what might they do to you?"

Saint-Germain shook his head. "The worst they know of me is that I am foreign. That might be damning but for my title. They will not risk bringing retribution upon themselves by attacking me. The report will not permit any to question my actions." He did not entirely believe this, but he did not relent. "Leave Jenfra to me, and she will not speak against anyone." There was no trace of threat in his words, but there was certainty. He handed the sheaf of parchment to Rogres, remarking with ironic amusement, "Read it if you like."

"I will, before I leave for Marsailla, which I will do directly," said Rogres, making his promise without apology. "She is in the reception hall. Mère Esmerauda is with her."

"Thank God fasting for Mère Esmerauda," said Saint-Germain in Provencal French, indicating the end of this discussion.

"Truly," Rogres agreed, and stood aside for Saint-Germain to pass him.

Jenfra was seated in front of the fire, so muffled in shawls that it was hard to see the simple woolen cote she wore beneath them all. She was less bedraggled than she had been the night before, but she was still pale; her hair had been unbraided and combed so that it fell around her face in ordered waves. Behind her Mère Esmerauda stood guard, her big hands resting on the back of the chair as if on the quillons of a sword. Jenfra did not look up when Saint-Germain came into the room; she stared into the flames, her expression remote.

"God send you good day," Saint-Germain said when Jenfra took no notice of his arrival.

She was recalled to herself at once. "Oh, mon Sieur. Thank my good angel—you are come!" She would have jumped out of the chair but Mère

Esmerauda laid a hand on her shoulder, a tacit reminder to her to remain seated.

These next few words were so crucial that Saint-Germain faltered as he said, "Your . . . your father must be worried about you? Where did you leave his train? Do you remember? How did you become separated from the others?"

Jenfra blinked. "I had to get . . ." Then she grasped his intent. "To shelter," she said quietly, color mounting in her face. "I did not know the storm would be so . . . so fierce."

"It was very bad," Saint-Germain concurred. He looked directly at Mère Esmerauda as he went on. "I am pleased to have you at Clair dela Luna, Jenfra. It was wise of you to come here, where you could be certain of your welcome in your father's name."

"My father . . . doesn't know . . . where I am," said Jenfra, feeling her way with words.

"If you lost your way in the storm, how could he?" Saint-Germain said, relieved that she had taken his lead.

"He might not even know I've . . . left," she said, her face darkening.

"Of course he does. You may be sure he is anxious for your safety," Saint-Germain said quickly, once again glancing at Mère Esmerauda. "He may have his escort hunting for you now."

"He will not know where to look," said Jenfra, her mouth pressed into a pursed, thin line.

"Then I will dispatch my manservant to find him." Without giving Jenfra a chance to protest, Saint-Germain went on, "And while you are here, Mère Esmerauda will be your companion. I will allow nothing to compromise the honor of your family."

Jenfra turned her face up to him, revealing a desolate expression. "But I thought—"

He cut her off before she could reveal anything that would compromise her still further. "It is the least I can do, Jenfra. Your father has done me good service and I can do no less for him."

Mère Esmerauda patted Jenfra's arm in a reassuring way. "You will be home again, and soon. Our Sieur will see to it."

At that, Jenfra burst into tears. "I want to stay here!" she wailed.

"And so you shall," said Mère Esmerauda as if she had not understood Jenfra's outburst. "Until your father comes to fetch you." She glanced at Saint-Germain. "You are overwrought, child." Bending down over the back of the chair she continued to comfort Jenfra. "Your good angel brought you here so you might be protected from harm; do not tax him further with rashness. The Devil comes by such paths."

"Then let the Devil come, if I can stay here," said Jenfra, crying with bitter determination.

Mère Esmerauda cuffed Jenfra with her open hand. "Never say so, not even in jest!"

Saint-Germain did not approach Jenfra, but spoke softly. "Jenfra, you must not be cast down. But I fear you have erred: whatever you seek you will not find it here. It is imprudent to act without your family's consent." There was little he could say to comfort her that would not encourage her attachment, which he had no wish to endorse. "Your father will provide—"

Jenfra shook her head vehemently. "Not he! He is waiting to have a son. He thinks nothing of me—nothing!"

"Curb your tongue, child," Mère Esmerauda said sharply.

"He has a wife. He has no need of a daughter when he can have sons!" She was sobbing loudly, her emotion making her shake.

Mère Esmerauda came around the chair and dragged the struggling Jenfra to her feet, shaking her as if she were a youngster. "Stop this at once!" she ordered. "You will do our Sieur an ill-turn if you keep on!" The tone of her voice was blunt.

Jenfra shrieked her defiance. *"I don't care!"*

"Then the Devil is moving you," said Mère Esmerauda decisively. "I will beat him out of you." And she raised her clenched fist to deliver the first blow.

It never fell; Saint-Germain moved swiftly to grab her hand. "No, bona Mère, no. She is not your child, nor is she mine. If she comes to any harm at your hands or mine, her family will—"

"She shames you, mon Sieur," Mère Esmerauda protested. "The Devil is bringing sin into her."

"Then it is for her father to decide how she will be chastised," Saint-Germain insisted, then gave his attention to Jenfra. "I am sorry for your unhappiness, Jenfra; it is not within my right or my power to change that." He took care not to touch her. "Your father will decide how you will best be happy." This assertion seemed ill-considered to him, but he knew any other observation would be unacceptable in Mère Esmerauda's eyes. "Pray his Good Angel will guide him."

"Yes, and pray your good angel will guide *you,*" Mère Esmerauda added, wrapping Jenfra in her arms. She met Saint-Germain's steady gaze as she tried to quiet Jenfra. "Never you fear, mon Sieur. None of the Devil's ramblings will be repeated by me." She patted Jenfra's head. "It would be wiser to leave us, mon Sieur, until she is herself again."

The sense of helplessness that went through Saint-Germain was barbed as a fishhook and set as intractably within him. "I thank you for all you have done," he said to Mère Esmerauda.

She waved him away as if he were a distraction. "I will be at your disposal, mon Sieur, but later. Later."

He knew that it was best to leave Jenfra in Mère Esmerauda's care, but every step Saint-Germain took away from the reception hall increased his conviction that he had turned his back on a disaster.

◦　◦　◦

Text of a letter from Hue d'Ormonde in Marsailla to Francois de Saint-Germain, Sieur Ragoczy, at Clair dela Luna in Provence, delivered by Rogres.

To the excellent Sieur Ragoczy at Clair dela Luna, the hurried thanks of Hue d'Ormonde in Marsailla.

I cannot express my gratitude in sufficient humility for your kindness to my daughter. Her malinspired actions have brought trouble to my house; your letter gives me reason to hope that she has not wholly fallen from reach of all grace, and for your good and Christian service to our honor, I can only reiterate my abiding gratitude.

I will come as quickly as I can ready myself; that you will protect my daughter until she is restored to me I thank God and your Good Angel. Your manservant has declared he will depart as soon as my clerk hands this to him. With the help of my daughter's Confessor and my wife I will determine the punishment she deserves for her sin-spawned flight. Nothing of her error will redound to your discredit, I pledge my Word upon it, before the Holy Roman Emperor and before God.

In as much haste as indebtedness, I commend myself to your continuing charity,

> *Hue d'Ormonde (his mark)*
> *by the hand of Frer Beneguet*

In Marsailla on the 21st day of November in the 1346th Year of Grace.

7

By the time Saint-Germain returned from his boar-hunt it was dusk; Hue d'Ormonde had arrived sometime earlier that afternoon at Clair dela Luna, his muleteers were finishing the care of the animals in the barn, d'Ormonde's escort of men-at-arms had already been sent to the servants' hall for hot wine and a place by the fire while d'Ormonde himself was visiting his daughter in her room at the end of the corridor. Consigning the two kills of the hunt to the cooks, Saint-Germain went to change his clothes from his fur-lined short riding-cotehardie, long braies, and boots, to his box-sleeved houppelande and thick-soled solers before sending word to d'Ormonde that he was at his service in the study on the ground floor.

"I am forever in your debt, mon Sieur," were the first words d'Ormonde spoke as he came through the door. He looked haggard and he slumped as he waited for permission to sit. "You are a lord; you had the right to use her in . . . any way you chose, yet you spared her. I am forever in your debt."

Saint-Germain studied d'Ormonde for a moment. "Don't be absurd," he said, hoping to rally the merchant from the desolation of spirit that had hold of him. "What man of honor would do less than I have? And if a deed is honorable, gratitude is unnecessary." It was also unwanted, given the nature of the times.

D'Ormonde shook his head once, his expression unchanged. "You show your quality in saying so, but I know that any merchant's child has no reason to expect the protection of a nobleman, least of all one who has behaved as my daughter has. You have been more—" He would not sit down although Saint-Germain motioned him toward the other chair.

"More shame to the nobleman, if he uses so volatile a child," said Saint-Germain with feeling as his memories brought incidents to his mind. Too often he had seen privilege used as a bludgeon; every time he felt as if he were lessened by such exploitation.

"Each is placed as it pleases God," said d'Ormonde, doing his best to be philosophical. "And each has the right as God gives it."

"That does not excuse corruption," Saint-Germain said, watching d'Ormonde narrowly. "As I understand Scripture, God does not countenance coercion, especially among those of rank." He knew as he said this that this was more aspiration than practice for most of the nobility he had encountered; he kept that observation to himself.

"The Devil will always strike as high as he can; he would rather debauch one prince than a village full of peasants." At last d'Ormonde sat down as if the weight of his bones exhausted him. "If your good angel has preserved you from the temptations of the Devil, then God be praised."

There was ironic amusement at the back of Saint-Germain's dark eyes. "Amen," he said, but did not cross himself.

Hue d'Ormonde sat still for a short while; Saint-Germain let him take as long as he wanted to speak. Finally d'Ormonde coughed and said, "She wants you to marry her."

Saint-Germain sat up very straight, alarmed by what d'Ormonde told him. "She what?"

"She wants you to marry her, so she can live here with you; she is unhappy with Benoita and her brother," d'Ormonde enlarged. "I told her it was not possible for you to take her to wife, that she is not well-born enough to hope for such an alliance, but she insists that I tell you."

"Jenfra is only a child," Saint-Germain said with a lightness he did not feel. "She has seen you marry and wants the same for herself. It is what every girl is eager to have, if she is not moved by God to a life in His service." He could not bring himself to believe that she was determined to defy her family so uselessly. "It is the fancy of her youth, and as she is unhappy, she supposes she may change that with marriage," Saint-Germain told her father; he did his best to make light of the suggestion. "You will have your hands full, showing her that she is mistaken."

"She is right: girls are often married while young and sent to the groom's family; some as young as six or seven. It is . . . You have seen it often. Not among merchants, of course, but the nobles have done so forever." D'Ormonde put up his hands to show he had no intention of going against custom. "Not that she should expect this from you, or from any man, after she has behaved in so degraded a fashion. She knows that is for the nobles; merchants do not often send young brides, but apprentices." His laughter was as feeble as his witticism.

"It is out of the question," said Saint-Germain, his voice flat. "She will have to understand that it is not possible."

"I know; I know," said d'Ormonde hurriedly. "There can be no such joining of our families. It would be unfitting for all of us. I have said she cannot . . . abuse your honor." He lowered his gaze to the hearth. "She has been fascinated with you, mon Sieur. She does not understand that she will not be permitted to have what she wants simply because she wants it. I fear I may have encouraged that fault in her, through my desire to assuage her grief. After her mother died, I permitted her indulgences that I must suppose were not seen for what they were—an attempt to lessen the pain she endured—and her bent toward willfulness increased." He looked directly at Saint-Germain, and put his hand to his brow to show his perception of his own sin. "It is my error—I am cognizant of it—for pampering her when her mother died. I tried to solace her by giving her as much of what she wanted that I could afford to give; it was intended charitably, but she has not been succored, but tutored in greed. I knew when she was very young that God made her capricious and I have not helped her Good Angel to curb her impulses. So she is determined to have you to husband, though all the world tells her this cannot be."

"She is only ten—" Saint-Germain began.

"Eleven, since Saunt Maurtin's Day in November," Hue d'Ormonde corrected him.

"Eleven. Still too young to know what marriage entails with anyone," said Saint-Germain. "She may think she does, but . . ." He turned his palms up to show how impossible her aspirations were.

"She supposes she does; God gave her many desires, and I fear the Devil will use them to her ruin," said d'Ormonde unhappily. "I have done all that I can to tell her she is wrong, but I have not been able to prevail. It will take a beating from her Confessor to bring her to a sense of her sin. He will have to persuade her to renounce all thought of you." He lowered his head again. "The Confessor will be aghast."

Saint-Germain shook his head. "I will keep this incident confidential. It would not be a tale I would want to hear of myself any more than you would want to hear it repeated of your daughter. No one, aside from her Confessor, need know of it if you do not wish it known." He got up from his chair and paced the length of his study.

D'Ormonde's face lost some of its hunted expression. "I am pleased to hear it. She will soon be gone from here and I had much rather she not see you again, in any case, but it is not for me to tell you, my host and benefactor, what you may do in your own house."

"You are her father," Saint-Germain said, growing impatient with the strictures rank imposed on them, "and I defer to you in all matters regarding your family. My rank confers no privilege upon me in that regard." He was aware that this was not entirely true, that as a noble he could command this merchant in anything not already commanded by the Holy Roman Emperor or the Church; it was a power he had no desire to exercise.

"I . . . I am most sincerely in your debt, mon Sieur. I had no reason to expect such leniency from you, and I will never forget I have received it." D'Ormonde rose from the chair but only to go down on his knee to Saint-Germain. "Nothing I can do will change the obligation: you have preserved me and mine from the machinations of the Devil and from public ignominy when you had no compulsion to do it: I am yours to command at any time."

"Then get up, for all the forgotten gods—" Saint-Germain held out his hand to help d'Ormonde to his feet; instead d'Ormonde seized his hand and kissed the eclipse-incised silver ring Saint-Germain wore on the first finger.

"I pledge myself, mon Sieur." D'Ormonde rose, still grasping Saint-Germain's hand. "For as long as there is breath in my body."

"Very well," said Saint-Germain; he was aware that he would insult d'Ormonde if he refused to accept his covenant. "Since you insist, what can I be but honored?"

"You have saved us from . . ." he began, getting to his feet. "From the burdens of shame. I will have to talk with my daughter about how you have preserved us, but not just yet."

"I should think you will want to wait until you have her safe at home again. You will have to address her unhappiness once you are there, and this will add to it; be careful how you deal with her, or you may bring about the very thing you wish most to avoid," Saint-Germain recommended. He could think of no other warning that would not evoke more distress in d'Ormonde.

"Her caprice is—" D'Ormonde stopped before he said anything more that might damage his daughter. "I will plan to leave in the morning, if that will suit you?"

"I am not about to turn you out into the night, not while you carry jars of my wine," Saint-Germain said, his tone sardonically amused in an effort to relieved d'Ormonde of the guilt he insisted on bearing. "I am sure Rogers has made you aware of the explanation we have given for Jenfra's presence: that she was traveling with you and was separated from the rest of your train by the storm? She came here because she knew the estate and hoped for a welcome in your name?"

"Yes, he told me," said d'Ormonde. "I think Jenfra has come to half-believe it herself."

"Just as well," said Saint-Germain. He indicated the oil lamps hanging from the sconce by the window. "Do you want to remain here until supper is ready, or do you want to stay with your daughter? I will have more lamps lit, if you would like."

"I think it would be best to visit Jenfra's room. Mère Esmerauda is with her—and I am most appreciative of her good work in tending to my daughter."

"Yes," Saint-Germain agreed. "Mère Esmerauda will let it be known that you are not angry with Jenfra, which will spare all of you."

"She is an excellent woman, for all she is the wife of a cook," said d'Ormonde approvingly.

"I think so, too," said Saint-Germain, his endorsement startling d'Ormonde more than anything else he had said.

"You praise a *cook's wife?*" he demanded.

"Why not? She has done worthy service for me, and for your daughter. That I am Sieur and she is, as you say, a cook's wife, makes no difference." He sensed he had alarmed d'Ormonde more than he intended. "This is not the land of my birth and my title is not from this estate. Those of us in exile cannot afford to hold ourselves up as those born to rank in Provence can, or assume all servants must obey us."

"This is greatness of heart, indeed." D'Ormonde lowered his eyes. "Coming here, I was certain you would want to sever all connections with d'Ormonde, that you would fear all of us were tainted with Jenfra's impulsiveness."

"Why should I do that?" Saint-Germain asked, wholly aware that it is what any other man in his position would do; he realized he had to do more to account for his lapse or risk suspicion. "I *am* a foreigner and my ways are not your ways," he reminded d'Ormonde to justify his inexplicable leniency. "Besides, we are engaged to establish land trade with the Hansa towns in the north. I would not like to jeopardize our dealings at this point. As an exile, I cannot dishonor my contract because of a . . . misunderstanding; only your own nobles have such privilege."

"The law does require much from exiles." The laugh that greeted his remark was as uneasy as it was relieved; he studied Saint-Germain, reassessing what he saw. "Ah, yes. You are not like the nobles of Provence. You have other heritage to uphold, and other traditions. You have foreign ways."

Saint-Germain had to resist the urge to explain more fully; that would draw unwanted attention to his foreignness and open the door for speculation that could only be damaging. "In this case, I must abide by my heritage," he said, closing the matter.

"So you must," said d'Ormonde in total acceptance, for he comprehended such strictures far more readily than he did Saint-Germain's flexibility. He bowed, less formally than before. "Then, if you permit, I will go to my daughter."

"I hope you find her well," said Saint-Germain, and turned away to cut short the prolonged social ritual demanded of him.

Some time later Rogres visited Saint-Germain in his study where he was poring over the contents of a portfolio of maps. He waited in the door until Saint-Germain raised his head; then he said, "My master, I have finished in the stable."

"The roof will hold?" Saint-Germain inquired.

"Through the winter. The tiles are sufficient for the time being. In spring it should be more fully repaired." He came into the room and closed the door behind him. "D'Ormonde's men-at-arms and muleteers have been fed, and a meal is laid out for d'Ormonde and his daughter. Monceau is seeing to their needs. I told them you would not join them."

"Thank you, Rogres. You anticipate me admirably," Saint-Germain said as he put another parchment sheet aside.

"I am afraid the child was displeased." There was a slight pause before he said, "My children died long ago, but I still recall how perplexing they could be."

"And Jenfra is a very perplexing girl," Saint-Germain agreed. "I take your meaning."

Rogres nodded. "It is possible she is filled with the folly of youth. She would not be the first to succumb to its lures. At another time I would say she will change, but . . ." He gestured the last of his thoughts.

"Yes: in this world where nothing changes but at the instigation of God or the Devil, she will not have any encouragement, out of fear that she is being lured into the Devil's control," Saint-Germain finished for him. "It is as if they are all pawns in some interminable spiritual chess game, each piece locked in move and function, either moved by God's ordination or wholly suborned by the Devil, and corrupt." He put the maps aside.

"Where were you thinking of going?" Rogres asked shrewdly.

"Does it matter?" Saint-Germain inquired, his voice so world-weary that Rogres began to feel alarm. "Denmark is as good as any place; I haven't been there in some time, and I ought to inspect my holdings, I suppose."

"Yet you hesitate," said Rogres, hoping for a response.

"Yes," Saint-Germain admitted. "For I will still be a foreigner in a world that is closed to foreigners."

"That has often been the case," said Rogres evenly. "Yet it weighs upon you now."

Saint-Germain gave a single nod. "It wears on me. Even those of my blood cannot escape such . . . encumbrance." He swung around to face his manservant; there was aching compassion in his dark eyes, and old pain in his tone. "It is not that they die—I accepted that long ago, and have treasured the brevity of their lives ever since, knowing that, but for the True Death claiming me, I will lose them all. No, it is not their loss that wears on me: what rankles now is their immutability; they are locked in such encompassing imposition that I can find no access to touch them, beyond dreams. Their minds are set, wary of questioning, defined by assumptions that are as fixed as Antares . . ." His shrug was so slight that most would not have seen it for what it was; Rogres did.

"And you cannot change it," he said, summing up the whole of Saint-Germain's malaise.

"I cannot even show most of them that change is possible without making myself one with the Devil," he said in resignation, then added with an ironic smile, "Which they would believe of my nature already, if they knew."

Nothing Rogres could say would soften that truth and both of them knew it. Rogres did not bother to try; instead he said, "When you decide to leave, I will be ready."

Saint-Germain sighed. "Thank you, old friend." He picked up the portfolio once more. "At least this is not Leosan Fortress, or Natha Suryarathas, or the Spain of the Emir's son."

"None of those," said Rogres, and prepared to leave Saint-Germain alone once again.

"Rogres," Saint-Germain said, halting him in the doorway, "I appreciate your kindness, little though I may show it."

"Yes, my master; I know," he said before he closed the door.

Shortly after the following dawn, Hue d'Ormonde was ready to leave Clair dela Luna. His mules, muleteers, men-at-arms, and Jenfra waited in the front courtyard; all were well-wrapped against the icy wind that drove clouds from the sky and heat from the air. He bowed to Saint-Germain, who had very correctly come to wish him Godspeed.

"The weather should be clear for the next two days," Saint-Germain remarked, indicating the empty horizon. "Your travel will go well."

"May God favor us," said d'Ormonde as he crossed himself. He had not yet mounted his mule, and he studied Saint-Germain as he held the stirrup. "I have said it to you before, but I must speak of it again: you have been most hospitable to my family; I am aware of it. I know I had no reason to hope for what you have done."

"It is nothing more than any good Christian should," said Saint-Germain, hoping to avoid another long, grateful expostulation.

"I will not forget your courtesy, nor will any of mine; you will be recalled in our prayers and in our thoughts as one who has spared us humiliation and treated us with regard. Your honor will be praised wherever I go, mon Sieur," he promised, then climbed into the saddle. "With God's care, I will return in spring."

"When it will be my pleasure to welcome you; get me a good price for the wine and I will be amply rewarded," said Saint-Germain, then cut short the decorous phrases. "You will want to make the most of the light when days are so short."

"Truly," d'Ormonde said, and signaled his train to start off, tugging the lead of Jenfra's mule with more force than was wise.

"Papa!" Jenfra cried in alarm as her mount balked.

D'Ormonde eased up on the lead and was rewarded by Jenfra's mule ambling after his own. "Cursed creatures," he muttered, but with good-natured condemnation; intractability was intrinsic to mules, making them a constant reminder of the perils of pride.

When they reached the gate, Jenfra swung around in the saddle and gave a last, speaking look to Saint-Germain. Then the party was gone down the lane to the merchants' road, and servants of Clair dela Luna closed the gate.

"She will not soon forget you," warned Mère Esmerauda, who had accompanied Jenfra downstairs. "Before her father came, she spoke much of you. I will not repeat what she said, although she may—to her Confessor." There was an implication of danger in her remark. "She will reveal her desires, and the priest will make what he will of them."

"I fear you are right; it is easy to think ill of foreigners," Saint-Germain responded. He looked down at the cook's wife. "You have done me good service. You will have a reward."

She shook her head. "With such a girl, it is not service to protect her." She shook her head and glowered at the closed gate. "God has given her much to bear."

"Which you helped her to do," Saint-Germain said.

"He has made me with patience," said Mère Esmerauda, "and I have practiced it to acknowledge His Will."

"Nonetheless, you will be rewarded," Saint-Germain told her. He opened the main door to the villa and motioned for her to go ahead of him.

She stared at him, astonished at his gesture of respect. "It is not right."

"I see no wrong in it," Saint-Germain remarked, and realized that once again he had erred.

"It is not right," Mère Esmerauda repeated firmly, and waited for him to enter ahead of her.

It was useless to argue the point, Saint-Germain knew from long experience. He gave a minute shake of his head and went into the house ahead of her. When they were indoors, he turned to her. "My manservant will bring a purse to you tonight. I pray you will not disdain it, for that would compromise my honor."

Mère Esmerauda looked at him in consternation, her face showing worry and dismay as she made a gesture as if to push him away from her. "How could I accept it? . . . I beg you show mercy, mon Sieur. How could I receive such . . . from you? My husband would cast me out for harlotry, and my sister would close her doors to me." She knotted her big hands together. "I am ashamed of causing you dishonor, but I fear for my life."

"Then my manservant will give it to your husband, in gratitude for his permission to use you in this difficult situation," Saint-Germain said with a half-sigh; these limitations were as vexing as they were arbitrary. "Will that spare you?"

She smiled at once. "For a foreigner you are a clever man, mon Sieur; you know our ways better than we do. My husband will rejoice."

"But will you?" Saint-Germain asked. "You are the one who deserves my thanks."

"You are Sieur. All Clair dela Luna is yours to do with as you like. You need have gratitude to none of us while we live in your household; we are part of Clair dela Luna," she reminded him as if he had suddenly become simple-minded. "If you were not a foreigner, my husband would not be pleased by any gift from you, but as you are . . ." She hitched her shoulder as if to make it clear that nothing could be done with foreigners.

"Yes; I take your meaning," said Saint-Germain. He did not add to her confusion by bowing to her; instead he turned away from her and went back to his study, his thoughts on the coming Nativity festivities and spring planting.

On Epiphany the ground froze and remained frozen for more than ten days and nights. The peasants and serfs huddled in their houses, listening for the howl of wolves in the forest, certain that the omens promised famine and a hard year. The priests in Orgon took advantage of the severe winter to castigate their faithful for apostasy and recall for them the threat of Hell, reminding them that hardships on earth were nothing compared to the eternal torments awaiting those who were not acquiescent in God's Will. At Clair dela Luna, Saint-Germain ordered a bushel of salt mixed with sand be spread on the lane leading to the estate, and tried to ignore the whispers of his servants condemning such a waste; he retreated to his laboratory and spent his time making gold and jewels, anticipating the return of Eudoin Tissant with the first sign of spring, and he was determined to be prepared for the tax collector's demands.

He was not disappointed. At the end of February when the first break in the weather came and the roads were not yet churned to muddy mires, the tax collector arrived at Clair dela Luna, his ledger in a heavy sack, to assess Saint-Germain's estate for the new year. He had a clerk with him— a tonsured monk in Cluniac habit—and to add to his importance, he wore a gold-link collar of office. As he and his clerk approached the villa, Tissant's eyes narrowed.

"God send you good day," said Saint-Germain as he came out to greet Tissant. "I have been expecting you." His cordial smile did not evoke an answering one in the tax collector.

"You are putting a new roof on your stable," Tissant accused Saint-Germain as he prepared to dismount.

"Alas, the worst storm of the winter damaged the old one. We made do with broken or short tiles for a time; now that the weather is better, the repair is being done properly." He signaled to his servants to take charge of Tissant's mule and the donkey his clerk was riding. "I will have my major domo bring you wine. You must be dry after your journey."

Tissant straightened his houppelande and fussed with the sleeves of his chamisa, as if making it clear he expected these two new garments to be noticed and admired. "And cheese. We are hungry." It was an audacious demand, one he would not dare to make of any Provencal-born noble-man; Saint-Germain's exile gave Tissant an opportunity he could not resist.

"Of course; tell my major domo what you would like and you shall have it," said Saint-Germain, his affability unruffled. He led the way into the house as good manners required, saying, "You know the way to the recep-tion hall. I will meet you there shortly."

Tissant glowered. "Why do you refuse to accompany us?"

Saint-Germain regarded Tissant for a moment, then said, "I thought you would like to review the household accounts. I was going to get them for you."

It was what Tissant came for; he glowered at this gesture of cooperation. "See that they are complete," he grumbled, motioning to his clerk to come after him. "Frer Loeis, come along."

The Cluniac obeyed silently.

Saint-Germain had put his account-book in his study, and he retrieved it promptly, returning to the reception hall in time to hear Eudoin Tissant ask for a comb of honey—an extravagant request at this time of year—and skewered duck as well as wine, cheese, and bread.

The look on Monceau's face was eloquent, though he said nothing; he bowed before he went to the kitchen.

"The bread was baked yesterday," said Saint-Germain. "The baker will make more tomorrow." He was certain that Tissant would decide that he intended to insult him if the bread was not new-baked.

"Why not today?" Tissant asked, his interest slight; he was inquiring out of habit and his inner conviction that everyone lied to him.

"Today he is adding to our supply of yeast." He did not add that the baker was using a technique Saint-Germain had learned two millennia ago that had not been used in Europe since the Caesars ceased to rule. "He does that every Wednesday."

Frer Loeis nodded his approval. "It is thus at all monasteries."

Saint-Germain had chosen the day for precisely that reason, but he said nothing of it. "We do not bake on Wednesday or Sunday."

"A good practice," said Frer Loeis. "Which is your fast-day?"

"Sunday," said Saint-Germain, knowing many of the Provencal house-holds fasted on Friday to remember Christ's Sacrifice. "It is the fast-day in my homeland."

"Lithuania?" Tissant asked, knowing he was incorrect.

"No; Hungary, near the eastern border with Wallachia. In the Carpathian mountains." He had told Tissant these things before, and knew it was the tax collector's intention to insult him; he refused to be goaded into a reaction that would provide a justification for punitive assessments. "Those of my blood have been there long before the Hungarians were."

His people had left the region three centuries before the founding of Rome, but Saint-Germain kept that to himself.

"And the King of Hungary has exiled you," Tissant said as if he needed to be reminded on this point.

"One of his predecessors," said Saint-Germain, his manner still courteous.

"Do you pay him tribute?" Tissant asked as if this had just occurred to him.

"In a manner of speaking," Saint-Germain said, making the statement final by holding out his account-book. "You will see the entries."

Tissant gave the massive, leather-bound book to Frer Loeis. "We will let you know what we will require from you," he said as Monceau came back into the reception hall with a tray filled with the food Tissant had requested.

"Of that I have no doubt," said Saint-Germain, and left them to their tasks.

Text of a letter from Pare Herriot in Orgon to his Bishop in Aix, presented in person on the Feast of Saunta Burgundofara.

In the Name of God the Father, Christ the Son and the Holy Spirit, Amen.

To the most revered Bishop Amadea at Saunta-Foi, the humble greetings of Pare Harriot, priest of Sauntissima Visitasion at Orgon, with the prayers that God will guide me aright in all I divulge to you, and that you will receive it with Grace.

It is with trepidation that I tell you that the Devil is present in our town. Already he has moved the souls of many good Christians to his damnable ways, turning their faith to adherence to his vile cause. Beatings and penance have been in vain, and so I implore you to come to our aid in this time of such great evil. The Devil has sent his Fallen Angels to seduce the souls of worthy men, making them prey to their lusts and the madness of desire that blinds the soul to the promise of Paradise. We of Sauntissima Visitasion have witnessed the manifestation of the power of the flesh, yet all our efforts have failed to drive the Devil from the bodies of those whom the Devil has debauched. Not fasting, not the rigors of prison have been sufficient to subdue his work.

We have witnessed the work of the Devil in the realm of sorcery: a most distinguished man in this town had a blight of one eye; it was covered with the white film that comes with injury or age. He, upon the thrice-execrable advice of Percevall, Vidame Saunt Joachim, consulted the foreign alchemist, Francois de Saint-Germain, who styles himself Sieur Ragoczy and is a known practitioner of pernicious arts. This so-called Sieur Ragoczy inserted a fine needle in the man's blighted eye, and through some machinations of the Devil, drew off the blight, restoring the sight of the man. We know only God and His Son may restore sight without the work being of the Devil. The people of the town have hailed this Sieur Ragoczy as a worker of wonders, but do not question in whose name these supposed miracles have been worked.

There have also been many acts of women that show the Devil has claimed his own: from the sins of Eve, we have learned that women are the tools of the Devil, always willing to enter into his service when he moves their hearts to his cause. Some have claimed in Confession that they have suffered a visitation of an incubus in the night, appearing in their dreams as a well-favored gentleman, who suborned them with honied lies and a confusion of the senses that left them hungering for more. We here have done what we can to eradicate the presence of the Devil in the women who come to us to Confess their trespasses, but it is not enough. Some women refuse to obey their husbands, and a few have refused to marry entirely, without a vocation for the veil. Since none of these women are ugly or simple, there can be no reason for what they have done than that the Devil has wooed them and set his mark upon them. Neither whipping nor more stringent measures have restored the women to Grace this side of the grave.

We see everywhere that it was not enough to send the Jews out of France; it is also apparent that not all of them have gone, for there are Jews still living in French cities, and in many others that are known to you in Provence, where so many fled. Not even holy Avignon is free of them, for it is said that the gold on the dome of the Papal palace was provided by the Jews of the city. Here, where the Holy Roman Emperor rules, the Jews have been allowed to thrive, and we of the Church must pay the price of their presence, for they stubbornly refuse to abjure the Devil and all his works, but cling to the discredited worship that is the delight of the Devil. Without higher authority, none of us may do what must be done to end the incursions of the Devil, which will continue as long as one man denies Christ's Salvation.

Those who have been made intractable by the Devil are bringing destruction on us all; how long can God endure the triumph of sin in this world? What price will God exact of us for refusing to purge the world of the Devil's servants? I beseech you to allow us to expand our work, so that all Provence may be made worthy of God's creation.

With submission to you and to the Holy Church in all things, I commend myself to you and to the God Who made me and led me to my vocation.

Pare Harriot
Sauntissima Visitasion

In the town of Orgon, in Provence, on the 3rd day of April in the 1347th Year of Grace.

8

Her cotehardie was slit up the front almost to her waist and its lily-shaped sleeves were unlined. The fabric was shiny silk, the color of peaches, and very nearly matched her skin which the garment revealed—she wore nothing under it—as she moved away from the inner courtyard door, saying over her shoulder to the visitor behind her, "Sieur Ragoczy, I should chide you for staying away so long. I do not often miss the men who come here." She admitted to being twenty-two, had fashionably high, small breasts, wide-set hazel eyes, and long, light-brown hair; her nipples were rouged and she had shaved her eyebrows.

"Yeselta, you are flattering me," Saint-Germain said as he went after her toward the door that led to the main part of her house. It troubled him to need this woman, for it lessened her and himself in his eyes; yet his esurience was becoming increasingly insistent, and Yeselta was the most easily accessible solution to his craving: he had resigned himself to the exigence of coming to her, for Pare Herriot in Orgon was preparing to advance himself in the Church by casting out the Devil, and was ready to increase his reputation for zeal at the expense of the women Saint-Germain visited in sleep; it was far safer to come to Yeselta in Marsailla than to expose the Orgon women to Pare Herriot's fervor, for the priest would demand they would pay for the pleasure Saint-Germain gave them in dreams with their lives. This courtesan would not have to answer to the clerics for what she did with him or anyone else. He was sure Yeselta would have no greater risk from him; there had not been enough time for that.

It was late May, and a warm day, when the sun shone like melted gold; the flowers in the small courtyard garden were in bloom: five-petaled roses and sweet peony flourished in small, walled beds, watered by a fountain, in imitation of the Courts of Love which had once flourished in France, and pots of thyme and rosemary added their fragrance to the air. The windows of the tall stone house were glazed, showing that Yeselta was successful, though officially her business did not exist; she paid egregious taxes every year to maintain her invisibility, for harlots and wantons were sent to prison and branded when they were publicly exposed. The privacy she had contrived for herself guaranteed her patrons of some position in the world.

The reception hall of the house was longer than most, with Arabic divans set out at various places down its length, a tribute to Yeselta and the men she entertained, who brought her gifts from their travels through the trading routes of Marsailla. Panels of murals took the place of tapestries on the walls, most showing gardens of delights in details that would earn most Catholic Christians a whipping at the hands of their Confessors, but here were tacitly permitted, given the debauched nature of the place. As if part of the murals had come to life, there was a Greek slave putting out platters of sweetmeats, his young, handsome form covered by a short page's tabard in Coan linen, which from the time of the Caesars was the sheerest in all the Mediterranean. The air here was perfumed with exotic sandalwood; the candles and lamps were scented, too, the candles with rose, the lamps with ginger, for both were known to be aphrodisiacs.

"Most of my women are . . . occupied," Yeselta said, pausing near the divan upholstered in dark-red leather, the most luxurious item in the opulent room; she turned toward him so that her body was easily visible. "None of them will be . . . available for some time." She ran her tongue over her lips very slowly.

"Then it is just as well that I came to see you," Saint-Germain told her, as he knew she expected him to do; he had chosen this hour so that his presence here would be known to as few people in the house as possible.

"It is, isn't it?" Her smile was so practiced that it lost most of its allure. She shifted her stance to tantalize him with more of her body. "My chamber is not so far that you will exhaust yourself getting there." She held out her hand to him, using the gesture as an excuse to shake out her shining hair. "In case you have forgotten."

"I think I can recall the way," Saint-Germain said in a low voice, going to her and taking her hand.

She continued to smile, her lips closed as if to keep a secret, as she led the way to the stairs leading up to the floor above; the noises coming from behind the doors they passed made no impression on her. The murals here were more specifically carnal than those in the reception hall below, executed with more verve than talent and clearly intended to inspire the visitors to sexual feats the Church roundly condemned when it admitted they existed at all. As Yeselta reached the end of the corridor, she took the door on the left, lifting the latch and swinging it back so that Saint-Germain could see the large, curtained bed that stood in the middle of the room. "You will like it here, mon Sieur."

"I have before, when I was here with d'Ormonde," he said, looking into her face. "Why should it be different now?"

"Perhaps because d'Ormonde does not come here now that he has a wife," she said with more bitterness than she knew. "So many of the men I have entertained leave wives at home when they come through the gate. But d'Ormonde is not one such." She gave a single, condemning shake of her head.

"He speaks of you fondly, Yeselta," said Saint-Germain, seeing the lost look in her eyes.

"I have heard nothing of it," she said, her demeanor petulant. "If he has such regard, let him come and show me for himself."

"His wife has a most demanding family; he would be unwise to cause them concern," said Saint-Germain, to offer her what solace he could. "Even his daughter is displeased."

"Then he is best disregarded; I will not trouble myself about him more." She reached out to caress his face, her act as practiced as his performance on the mandola. "This is better than he ever was. It is a rare pleasure to have such a lover as you, mon Sieur."

"I am pleased you should say so," Saint-Germain said before he kissed her.

Yeselta's response was so masterfully executed that Saint-Germain almost despaired of evoking genuine fulfillment in her, but he held her when their kiss was done and told her, "I am happy that you come to me thus willingly. You give me hope. May we discover your joy."

The seductiveness of her smile changed to a friendlier expression. "That is what I like most about you, mon Sieur: you are as bent on achieving my gratification as yours." She abandoned her coquetry; taking his hand she tugged him through the door and closed it behind them. "There. Now we need have no worry about the rest of them. Not," she added cynically, "that they are not otherwise occupied."

"But you would prefer to be private," he said for her, aware of her denied longing for the love of which troubadors sang.

She went toward the bed, her smile back in place. "Then from now until sunset, I am yours to do with as pleases you."

Saint-Germain followed her, his dark eyes compellingly on hers. "I would far rather do what pleases *you*, Yeselta," he said; he made no move to take off his clothes. As he reached her, he stroked her shoulder, then down her back to draw her to him again.

"More generosity—it is not necessary." She waited for him to move; he did nothing. "Come now, mon Sieur," she rallied him, not daring to take what he said to heart. "We all know what my house is and what is sold here."

Saint-Germain bowed crisply. "Then I am most sorry to disappoint you, Yeselta, but I do not bargain in bed."

Yeselta was taken aback by his sudden remoteness, and moved away from him as if to account for it. "Of course not. I didn't mean . . . I . . . I do not . . . No, you are right. I wanted to haggle. But not for the reason you suppose: I . . . am unaccustomed . . . to how you are. If I can fix a price, I will know what value you put on our pleasures." She tried to find the words that would shield her from his sensuality and his gentleness.

"Must they have a price?" He asked, anticipating her answer. He held out the wallet that hung from his belt, adding wearily, "I will not cheat you."

She shook her head. "No, you would not." Her eyes were very bright.

"I would not slight you, either," he went on, and saw her blink. "If I could show you . . ."

Her laughter was high and musical, a practiced art. "What a reprehensible creature you must assume I think you are: it is nothing of the sort. I am . . . not used to your ways." Again the counterfeit laughter sounded and she walked directly up to him. When his searching kiss ended, she broke away from him; her sense of him was becoming too overwhelming. "Well, you do not want to waste the afternoon, I suppose. Do you want me to undress you?" she offered with a wide smile no more genuine than her laughter had been.

"Not just at present," Saint-Germain replied; he was not deceived by her attempt to restore her command over him. "If you would like it, I will undress you."

She shivered in the warm afternoon. "Not yet," she said, her breath catching in her throat, her hands rubbing her arms.

Saint-Germain knew she expected him to pursue her; he remained where he was, the expression in his eyes enigmatic as he watched her go to the three narrow windows placed close together, and look out into the courtyard. "Yeselta, if my presence here disturbs you so greatly, I will go." It would mean he would have to find a woman to visit in sleep that night, but here in Marsailla there would be no danger; no priest here would use any Confession of dreams to show the Devil was loose in the city, and the visit would never be repeated.

She turned around sharply, making herself a shadow in the light from the windows. "You do disturb me, mon Sieur. But I do not want you to go because of it."

"Ah." He waited for her to speak again.

"Do the nobles of Hungary always wear black?" she asked, not moving from her place by the windows. "I have seen you in no other color."

"It is my custom, though I also wear dark-red." He touched the pale chamisa sleeve under his houppelande. "And white."

"One would think you were in mourning for the dead," she said, and put her hand to her mouth as if to keep the words from being heard; this was an unpardonable lapse in courtesy.

Saint-Germain gave no sign of being offended. "So many of my House have died," he said as if this were an explanation.

"Yes. Death is everywhere, the priests tell us. They say it comes, like birth, from the wombs of women." She made a gesture of disgust; after a short silence she found something safe to talk about. "There was a Captain off a Genovese hulque who came here a few days since; he told me there was fever in Sardinia, that many of the people are ill. The sickness is a hard one, striking down many it touches. His own men did not want to remain in port, for fear of it. He thinks it will be bad for shipping if captains are afraid to put in there; the Sardinians will want the goods they expect; they will seize them if merchants will not bring them willingly. There are smugglers and pirates everywhere in Sardinia, and Corsica as well," she remarked as if they had been discussing trading and the sea. "He said the Church called the fever God's Wrath."

"That is not surprising," Saint-Germain responded calmly.

"It must not come here," she declared.

"I hope it will not," said Saint-Germain with conviction.

Yeselta suddenly stamped her foot. "Oh! why do you not take—" She came toward him. "What use does a courtesan have for compassion? Use me and be done with it."

"That would profit neither of us," Saint-Germain said, his voice low and steady, his dark eyes fixed on hers.

As she reached him, she closed her hands as if to strike him. "I can give you nothing but the use of my flesh. God made me for carnality, for the satisfaction of men's appetites. Why will you not accept that?" Her clenched hands remained at her sides; as great as her aggravation with him was, she could not bring herself to attack him.

"I will accept it, if you insist, but not as an excuse to deny you your fulfillment," he said, knowing he could not argue with her regarding the fixity of her character; she had been taught since infancy to think of herself as an artifact of God's Hand and nothing he told her would change that.

"Why not?" she inquired sharply.

His half-smile was ironic. "I suppose because God did not make me that sort of man."

She did her best to break away from him and failed, more because of her lack of resolve than any effort on his part. With a sigh of capitulation, she stood before him. "Very well."

"What?" he asked persuasively. "Very well, you will release me from your house? Very well, you will comply with my . . . demands?" His voice had become harsh. "Very well, you surrender your will to mine?" He took hold of her hands. "I want you to reach the fulfillment that is within you, so that I may share in it; without your satisfaction I can have none."

She laughed. "It is what you said before, and you were most . . . attentive, I will grant you that. Not like the noblemen, who want to try out every perversion they hear of; or the clergy, who are angry and shamed when they are debauched; or the fighting men, who are abrupt and rough; or the foreigners, who are famished for women and exhaust us all; or husbands, who would not contaminate their wives with the desires they expend on us; or merchants, who want their money's worth and take it however they can; you are . . . tender." She said the word as if it were in a foreign language.

"Is that so intolerable?" he asked, and heard the loneliness in his voice.

"It can be," she whispered, and pulled her hands away from him. She began to stroke the front of her peach-colored cotehardie suggestively, as if she wanted the silk to purr. "Isn't the appearance of passion enough? Will you not acquiesce in it, as you do when you see a player fall dead on the stage? You applaud him for dying well; you do not rush to dig his grave."

"If I were another player, I would," said Saint-Germain with such kindness that she winced.

"But you are here," she persisted. "You know courtesans supply illusions as much as they purvey flesh." She continued to stroke her clothing, giving the appearance of stimulating her body; her eyes showed no trace of arousal though she arched her back and stretched languorously. "Why be so fastidious, when this is so readily obtained?"

He watched her fighting his own despair. "Yeselta." His dark eyes held hers. "If you do not wish to seek what I aspire to have, then I will trouble you no longer. You were gracious to receive me, Bondama, and I am grateful to you for—"

"It is so difficult!" she cried. "You make me forget my anger," she said in an accusatory rush. Then she became very still. After a moment she laughed uneasily. "What an odd thing . . ."

Saint-Germain took her hands again. "You need not deny your anger for my sake. I will not think less of you for it. If you would like to rage at the heavens, I will not stop you, nor will I reveal anything you say to anyone." He bent and kissed her palms. "Your anger will not hurt me, Yeselta; your deception would."

Her laughter was false even to her. "Nothing of the sort, mon Sieur. Why should any woman be angry when fortune has smiled upon her as it has on me? I came from a weaver's family; my father went blind and we had to make our way in the world as best we could. I have achieved more than my father or his father before him, and more than any of my brothers. I have one brother still alive, I think; a sweeper in Aix: the rest—" She shrugged. "I thank God every day that He made me as He did, or I would have starved in a ditch or . . . or become the lowest servant in Marsailla."

"And it infuriates you," said Saint-Germain; his small hands tightened on hers. "Who would not be outraged at such choices?"

Abruptly she burst into tears—not soft, plaintive ones calculated to get sympathy, but strong, deep, wrenching sobs that frightened her more than they did him. She was grateful for his hands to cling to, for they held her upright; she could not endure the thought of collapsing on the floor in front of him, for it was too much like groveling.

Saint-Germain discerned her conflicts more fully than she did; he made no effort to restrain her or to call her to collect herself. He had seen this fury before, and because of his nature and the perceptions he gained through his intimate knowledge, he shared it, recognizing it for what it was—the legacy of millennia of male contempt, which had waxed and waned throughout that time, but was never eradicated, so that it continued to flourish. Yeselta had taken the brunt of it most of her life and it had left her maimed in spirit, blighted in soul. For an instant he recalled Ranegonda, so outwardly unlike Yeselta and inwardly so similar, both compelled to live lives defined by religious men. Any apology he offered, or any cheer, he had realized long ago, would serve only to make the despair worse, so he let her cry herself out and gave her his strength to work against.

Finally she jerked herself out of his grasp and wiped her face with her fingers. "I am all blotchy," she declared.

"Yes," said Saint-Germain, who was aware that trying to cajole her just now would be disastrous. "But it will fade."

"Do you intend to wait until I have . . . restored myself? You cannot want me like this." Her challenge held the vestiges of her anger, and there was an obdurate set to her jaw.

"If it is what you would prefer, I will," he answered calmly. "I do not demand that perfection of you. Your face need not be waxen for me."

She glared at him, as if certain he was criticizing her. "It will fade. Soon," she insisted.

His smile was genuine, sad, and private. "What can I be but complimented."

She made an abrupt, impatient gesture. "Why do you do this? Why will you not do what you have come to do and—"

"What I have come to do is give you pleasure," he told her. "Believe this."

For a short while she said nothing; her shoulders were tense, and she shivered from the impact of her emotions. "If you require this of me, I suppose I must," she said at last.

Saint-Germain gave a single laugh. "Am I so unpleasant a duty that you have to make yourself submit to me as if I were a tax collector? You must pardon me if I decline the—"

"You are not unpleasant; that is the trouble," she said, sounding tired. "I forget what I am when I am with you, and that is a burden I do not want." She took hold of his arm. "But I do not want you to leave, mon Sieur."

He did not know what would be the most sensible thing to do: he was aware that sensibility was not the issue, and that to impose it was simply an attempt to buffer himself against her rejection; he would be able to persuade her if he put his mind to it, but he balked at such coercion, for he had learned over the centuries that any gain made through those methods was illusory. He took her free hand and met her gaze. "If I stay, what will you do?"

Yeselta became more seductive. "You know what I do, mon Sieur."

"Yes," he said. "But that is not what I desire." There was no blame in his demeanor, no slight in his tone of voice. He released her and was about to step away when he felt her grip tighten on his arm.

"I will miss you," she cried. "If you give me now what you have before, I will miss you when you go." She tugged his arm. "Don't you see?"

"It is painful, missing those who are gone," he said, his eyes becoming distant and enigmatic. "I have no wish to cause you pain, Yeselta."

"But you will, no matter what you do. If you stay, I will miss you for giving me pleasure and . . . all the rest. If you go, I will miss the pleasure I will not have." She let go of him with great deliberation and moved away from him as if she could not trust herself if she remained too near him.

He studied her, watching how she moved; she was eloquent in her conflict. "I apologize, Yeselta. I should have stayed away."

"Probably," she allowed as she walked into his arms. "But now you are here, I would be a fool not to have what you can give me." She pressed her body close to his. "You had better make me rejoice in my decision." Her kiss was as practiced as before, as artful; it almost concealed her longing.

Saint-Germain responded to her, his small hands sliding over her satin clothing, searching for some hint of passion in her feigned excitement, some means of touching more than her skin. "Then I am on my mettle," he said when she released him.

"You are, mon Sieur." She went to the side of her bed and climbed onto it. "This is where you will find your lists, my jouster." With that, she lay back, lifting the skirt of her cotehardie over her head. "The field of honor awaits."

This was not a promising beginning, he knew; he went toward the bed even as he felt his doubts increase: would he be able to stir her, to evoke her ardor? He stood beside her and pulled the cotehardie down. "When you are ready," he murmured.

"I am ready," she said, resignation in her words.

"For another, perhaps; not for me." He sat down next to her and touched her face lightly, the backs of his fingers just brushing her skin. "For me there must be more than acquiescence."

She sighed. "Yes. So you have said." Opening her eyes, she contemplated his face. "Why should you be so different from the rest?" Her expression hardened, and her smile vanished. "If you lie to me, I will be indifferent to you."

Because he believed her, he said, "It is how I live, Bondama."

She considered this for a long moment. "That is the truth," she declared. She turned on her side to face him. "If you did not live this way, would you be like the others?"

"I would have died long ago if I were like the others," he said, his voice low and musical.

Her expression changed, becoming more determined. "Does that make you angry?"

"Occasionally," he replied, his fingers still light on her face, his manner tranquil.

When she kissed him again she was less expert, more tentative; her mouth was no longer hard, and she let him explore her face with his lips when the kiss was over. She thought of all the songs she had heard sung of loves who fainted at the sight of their beloved, of men so wholly in tune with their women that they would sleep and wake at the same time as their distant loves. For most of her life she had scoffed at such notions: she knew men and how they were, and because of that she decided that these happy fables were without substance; she rarely allowed herself to dwell on them, because they made her feel so lonely. Only when she was with Saint-Germain did she feel any hope that the troubadors might be right, and such love might be possible; she adored and despised him for revealing this to her, and her ambiguity was expressed in her impatience. "Now. Now. Hurry," she whispered to him as his kisses moved to her neck and the soft rise of her breasts.

"You haven't reached your fulfillment; the rest is nothing without it," he said as he opened the front of her cotehardie and tongued her rouged nipples. His movements were slow, yet they did not lack fire. "Let us make the most of the time."

His short beard was rough on her skin but not unpleasant; its crinkly texture was stimulating as he moved down her body. He folded back her cotehardie so that it lay around her like moth-wings. "You are very lovely," he said softly as he caressed the arch of her hip, the top of her thigh.

"You have not taken your clothes off," she said, the words a bit unsteady from the onslaught he gave her senses.

"There is no rush," he said as he continued his tantalizing perlustration, finding responses and taking the time to develop each one before going on.

"And you will not, will you?" She recalled his other visits when he had not undressed even the small amount many of her visitors did.

"If there is cause," he answered soothingly. He could sense her resignation in her compliance and he wondered if he would be able to break down the barriers she had imposed against intimacy.

She opened her thighs and arched her back. "There. Now."

Saint-Germain persevered in his quest. "When you are ready." His kiss as he moved up her body made her tremble with its intensity.

When she could speak, she said, "How do you . . . you find . . . There was never such . . ."

He soothed her, his small hands working her body to a state of expectant languor, his mouth awakening sensations she did not often permit herself to feel. His lingering ministrations began to wear down her resistance to his touch, to the intimacy he offered and sought. Finally she became pliant, her body answering his in harmony no instrument could play. As he at last slid his fingers to the soft recess at the top of her thigh, she shivered luxuriously; when his finger penetrated her, she gave a small, high cry. His lips and hands continued their excitations, coaxing more responses from her than he had ever done before. Slowly her breathing changed and her face and neck grew flushed as her whole being was engulfed in her concupiscence. He felt release gather within her, and he bent his head to her neck, holding her close as the rapturous spasms went through her.

Gradually Yeselta came back to herself; she stretched and reached out for him in a single motion. "I should hate you," she said as she snuggled to him.

He was certain that in time she would, but he responded mildly, "Why?"

"You make me want what I cannot have," she murmured as she curled against him.

"Are you certain you cannot have it?" he asked as he smoothed a stray lock of hair from her forehead.

"Yes," she said with great finality.

He could not deny this, for he knew her through her blood; instead he held her as he might hold a child, trying to provide a little surcease of the despair that tinged every aspect of her life.

A short while later, she asked in a small voice. "Will you see d'Ormonde?"

"No. He is in the north," Saint-Germain answered gently. "He won't be back for six or seven weeks."

She said nothing in response to this, pretending to doze in Saint-Germain's arms. For a while she let herself imagine that she was the object of courtly esteem; later she would be angry with him for waking her heart as he did, but for now she let herself be convinced that something had passed between them, although he had not entered her body as other men did. That alone served to give her hopes credibility even as they became suffused with the gauzy light of imagination.

He did not move as the day faded; his thoughts were somber even as he felt a welling gratitude to Yeselta for restoring him. He wanted to be able to guard her from her inner pain, but knew if he acknowledged it, she would condemn him; so he cradled her and with his emotions banked against her anguish, tried to determine how best to leave her.

Text of a letter from Atta Olivia Clemens in Trieste to François de Saint-Germain, Sieur Ragoczy, at Clair dela Luna near Orgon in Provence.

Sanct' Germain, my dearest, oldest friend;

Word has come from Constantinople that Black Plague is in the city, and so my worst apprehensions have been realized. It is not Swine Plague, or Well-water Plague, or smallpox or any of the other, dreadful roster: no, it is the Plague that is marked by black swellings in the pits of the arms and the legs. There are rumors of it in Alexandria as well, and possibly in the lands of Arabia, which may or may not be true, but if it is, does not bode well for any of us. I do not know how long it will take to spread, but I must say I am glad I am no longer in Rome, for if the Plague is in Constantinople, it will come to Rome, which has enough to bear with Cola di Rienzi. Do not remind me that the Plague will come to Trieste—I am well-aware of that, and have made plans to go to the villa on the northeast side of the city. It is called Il Capolavoro, which may be a trifle extravagant. The villa itself is not large but it is made with something other than war in mind, which lends it a kind of grace that one sees all too rarely these years. Still, it is a pleasant location, and the wells are good. I will have the villa fumigated as you taught me to do, and I will be able to wait out the worst of it unnoticed. The villa is remote, in a high valley that is two leagues from the merchants' road to Vienna. The place was once a hunting retreat, isolated and well-fortified but not armed, not unlike that small castle you had in Trebizond, though not so luxurious. I have made a few Roman improvements, so that it is a tolerable haven. The baths are small and the tepiderium cannot be used for swimming, but I will get on well enough.

Of course the Church here—Catholic and Orthodox—is spending long hours in prayers and Masses to persuade God to keep the Black Plague from coming here. They have told their flocks that God will save them if they will renounce the Devil, as if the Devil embodied the Black Plague and selected those who would have it from those who had sinned the most. The assurance that only the damned will be infected lends a certain authority to the rest of what the clergy says: the people are exhorted to fast and pray as well, and to abstain from bathing. I cannot see the use of this, but it does give them all something to do, and makes the clergy feel less helpless.

It might be wise if you were to plan to leave Provence, as you have been saying you intend to do. You may not want to remain where you are while the Black Plague comes. As you have seen, it is a deadly thing, and those of our blood can do little to stop it. I have witnessed it only once before, and that was enough to make me realize that its virulence was beyond that of any other illness I have encountered. You do not need to be reminded what Black Plague is, though I fear you may try to help those who have contracted it. That is not entirely wise. If you save too many, you will be suspect, and if your patients die, you will be hounded. Either way, you will be subjected to scrutiny you have long striven to avoid.

It is probably useless to ask, but I will: join me at Il Capolavoro. You will be safe. The villa is isolated enough that you need not worry that we will be found. Niklos has taken over all the servants' duties; he has poultry enough to take care of his needs and more. If you and Rogerian should come here, it will not be difficult to make arrangements for Rogerian as well. I have three chests of your native earth with me and I will carry them to the villa, in the hope that you will be sensible for once. Not that I do not admire your courage, for I do. But in your determination to help those stricken, you have as much to lose as they. I feel I must remind you, in case you have forgot. And, Sanct' Germanius, I would not like to be alive in a world without you.

I will remain at Il Capolavoro until winter at least. If the Plague has abated, I will go back to Trieste. If it has not, I will stay at the villa until the Plague is over. It has been many centuries since this part of the world has had Black Plague to contend with, and I fear that they will not do well now, not with priests making the decisions about treatment and the most gifted physicians more inclined to bleed their patients than to treat their ills. I do not worry about finding sustenance while I am here: with the merchants' road so near, there will be travelers I can visit in dreams, and, with the perils of the times what they are, this is a most reasonable solution for the time being. I will not bother myself with a new lover until the Plague is gone: it is hard enough to see them die full of years; to have them perish from so hideous a disease is more than I am willing to tolerate. Do not hold me in contempt, Sanct' Germain; I am unable to watch them die without more grief than I can bear. If that means I lack courage, then so be it.

At least consider my invitation, and if you will not come here, promise me you will take yourself north. And no matter what you do, let me know of it. Niklos goes to the village of Sezana once a week and will get messages at the travelers' inn.

With all my love and most of my anxiety, as well as

My enduring devotion,
Olivia

On the 23rd day of July, in the year 1347.

9

By midday, Saint-Germain knew something had gone wrong; as he rode past his fields, he noticed that some of the men avoided looking in his direction, while a few stared at him as if they were not laborers but men of substance; one or two appeared defiant. What had happened? Saint-Germain asked himself as he left his horse in the stable to be groomed and fed. He usually performed the chores himself but today he was too preoccupied; he knew the groom would rather do the task, for taking care of horses was not the work of lords, but of their servants. Going into the villa, he wondered if Pare Herriot had spoken out against him. He went directly to his study and sent Rogres to fetch Monceau, hoping the major domo would be able to provide him an answer.

"What is it, mon Sieur?" Monceau asked in trepidation as Rogres opened the door for him; this remarkable courtesy only served to instill more dread in the major domo.

"Leave us, Rogres, if you will," said Saint-Germain, then turned to Monceau. "I have noticed that some of the workingmen seem . . . shall we say, troubled? I was hoping you might know what the matter is, and why they are so—" He lifted his hands to show he was at a loss.

"I told them of your orders," Monceau answered obliquely. "And I said they could leave if they were unwilling to abide by your orders, as you said I should."

"Yes," Saint-Germain said, and waited for the man to go on.

It was difficult for Monceau to look directly at Saint-Germain. "But you see, mon Sieur, that the men are afraid, don't you? It was because you have done . . . such things as they cannot understand. You are . . . not . . . not . . ." He stopped and cleared his throat. "They are certain that God makes nothing without also providing its remedy, and without a remedy—" He touched the medal of Saunt Loys that hung on a leather thong around his neck. "Pare Herriot has said that if the remedy is not of God, then it must be of the Devil, and anyone using such remedies does so in the Devil's name. And the men will not put their souls in peril. I . . . I regret to tell you."

"And so they risk their bodies." Saint-Germain went to the window and looked out on the fields beyond. "How do they conclude that what I am doing here is of the Devil?" He waved Monceau to silence as he gave his attention to the major domo once again. "Never mind. I have heard it all before." He recalled the madness in Lyons that had ended the lives of the last of Csimenae's company. "Tell me about the men; the ones who want to leave."

Monceau was still unable to meet Saint-Germain's steady eyes. "There are . . . There are eight men who will not do as you have ordered them, no matter what your rank; they say they fear for their souls before God; the harvest is not enough to make them stay," he reported as if he were the cause of their recalcitrance. "I told them that they were disgracing their—"

"You do not have to apologize, Monceau; yours is not the fault, if there is any fault," Saint-Germain cut in, knowing that his major domo would recite his supposed errors until he was stopped. "The men were given a choice: the harvest has not begun. You were never in charge of their judgment. They decided they would rather leave, which is their right: I gave them my Word and I will abide by it: you may tell them. You do not have to answer for their choices." Such discontented servants were often the source of rumors that brought unwanted attention to him. He looked around the room that had served for his study, his eyes caught by the high shelves where he kept his maps rolled. Recently he had been examining them again, knowing he would have to make up his mind shortly whether or not he would stay at Clair dela Luna or go north to the Low Countries and Denmark; Olivia's warning of spreading Plague was starkly impressed upon him and he could not make himself believe this part of the world would remain unscathed for much longer, not as long as ships plying the Mediterranean counted Marsailla as one of their ports; the Plague would come.

"Three will stay through the harvest, the others want to go now, before it starts," Monceau said as if confessing to theft and the loss of his right hand in consequence. "They will not remain even if they are not paid for any of their labors, nor their lords."

"I will give them what they are owed," Saint-Germain said, his calmness concealing his increasing dismay. "They will not be cheated of their earnings." His thoughts shied away from the images of sickness that rose in his memory, images he feared would be realized here in Provence.

Monceau looked away, embarrassed. "They will be relieved to hear this." He coughed once. "Not that they had any reason to think you would not pay them."

"No reason whatsoever—I am not so petty as they must suppose I am," Saint-Germain said dryly, deliberately shutting out his recollection of the Temple of Imhotep, and those who came there to die so long ago.

"Oh, no, mon Sieur, you are not petty. That was never their . . . No one could say you had been petty. You have always been more than fair, more than the law required of you; more lords could learn from you. You do not beat them, and you do not demand the use of their women. You see . . . it was the bathing. The smoke would trouble them, it is true, the bathing— Pare Herriot has said that in this dangerous time, all sin is to be avoided, and bathing is vanity, so . . ." He shrugged miserably.

"I understand," said Saint-Germain calmly, wishing he knew what to say to reassure his major domo. "You have no cause to be so—"

"These men listen to Pare Herriot and they worry, as do all faithful Christians. He shows us the danger all about us, and the price we pay for disobeying God." He looked around as if he expected to be blamed for disappointing Saint-Germain. "The men fret about what you have required of them. No other lord has done the things you have done; they know you are foreign, but it does not suffice to explain your . . . The men are troubled by the smoke you fill the house with, as I have said," he confessed in a rush. "They are told that these are signs of the Devil. Hell is filled with smoke from the eternal fires. To have so much smoke at a time like this is to invite . . . They have said that this smoke you make may be the work of Hell, and they—"

"—put their souls at peril if they remain," Saint-Germain finished for him and watched him cross himself for protection. "I do not know how to show that what I do is not the Devil's work if they have already decided it is." He knew the reason for their apprehension: he had fumigated the villa and its outbuildings twice in the last ten days and would do it three times more in the next two weeks. He lowered his voice. "You may tell me the truth, Monceau, and I will not hold it against you: does what I have done here trouble you? not the other men: you."

"I am a loyal servant," Monceau declared, still refusing to meet Saint-Germain's gaze.

"Yes, you are, but that does not answer my question," said Saint-Germain kindly. "Are you troubled by what I have done?"

"They say that to use smoke for cleansing is to court the fires of Hell; I have heard this all my life, and I have no reason to doubt the priests," Monceau answered obliquely. "When the French sent the Jews out of their country, many of them came here, and Pare Herriot says their presence draws the Devil to us. They are all sworn to the Devil and they seek to lure Christians from the promise of Grace. If we had done the same as the French—cast out the Jews as they have done in France—Hell would have forgotten us. The smoke only confirms our hazard, reminding us what is waiting for us in the life to come."

"If the priest says that the Jews bring the Devil," Saint-Germain marveled, although he knew it was reckless to express himself so directly, "I wonder that he can worship a Jew, for Jesus was surely one."

This time the major domo crossed himself three times to invoke the protection of all the Trinity. "He was the Savior, and the Son of God, which is more than anyone has been before or since. The Jews bring the Devil because they refused to know Him for His Godliness, or to honor His Sacrifice for them. The Devil will always come where His Grace is denied," Monceau recited.

"Jesus had Jewish apostles, as I recall," said Saint-Germain lightly. "Were they not the first to honor His sacrifice?" It was unkind to foist such questions on Monceau; he said, "Doubtless the priests have explained it all to you."

"Yes," Monceau said, relieved to be able to give Pare Herriot's answer rather than to struggle to find one of his own that might put him in danger of heresy from imperfect understanding. "If the Jews had remained in France, you would not be blamed for the smoke you use. With the Jews here, there is more to fear, for the Devil loves them, and abides where they are, and you summon the Devil with smoke. When you, mon Sieur, use smoke that you claim can cleanse the villa, you make many of us wonder what else it may do."

"But the priest uses incense, and that is holy," Saint-Germain reminded his major domo, though he knew it was useless.

"It is not the same thing at all; you must know that it is not: only one who had forsaken God, or never known Him, could mistake the two. You should listen to Pare Herriot: he will make it all clear to you, as he has for all Orgon. He has been shown things of God that are for priests to know, not the worshipers." He hesitated, but when Saint-Germain said nothing, he went on. "We have been given incense to please Heaven. Incense is blessed and the Devil is cast out by it, for the priest has the power to banish the Devil. Without a priest, the Devil will be present. A priest is already given to God. He is in no danger from Hell; others cannot be so certain of their salvation. Unless he is a false priest, or an apostate one, in which case, he will be the most tormented of all damned souls." He crossed himself again, this time very quickly.

Saint-Germain sighed, his thoughts in disorder: his simple precaution was intended to kill vermin, but the servants would not believe it. He could offer Monceau no explanation the man would respect, so he fell back on rank. "It is my will that this be done, in accordance with the traditions I have followed for . . . most of my life. As the master of this place, if there is any risk of Hell, it is mine. I will answer for what I did to you when the Last Trumpet raises the dead for Judgment."

"Pare Herriot would not like to hear that you say so," Monceau warned. "He is certain the Devil has come to Orgon. He has been diligent in casting out those who serve the Devil."

"Yes; and six women have burned because of it, and one feeble-minded boy who said he had seen demons in a tree." Saint-Germain crossed himself as Monceau did this time, though for very different reasons.

"Those with simple minds are sometimes given better vision than most, to see what is hidden to others," said Monceau. "The boy had often been left in a fit for what the demons did."

"And he would have had the fit had he seen demons or not," Saint-Germain could not keep himself from saying. "No one with his condition could keep from succumbing to fits."

"Pare Herriot says—" Monceau began and then stopped himself. "You are not like the other well-born; you are not of Provence. You come from a distant place."

"I am an exile," Saint-Germain said tranquilly.

Monceau nodded. "It is more than your foreignness. You are an alchemist. You have summoned great forces for your work."

Saint-Germain's smile took Monceau by surprise as much as his self-effacing attitude. "Actually, I summon no forces that do not already exist in the nature of the work, the nature is already given by God; anyone who believes otherwise is ignorant of the Great Art." He saw Monceau scowl and went on easily. "There are those who will say anything they do not understand must be of the Devil because they do not understand it. If Pare Herriot suspects deviltry, let him say so to me, and stop frightening my servants." There was small chance of that happening, he knew, so long as Saint-Germain had friends in Avignon. He pointed to the chalcedony cup that stood on the end of the table, a good-sized vessel with a careful carving of his eclipse device cut in low relief upon it. "You have seen that cup change color when a candle is lit within it. That has nothing of the Devil or God in it, only of the stone, which is as God made it when He made Heaven and Earth. I have made nothing in this stone that was not there to begin with. The carving was the most difficult part of its forming, and the only art used to shape the stone."

Monceau wanted to hear none of this. He had taken two steps back while Saint-Germain spoke and now he held up his hands with his palms outward. "I beg you, mon Sieur, nothing more. I would have to Confess it, and that could bring you grief."

"So it might," said Saint-Germain, his tone of voice sardonic, his dark eyes hard to read. "I will not ask you to put yourself at risk for my sake."

Monceau looked relieved. "I thank you, mon Sieur." He paused. "The men who are leaving—shall I ask for replacements for them?"

Saint-Germain thought about his answer a moment. "No; it is hardly necessary. I will wait until spring, and if it is appropriate then, I will request more hands from the nobles. Most of those living in Provence are willing to lose a few weeks' labor in exchange for gold, and if not—" He shrugged. "We will be able to manage the harvest with the men we have, don't you think?" He was not sure he would still be in Provence come spring but did not want to speak of it; it would smack too much of flight, and that would turn the suspicion of his staff on him.

"Do you want the men who are leaving summoned here, so that you may know them?" Monceau looked at the heavy leather books in which Saint-Germain kept records of this estate. "You have their names written."

"If they will come at the end of the day, yes," said Saint-Germain. "And see they are given fresh goat cheese to take with them."

"A most generous gift, considering their departure." Monceau was try-ing hard not to be too inquisitive, so that he would not find out something that reflected badly on Saint-Germain. "I have been most sorely tempted by curiosity since I was a child. No beating could mend my ways, though both my father and the priest tried. It is wrong, and I have prayed to God to send me the strength to deny it: I have regretted it most of my life, and have asked God to take this bane from me before now, but never as I have done in the last year." This admission made him feel less at fault, but he was surprised to see the frown on Saint-Germain's face. "What offense—"

"You do not give me offense," Saint-Germain said quickly. "I am . . . vexed that my ways are so unwelcome in this place where they could—" He broke off, knowing that if he said anything about learning and curios-ity Pare Herriot might twist it to Monceau's disadvantage, and his own. "May God give you His Angels to protect you."

"Amen," said Monceau at once, and lowered his eyes. "I went beyond what is seemly."

"Not in my opinion," Saint-Germain said, adding genially, "In fact, I am grateful to you for your candor." He paced the length of the room, turned on his heel and said, "Well, let the men go, and warn the rest of the house-hold there will be more smoke and more baths; if this is unacceptable to them, they need not remain. Their work is appreciated here, and they have my thanks. But tell them this for me when you—" He stopped and steadied himself. "If I have learned nothing else in my travels, I have learned this: that where there are vermin there is sickness."

"Vermin were sent by the Devil," Monceau declared, relieved to find some point of dogma on which Saint-Germain and Pare Herriot agreed.

Knowing it was useless to dispute this point, Saint-Germain went on, "And in recognition of verminous . . . emanations"—he hoped the word would satisfy Monceau and Pare Herriot—"there must be cleansing. The Great Art teaches the same wisdom as the Church does."

Monceau made a sign of assent. "Yes. That is why the witches were burned: their sins were cleansed in the flames."

It was difficult for Saint-Germain to keep from arguing with Monceau, though he knew it was useless; the despicable act still had the power to appall him. He could not keep from feeling some apprehension: he knew how easily suspicion could point to him; his doctrinal disputes would not spare the women their suffering now. "Just so," he said curtly, and made himself continue without protest, "And as I have heard it explained in years past, the flames purify, so the smoke they generate will carry the purification they bring. It is a great truth." He had said something of this sort before, many years ago, and had been able to avoid a Church prison; he was not convinced he would be so fortunate if he were put to the test this time.

Apparently Monceau was willing to accept his logic as well; he brightened visibly. "I will tell the household. It will make them all less apprehensive." He waited to be dismissed. "Is there anything more you require of me just now, mon Sieur?"

"No; not just now," said Saint-Germain, acknowledging Monceau's short bow with a sign of blessing. "You serve me well."

Monceau faltered, uncertain of what to make of this; it was incorrect for him to question his employer, and so he left Saint-Germain alone in his study.

It was several hours later that Saint-Germain emerged from his study; he carried two rolled maps under his arm as he made his way to his private apartments. Only one servant saw him: Mère Esmerauda stopped in the entrance to the kitchen to watch Saint-Germain, thinking as she often did that it was a shame her master was a foreigner; he was a good master in so many respects that were often overshadowed by his many strangenesses. Comte though he was, she knew his rank was not so important as his alienness, for people would always notice the unfamiliar; it was all anyone talked about—how unlike the other nobles he was: their Comte was an exile, living in a place not his by birth. No, she thought, he might have rank and privilege by right of lineage, but it would not sustain him. She blessed herself and went to see that the churn was ready for use tomorrow morning.

"Were you planning to go out later?" Rogres asked in Byzantine Greek as Saint-Germain came into his private apartments.

"I have men to pay," said Saint-Germain with a slight sigh. He lifted his hands palms upward to indicate he could do nothing until that task was complete.

"When that is done, do you intend to . . . spend time away from Clair dela Luna?" There was a sternness in Rogres' question that went beyond what Saint-Germain expected. "You have not gone beyond your gates for some time."

"No, I have not; it has been . . . imprudent. Why do you ask?" Saint-Germain inquired with interest.

"Orgon will not be safe for you, my master. The monks at Saunt-Joachim are conducting a vigil for the town tonight. I just heard it from the miller's boy: they will be walking around the walls of the town reciting prayers until dawn." Rogres' expression revealed nothing, but he could not help but add, "Pare Herriot is looking to root out the Devil. He will be disappointed if he does not find one."

"Ah," said Saint-Germain.

"He will not stop at this night." The warning was given flatly, as if he were describing nothing more than an inconvenience.

"No," Saint-Germain allowed sadly.

Rogres stood silently for a short while, then cocked his head. "My master?"

Saint-Germain did not answer at once; he went to the red lacquer chest and opened it, taking out a bag of coins. "Is it more sensible to give the men a few extra coins in spite of their leaving early?"

Rogres made an impatient gesture. "Do not answer, then." He stood still, waiting for Saint-Germain to speak to him. "It would be prudent to keep Pare Herriot in mind while you make your decision about the men; he will be sure to question them when they return to their homes. You do not want it make it appear you are bribing them."

"Nor should it seem that I am punishing them," said Saint-Germain. "Well, I have until sundown to decide."

"Sundown," echoed Rogres. He was silent a short while. "You know what is coming, don't you?"

"Yes; better than I would want to," Saint-Germain said quietly. He looked toward the window, his dark eyes seeing horrific images of other places in other centuries; his voice was remote. "So many of them die. So very, very many."

"You told me not long ago that you can accept their deaths," Rogres said in stern sympathy.

"Perhaps," Saint-Germain replied. He turned his attention to Rogres. "We will have to make ready. I have begun, but—"

"Tell me what I am to do," said Rogres.

Saint-Germain came near to smiling. "Yes. Yes, old friend, I will." He stood a bit straighter. "There are compounds I must prepare."

"Very good," said Rogres. "Tell me what is needed and I will—"

Saint-Germain interrupted him. "If you busy yourself on my behalf, you will only draw more attention to what I am doing, and that would not be wise. Too many people are watching what I do; I must give them no cause to suspect the worst of me." He shook his head once, his dark eyes fixed on the middle distance, the beginning of a frown between his brows. "So: you will need to find one of the servants, and give orders to him. Otherwise Eudoin Tissant will be here, inventing new taxes for me to pay, and he may bring Pare Herriot with him."

Rogres considered these things. "It is what Tissant would like. He is still trying to find ways to tax your chests of earth."

"And if he has a long tenure, he may yet discover one," said Saint-

Germain sardonically. "His designs are only worldly; Pare Herriot is the more dangerous of the two."

"I am consoled to hear you acknowledge it," said Rogres, an edge in his voice.

"Consoled, not relieved?" Saint-Germain inquired, one fine brow rising to punctuate his question; he did not hurry Rogres to reply.

"No. Not relieved," Rogres admitted. "You will not leave yet, will you?"

"And that bothers you," Saint-Germain said, conceding awareness of his manservant's anxiety; he abandoned his ironic manner. "It bothers me, too, old friend. We have seen his sort before, and we know what his dogmatic vision can do."

"Which is why you are lingering here, I suppose, when experience says it is folly," said Rogres. "You want to guard them all from—"

"From what is coming," Saint-Germain finished for him. "I know what will happen; I cannot abandon them to their agony. The Plague cannot touch me, nor any other illness."

"But fire can," Rogres reminded him grimly. "Even you are not proof against flames. While the Plague is with us, so will fire be."

"Yes. And beheading, or anything that destroys my head or my spine, you needn't remind me, will give me the True Death," Saint-Germain supplied. He took two sheets of vellum and reached for his ink-cake and the small pot of water. "I will make a list of herbs I will need. Several lists, in fact."

Rogres' faded blue eyes softened. "You cannot leave them, can you?"

Saint-Germain answered as he selected two trimmed quills and dipped them in the ink. "Not while I can spare them suffering."

"You put yourself in danger," Rogres said, exasperated.

"Not as great as the danger they are in," Saint-Germain said with quiet certainty, and taking a quill in either hand, began to write on both sheets simultaneously.

Text of a letter from Hue d'Ormonde in Marsailla to his second cousin, Fabrice Rocene, in Pont Sant-Pierre, County of Hainaut.

To my much-loved kinsman, the greetings from Hue d'Ormonde in Marsailla, Provence, in the Holy Roman Empire, with profound thanks that you have consented in what I proposed in spring.

This letter is being carried by my daughter, Jenfra, who will, by the terms of our agreement, live with you and your family until she is sixteen or married. She will herself present you with the agreed-upon sum of twenty-eight gold crowns and five bales of good cloth for her personal use. Again, I must express my gratitude that you will undertake to help my child reform herself before her willfulness is inexpugnably fixed in her character. The prayers and the prayers of my wife for your success in this worthy Christian enterprise accompany my daughter; your charity in re-

ceiving her has eased my mind in many ways, for it is rumored that there is sickness in the East and many fear the miasma will spread here. To know that my daughter is far away from Marsailla will pain me, but that will be eased with the certainty that she is beyond all danger.

You may hear my daughter speak against my wife and her brother, Josue Roebertis, who has shown her such kindness. It is the belief of Jenfra's Confessor that she is troubled because the Roebertis family has, in times past, been Jewish, and came to Marsailla from France when the Jews were expulsed from there. The father of Josue converted shortly after his family arrived here and Josue has embraced the Church as well, so there can be no reason to hold the family in distaste.

There has also been an episode—now thankfully over—when my daughter, though a child, conceived a violent attachment to a foreign nobleman who keeps a villa on the merchants' road between Marsailla and Avignon. She urged me to arrange a betrothal and would not be persuaded that this was unacceptable, not only because the man is of higher rank than we, but is an exile as well. He has told me that he has no wish to ally himself with Jenfra, and I know him to be a man whose Word is binding. But Jenfra is not yet a woman, and as soon as she becomes one, even so honorable a man as this one has been might be tempted to change his mind. That you have taken Jenfra into your household is most beneficial in this regard, for although this foreigner is a man of impeccable conduct, he is also a lord, and it would shame me if he should change his mind and demand she become his mistress; we are merchants, not serfs or servants or farmers, and we are not so beholden to our lords as others are. It would increase my indebtedness to you if you would be willing to look about for a husband for her while she is in your care. I have settled a handsome sum on her and her children to come, which should make her more marriageable than if she had no portion or only a small one.

It will be a year or more until I come as far north as Hainaut, and for that time I pray you will guard my child as I would do were she still with me. The times are precarious, as you are more aware than I. If the war between France and England continues so ruinously, I may have to wait longer; I do not want to risk finding soldiers on the road in my travels, for in such encounters, the merchant always does poorly, being lucky to keep his life. How have the Hansa towns fared through the conflict? I have heard many reports, each one contradicting the last. First one says that all trade has stopped, and then another says that those who could flee need everything from clothes to pots and pans, which they left behind. Then another says that the looters have taken everything in the warehouses and all the merchants in the north are without goods to sell or money to purchase new stock. Then they say that cities that were besieged are now longing for new goods. I would be willing to undertake the trek if there is a chance to make a profit upon my arrival. If you can sort this out for me, I can better decide when I will come north again. My trading with Avignon has always done well, but if I can find other markets, I will not have to depend on the vagaries of the Papal court and the fashions of the Church for my profit. As you must know, we who serve the Papal Princes often serve despots.

My wife was brought to bed of a stillborn son, some weeks before the delivery was expected, but we continue to hope and pray that our union will be sealed with children. My wife is eager to have more children, and I confess I am longing to father a proper heir for my business. Your prayers will be a welcome addition to ours in the days ahead. It is important that the d'Ormonde name continue in this place, for we have long striven to make our reputation one that any merchant could envy. Without a son of my own to leave it to, my business must go to relatives who would extinguish d'Ormonde in Marsailla forever. That would cause me grief, and shame as well.

I commend my daughter to you, and once again ask God to bless you for showing her such benevolence as your letter to me ensures. You will find her lively, but not unbecomingly so. Her maid, Ancella, will remain with her. I have provided separate monies for her maintenance and for her wages; you will not have to pay for her presence among your servants. You have my full authority in every regard, from Jenfra's conduct to her suitors. Your wife has always been mindful of her place; let her set an example for my daughter to follow and I will praise your devotion in my prayers and in all my dealings in the world.

I pray you will send me word as soon as Jenfra arrives, so that I may be calm once again. It is my father's heart that speaks here now: Jenfra has been my treasure, and now I entrust my treasure to your care, certain you will not fail in your protection of her.

> Hue d'Ormonde (his mark)
> by the hand of Frer Beneguet

In Marsailla, in Provence, on the 9th day of September in the 1347th Year of Grace.

PART II

ROGRES DE GADES

*T*ext of a report from Pare Pascale of Marsailla to Abbe Enigo, secretary to His Holiness Pope Clement VI in Avignon.

In the Name of Father, Son and Holy Spirit, Amen. May my salvation be forever denied if I speak deceptively or tell anything that is false, or intend to lead any into error. May my name be stricken from my Order and may my family know me no more if I mislead any in what I say in this report. I pray you, reverend Abbe, will attend to my words and follow them with a desire to do right in the eyes of God and the honor of the Pope.

Surely Marsailla is a sinful place, as are all places on earth, but not so sinful, I hope, that we are cast out from all Grace in this difficult time, when the faith of all is tested and the very confines of Hell would seem to have been breached and our souls brought low in this ordeal. We have endured much in the past, but nothing so enormous as the catastrophe which has overtaken us in these days. I must assume that you have heard that we are beset with the Black Death in five of the eight quarters of the city, and in those places, the Devil may be said to reign. The ravages of this fever are beyond recounting; if it spreads as it has begun we will not have enough living to bury the dead.

Every family lives in fear that the Blood Rose will bloom in their flesh, and the household be boarded into their houses until the crisis is past; the only reason to step into the street is to put the dead into the death carts. The men who had offered to drive the carts, for the service of God and the glory of sacrifice now hide in their churches and will not venture forth; the carts are in the hands of the lowest denizens of the prisons and the repro-

bate soldiers who have come here to profit from our misfortune. I pray they will not enact sins that will make the visitation of the Plague worse than it is so that we will all atone for their faults. The churches are no longer able to say Masses for the repose of single souls, and no graveyard is adequate to the demands that now confront us. Great pits have been dug outside the walls of the city, where the dead are carried, blessed, and buried. It is not suitable to dispose of good Christians in this way, but any other would increase the spread of the miasma that already penetrates most of Marsailla. God has shown mercy to those left to rot on the fields of battle, so perhaps He will take pity on those whom the Plague has touched with its black fingers, and raise them up as He promised on the Last Day.

It is my fear that in spite of all we have done to stop it, the Plague will spread. I am sending this report to you in the hope that it will spur you and those around you to some action that will serve to end the miasmic spread, and make the Devil turn from his purpose of bringing us all to perdition through his wiles and the sin of Despair, wherein all activity is abandoned as useless, and hope is forsaken. The physicians of the city have given their recommendations to board up houses where the Plague is, and have themselves left for Avignon and other places thought to be safe from its fevers. With the physicians gone, we must place all our trust in God.

I fear that in the throes of this terrible fever, the people will give way to debauchery and carnality; surely we have already seen that death has made many forget the respect they owe those who are suffering; it is an appalling thing to realize that there are men and women—I dare not call them Christians—who dare to enter closed houses with the purpose of robbing the afflicted.

We will soon bring the most flagrant sinners to trial and offer them to the flames, our faith promising deliverance if only we will put all the works of the Devil behind us. If we are not zealous enough, it may be that all the city will succumb; God's Will be done. Already we see that the trespasses of the city's people have laid many deaths at our doors to remind us that God will not look kindly upon those who do not obey His Rule implicitly, with innocence and unquestioning devotion. It will not be much longer that I will deem it safe to send reports to you, for it is said that the Plague may soon be found in the country as well as within the walls of Marsailla. Address these concerns to His Holiness, I urge you in all humility and piety, with my admonition that even so great a city as Avignon may yet know the scourge of the Black Death if God is not sufficiently appeased by the acts of those of us who are devout in all we do, and prepared to cast out sin even at the cost of our lives, for the salvation of our souls and the glory of God. I have begged to know what unthinkable iniquity has brought this upon us, but God has not revealed Himself to me. I must suppose that the sins for which we are so horribly redressed are beyond anything we have feared; the devices of the Devil ensnare us every hour, and nowhere is this more evident than in the presence of the Plague: where Blood Roses bloom, *virtue cannot flower. All of us who have vowed to live exemplary lives are now being tested, to determine if our will to do God's Will is genuine, or only a vile calumny in the roles of Heaven. It is my intention to maintain God's Law on earth until I have no breath in my body, and I offer you the opportunity to reform any ungodly acts that might cause God to judge you as stringently as we are being judged.*

Never before have I besought God to send a hard winter, but now I do, so that the miasma may be restrained, as the physicians of Alexandria claim will happen; they have taught that miasmas are contained by cold and stirred by heat. Nothing in God's Word says that these physicians err, or that they are guided by the nefarious intentions of the minions of Hell. It is unwise to ask for hardships, I know, and at another juncture I would not do it, but there has been such a calamity visited upon us already that a hard winter would not make our situation worse than it is and might in a few months spare us from disaster which is now gathering to overtake us. There can be no question that God has shown us His displeasure with His erring children: what other sign is needed when the proofs are all around us? All those who question the hand of God in these things increase the danger of damnation to all of us. The heretics are everywhere, saying that God is not so unjust that He would punish the virtuous with the guilty, forgetting the glory of martyrdom in dying for the salvation of sinful humanity: what Christian can aspire to more than that? If God will allow His Own Son to suffer for all our failings and raise Him up for eternity, what shall those souls who have in all purity of heart be given in Heaven after their travail on earth?

From the mouth of a man who knows he is already dead, the blessing and protection of God upon you and His Holiness.

Pare Pascale,
Order of Intercessionist Fathers

At Saunt Victorio in Marsailla, the 28th day of November, in Our Lord's Year 1347.

Post Scriptum: We have heard that the Holy Roman Emperor, Loys of Bavaria has died; we pray that this is a falsehood, spoken to make the faithful succumb to grief, for if this is true, it is yet another portent of evil, for if it pleases God to take away the Holy Roman Emperor at such a time as this, to whom can we turn to relieve our earthly suffering? God has laid his hand upon us most potently if this has come to pass. If it is not true that Loys is dead, then send word of that great news hastily, for in this city we yearn for any intelligence that will save us from despair.

1

What struck them first was the smell: it was not just the cloying, metallic odor of rotting bodies of hanged men at Marsailla's gates, it was a massive stench, palpable, permeating; it hung on the cool winter air, making every breath a ghastly reminder of what was inside the city walls. No prison, no battlefield had such a presence of death about it as the city of Marsailla.

"No Guard," Rogres observed in Greek as they approached on the broad merchants' road. "And it is not the hour of repose; that should have ended by now. Someone should be there."

"There is a monk in the entryway," Saint-Germain said in the same language, holding his fretting horse with firm hands and strong legs, keeping the reluctant animal directed toward the gates. He was dressed for hunting in a short, full-skirted Flemish haincelin of soft black leather over a Hungarian chamisa of dark-red silk. His black gloves were Italian, lined in marten-fur. His thick-soled heuze, worn without spurs, reached to his knees; his short, loose curls were covered by a soft Pisan hat in dense, black Antioch velvet; his only jewelry was his eclipse device worked in silver depending from a heavy silver collar.

Rogres had chosen a grey-leather skirted pourpoint over long hose and brodequins; the fashion was a bit grand for a manservant, but served to underscore Saint-Germain's simplicity of clothing.

It was early afternoon, when the markets would usually be opening for the second half of the trading day, but there was no indication anything was happening; the streets were empty. No one looked from windows along the broad avenues on the other side of the gate, and no one came out of doors, baskets and sacks in hand for purchases. "They are afraid to be outside," Saint-Germain said quietly. "They will not venture to any part of the city where the Plague has struck."

"But it is said some of the city is not yet . . ." Rogres could find no words to finish; he had seen too much in his centuries with Saint-Germain to believe that Marsailla could be spared. He tugged the lead rope that kept the six pack-mules in line behind his horse. "Where do we take these?"

"The monk will tell us," said Saint-Germain. "If there are churches ministering to the sick, he will know of them." He clucked to his horse to encourage the big grey gelding to keep walking, no matter what the animal smelled.

As they reached the gate, the monk, a painfully thin man in a Franciscan habit, stepped out of the shadows and held up his walking staff. "Mon Sieur," he said in a loud, harsh voice, "do not continue into the city unless you are shriven."

Saint-Germain pulled in his horse, which stamped and nodded his head with anxiety. "Good monk, we are bringing flour and honey and cheese and wine to Marsailla. We have heard that there is not much food left in the city; in such distressful circumstances as the Plague brings, I would like to do my part to be certain that famine is not one of them." The goods he brought were little more than a gesture; he had seen disease many times in his thirty-four centuries of life and had learned that when the fevers were severe, they were inevitably accompanied by famine and rapine. "What churches are providing succor to the sick? I will donate what we have to their use."

The Franciscan stared, clearly astonished at this foreigner's presence; he took a little time to answer, as if he expected Saint-Germain to change his mind. "The monastery of Saunt-Gregorio is giving food, and the church of Saunt Esprito; Saunt Esprito is nearer and more of the people come there." He continued to look at the sacks and barrels on the pack-saddles. "God will bless you for your kindness; there are many in need and few to care for them," he said with fervor.

"And which street do we take to reach Saunt Esprito?" Saint-Germain inquired levelly.

"That way," the monk said, pointing along the cobbled street inside the gates. "At the market turn to the right." He began to pray loudly as Saint-Germain used his heels to make his grey enter the city.

"Do you think we should watch for—?" Rogres called as he and the mules he led followed after.

"I think the robbers are too frightened to attack us, or they are boarded into their houses," Saint-Germain answered, his voice carefully flat as he indicated several building fronts marked with painted crosses on massive planks.

Rogres lifted his head. "Is it all through the city, then?" he asked.

"Oh, yes," said Saint-Germain, sounding tired; he had first seen the effects of epidemic illness in Nineveh, where it had meant nothing to him; the next time, he had been a slave in the Temple of Imhotep at Thebes, and the experience still haunted him. "And beyond, by now. The people may hope it is not, but . . ." He let his thoughts trail off as they entered the market-square where foodstuffs were usually offered for sale. Today the place was empty; two vacant stalls stood as reminder that this had been a busy site until very recently. Heaps of rotting straw with bits of inedible garbage mixed with them were piled up where they had been left more than a week before; no scrap of food remained, silent testimony to the ravenous dogs and rats that had made the place their own.

"It is very bad, is it not, my master?" Rogres asked quietly, as if speaking more loudly would make it worse.

Saint-Germain nodded. "Um." He made his horse pick his way across the square toward the street on the right that would take them to Saunt Esprito. He drew in when he saw two bodies rolled in sheets and left at the side of the nearest boarded-up house. "The death carts have not come this way yet today."

"Do you think they will?" Rogres kept his voice uncritical, but it was apparent that he was appalled at what he saw. "Not even Cyprus was—" He made himself stop.

Saint-Germain spoke for him, coolly, his emotions banked like the smoldering coals that heated his athanor. "I think that until the whole city is filled with the dying, those who can will insist that the death carts tend to the business of retrieving the dead. No one wants to be reminded of how the numbers are growing: so the dead cannot be left to lie in the open, and if anyone suggests it might happen—that the dead would so outnumber the living that there would be no one left to bury them—he would become the object of suspicion—and the penalty for that lapse has become severe. There have been cats and old women burned here yesterday, dead because someone was troubled by them." He pointed ahead to the small, ancient church of Saunt Esprito; the building was at least eight hundred years old, laid out in a design that had been abandoned centuries ago. "You see? There are a few brave souls who have come to be fed. In this place. By all the forgotten gods, what their lives have become, and in so short a time." His musical voice was sad, the tone so quiet he was almost inaudible. "I feel I am cheating them."

Rogres heard Saint-Germain and would have asked why he felt so, but he knew he would receive no answer from him now; their goal lay just ahead of them. From his long centuries with Saint-Germain, Rogres knew his master often felt the weight of the mortality of the people around him more intensely than they did themselves, and never more so than in catastrophes like the Plague; nothing he had said to Saint-Germain had eased his abiding burden in the past, or would be apt to lessen it in future. The braying of one of the mules brought him out of his glum reverie and he gave his attention to the church they were approaching.

At the broad steps into the church about twenty persons were gathered, many holding baskets or sacks in their hands. Each remained silent, as if speaking would bring them into danger; they were like deer gathered at a waterhole: watchful, prepared for flight. A few looked up in dazed uncertainty as Saint-Germain rode directly to the front of the church and swung out of the saddle. "Good priests!" he called out in Marsailla's French. "Send one of your company out."

"We do not give food for another hour," came the exhausted answer from inside the door. "You will have to wait with the rest. Everyone is hungry."

"Then you will want what I am bringing you," Saint-Germain responded at once; he realized he had the attention of everyone waiting: a few of those waiting pressed closer to him, but not so close that they could be at risk from him.

The door at the end of the narthex opened and an elderly priest poked his head out. "What is this about? And God will not look kindly on any deception you may attempt in this wretched quarter."

"No deception," said Saint-Germain, motioning to Rogres to bring his horse up nearer, and with his mount, the pack-mules. "Unless these provisions are illusions." He knew better than to laugh, for the priests as well as those depending on them were incapable of any amusement.

The old priest opened the door a bit more. "Provisions?" he repeated as if he had learned the word long ago but had forgot its meaning.

"From my estate, near the town of Orgon," said Saint-Germain. "I have brought what I can to this city." He signaled to Rogres to dismount. "My bondsman will bring the food to you if you will not send your priests out to get it." He looked about, his expression neutral; he could see the hunger and need in the faces of the men and women waiting for what little the priests could provide; his sympathy for them was as real as pain. He was relieved there were so few of them, for it would take little for these frightened people to become unruly; had there been twice their number, Saint-Germain would have found another way to approach the church so as not to provoke them to violence. He stood beside his horse, the reins held firmly in one hand, and spoke again. "I have to go to the house of Hue d'Ormonde when we are through here." His concession was more than what most nobly-born would make, and those gathered at the church were keenly aware of this.

A man in a greasy scholar's gown—probably an itinerant clerk—made a sound that was not a laugh. "So you will feed us and run away?"

Saint-Germain rounded on the man. "Would you rather I had not come?" The challenge was delivered conversationally, even affably, but the man was not fooled.

"You are the only one in three days, though it is the Nativity," he said quietly, all his defiance vanishing at once. "We have begun to despair." He crossed himself for admitting to so great a sin; the priests could refuse to give him charity for such a failing.

"Then help the priests," Saint-Germain recommended, indicating the packs on the mules. "My bondsman will carry some of the barrels if you will assist him." He could have lifted the barrels and sacks and crates easily himself, but it was not fitting for a man of rank to do the work of servants, and he dared not give these people reason to doubt him; he would load his crates of earth later, when he fetched them from d'Ormonde's house and strapped them on his mules' pack-saddles for the long ride back to Clair dela Luna.

At this suggestion half a dozen priests surged out of the church, swarming around the mules and busying themselves with unloading what Saint-Germain had brought. They spoke little, and they refused to look at the people waiting for their help; Saint-Germain recognized the beleaguered manner of the priests, who could do so little for those who came to them. A straight-backed old priest with whited eyes felt his way with a stick, giving an occasional order to the others and listening to what they said as they worked. "Cheeses. I smell them for myself." He made his way to Saint-Germain. "Who are you?" he demanded without ceremony.

"I am Francois de Saint-Germain, Sieur Ragoczy," he answered directly. "I have an estate near the village of Orgon on the merchants' road to Avignon."

The old priest rapped on the uneven steps with his stick. "You are not from Orgon."

"No. I am from an old Carpathian House. I am here in exile," Saint-Germain answered easily enough as he watched the priest measure what he heard; the small crowd would be guided by the old priest in their reaction to Saint-Germain.

"You are well-born," the old priest declared.

"Yes." He waited for the next question while Rogres supervised the last of the unloading.

Apparently satisfied with what he had learned, "God will bless your service this day," said the old priest, then turned and started back toward the church. The priests carrying barrels and sacks stepped aside for him, and one of them put his small chest down to cross himself.

"He is a saint, that one," said one of the women; her voice shook with fervor. "God reveals Himself to Pare Simone."

The rest murmured their agreements, and one of them began to sing; the song was plaintive and rhythmic, of the sort that were often sung at public gatherings. Soon the rest had joined in, a few clapping in time to melody.

"The praise of God rises even from the tomb," said the old priest as he reached the door.

When the old man was gone, the other priests hurried to finish their tasks. The people waiting continued to sing; one or two began to dance, doing the slow prance that was reserved for religious celebrations. The singing got louder, the clapping more emphatic; more of the people began to dance, their hands raised in a gesture of ecstasy. An underlying panic made this impromptu ceremony seem less an expression of thanksgiving than a venting of something darker, more explosive.

"It is time we left," said Saint-Germain with apparent tranquility, though he sensed the frenzy in the people around him. Without any sign of haste, he swung onto his horse, his shadow falling across the dancers as he did; a few of the people cried out, partly in wonder, partly in accusation. "Rogres: d'Ormonde's house."

Rogres heard their destination over the growing clamor of song and clapping. He took up the lead as he remounted, pulling the mules sharply; for once they had no objection to moving, breaking into a trot in their hurry to put Saunt Esprito behind them.

Holding his horse to the slow, sweating trot, Saint-Germain led the way through the silent, reeking streets, toward Hue d'Ormonde's house; neither Saint-Germain nor Rogres spoke as they rode and their passage went largely unnoticed, although occasionally there were distant cries for help that made Saint-Germain wince. As they reached the edge of the merchants' quarter there was less squalor than they had encountered before, but most houses had a cross painted on the door and boarded windows: there were bodies wrapped in sheets laid out beside these houses; a few had black crosses painted on the side of the house, indicating all the inhabitants were dead.

At d'Ormonde's gate four sheet-wrapped corpses lay, ready for the death carts. The gate was slightly ajar, so that the cross painted on the gate was cut in half; this was an ominous sign. Saint-Germain dismounted with care, holding the reins securely as his grey stamped anxiously; Saint-Germain stood by the bodies and crossed himself in respect for the dead. Then he looked up at Rogres. "I'm going in," he said. "Keep watch for me."

"And hold your horse," said Rogres, extending his hand for the reins. "Shall I call if anyone approaches?"

"Yes," Saint-Germain said. "But call for d'Ormonde, not for me." With that, he gave a curt nod and slipped inside the courtyard of the house: how changed it was from the last time he had seen it—the day of Hue d'Ormonde's wedding. Then flowers had bloomed in pots around the fountain; there were no flowers now and the water in the fountain was brackish, what little trickle came from it marked its path with slime. Saint-Germain stood in the courtyard for a brief while, his thoughts as still as his body. Then he went into the house. He knew his chests were in the storehouse behind the creamery, but he searched the rooms first, looking for anyone who might be alive.

In the servants' parlor in the rear of the top floor he found two young women; they were in their shifts, sitting on the padded benches where the servants met for evening prayers. Both had buboes developed in their armpits and large discolorations on their bodies, which were easily seen through the worn linen of their shifts, and both were nearly delirious with fever and hunger; neither of them had bathed in several weeks, and the odor of old sweat vied with the stench of sickness and death. One of them was thin, the other was emaciated, as likely to die of starvation as of Plague; no food was brought to houses where the Plague was. Both of them looked up at Saint-Germain in utter disbelief, and crossed themselves to keep their souls from harm.

"May God protect you," Saint-Germain said quietly. "And the house of Hue d'Ormonde."

The thinner woman shook her head, laughter grating from her. "There is no House of Hue d'Ormonde. They're all dead. We're the last." She sagged in her place, almost reclining as she waited to die.

"No others are left in this house?" Saint-Germain asked, knowing that neither woman was capable of thinking clearly now that the Plague had its talons in them. He tried to keep their attention. "When was a physician here last?"

Both women looked at him in astonishment; the woman who was still sitting upright answered. "No physician. No apothecary. All gone. All gone, all gone, all gone."

"You put the dead at the gate?" Saint-Germain kept his question level to keep from giving either woman greater alarm; his incredulity mixed with recollections of similar feats from the past: the camp-follower in the mountains of Greece who had carried her Roman officer on her back for a day and a night to reach safety although she herself had been raped and beaten, the ten-year-old eunuch in Tunis who had lifted a fallen marble pediment from his brother's body, the grandmother in Karakorum who raised a fully laden wagon to free her grandchildren pinned beneath—those incidents and many more flickered in his memory.

"There is no one to do it but us," said the reclining woman.

"Hue d'Ormonde and his family?" Saint-Germain knew the answer but could not keep from seeking confirmation.

"All dead. All dead," said the first woman.

"We are going to wrap ourselves in sheets tonight," said the second, very seriously. "We will go and lie in the streets. Otherwise we will be devoured by rats, and . . ." Her voice rose to a shriek.

"Did anyone leave? When the Plague began?" Saint-Germain persisted. He knew these women were beyond any succor he could provide but one, and neither would welcome what he could give; neither was prepared for what his blood could do, and would not accept it if he offered.

"The brother . . . The brother, her brother," said the thinner woman, and began to convulse, spasms wracking her unmercifully. The foam at the corner of her mouth went red as she bit off the end of her tongue.

Saint-Germain went to her, kneeling down to hold her, to whisper futile words of comfort while the Plague shook her like a rat in the jaws of a wolf. Only when it was past, when the woman lay still, did Saint-Germain release her; as he stood he said to the other woman, who had watched her companion die with dull resignation. "I will fetch a sheet."

"And carry her down," she replied. "I . . . I can't . . ." Her voice trailed off.

"I will," Saint-Germain promised. As he went out of the room, he realized he had not learned who, if anyone, from the household had left the city.

By the time the death-cart reached d'Ormonde's house at sunset, there were six sheet-shrouded bodies at the door; Saint-Germain, with Rogres and his chests of earth loaded aboard the pack-mules, was gone from Marsailla.

Text of a letter from Eudoin Tissant to Percevall, Vidame Saunt Joachim.

To the most gracious Vidame Saunt Joachim, the respectful greetings of the tax collector of Orgon, at this most holy time of the year, with the prayer that God will give each of us to know His Will and the courage to persevere in His Name.

As Your Excellency is certainly aware, the Black Death has come to Marsailla; it is said that the city is now marked by the presence of birds of prey circling in the skies, ready to feed on the dead who are no longer buried but are left to rot in the streets, so greatly do they outnumber the living. Mindful of this, the town of Orgon, in a desire to save its people from a similar fate, has enacted certain new and stringent taxes and penalties for those who might bring danger to us. You, as Vidame Saunt Joachim, will be called upon to enforce these taxes and penalties, as I am required to record and account for them; further, you and your armed men are charged with the task to keep away anyone coming here from Marsailla by any means you deem appropriate. These measures are to be put into effect on the first day of January, and will be enforced until they are no longer necessary.

For those giving succor to any coming from Marsailla, including the monks and nuns who would usually provide charity to all unfortunates, the penalty for such laxness will be a fine of four golden crowns for the first offense, a fine of ten golden crowns and a beating of ten lashes for a second offense, a fine of twenty golden crowns and thirty lashes for a third offense, and a seizure of all monies and goods and a public burning of the criminal for a fourth offense.

For those failing to report any case of Plague, though it be within their own household, the penalty shall be ten golden crowns for a first offence, twenty golden crowns for a second offense, thirty golden crowns and twenty lashes for the third offense, and a seizure of all goods and monies and a burning of the criminal and those infected with the Plague for a fourth offense; their ashes are to be buried outside the town at a distance of not less than two leagues.

For those receiving any goods determined to bring the miasma, the penalty shall be a fine of five golden crowns for the first offense, ten golden crowns and five lashes for the second, twenty golden crowns and ten lashes for the third, and a seizure of all goods and monies as well as permanent exile from Provence for the third.

For those whose conduct is known to promote the miasmic presence, the first lapse will carry a fine of twenty golden crowns and twenty lashes, a second lapse will result in seizure of goods and monies and the criminal will be burned.

For those whose wits are addled, or who have traffic with familiars, or who prepare philters for the seduction of men, any instance of such activities reported will carry a sentence of seizure of all goods and monies and the burning of the criminal.

For those unable to pay the fines, the lashing shall be doubled and burning or exile imposed at the third offense.

For those unwilling to be confined to their houses once Plague is discovered there, the penalty shall be burning at the first offense, the ashes to be buried not less than two leagues from the town walls.

With the sole exception of physicians, no person will be permitted to enter a house where Plague is, and then leave it until the Plague has passed without being subject to burning upon leaving the house. This will apply to all persons, including pregnant women, for the innocence of the babe will not be lessened by a martyr's death.

I commend these new measures to you, and pray you will be diligent in enforcing them, as I have sworn to be. In duty and in honor, I am always at your service and the service of the town of Orgon,

Eudoin Tissant

In the town of Orgon, in Provence, in the Holy Roman Empire on this 29th day of December in the 1347th Year of Grace.

2

"I realize we should not have come here—those in the town will hold this against you, I fear," said the leader of the players as Saint-Germain closed the gates of Clair dela Luna behind them. He was a lean, middle-aged man with a prominent aquiline nose under deep-set green eyes and straight dark-brown brows. In conversation his voice was a deep, internal rumble; when performing, it was as moving and clarion as the peal of great bells. He had called himself Faustino for so long that he had almost forgotten his childhood in Flanders and his loomsman father; he had been a player since he was ten and had never regretted his choice that had made him an outcast from his devout, austere family.

"I doubt they will notice. They have other grievances that are more . . . pressing," Saint-Germain replied, making a gesture of welcome to the troupe of fourteen—nine performers, two men-of-all-work, and three women, wives of the three senior men, who made most of the costumes, masks, and properties for the actors. Aside from the extravagant scenes painted on the sides of their wagons, they might have been a group of ill-assorted merchants; they were plainly dressed without frills or excesses and they had the same stolid exhaustion about them. "The evening meal will be ready shortly. There is a boar and two geese on the spit, and fresh cheeses being baked. Come in and have something to eat; you look as if you have missed a supper or two of late." The words were light enough to earn him a smile from a few of the players, but their eyes were grim.

"No one will eat soon, if the Blood Roses continue to bloom," said the hard-faced young man who was Faustino's stepson, and his lieutenant. He had a cap lined with rabbit-fur pulled down over his forehead; he glowered as if his head ached. "The peasants will not go into the fields to make the ground ready for crops, for fear the miasma will rise through the ground and kill them."

Saint-Germain's voice dropped. "But it doesn't save them."

"We reached your villa before that rain did, for which we are thankful," Faustino said, indicating the massing dark clouds to the southwest, and bowed deeply to Saint-Germain, flourishing his hat as if he were facing an audience of dozens and not a solitary man in black. "So we are the more grateful for our welcome here. We have heard it said as far away as Avignon that your villa and estate is safe, at least for now. Pray God you do not become a haven for all the scaff and raff of the road." He glanced in the direction of the stable. "Do you have grooms still, or are they . . . gone?"

"None of them have died, if that is what you mean, or none that I am aware of," Saint-Germain said readily enough. "But two have left, out of fear, and what may have befallen them I have no knowledge. It is as you've said; they wait in their houses, certain they can hide from the Plague. I am sorry to tell you: you will have to look after your own donkeys and mules. There is fodder for them, and the stalls are clean." He continued across the icy courtyard toward the entrance to the villa, the heels of his heuze ringing on the flagging as he went. "I will give the order as soon as your men are in from the stable: the bath-house will be ready for you in an hour or so. You may use it after you have dined. There will be enough hot water for all." The baths were built long ago, with old Roman sensibility; the tepidarium was missing, but a calidarium and a frigidarium were in good repair and of sufficient size to accommodate up to twenty.

"Thank God for that," said Faustino. "We are grimy from the road. And the winter is hard this year, Plague or no Plague."

"At least you have been able to travel," Saint-Germain said as he opened the door for his guests, allowing them to enter ahead of him in spite of custom which dictated he precede them. "Or has there been trouble?"

"No one stops us, if that is what you mean. Players are going everywhere, as we always have. Merchants are being restricted, and vagabonds. Religious men travel unhampered, and so do we." Faustino laughed. "In times like these, people need to have their minds taken off their fears. So they let us come and play for them. Troubadours are free to travel for the same reason." He remembered the way to the main reception room and went there directly, his voice ringing as he went, making his arrival an entrance. "We have entertained the Pope himself at Avignon because we were coming from the north. Even His Holiness is worried about things from the south—other than Rome, of course." He laughed at his own jest; the rest had heard it and groaned.

"The Plague has reached Avignon?" Saint-Germain inquired, his face showing nothing of his dismay; he had not supposed the disease would arrive there before spring.

"They claim it has not. I am not certain it is so. The Plague moves swiftly as the dead." Faustino folded his arms and fixed his gaze on the large log blazing in the fireplace; his face was stark with emotions he readily expressed only on the stage. With an effort of will he shook himself and did his best to smile engagingly. "You are always hospitable, mon Sieur."

"And not an hour too soon, with the storm coming," said his stepson, who was called Palot. "I will go to the stables when Dormahn and Ettore are finished, to see our mules and donkeys are properly brushed, fed, and watered and have—" He stopped, taking in the reception room. "For a small villa, you have an elegant fashion here, mon Sieur. I had forgot how—"

Saint-Germain looked seriously at the player. "You are kind to say so." He had a fleeting recollection of many of the lovely things he had had and now had lost; his jade lions, waiting in his house in Antwerp and his red lacquer chest which was now in his laboratory in the tower were among the few survivors of his long wanderings.

Faustino's wife, a rawboned woman from the far north of Lombardia who had an ancient, puckered scar on her forehead indicating she had once been a slave, put her hands out to warm them; her knuckles were chapped and cracked. "The last two nights we have slept in the open. We have had a fire, but nothing like this, where the wind cannot reach us."

"Then I hope you will enjoy it," said Saint-Germain, signaling for Monceau: to his surprise, Rogres appeared.

"I must have a word with you, my master," Rogres said in his calm way.

Saint-Germain gave no indication of distress. "Of course."

Faustino dropped into the X-shaped chair, turning toward the fire. "I used to love the hours of travel, of how the scene changed and new sights were always before me. Now my bones demand more attention than the scenery. And my stomach demands its due." He sighed heavily, adding for emphasis, "The penalties of age."

"I will return in a moment," Saint-Germain said to the players, and nodded to Rogres to step down the corridor; he could not hide a tense little frown that settled between his brows, for he knew Rogres would not alert him in this way unless something was sadly awry.

"Is everything . . . all right?" Palot asked, stopping Saint-Germain as he noticed his host's demeanor; his question sharp enough to have the full attention of the rest of the troupe, and the sudden flare of their anxiety as well.

"Yes," said Saint-Germain somewhat distantly; then he gave himself a mental shake. "I shall not be long. Then you will tell me how the broad world fares."

"Very good," said Faustino for the rest.

"Is there some trouble?" Saint-Germain said to Rogres when they were out of earshot. "I imagine there must be. It is in your eyes." He spoke in the language of Rogres' native city Gades, which the Moors in Spain called Cadiz.

"It is more than imagining," said Rogres, grateful to be using his native tongue; it provided him a comfort that took the worst burden from unwelcome news. "I made certain of this before I came to you: Monceau is nowhere to be found; his things are gone from his apartment, and Mère Esmerauda tells me that she saw him leave by the side-gate at midafternoon, while it was still raining."

"Did he say anything to anyone?" Saint-Germain asked, more to fix the time than discuss the weather.

"Not that I have been able to discover. Mère Esmerauda said she was puzzled to see him leave, for he had told no one of his intention; she took the time to speak to the others before coming to me. I think she is trying to reassure the rest of the household, for she is reluctant to tell me anything more. I doubt the others are convinced." Rogres kept his voice level, but his faded-blue eyes were becoming more troubled. "He did not ask for his wages. He may indeed intend to return."

"You do not believe that any more than I do," said Saint-Germain. "We will have to find out if any message came for him—that could account for his departure. If his family sent him word of trouble—" He tapped his fingers impatiently on the hilt of his short sword. "I suppose we should be grateful for this warning."

"If that is what it is," said Rogres carefully.

Saint-Germain gave a one-sided smile. "Oh, that is what it is, no matter what Monceau intended. We know now that the partial acceptance we have had in this place has come to an end. What was excused or overlooked in the past will no longer be tolerated." He stared toward the light from the kitchen at the far end of the corridor. "Not today, and not tomorrow or the next day, but soon we will have to leave; the winter storms will provide us a little time to make ready. We had best prepare Mère Esmerauda for what will come."

"She will want to help you," said Rogres. "You have treated her well and she will want to acknowledge what you have done."

From the reception room, the babble of conversation among the players grew louder and more animated as they gathered around the fireplace.

"That might be difficult," Saint-Germain said thoughtfully. "For both her and me. And you as well, old friend." He looked down at the floor, where the thin flagstones were laid over a layer of his native earth. "She cannot be allowed to appear in complicity with either of us, for suspicion could turn on her. No matter how we try to keep it from happening, I am certain Pare Herriot will turn our departure to his advantage; he needs to exert himself if he is to continue to impress the people and the Church with his zeal: if he can claim to have driven me away, he will make the most of it, and you and I cannot change that. He is reluctant to attack me while I am here, for he is a miller's son and village priest and I am well-born, though an exile. But once we depart, he will be eager to show that he has driven the Devil and the Devil's foreign deputy out of the God-fearing regions of Orgon. If condemning Mère Esmerauda will strengthen his position, he will not hesitate to lay all our supposed sins at her door. That would be poor recompense for her devotion." He sounded more weary than bitter, but his tone was such that Rogres knew Saint-Germain was recalling similar incidents from the past. "Not that any of this will stop the Plague."

Rogres nodded. "It is hard to watch them die," he admitted slowly.

"And no consolation to know that neither Plague nor any other illness can touch either one of us." Saint-Germain laid his small hand on Rogres' shoulder, an ancient, blind ache in his dark eyes. "I wish I could summon up some deliverance that would—"

"It is not possible for you, my master—nor for me," said Rogres, stepping back from his black-clad master. "You will want your alchemical supplies readied for travel, I suppose."

"Along with the rest of anything we wish to keep. Do not let your initial preparations be too obvious; I do not want the staff thrown into panic. We must prepare for what is likely to happen, once we are gone from here. I doubt this place will remain untouched in the months to come." He sighed once, a short, perplexed sound.

"Your crates of earth?" Rogres asked, now wholly remote in his demeanor.

"We will take as many as we can in wagons. The rest we can leave under the floor of the creamery. No one would look for anything of the sort there." Saint-Germain glanced back toward the reception room. "I must get back to them."

"And Mère Esmerauda is waiting for me, as well," said Rogres.

"Put her at ease if you can," Saint-Germain said quietly. "She has had enough to endure because of me."

"I will do what I can to reassure her," Rogres said calmly.

As Saint-Germain started to turn away, he said, in the French of Provence, "Thank you, my friend. I am in your debt yet again."

Rogres bowed. "If it pleases you to think so, my master," he said and went toward the kitchen while Saint-Germain returned to the players in the reception room.

"Is there anything wrong?" Palot asked without apology as Saint-Germain stepped out of the gathering shadows.

"Not that should concern you," said Saint-Germain with a self-possessed smile. "My bondsman is worried about the major domo, who has been suddenly called away."

"Do you mean that Plague—" one of the women asked, crossing herself and unable to say anything more. "They have walled up Saunte-Barbara, so we heard, and all inside."

"I mean," Saint-Germain said with no sign of dismay or deception, "that he was called away." He looked at Faustino. "My manservant will assume the duties. You will not be at a disadvantage if that is troubling you."

"I am quivering with fright," said Faustino in a mixture of humor and apprehension. He signaled to Palot. "Everyone is quivering with fear." He saw his stepson's impatient glare, and changed his tone to a crisper one. "Go check our animals and tell Ettore and Dormahn to come in. The mules and donkeys must be brushed down and watered by now."

"The bay mule was about to cast a shoe," one of the men reminded Faustino. "That could be delaying them."

"So it might," said Palot. "I will find out." He could not hide the expression of ill-usage that flickered over his features.

Saint-Germain held up a hand to stop the young man. "If your mule needs new shoes, I will attend to it. You have only to inform me." He did not mention that he would tend to the shoeing himself, for that was something no titled man would lower himself to do.

Palot favored Saint-Germain with an expression of surprise. "We are players, mon Sieur," he began, as if to remind his host of their relative positions in the world.

"That means little to your stock; they will go lame as easily for a high-born lord as a player, and suffer as much," said Saint-Germain. "They will have what they require, I give you my Word." He motioned for Palot to go about his task, then looked at the troupe sitting in chairs or on the floor at the edge of the fire's warmth. "Your stock will not be better served than you. There will be beds for all of you, though most of you will have to share them in pairs."

Most of the players chuckled for they usually lived in the close confines of three wagons—separate rooms with only two to a bed was a luxury to them. The youngest of the women put her hand to her swollen belly and said, "I am already sharing."

There was genuine laughter at this familiar complaint; Faustino slapped his knee in appreciation. "When we travel, and we have no crowds to entertain, we have many things to occupy our minds; plays are the least of it." He looked uneasily at Saint-Germain. "I don't mean that you . . . that your work is not . . ."

Saint-Germain made a gesture of dismissal. "I know what you mean; I am not offended. Words on a page are important to one part of your playing—the demands of your work are more important than that, and there are many more of them."

Faustino looked relieved; he had often known the well-born to be capricious, and never more than when their talents were in question: players had been thrown into prison for more minor slights than this was. In the five years that Saint-Germain had received his troupe he had also supplied them with four scenarios to perform; Faustino did not want to appear unmindful of this gift. "Five of our company are new."

"So I noticed," said Saint-Germain, minor curiosity in this statement; most companies of players changed personnel fairly often.

"The new ones. They don't understand, mon Sieur. It might be different if the others could read," Faustino said lamely.

"Possibly," Saint-Germain allowed; he had realized long ago that few players cared who made the scenarios for them: only when their performances were given a generous reception did they remember the originator of the work, and then with the hope that there would be more that would bring them favorable attention. When their performances went badly, they cursed everyone, beginning with the author of the scenarios.

"We will not remain here long," Faustino said, as much for his company as for Saint-Germain's benefit. "If Plague is coming, I want us to be well-away from this place as soon as the weather will permit us to go. The longer we remain in one place, the greater is the chance that the Plague will find us." He shrugged his apology to Saint-Germain and did his best to take the sting out of what he had said. "Your villa is wonderful, but we do not want to wait for the miasma to envelop us simply because the place is pleasant and there is sufficient food for all of us."

"True enough," said the craggy old man who played most of the aged roles. His face was pock-marked and his hair was little more than fine white wisps, but his presence was immediate and he was able when he chose to, to command attention with his posture alone.

Saint-Germain made a sign of acceptance. "You have nothing to fear: I will not ask you to stay in danger for my sake," he said, aware that traveling would not spare them; he was able to keep from saying more by the appearance of Mère Esmerauda with two scullions in her wake carrying huge trays with trenchers of fresh bread upon them.

"Cheese and a soup of chicken and herbs first, and then the boar and the geese, with roast onions and butter. You may have another trencher if you need it after the soup," she announced, sounding both awkward and self-important for announcing the meal, a task she had never performed without Monceau to manage it. She looked in Saint-Germain's direction. "Will you want beer or wine served, mon Sieur? I have no orders."

"Let each choose what he would like," Saint-Germain replied, going toward the passage to his study. "God send you good appetites, my guests," he added as courtesy demanded.

The players scrambled toward Mère Esmerauda and the scullions; they made no excuses for their hunger. The aromas from the food perfumed the air more than roses and sandalwood, for they promised something good to eat. Their eagerness created some confusion until the players restored themselves to some order.

"Save some for Palot. And Dormahn and Ettore. They will be back in a moment," Faustino reminded his company.

"Do you think there will be enough?" The woman who asked was skinny, her face pinched and her voice quarrelsome; she was the nominal wife of the handsome-but-irascible Timoteo, who played many of their heros.

"In this lord's house, you need not fear," said Faustino, color creeping into his face. He glanced toward Saint-Germain and was relieved to see that he was not offended.

Timoteo raised his hand to cuff his wife, then thought better of it. He seized his trencher and glared at anyone who glanced his direction.

Wind rushed through the room, coming from a newly opened door. "That will be Palot and Ettore and Dormahn," one of the players announced; a moment later the sounds of their footsteps could be heard approaching and the wind disappeared.

The three men arrived in the reception room; Ettore said something privately to Faustino as Palot and Dormahn went to get their trenchers.

Faustino rolled his eyes at what he heard and muttered something that made Ettore scowl. Then, with an assumption of casualness, Faustino clapped Ettore on the shoulder. "Well, we cannot do anything about that mule just now. Let us put our time to better use and have some of this excellent food Sieur Ragoczy has been kind enough to provide for us."

Mère Esmerauda watched carefully as the meal was set out for these unusual guests; she knew other men of Saint-Germain's rank would require the players eat with the servants, or with the laborers. She decided it was a show of good-will that caused him to entertain the players as if they were worthy merchants or men of substance. "There is plenty in the kitchen," she announced to forestall any more slighting remarks.

One of the scullions was sent to fetch a keg of wine, an errand that earned a stifled cheer from the players. "Bring tankards, as well!" called the white-haired actor.

"Right!" one of the others agreed. "We don't want to lap it like dogs."

"We will drink your health," Faustino declared as he took his trencher in his hands and went toward the table where the meal was being laid out. He paid little attention to Saint-Germain's departure—the high-born did not often dine with players, and this was not a Day of Humility, when it would be expected of men of rank to invite vagabonds and beggars to their tables.

"I thank you for that," Saint-Germain said before he walked away.

Text of a memorandum made by Pare Herriot, filed in Orgon and in Avignon.

To the notice of the most reverend and learned judges in Orgon, in Provence, in the Holy Roman Empire, and in Avignon, the Pope's city, this record is offered most zealously for the preservation of our faith in this time of trial.

The Wrath of God is surely visited upon us, for the Plague is all around us, its grip more deadly than the chill of winter. No wolves ravening in the forests can claim so many souls as the Plague has in the last two months.

If the ground were not so hard, we would dig pits to lay the dead in as a common grave, but as it cannot be worked, a pest-house has been set up near the monastery of Saunt-Joachim, where the sick are taken for the last of their days on earth. Those among the monks who have declared themselves ready to die have sworn to care for the sick while there is breath in their bodies. We offer prayers for them three times a day, and each morning we recite the requiem for those who have died in the night. When the ground softens, we will bury them.

In order to ward off the Devil and his servants who bring the Plague, we have captured all the cats in the town and have put them to the torch. Our efforts were not sufficient, for there have been more cases of the Plague since that was done, showing how obdurate the Devil is in his purpose of destruction. We will put Saunte-Barbara to the torch, to cleanse our worship. We will have to discover the greatest sinners in Orgon and put them to the flames next, as well, or we will face the loss of all—our lives and our souls. Even Vidame Percevall has declared he will stand with me in this contest, for he fears the triumph of the Devil in his Vidamie will mean that God is forsaking Provence.

With the unaccountable departure of the foreigner, Francois de Saint-Germain, Sieur Ragoczy, his estate, Clair dela Luna, has been seized by the town of Orgon, and until such time as a legitimate claim may be made for it and all assessments against it be paid to the town, it will be managed by Eudoin Tissant, who is granted a portion of the taxes he levies for his efforts, as he has been for all such abandoned land in the area. He has also been authorized to order the slaughter of starving animals if no one may be found who is willing to undertake their upkeep. I have approved all these measures, along with the leaders of the town, who are willing to listen to my advice.

The five vagabonds detained last week have been judged and will be consigned to the flames on the Feast of Saunt Savion, eight days hence; their guilt is beyond question and I cannot do other than uphold the Church in this desperate hour. All five have protested their innocence, which is to be expected, but all five cannot deny they have been to Marsailla and not been touched by Plague: what else can any pious man conclude but that they have entered into a pact with the Devil for the purpose of carrying the disease afar? They must have poisoned our wells, for they would not otherwise refuse to drink from them, preferring to quench their thirst in running water. Their deaths may yet save us from the hideous losses we are told of in other villages nearer to Marsailla.

Nothing will stay me in my work to preserve this place from all evil and

death. May the Bishops and Archbishops add my name to their prayers to
strengthen me in my endeavor. And to this I say Amen.

Pare Herriot

In Orgon, on the 12th day of February, in the 1348th Year of Grace.

3

Around the square in front of the imposing, fortresslike Papal Palace in
Avignon many terrified faithful had gathered in the hope that the nearness
of Clement would preserve them from harm. The crowd had been growing in size for more than a month and showed no sign of diminishing in
spite of the increasing number of Plague victims within the city walls; the
people were fleeing the countryside and villages faster than they could die
in the streets of Avignon. Every morning and evening the death carts came
and took away the bodies of those God had not spared, and this evening
would be no exception, although the air was icy; those who would not live
until dawn would not all be victims of Plague—some would freeze in the
night. A dozen harried monks were trying to distribute the thin soup and
hard bread charity required they provide, but the crush of people made
this nearly impossible.

Saint-Germain avoided the center of the huge square fronting the
palace; his companion, the wine merchant Jehan Nemout, a broad-
shouldered man of good stature and crafty mein, shook his head in pon-
derous disgust, while taking care not to get too close to the crowd. "Look
at them all," he said to Saint-Germain; he swung the hem of his fur-lined
huque up to avoid brushing it against any of the wretches. "Nothing but
vultures, the lot of them."

"So would you be as well, Jehan, if you were starving," said Saint-
Germain quietly.

"They are desperate to come here, and foolish. The Plague may take
them before hunger can." He made a sign to ward off the Evil Eye as he
looked for an unhampered path at the outskirts of the crowd. "It is unfitting that they should hang upon the Church so—" He waved his hand to
dismiss them. "They have turned from the work God and the world has de-
creed for them, and like frightened children, come running as if to hide
under their mother's skirts." His long years of prosperity and unflagging en-
ergy had given him no patience with those who where not as industrious
as he; God had given him purpose and ambition—why should others lack
those qualities?

"Their lives are not like yours. You only sell the wine, Jehan," Saint-Germain reminded him. "You do not raise the grapes and fill the vats yourself. You do not fret every time there is an unseasonable shower, or when the spring is too dry, or too cold, as they do. Animals do not raid your orchards and vineyards, and you have no local lord to placate, or greedy Bishop to appease. Do not condemn them for being countryfolk." He cocked his head in the direction of the Papal Palace. "You are certain we will be received."

"We were sent for; they will not send us away," said Jehan Nemout. "Cardinal Montantica is concerned for the towns to the south of here. He comes from Torino, and he has had little news from there, and all of it bad. He is mindful of his duty to his flock, and he seeks to learn from you. Provence is not Torino, but you have come through towns and villages on your way here, and you must have heard things on the road. You are not a credulous man, nor an ambitious one, so your views are not suspect. Therefore he and a few others would like to hear what you have to say." He smiled, confident that this act would bring him favorable notice of these high-ranking clerics. "It's a pity about Hue d'Ormonde and his family. I understand one of the wife's children survived."

"So I understand," Saint-Germain concurred, more brusquely than he had intended.

"Where is the lad?" Nemout inquired with a modicum of genuine attention; the ownership of Hue d'Ormonde's warehouses was of interest to him.

"I do not know," said Saint-Germain sadly.

This did not please his companion, who covered his annoyance as best he could. "Well, God will reward him in Heaven and make amends for his suffering on earth," said Jehan Nemout with automatic piety. "And when the Plague is over, the matter may be put before a magistrate or the Bishops for a determination."

Saint-Germain plucked at Jehan Nemout's sleeve to pull him out of the way of two tussling youths who were tearing a small loaf of bread to pieces, egged on by those waiting at the edge of the crowd; it gave Saint-Germain an excuse not to respond to Nemout's last remark.

"Stand back! All of you—back!" shouted one of the monks in frustration. "You will all be fed. Stand back!" His orders inspired grumbles but no action, and the monk went back to his work with a hard face.

"Be careful," Nemout barked at a man pulling a two-wheeled barrow filled with wooden bowls and cups, clearly intending to sell them to the people waiting for the Pope's charity. Unlike most of those gathered in the square, this man looked happy, even jaunty, as he went along, calling merrily, "Two coppers a bowl, two coppers a cup."

The crowd was almost behind them now as Jehan Nemout and Saint-Germain made their way between the massive walls of the palace and the two small chapels to Saunts Cosmo and Damieno on the other side of the narrow street. The sounds of the crowd behind them echoed on the stones, turning into the howls of storms, or demons.

"Are your accommodations to your liking? You may command an apartment in my house if you are not satisfied by the inn." This belated offer of hospitality fooled neither of them.

"There is no need. The inn suits my purposes very well," said Saint-Germain with such firmness that it was doubtful if Nemout would have the temerity to ask again.

Jehan Nemout dodged the issue entirely. "I think you must be singly honored, to have the Cardinal summon you in this way."

"He summoned you as well," Saint-Germain pointed out. "The honor— if there is one—must be shared."

"I suppose it must," said Jehan Nemout, looking a bit smug at this. "But I have lived in Avignon all my life. You are a foreigner. The Papal court knows me."

"And you have long been of service to all the court." Saint-Germain's smile was ironic.

Nemout was unaware of Saint-Germain's intent. "As all good merchants in Avignon hope to be," he said with a sincerity that revealed his aspirations eloquently.

"Then I must hope that I will have knowledge that is useful, to uphold the tradition," Saint-Germain said, his tone neutral.

"You will be expected to tell them everything you saw, if that is the whole of the Cardinal's purpose. If it is not, you will do all you are able to in order to accommodate his requests. In these days, it is wise to have the Church hold you in high regard," Jehan Nemout reminded Saint-Germain for the third time since he had called at the inn where Saint-Germain was staying. "You are noble and your report must be believed more readily than the reports of commoners or worse."

Saint-Germain noticed that this last admission did not trouble Jehan Nemout, who accepted the world and its rules as he found them. "I should think the Cardinals would want all the information they could get at this time, no matter who the source might be, noble or common."

"But that is just the trouble—the source," said the wine merchant, stepping carefully past a group of children huddled together for warmth; he ignored their crafty smiles and the pinched faces with the ease of one who had never questioned his place in the world. "Men of God and men of Honor will bear the truest witness. They will uphold their oaths or they will face Hell in eternity. We all know the truth of it; their vows preserve them from errors. The rest of us are more worldly, and are more apt to be snared by the world, which is—"

"—the dominion of the Devil," Saint-Germain finished for him, adding wryly, "No doubt."

They were nearing a small door, its thick planking banded with iron: Jehan Nemout walked directly to it and slammed the flat of his palm against it twice; the sound in the stone alley reverberated dully as distant cannon fire. He lowered his head and pulled off the long-tailed liripipe, holding it tightly between his big-knuckled hands. Under his breath he ordered the monk who kept this door, wishing perdition upon him if he were not prompt; a moment later the bolts inside were drawn back and the door was pulled open a crack. "Jehan Nemout brings Francois de Saint-Germain, Sieur Ragoczy, to see Cardinal Montantica. *Deo gratias.*" He crossed himself.

The door was opened somewhat wider and a man in a Cluniac habit motioned the merchant and the foreigner inside; the abandoned children looked up briefly at this unusual incident, and then put their minds to more important matters.

Saint-Germain stepped inside the palace of Clement VI, tossing back the hood of his black velvet, fur-lined balandras, thinking as he did that the garment had not much changed from the version of it he had worn a millennium ago, when the Romans called it bardocucullus. Beneath he wore a deep-pleated amigaut of red-and-black brocade the hem of which just brushed the rolled tops of his thick-soled brodequins. While elegant his clothes were not elaborate as the law allowed him, and this gave an impression of austerity that the Church assumed showed piety. His only jewelry was a pectoral of silver links with his eclipse device hanging from it in the center of his chest. He crossed himself and gave his full attention to the Cluniac monk who faced him. "I am most grateful to be received."

The Cluniac heard this and nodded; his answer was more sung than spoken, in accord with the old Cluniac traditions. "You are welcome in the Palace of the Pope. May God keep you in His Hand while you are here."

Jehan Nemout crossed himself again, betraying his nervousness, saying, "The Cardinal . . . Cardinal Montantica? he sent for us."

"So you have told me," the Cluniac intoned. "And you are expected. Both of you will be received."

Saint-Germain glanced at the corridor ahead. He was about to suggest they move on when Nemout cut into his thoughts.

"And we are here, in accordance with his summons," said Nemout a bit testily, unwilling to embrace the elaborate civility of the Papal court. "No doubt he is expecting us."

"He is waiting for you," sang the monk, and started away from Jehan Nemout and Saint-Germain with such uncanny grace that he seemed to float over the stones of the floor.

"What do you think?" said Nemout, pointing at the retreating monk. "He gave us no order. Do we follow him?"

"Why not?" Saint-Germain replied. "He knows this place and we do not. I have no desire to wander the corridors looking for Cardinal Montantica." He found the place magnificent and oppressive at once, a huge pile of stone that was more like an enormous mausoleum than a place for the living. He followed his own suggestion and went after the Cluniac, hearing his heels strike and echo in the vaulted hallway.

Jehan Nemout came after him, his manner flustered. "Very well, very well," he muttered; he glanced around uneasily as if he suspected they were observed.

Saint-Germain was certain they were: he had been aware of scrutiny since they entered the building, and he had had experience enough with priests to behave in a seemly manner—no priest, no matter what god he prayed to, wanted to see his faith made mock of. He thought back to his own initiation into the priesthood of his vanished people in that grove at midnight, so many, many centuries ago. He had long since put that worship behind him, but he could recall with chagrin the bloody revenge he had exacted in the name of his god and his family.

"This staircase will take you up to Cardinal Montantica's apartments in the South Tower," the Cluniac chanted, indicating a staircase that was wider than most, and lit by narrow windows as well as clusters of hanging oil-lamps.

"You are not escorting us?" Nemout demanded, looking narrowly at the monk. "Why should we go up alone?"

"I am not bidden to come beyond this point. A Dominican will meet you at the door. I am wanted in the choir. *Pax vobiscum.*" He blessed them and nodded to show his work was done, then stepped away.

"But—" Nemout protested, trying to call the monk back.

"Never mind," said Saint-Germain as he put his foot on the lowest tread. "The Cardinal must have had his reasons for wanting us to come alone. We would offend him, perhaps, if we failed to do as he has ordered." He continued to climb the broad curve of the staircase, moving steadily, progressing upward as if wholly unconcerned with what might wait for him at the top.

Reluctantly Jehan Nemout followed him, not quite lagging, but making no haste either; as he climbed he spoke in whispers, as if he could not be overheard if he did. "Why did the monk leave? What does the Cardinal want?"

"I suspect he does not want to order wine," said Saint-Germain with a sardonic lift to one fine eyebrow.

"I fear not," Nemout agreed unhappily. "But why should he send for—"

Saint-Germain cut him off. "I do not know the Cardinal's purpose, nor do you. Let us wait until he explains this all to us." He was almost at the top of the stairs now, and the patterns of light and shadow from the narrow windows marked their upward progress on the opposite wall.

Jehan Nemout was not brave enough to pout, but he fell huffily silent as he completed the climb; he stepped out onto a wide gallery made lustrous by the many-colored splendor of a rose window high in the tower above them; this was the west-facing square tower, one of four; there were six round towers as well, but they did not boast rose windows. The fine window could not entirely disguise the defensive nature of the building, which could withstand siege and assault. Two more colonnaded galleries soared above them toward the window, as if all the palace, even the stones of which it was made, aspired to Heaven. Nemout crossed himself in awe as he stared upward. "God above . . ." From some recess below a choir was singing the Office of the Hour, the voices echoing the wonderful light.

"So it would seem," Saint-Germain remarked as he looked along the gallery for the Cardinal's apartments. Finally he noticed an open door. "There. I think that is where we must go."

"There?" Nemout asked, doing his best not to be awed by all he saw and heard. He stumbled and recovered himself as he accompanied Saint-Germain along the gallery toward the open door.

A young Dominican stood just inside the door. He raised three fingers in honor of the Trinity to welcome Jehan Nemout and Saint-Germain, then pointed toward the long chamber just ahead of them.

At the far end of the room stood a square-bodied man in Cardinal's vestments; he was between thirty and thirty-five, a powerful figure with a long head and a broken, red-veined nose. He held out his hand with its ring to be kissed.

Rising from this duty, Saint-Germain once again wondered what it was that Cardinal Montantica wanted of him; he watched as Nemout knelt to kiss the ring and be blessed, thinking all the while that there was apprehension beneath the Cardinal's imposing manner, an ambiguity of purpose that served to whet Saint-Germain's curiosity. "You were most gracious to send for us, Eminence," he said when the Cardinal glanced his way again.

"It was not for grace that I did it," the Cardinal replied. "I must require you to help me." He folded his hands as if to guard against taking more aggressive action.

"If it is in my power to do so, I will," said Saint-Germain, this concession without subservience.

"I am pleased you are willing to comply." Cardinal Montantica scowled down at his folded hands; when he spoke again his question startled Saint-Germain. "You know Percevall, Vidame Saunt Joachim?"

"We have met," Saint-Germain answered carefully, now fully alert to what might be real danger.

"You saved him," said the Cardinal, making this a challenge. He paid no attention to the shocked expression on Jehan Nemout's face.

"I helped him recover, Eminence," Saint-Germain corrected gently, his mild response masking his sudden foreboding. "There is a difference."

"He says that without you he would have died," Cardinal Montantica declared; he would not brook more dispute on the matter.

"Such things are in God's hands, not mine," Saint-Germain responded; he realized he would have to offer the Cardinal something more than pious saws if he was to avoid unwanted scrutiny. "In my travels, I have learned something of medicaments. Occasionally they are of benefit to those who are suffering. Such was the case with the Vidame Saunt Joachim."

"He said you brought him back from the shadow of death," said Cardinal Montantica; the Dominican behind him was watching Saint-Germain narrowly.

"He may have assumed the worst for himself; to my eyes, he was ill but not yet in mortal danger." Saint-Germain spoke easily enough, but he could not rid himself of anxiety.

"Still, that is a gift from God in its way." Cardinal Montantica paced down the room, away from Saint-Germain and Jehan Nemout. He paused at the window that looked out on the main square inside the Papal Palace. "The Plague is getting worse," he said conversationally. "It is in the Hands of God, as is everything in this world. God has allowed this Plague to come, and we are as nothing in its path." He indicated the square below his window. "Everything is becoming dangerous. We have Masses six times a day, and God will not relent. We have punished the faithless and the heretics, but to no avail. We have cast out those of simple minds and deranged wits, but it is not enough. Sinful women from Marsailla have come here, and the miasma is strong in them, nurtured by their sin. They will face judgment tonight; when the flames here have been put out, the eternal ones will have just begun." He motioned to Saint-Germain to join him at the window.

Saint-Germain knew it was folly to show any reluctance; he made himself walk briskly to the Cardinal's side and look down into the vast courtyard below: a dozen stakes were erected on platforms above piles of faggots; the number of the stakes was in honor of the apostles, Saint-Germain recalled with distaste. "Women from Marsailla?" he asked because it was expected of him.

"A courtesan and her women," said the Cardinal. "If you wait a moment, you will see them for yourself." He glowered at Saint-Germain. "You know of these women?"

It was an effort to smile. "I have . . . appetites; all men have appetites," Saint-Germain said. "I have no wife or mistress, as I am sure you know, and I do not keep any men or boys for my pleasure." He met the Cardinal's gaze steadily. "So, yes, I do know courtesans."

"And whores?" Cardinal Montantica asked bluntly.

Saint-Germain shrugged, letting the Cardinal assume whatever he wished. Finally he said, "It is not . . . honorable to debauch virtuous women."

"No, it is not," the Cardinal agreed at once. He licked his lips, the movement of his tongue quick and finicky. "If these women die, the Plague may abate."

Saint-Germain shook his head slowly; he was aware how dangerous it was to contradict a man of the Cardinal's rank, but he was too repulsed by what he was about to witness to show any endorsement of it. "You may kill these women, and a thousand more, and you will not stop the Plague."

"This is the Great Dying," said Cardinal Montantica.

For once Saint-Germain could not dispute the Cardinal's pronouncement. "I fear it may be."

"So says your master?" The Cardinal all but pounced on the question.

"I am without master or country," Saint-Germain reminded him, his voice lowered to show respect; he concealed his consternation at the change in the Cardinal's tone with a combination of deference and hauteur, as any man of noble birth would do.

"Not in this world, perhaps," Cardinal Montantica said, all but accusing Saint-Germain.

It was Nemout who answered. "Eminence, Eminence. What are you saying to this good man? He has provided wine for your table and you have always praised its quality. No one has spoken against Sieur Ragoczy whose complaints have been upheld, by the civil authorities or the Church."

"The Devil is subtle," said Cardinal Montantica. He pointed at Saint-Germain. "Pare Herriot of Orgon has said you are a dangerous man, an alchemist working with ungodly forces. He says you spared the Vidame in order to keep the men of the Church from watching you and discovering what you truly do in the world."

Saint-Germain made himself chuckle. "Is that what bothers you?" He did his best to look amused; the inquiry was too near the truth for his comfort. "I make a few medicaments in the manner I was taught, when I went to study in Egypt. That was more than half a lifetime ago." The last was not only to impress the Cardinal, but to make it plain he had not brought the miasma with him from that distant place: he had seen this Plague before, but not in Egypt—in China more than a century ago he had witnessed an outbreak of it near Lo-Yang; the disease had not been as ferocious there as it was proving to be here, but the symptoms were unmistakable.

"Egypt, was it?" Cardinal Montantica managed a skeptical frown.

"Yes. I went there after my family was driven from their lands." That more than five hundred years had passed between his family's slaughter and his arrival in Egypt, Saint-Germain did not mention. "I thought an exile should have some skills to use in the world beyond simple royal birth."

"Royal birth—simple," said the Cardinal, too much bemused to be offended.

"Why, yes. To an exile, it is of less importance than his capabilities." He regarded the Cardinal with a look that was part respect, part evaluation. "Would you think it honorable for me to batten on another royal house for my keep, and offer nothing back to them?"

"There is your blood," said Cardinal Montantica, referring to the value of royalty in marriage.

"Yes: there is my blood," Saint-Germain said, meaning something else entirely.

Once again Jehan Nemout spoke. "You said you were curious, Eminence, about what has become of Marsailla, and the cities of Italy." His face showed his dismay, as if he expected Saint-Germain and Cardinal Montantica to come to blows.

"Yes," said the Cardinal as if recalled from a distraction. "You associate with merchants, Sieur, as we see." He pointed to Jehan Nemout. "Have you learned anything from them?"

"Tell him; tell him," Nemout urged, almost poking Saint-Germain's arm to goad him to reply.

"Word from the sailors—those few who are bold enough to put into port—say that Corsica, Sardinia, and Sicily are full of Plague," Saint-Germain said bluntly. "If their reports are accurate, the situation on those islands is as bad as what I, myself, saw in Marsailla. I have not met anyone coming overland from Italy in three months. What may have happened now, I can only guess, and pray that my guesses are in error." He waited for the Cardinal to ask him questions; his memories of the Black Plague in China were more than a hundred fifty years old, but as vivid as the terrible carnage wrought by the horsemen of Jenghiz Khan, thirty years after the Plague.

"The word we have from Marsailla is that six out of seven are ill or fled." It was not easy for Cardinal Montantica to admit this much.

Although Saint-Germain was certain that the figures were higher, he responded, "At least that. And they burned the simple-minded and the whores and the Jews in Marsailla, though it did not save them." This was a dangerous observation, one that could bring about accusations he could not refute: he saw distress in the Cardinal's eyes and relented. "I fear Death has no regard for sacrifice." In his more than three millennia of life, he had realized this as he had learned no other lesson: Death sought no acolytes and honored no offering.

Cardinal Montantica crossed himself. "But God does, and we are in God's Hands."

Not knowing what else to do, Jehan Nemout crossed himself.

Text of a letter from Rogres de Gades in Avignon to Atta Olivia Clemens, at her retreat near Trieste, written in the Latin of Imperial Rome.

Bondama Clemens, from Rogres, the manservant of Sanct' Germain, my greetings both from myself and on his behalf.

As my master has informed you, we have left Clair dela Luna and have come to Avignon. Now my master has said we cannot remain here: we are to travel northward to his holdings in the Low Countries, or perhaps as far as Denmark. He is certain that the Great Dying, as it is now being called, is just beginning, and he wants to put himself far beyond it if he can.

Not that this Plague is a danger to him: as one of his blood, you know no illness can touch any of you. But the dread and rancor of the people who are sick can, as we see here every day. The courtesan whom my master sometimes visited in Marsailla fled to this place and for her efforts was burned at the stake with twenty-three other women who had come to Avignon to escape death. The stake—through the back, or as a site for burning—is as fatal to you who share Sant' Germain's blood as they are to all the living. You have reminded him of this many times over the centuries; for once he is taking heed of the danger without your warning.

He is torn between his desire to treat those who are ill and his certainty that to do too much to heal the sick would bring suspicion upon him that would result in imprisonment at the least. So he has ordered me to make ready to go while we can. It rankles with him to leave this city when the disease is not yet at its full force, but to wait longer would mean risks that he will not accept.

If you were here, you could coax him out of his despair. I have not seen him so since T'en Chi-Yu fell in battle, when he was as remote as the heights of the mountains through which we climbed after her death. You recall how he was when he and Niklos faced the Huns: this is much the same, but without the battles to comfort him.

You may be certain that I will remain with him while he travels, and should any misfortune befall him, I will do my utmost to preserve him from harm. Whenever it is possible, I will send you word of where we are bound and what has transpired. It is fitting that you should be informed of what has become of him so that you will know what you must do. I was relieved to have your message that the packet of Wills and Deeds had arrived. Sanct' Germain will not now admit so much, but I am convinced he is less vexed now that he knows his affairs are in your hands. You and I would prefer that there be no need for these measures, but is it not better that this preparation be made?

We are bound for Valence, but not on the main road. When we arrive there, if any reliable merchant or other travelers are bound for Trieste, I will ask them to carry another message for me. For now, I will entrust this to the pilgrims bound for the Holy Land, for they plan to travel overland to Trieste to avoid the Plague at Venice.

Keep yourself safe, Bondama, and hope that Sanct' Germain will be safe, as well.

With profound regard,
Rogres
Manservant to Sanct' Germain Ragoczy

In Avignon on the 27th day of March, 1348 Christian years.

4

Spring was beginning to take hold of the countryside, but its beauty was forlorn and unseen by most of those who might have enjoyed it in another year, and the promise of richness for the harvest was ignored. Fallow fields and neglected flocks were everywhere and they were increasing; a few small villages and hamlets were nearly deserted, the peasants driven away by the rumor of the Great Dying as by its presence. Where the Plague had taken hold there were isolated peste-houses, places where the dying went when there was no one left to care for them, or when those left were as stricken as they. Many attempted to flee the disease, although such travel had been forbidden; there were not enough men-at-arms brave enough to force peasants back into Plague-ridden hamlets and villages to make the threat anything more than perfunctory. Market towns were shunned, their easy commerce a thing of the past now that everyone was in danger; not even the precaution of burning cats and flagrant sinners could lull the peasants and artisans back into the towns. Once winter was over, the roads were filled with small groups of people, most with their households on their backs, trying to get beyond the limits of the Black Plague.

"And probably carrying it with them," Saint-Germain observed to Rogres in Magyar as they passed four goatherds, each with young kids across their shoulders, tied to their small packs of belongings.

Rogres, riding behind him, said, "If you are right in how it is spread, it is certainly possible; more than the chance of wells being deliberately poisoned, at least. There is not much consolation in knowing that you and I cannot be touched by it." He looked back at the loaded mules he led, and frowned. "Will it spread quickly, do you think?"

"It has already spread quickly," Saint-Germain said, his voice disheartened; with a nod he indicated the goatherds. "One of them is sick already. The others will be soon."

"Are they beyond help?" Rogres had seen the Plague in China, too, and remembered its deadliness. "Can they not be saved?"

Saint-Germain looked away toward the line of trees that ran along the edge of the untended fields. "The wolves will do well; they will become bold, and the sheep, and goats, and hogs, and cattle, will be weak," he said distantly, remembering how many times he had seen the wolves prey on abandoned herds. Then he shook himself slightly and answered Rogres' question. "They might be, if they would accept my remedy. But they will not. Stop the goatherds and see for yourself."

Rogres considered this unexpected gesture. "Yes. Let me at least make the offer."

"Certainly; as you wish," Saint-Germain said, still sounding remote. He spoke next in the Avignon dialect. "If I can help any of those men, I will."

Rogres pulled in his horse and secured the mules' lead to his saddle before dismounting. He stood facing the approaching goatherds, his soft Italian cap in his hands as a sign of good-will. As the men approached, he said, "God give you good day, Goatherds."

The oldest of the group—a scraggly fellow without many teeth whose bald pate was fringed in a long wreath of white hair—looked narrowly at Rogres. "You passed us a way back," he said in a patois that was hard to follow.

To the west of them a small group of peasants' houses were nestled in a compound; there was almost no activity around them, but for a young donkey, still shaggy from winter, pacing restlessly in his pen, and a cow with full udders bawling out her discomfort.

"Yes; my master and I are traveling to Valence." Now that he was speaking to the goatherds he did not know how to continue. "You have fine kids with you."

"Yes, we do," said the oldest. "You are looking to buy one?"

Wanting to keep the man talking, Rogres nodded. "That's right," he said, and saw the greedy light in their eyes.

"Five silver Emperors," said the oldest at once: it was three times the amount he would charge at market. "Your master is wealthy."

"So I am," said Saint-Germain, surprising Rogres as much as the goatherds. "And I will pay your price." He watched the men exchange eager grins. "If you will do one thing I ask."

Rogres saw the men grow wary, and said, "My master is an honorable man, Goatherds. You have no cause to fear him."

"What does he want us to do?" The oldest goatherd glared at Rogres since he would not dare to confront a man of noble birth. "We will touch no one who has died with Blood Roses on him."

"No, no," said Rogres hastily. "That is not what we are to do." He crossed himself, hoping to reassure the goatherds. "He will give you something to drink. It is quite harmless, but it can bring a blessing, if you will take it."

"From a saint's fountain?" asked one of the other goatherds suspiciously; miraculous cures from saints' fountains had been common enough before the Great Dying began, but now nothing seemed to help. "Your master is offering it for charity?"

"Not from a saint's fountain," said Rogres, then realized his mistake, and strove to correct it: he knew they would not accept a remedy that was extracted from moldy bread, and so he improvised. "It is from the Papal

Palace at Avignon. Pope Clement himself has blessed it." He hoped he had recovered himself enough to make this an acceptable explanation.

"The Pope!" the oldest goatherd scoffed as he glanced back at his fellows. "Understand me: I ask no charity, not from God, who has sent this Dying, nor from the Pope. The Blood Roses accommodate the prayers of no man—not beggar or Pope. Water is water, no matter who has touched it: to the Black Plague it makes no difference." He shook his head, then he took the kid off his shoulders. "Five silver Emperors," he said, holding out his hand; the kid struggled against the cord holding it, bleating in discomfort and thirst.

"The offer included the drink," Saint-Germain reminded him.

If the goatherd was impressed to have a man of rank speak to him, he showed it by spitting.

"That changes nothing," said Saint-Germain mildly.

The oldest goatherd had prepared himself for a beating, and found this reasonable response more ominous than anything he had heard thus far. "Four silver Emperors, for the kid. No drink." He made a sign to the others. "I have lost all hope in God, and the Pope cannot change me." This was clearly for Saint-Germain's benefit; the goatherds understood one another already.

"I'll have some," said one of the younger goatherds, a youth with a long, lean face, large ears, and big, knobby hands. "If the Pope has blessed it, what harm can it do?"

"What *good* can it do?" the oldest countered. "And what if the well it came from was tainted? Do you think the prayers of the Pope would cleanse it?"

"Why would the Pope bless tainted water?" Rogres asked, doing his best to sound shocked at the notion.

"The Devil would deceive him," said the oldest goatherd. "We've seen it for ourselves. The priest at the church where we heard Mass drank from the Chalice and died with it in his hands. Now he is waiting for Judgment Day when he will learn why God was so displeased with him that He allowed him to die on the altar."

The young goatherd who had accepted the offer of a drink now faltered. "Yes. He is dead. God did not lift him up." He shook his head and stepped away from Rogres. "I won't take any, after all."

"But it will save you. It is—" Rogres began, then tried again. "It is the one thing that may be proof against the Dying."

"And the miasma might be in it," said the man whose face was scarred by the Great Pox. He hitched his pack and the kid tied to it a bit higher on his shoulders, and in a display of defiance, walked on without being dismissed; this was an insult both to his companions and to Saint-Germain— he clearly had intended it to be.

"Do you want the kid or do you not?" the oldest goatherd persisted after an uneasy glance at his departing comrade. He raised his voice as if speaking louder would make the other goatherd's behavior less noticeable. "If you do not take him, another will." He toed the kid to make him squirm; he was becoming impatient. "We have a way to go before night comes on. We have no shelter and will have to find some. Tell me what you want."

Rogres had to resist the urge to upbraid the goatherds, to call them obstinate fools; he reached into his wallet that hung from his belt and pulled out five silver Emperors. "There," he said.

"I asked for four," the goatherd challenged, aghast at the generosity Rogres showed him; he was half-expecting a kick in the face for his trouble: the high-born were capricious in such matters, as the goatherd had reason to know. Hunching over, he stared down at the ground, saying, "I don't want to lose my hands for theft."

"You will not," said Rogres, knowing the goatherds were not convinced. "I will pay the first price." He dropped the coins at the goatherd's feet. "If you want them, take them." With that he picked up the kid and slung the protesting animal over the sacks on the saddle of the second mule, taking care to secure it in place before he remounted his horse; he said, "May God guide your travels and keep you from harm."

"Amen," answered two of the goatherds as Saint-Germain signaled his horse to move on; as he and Rogres passed the pockmarked goatherd who had already resumed walking, Rogres turned back to see the oldest goatherd pawing through the dust in search of the five silver coins.

"Do not think you are to blame," Saint-Germain remarked a short while later; the goatherds were now out of sight around a bend in the road behind them.

"I have observed this many times when you had made such a gesture, and *you* have not believed *me*," Rogres replied with a trace of amusement in his annoyance.

"True enough," Saint-Germain agreed. "Still, you gave them the opportunity. They were the ones who refused. You cannot hold yourself accountable."

"Why not?" Rogres asked. "You have, many times."

"So I have," Saint-Germain said, his voice remote again.

"If they had known what it was, they might—" Rogres interrupted himself. "No, they would not. They would probably have thought it was diabolical, because it was made of moldy bread." He looked back as the kid baaed his complaints again.

Saint-Germain stared off at the peasants' compound on his left; they were almost abreast of it now. He could see the young donkey pacing in his pen, his shaggy coat matted with mud. On impulse he drew rein, saying, "Wait for me. And give that kid some water."

"Where are you going?" Rogres called out as Saint-Germain spurred his grey down the track toward the compound.

"To see why no one has fed that donkey," Saint-Germain answered loudly. Riding into the circle of houses within the stockade, he shouted,

"Good peasants! Good peasants! Is anyone here?" He made a quick circle of the central well, and was about to ride toward the fields when the stench hit him: the village had been struck by Plague, for nothing else could create such a terrible odor without goading the people in the place to do something to stop it. His horse nearly sat back on his haunches, his head angled in distress; he minced forward in answer to the insistent pressure of Saint-Germain's legs. "Courage, my lad," he said, trying to steady the gelding with his hands and his voice; the grey's back was tight, his shoulders moving stiffly. Glancing at the houses, Saint-Germain saw two of them had open doors marked with the cross to indicate Plague within; the doors should have been boarded shut; the little chapel had a crude cross on its door as well; the priest had taken the Plague. High squeals told him rats had got into the creamery and were feasting on the cheeses and smoked meats stored there. No dogs barked, no chickens squawked, sure signs that any survivors had left.

On the far side of the compound near the midden there were nine bodies laid out, all with Blood Roses in their armpits and groins and marks like great bruises in several places on their flesh: one was an infant not more than a few weeks old. All were naked and had been dead for at least two days; they had nothing to protect them now but their disease; only two showed signs of being gnawed on—an old man and a girl about fourteen, both of whom were missing parts of fingers and toes. "Rats, not dogs," Saint-Germain murmured as he swung out of the saddle and secured his horse's reins to a stout post; then he went in search of a shovel so that the bodies could be covered. He dug fresh earth, working steadily to bury them, though he knew it made no difference to their repose; they were beyond all succor. As he continued his self-appointed task, Saint-Germain paused from time to time to assess his progress; the bodies began to disappear: first features, then shapes and finally the distinction of individual corpses vanished under the rich soil.

When that was done, he turned to more mundane problems; he opened the byre and let out the cow, trusting that one of the groups wandering the roads would find her and milk her. He was about to do the same with the young donkey, when he changed his mind: he improvised a halter and a lead from a length of rope he found hanging on the side of the byre; the donkey spent that time eagerly consuming the bundle of fresh, green grass Saint-Germain cut for him and dropped into the pen. When the donkey had eaten, Saint-Germain tied the halter into place, took the lead and got back on his grey; in answer to a first tug on the lead, the donkey responded at once, ambling forward as if glad of company. "Come along," Saint-Germain ordered him and signaled the grey to walk on.

Rogres showed no sign of surprise when Saint-Germain arrived back on the road. He glanced at the mud on Saint-Germain's sleeve and remarked, "The people back there are gone."

"Yes; they are gone," Saint-Germain confirmed, turning his mount north along the rutted road leading to Valence and the bridge that would take them across the Rhone.

"You are taking the donkey?" Rogres asked, expecting the answer he got.

"I am," said Saint-Germain, and moved on.

Travel was slow. Many of the villages along the way had closed their gates to most travelers in the hope of keeping the Plague out: they held off everyone but religious and entertainers with barrages of stones and flaming arrows: other places were already in the grip of the Great Dying, and those places were being emptied as rapidly as the sound could flee and the grave-diggers could work; in many places the only care left to the stricken who were not quite so ill as they.

"How far will we have to go to escape it? how long?" Rogres asked one night as they stabled their animals in the narthex of a deserted church at the outskirts of the village of Saunte Sophia; the village was one of the many hilltop towns that could easily be closed off—now barricaded and all travelers but religious pilgrims and mummers were being told to move on, encouraged to go by peltings of dead mice and rats, and the charred corpses of cats. This church offered the nearest shelter below the town; it stood half-way down the gentlest slope of the hill, built of native stone, and of a design that was at least five hundred years old.

"I wish I knew," Saint-Germain said as he helped Rogres to lay a fire in the middle of the nave. "In China, it was more than half a year before the disease abated. But here?" In his long centuries at the Temple of Imhotep he had seen epidemic disease before, but never one as relentless and virulent as this Black Plague. "Who can say when it will lose its venom?"

"Will it? Lessen?" Rogres made his voice steady and without inflection, but he could not conceal the trepidation in his eyes.

"Eventually, I think it must," Saint-Germain answered in much the same tone as Rogres. "It abated in China."

"They did not die in China in the numbers we see here," Rogres pointed out, his careful neutrality slipping.

"No," Saint-Germain sighed, adding, "But in China the disease was not new; it has not struck here in nearly a thousand years. New diseases are more . . . ferocious than old ones." He changed the subject without apology. "Traveling by day is exhausting; my native earth provides some protection, but still, the sun is enervating."

"We could travel at night," Rogres reminded him as the kindling took the spark from the flint-and-steel. "There is no reason that you and I must be abroad in the day."

"True enough," Saint-Germain agreed. "And at night, be exposed to the brigands who are growing bolder, or to the accusations of those who are afraid, and dread everything and everyone they encounter in the night. To say nothing of risking our animals on bad roads in the dark." Saint-Germain had opened the sack containing grain; he distributed a portion to the horses and mules and donkey, saying to Rogres, "I will take them down to the stream shortly. They will need water."

"Do you intend to keep the donkey?" Rogres asked: Saint-Germain claimed the creature; now he supposed that his master had needed to save something from the empty compound.

"I think so. He may come in useful." He watched the animals eat, listening to the regular sounds of their chewing. "It was warmer here, six hundred years ago."

"So it was," Rogres said, adding wood to their fire; he wondered what Saint-Germain intended by this remark.

"How long until it warms again; the seasons do not change their temper quickly." He shook his head. "In Caesar's day, they made wine in England. Now—" he broke off. "I'll tend to our animals." With that he went and led the horses, mules, and donkey out of the narthex and down to the stream that ran down to the Rhone. When he returned he found Rogres completing the plucking of a duck; feathers were everywhere and Rogres had a pail of hot water into which he plunged the duck from time to time. "So you found something to eat."

"It will do for tonight," said Rogres as he battled the feathers out of his face.

"No doubt we can find you a lamb in a day or two," Saint-Germain said as he tied their animals to the screen in the narthex for the night.

"You can have the blood and I the flesh?" Rogres ventured, his faded-blue eyes keen in the general darkness of the church.

"Why, yes. It will do for the time being." He patted the rump of the donkey as he came into the nave, walking up to Rogres directly, duck feathers eddying around his feet with each step. "Do not fret about me, old friend." He found an old bench at the back of the sanctuary and dragged it out near the fire, straddling it as Rogres continued on the duck. "We should reach Valence in two days, if the weather gets no worse and the roads are not blocked. I do not want to speculate on what we might find, not after what we saw in Marsailla."

"This journey has taken twice as long as usual to reach Valence," Rogres remarked. "That is assuming we reach the place in two days."

"We are fortunate it is not more; the roads are neglected and filled with those looking for sanctuary, and those preying upon them," Saint-Germain reminded him. "Think how long it took in China, and the Plague was not so advanced as this is." He rubbed his face. "I am going to unpack one of the chests of my native earth; I intend to restore myself as much as possible." He did not rise from the bench quite yet; he stared toward the altar and the peeling frescos of the lives of Saints; he perused the nearest, remarking as he did, "Saint Bernard spoke against learning. He said it would pollute faith." There was an emotion in his enigmatic gaze that was very nearly grief. As Saint-Germain rose, he added, "How sad, when ignorance is praised and learning despised." He studied the wall again, saying after a short silence, "Ignorance is the greatest ally this Plague has."

"You cannot convince them; the goatherds were nothing compared to what the clergy would do if you gave them the same offer," Rogres said, removing the guts and the organs of the duck; he set the liver and heart aside, but prepared to toss the rest outside.

"Make sure you take them a short distance from the church," Saint-Germain told him. "You do not need any stray dogs coming here."

Rogres made a sign of agreement. "No. I do not want that."

"Or those who might follow the dogs," Saint-Germain added. "The Polish marshes should have taught us circumspection."

"I will take care, my master, you need not worry I could forget," Rogres assured him as he gathered up the duck's innards and dropped them in the pail. "I saw a few old gravestones out behind this place; I'll dump this there."

Saint-Germain cocked his head. "I do not mean to harry you, Rogerian. I have been visiting all my apprehension on you; it is a fault. Will you pardon me?"

Rogres gave a dry chuckle. "Haven't I always?"

"Truly," Saint-Germain said as Rogres left the church.

By the time he came back, Saint-Germain had taken the smallest of his chests and put it between two benches, making a rough but serviceable bed. He was sitting on it, his dark eyes distant, a grimness about his mouth that gave his features a severity that they rarely revealed. As he looked toward Rogres the bleakness left his face and he said, "Would you mind leaving very early, old friend?"

"Of course not," said Rogres as he prepared to quarter the duck and eat it. "You need only wake me shortly before we are to saddle the animals." He paused as he cut off a wing. "You will not neglect your hunger too long, will you?"

"I will try not to," said Saint-Germain. "When we reach Valence, there should be someone I can visit in her sleep. That will suffice." He swung his legs up and lay back on his makeshift bed. "Make sure to set the bolt on the door. I would not want to be . . . surprised in the night."

"Of course," said Rogres at once, doing his best to eat quietly; occasionally he shot a glance at Saint-Germain's supine form, wondering how much longer his master would endure his privation: he had come to the conclusion many centuries ago that life was easier for a ghoul than a vampire.

Text of a letter from Josue Roebertis in Constanz in the Duchy of Swabia, to Fabrice Rocene in Pont Sant-Pierre in the County of Hainaut.

To my late sister's late husband's kinsman, my dolorous greetings in this most calamitous of times, and with the prayers that you will not have been touched by this tragic Plague which has so devastated the lovely lands of Provence, the greeting of a most grief-stricken brother.

By the Grace of God I have been spared the fate that overtook my sister and her new family. It is the greatest sorrow to me that she did not escape the Plague, and that her new husband should fall to it so soon after their marriage, before they could produce an heir. As things are, until a magistrate decides who is to inherit the business of Hue d'Ormonde, nothing more can be done to enrich the family, or to determine who will take its helm.

It is for that reason that I write to you, for it is my understanding that the daughter of Hue d'Ormonde has been sent to be part of your household, with the assurance of money for her keep. With her father dead and the estate undetermined, I must regretfully inform you that I am in no position to meet his obligations to you, at least not under the generous terms he proposed. As she and I are related only through the marriage of her father to my sister and their union had no issue, I have no compelling reason to do anything for the girl Jenfra, and no law dictates what my obligation to her is beyond any I am willing to assume to honor the memory of her father.

But I am also mindful of my duty as a Christian, and so I will send to you half the amount her father had promised you. This will not make much of a dowry for her, I am aware of it, but it will save her from becoming wholly dependant on you for all her keep and her bride-price. Should she discover a vocation for the religious life, I will gladly pay the fee for her entering the convent as a novice. If she decides on that cloistered life, I want no hinderance to her dedication. When the father she so loved has been taken from her so horribly, I would think she might want to devote her life to contemplation and prayer. I know my sister would be overjoyed to know that her husband's daughter was willing to dedicate her life to prayer and contemplation.

Anyone who supposes that my purpose in this offer is anything other than for the benefit of the girl, to such calumny I say that even should she marry and produce a male child to claim Hue d'Ormonde's estate, it could not be done until the boy was twelve, and then it would have to be administered by a guardian until he achieved his majority or until the courts assigned him the estate by default. You may say what you wish, I believe that prayer is the best occupation for any woman lacking the means to secure a worthy husband.

I have instructed that any monies owed to Hue d'Ormonde be sent on to me; I will determine the daughter's share and have it carried to you when the full sum is determined. I hold little hope that the amounts received will be great, but, with God's Grace, if I am alive when this catastrophe is over—as we must all pray it will be soon—I will make more regular arrangements with you in regard to the child.

The messenger who brings this will remain with you until you have arrived at your reply to this. I have heard you are a reasonable man, and *therefore I do not hesitate to give the messenger such instructions, for it is apparent to me that you will want these questions resolved as soon as may be.*

I beseech you to extend my condolences to Jenfra: she has lost a father; I have lost a sister and her son, heavy burdens for all of us. I will pray for her, as I hope you and she will pray for me.

Josue Roebertis
(his mark)
By the hand of Frer Nicolas, Passionist

In the city of Constanz in the Duchy of Swabia on the final day of April, in the 1348th Year of Grace.

Post Scriptum: I have had no word in regard to my sister's older boy, Hilaire, who is with his uncle. If God is kind, he will escape this terrible Plague. Should I have news of him, I will send it on to you at once.

5

All three magistrates looked haggard; two of them had not been shaved in several days, and each of them had the wary demeanor of ducks near a fox. Their court had been moved from the town hall to the Chapter House adjoining the church on the main square in Valence; the town hall had been pressed into duty as a hospital and none of the officials were willing to go near it. As it was on Church property, the clerks were monks of the Hieronymite Order, and dedicated to maintaining records of everything that took place within the church grounds. The sounds of chanting echoed in the Chapter House as the prayers for the dead continued unceasingly; the odor of incense and the presence of death intruded on the hearing that was taking place.

"Well, sir? You have had three days in a cell to consider your answers; what will you tell us now?" the center magistrate asked. He was a judge, and although his robe of office was in need of more than washing, he still retained the dignity of his position. He addressed the man in the fastidious black houppelande in stern accents, as if the prisoner's very neatness made him suspect. "You are a foreigner with no connections to this place but those of merchant concerns, and you a nobleman!" He relished his scorn. "By your own admission, you are an exile in this place. You have come into our city by stealth—"

"With respect, I should remind you, as I told your Guard when my servant and I were arrested, that the gate through which my manservant and I entered the city was unmanned and open: it was not my intention to do anything by stealth." Saint-Germain was not flustered, which served to exacerbate the already-strained sensibilities of the judge; his manner was a nice blend of hauteur and concession: he knew better than to accommodate the magistrates, who would view any sign of adaptation to their demands as capitulation.

"By *stealth*," the magistrate repeated in a tone that brooked no contradiction. "You entered through a gate you knew to be unwatched, and you sought out a hiding-place before your presence was known. This is stealth, mon Sieur."

"I did not seek a hiding-place, only a safe haven where I could rest." He did his best to sound as if he were not repeating himself, but it was an effort. "All but two of your travelers' inns have crosses on their doors and I could not ask for quarters in one of them, could I?" This was not offered as defiance and Saint-Germain hoped it would not be so construed.

"A most facile reply," said the second judge, whose lips were chapped and whose face was flushed; he was a tax-collector pressed into service of the courts since most of the magistrates were ill or had fled the town. "Credible in its way, but too easy—much too easy." He subjected Saint-Germain to a squint-eyed scrutiny that was intended to intimidate, but only succeeded in giving Saint-Germain a moment of sad amusement.

"I regret that the truth is not more acceptable to you," said Saint-Germain in a steady voice.

"If it is the truth," said the center magistrate. "We have not yet been satisfied on that account." He clutched the crucifix he wore on a chain around his neck and hung on to it as if it were nothing less than his protection from disaster. "You may have come at the order of the Devil, whose minions are everywhere and whose works are for the ruin of mankind."

"So I might," said Saint-Germain. "But if I were such a creature, why would I remain in your prison for three days? Would the Devil not open the locks of the place to release me to do his work?" He stared from one magistrate to the next, taking care to force them to look away from him to establish his position in relation to them; as a noble, he was entitled to deference, and in this place, that deference could keep him from accusations and worse. He rose, using the authority he had just demonstrated to command their attention and to impress them with his station in life. "Good magistrates, you are asked to labor in trying times, and I cannot question your devotion to your task. But I must tell you that I am no servant of the Devil, and I am not eaten up with Plague. You have had your monks examine my body and they found no Blood Roses on my flesh."

"True enough," said the third magistrate; his voice was hoarse and his complexion grey with exhaustion. He had retired from the magistrates' bench five years ago, but press of circumstances had returned him to his post. "The monks have already told us that you are not ill. They have said, however, that you are severely scarred." He made this a condemnation.

"God has been kind to me, and delivered me from death," said Saint-Germain truthfully; he saw the magistrates make the sign against the Evil Eye, and he said, crossing himself for emphasis, "May He show a like goodness to you all."

The central magistrate spat suddenly, then lowered his head to indicate his chagrin at this lapse. "You claim God's support readily enough, mon Sieur," he declared. "We must know you are rightfully entitled to it before we reach any decision." He signaled the two Hieronymite clerks who had been taking down all that was said. "You need not write what we say now."

One of the monks looked startled, then nodded to show his compliance; he and his fellow-monk put their quills down and folded their hands.

"You have come from the town of Orgon," the central magistrate intoned. "You confess this much."

"Yes; I have kept an estate there for some years, as I've already told you. You may send to the tax collector for confirmation, if you wish. His name is Eudoin Tissant," Saint-Germain said, adding, "I lived there gladly for many years, but it was not my native earth." He saw the three men exchange nods as if this were new information and not something they had heard many times before.

"And you say that you have passed unscathed through Avignon, where we know the Plague is found everywhere." The third magistrate rapped out these words like the tattoo of a mustering drum.

"When I was there, it had just begun. I thank God that I was permitted to escape." Saint-Germain glanced toward the door, aware his answers would satisfy the monks more than the magistrates. "If this is the whole of your inquiry, you might as well return me to my cell; I can tell you nothing more than what I already have."

The central magistrate studied Saint-Germain briefly, then said, "We have the right to detain even a man of your rank, mon Sieur."

Saint-Germain bowed slightly. "I do not doubt this. But unless you have some new challenges to put to me, I have nothing more to tell you. I have no wish to give you answers that would not prove reliable. What I reported when you first questioned me was accurate; I cannot tell you anything else without falseness, which would dishonor me as well as this court. I will not compromise my honor in exchange for fewer days in a cell, or a more lenient fine." He let them consider this; he went on only when he was certain they had thought about his remarks. "Because you fear the Plague, you have imprisoned me, and many others: you are afraid we will poison your wells, or summon the miasma, or loose the Devil on you, or—" Abruptly he stopped. "Why should I do such a thing?"

"Why?" The third magistrate found the question baffling. He stared down at Saint-Germain as if he had never considered the matter before. "Why?" he mused aloud.

"You . . . you have sworn to destroy all works of God," said the second, trying not to cough.

"But why?" Saint-Germain persisted. "If I have done this, why have I done it? And if I have done these things, why should I not depart at once? I put this to you again—if I am what you fear, how is it your prison can hold me? Surely, if I have the power you suspect I have, I might have escaped by now."

"The prison is under a church. The Devil has no power in such places," said the third magistrate; there was a slick of sweat on his face now.

"That may be," Saint-Germain allowed. "But suppose you are wrong? There are as many priests and monks fallen to the Great Dying as there are merchants or millers or smiths; their vows have not protected them. Suppose I have remained in the cell where you put me because, like other men, I am unable to pass through iron-bound doors?"

"The servants of the Devil deceive men," said the third magistrate. *"Apage Satanas,"* he pronounced, with an uncertain glance toward the monks. He leveled an accusatory finger at Saint-Germain. "You have not eaten since you were put in a cell."

"No," said Saint-Germain at once. "I fast for . . . humility."

"Humility, is it? Are you sure you have not poisoned the food so that others will succumb to Plague and you will not?" said the second magistrate. "Every man must eat."

"But not every day," Saint-Germain reminded them. "It is for the good of the soul that we go hungry one day in seven. Saunt Bernard taught that, and all good Christians follow his Rule." He saw one of the monks nod in approval.

The central magistrate nodded emphatically. "And those who serve the Devil sup from the teats of his familiars. And the Devil knows Scripture," he countered sharply. "You have not shown how you have preserved yourself from the Plague." He signaled to the monks. "When he says something new, write it down."

One of the monks crossed himself and both prepared to record the questions put to Saint-Germain.

"I have not preserved myself," said Saint-Germain. "It is God who disposes of us in life and death."

This was the answer that the Church required, but the magistrates were not pleased with it; the central magistrate glowered fiercely at Saint-Germain, his brow thunderous and his voice nearly breaking with emotion. "God and the Devil. This Plague is not of God. If it were, none of the priests would die of it, and you have said already that they are its victims."

"For the glory of their faith?" Saint-Germain asked, knowing it was dangerous to ask such a thing; he might well be denounced as a heretic for doubting Providence. "Does not the Plague bring a martyr's crown?"

"We pray so," said the third magistrate, his voice wheezing. He looked covertly at the monks to see what their response to this would be: the recording monks paused to kiss their crucifixes before continuing their transcription.

"What God's servants endure is not the question here," said the second magistrate. "The act of bringing Plague is damnable, and it is for those of us who are sworn to protect the country and the Church to stop those agents of the Devil from carrying out their pernicious work." He began to cough. "The prayers of the righteous will be heard, and God will answer."

The other two magistrates endorsed this, the central magistrate lifting his mace of office and bringing it down on the high bench before him. "You will be returned to your cell, mon Sieur, until you can give a more acceptable account of yourself. You may seek to wait us out, thinking that the Plague will free you, but we will be here when you are brought out of your cell." He regarded Saint-Germain sternly. "Prayer and fasting may give you a better grasp of the truth."

Saint-Germain crossed himself. "Amen to it, good magistrates," he said, troubled by this decision, but aware that he must show nothing of his misgiving. "In three days, I will have no other answers for you than the ones I have given already; would it were otherwise, for all of our sakes."

This was a much greater concession than anything the magistrates expected from a nobleman, even a foreign one, and the third magistrate frowned. "Why are you not demanding your release? You are of noble birth—why do you not insist we put you in the prison of a man of equal rank?"

"One dungeon is much like another." Saint-Germain was almost to the door, knowing armed monks awaited him beyond it. "I make no such demand because it is what you expect me to do; you would then condemn me, would you not." He inclined his head. "I believe there is enough dying in Valence without giving you grounds to order my execution."

The central magistrate pointed at Saint-Germain. "You will have three days," he announced.

As the monks opened the door, preparing to escort Saint-Germain back to prison, the second magistrate said, "Your manservant will be examined separately. We will see how well his accounts match with yours."

"What else is possible?" Saint-Germain asked. "He and I have come by the same road to get here." He wondered where Rogres was being held, for he had learned that Rogres was not in the same prison as the one where he himself was confined. "Treat him well. He is a worthy servant." He saw the magistrates exchange glances and added, "In praising him for his long duty in my service, I pray I have not caused him any greater trouble than what he encounters now."

"This man is going back to his cell," the central magistrate told the monks. "And since he claims to seek humility through fasting, do not feed him until you bring him here again."

The monks hefted the mauls they carried and motioned Saint-Germain to walk between them. Neither would speak to him; both watched him carefully, as if they expected him to vanish in a puff of smoke.

Narrow stairs led down beneath the church to catacombs where monks and priests had been laid out for centuries; among the niches for bones were penitents' cells. The monks led Saint-Germain to the one he had occupied for the last three days; it was dark and small, with a pile of rags to serve as a bed, and a grating high in the wall that let in a sliver of light as well as the odors of the city's open sewers. The monks shoved him inside and slammed the door closed behind him, turning the huge key in the lock with decisive intent.

Saint-Germain heard this with an emotion that bordered on despair; he had once before been confined while catastrophe overtook his jailers, and the long time it had taken him to escape had left him ravenous. That could happen again, he knew; if he had to wait much longer, he would overpower the guard and flee. But he would not leave Rogres behind: such betrayal was unthinkable. He sat down on the rag-heap and leaned back against the cold stones of the cell; at least he was being held in darkness, which mitigated the worst of his hunger. What were the magistrates doing to Rogres? The question haunted him as he waited for nightfall.

The Hieronymites were preparing new sheets of vellum when Rogres was led into the Chapter House for questioning; they made a note of his name and his station in life, and then they nodded to the magistrates.

As before, the central magistrate asked the first question. "You are the manservant to Francois de Saint-Germain, Sieur Ragoczy?"

"I have already said so," Rogres replied, his demeanor more respectful than his words; he had been kept waiting for some little time and he wondered why. "I have served him many years, and been honored to do it."

"Many years," said the central magistrate. "More than ten?"

"Yes," said Rogres. "A number more than ten." He stood with apparent patience while the three magistrates conferred in whispers.

"You say you are from Spain?" The second magistrate made no attempt to hide his skepticism, for Rogres' sandy hair and blue eyes did not seem Spanish to him.

"From . . . Cadiz," he said, giving it the modern pronunciation; when he had lived there, thirteen hundred years before, it was called Gades.

"And you entered his service in Roma?" asked the second magistrate.

"As I have already told you, good magistrates," said Rogres, still maintaining his equanimity in the face of their charges.

"Then you can speak to your master's comportment," said the central magistrate, as if the matter had finally be settled to his satisfaction.

"As far as I have observed it, yes," Rogres replied.

"It is claimed that he has powers and skills," the second magistrate said sharply.

Rogres brought his head up. "My master is very learned," he answered, puzzled. He knew he would have to be careful in what he said now, for if the magistrates decided that Saint-Germain's skills were diabolical, they would sentence him to burning without hesitation.

"And his learning is to the glory of God?" The second magistrate wiped his brow with the hem of his sleeve.

Rogres crossed himself. "All men of honor must be so dedicated," he said; he had answered many versions of this question over the centuries and had evolved this response which satisfied both his interrogators and himself.

The third magistrate looked dazed, but he managed to ask a question. "Does your master know the Vidame Percevall de Saunt Joachim?"

Now Rogres was alarmed, though he concealed his apprehension with surprise. "Yes, he does; my master was once given the opportunity to relieve the Vidame's suffering."

Again the magistrates spoke in whispers, the second magistrate, the most heated of the three, pointing at Rogres emphatically while he hissed in his colleagues' ears, his gestures increasingly assertive; the monks sat impassively while this altercation went on, their quills at the ready for when the questions should resume.

"Does the Vidame credit his recovery to your master?" the central magistrate demanded suddenly.

"I do not presume to know what the Vidame believes," said Rogres with a deliberate show of subservience.

"Did the Vidame have Blood Roses?" the third magistrate ended on a racking cough.

"No," said Rogres. "He had been bitten by a venomous spider, or so my master determined." His admission was so direct and calm that the magistrates were unnerved by his candor, as he had hoped they might be.

"How do you know the spider—if it was a spider—was venomous?" The central magistrate scowled at Rogres, making it clear he would not tolerate a deceptive response.

"I do not know. My master has much understanding of poultices and tinctures, and he uses them according to the teaching he had in Egypt. He studied there with the great physicians for some years, I understand." He also understood that Saint-Germain's years in the Temple of Imhotep were reckoned in centuries. "That was before I came to serve him." He paused. "If you wish to know how he did this, you should inquire of him. The Vidame had an injury filled with corruption."

"But you saw what he did? If this was venom, how did your master treat it so that the venom was no longer deadly?" The third magistrate sounded as if he were drunk, and he passed his hand over his eyes as if to clear his vision.

"I saw some of it," Rogres told the magistrates. "And when he gave me orders, I followed them. The Vidame recovered."

The central magistrate fixed Rogres with his gaze. "What orders were those?" He made a quick sign to the monks so they would give particular attention to the answer.

"Nothing beyond doing those tasks he instructed I should do," Rogres said, and added, "He has not taught me his arts."

The third magistrate slumped in his chair; the two others stared at him in astonishment and rising dread; the two monks stopped writing and crossed themselves.

His voice taut with fear, the central magistrate muttered, "He . . . he said . . . he swore . . ." He stumbled to his feet, his features set in a rictus of terror.

The second magistrate bolted from the room, crossing himself and whispering prayers as he fled; the monks followed after him.

Rogres came toward the bench. "It may not be Plague," he said calmly. "My master could determine this for you, if you would rather not touch him."

"I . . . I . . . yes," said the magistrate as he recalled himself from his rising panic: that he should succumb to trepidity when this foreigner's servant remained staunch. . . . He strove to maintain his dignity as he addressed Rogres. "You believe your master could . . . help him?"

"It may be," said Rogres cautiously. "He would be the one to tell you." He noticed that the collapsed magistrate was wheezing badly as he tried to breathe; his body shook with the effort. "If you do not send for him at once, nothing will avail this man."

Glad for a reason to move away from his stricken colleague, the central magistrate backed toward the door in unseemly haste. "Bring Sieur Ragoczy from his cell," he ordered the armed monks. "At once! *At once!*"

The guards had seen the second magistrate and the monks leave, and their fright was rising; they hurried to carry out the order, going with unseemly haste toward the narrow stairs leading down.

Saint-Germain was startled to hear the monks approaching; he rose from his place against the wall and tugged his houppelande into the correct line, then waited for the lock to be turned and the door opened. When the monks saw him, he said, "Something has happened."

"How . . ." The monk made the sign against the Evil Eye.

"This is not sorcery," said Saint-Germain with more asperity than he had intended. "I was told I would be confined for three days, but you return to me in less than . . . what? an hour? What am I to think." This last revealed his apprehension; he looked at the monks with an air of resignation. "I am ready to go with you."

"This way," said one of the monks, standing back so that Saint-Germain could leave the cell without touching him.

The central magistrate was still in the Chapter House with Rogres when Saint-Germain reached the place, but the second magistrate and the two recording monks were gone; Rogres turned, saying, "My master," as Saint-Germain came toward the raised bench.

"He was well yesterday, only yesterday," said the central magistrate, pointing at his collapsed fellow-authority. "He was quite well."

"No longer," said Saint-Germain, going to the man and beginning to examine him. He drew back as he saw the buboes on the magistrate's neck.

"Blood Roses!" exclaimed the central magistrate, crossing himself and turning pale. "So fast?"

"It can strike very quickly," said Saint-Germain quietly. "He is beyond anything I can do for him; he will need Extreme Unction, and quickly." He crossed himself, and saw the central magistrate do the same. "Rogres, be so good as to summon a priest for this man."

"None will come," said the central magistrate, his expression a little wild. "It would be their death to come near him. As it is mine. And yours." He dropped to his knees and began to pray in a breathless, terrified whisper.

Saint-Germain could not deny this possibility. "This man cannot live, but it may be that something can be done to ease his agony." He signaled Rogres. "In my lacquer chest, the vial of pansy-and-willow."

"Not the syrup of poppies?" asked Rogres, knowing it was the more potent medicine.

"Pansy-and-willow will ease his hurt without making his breathing slower. That will happen soon enough," said Saint-Germain, and nodded.

Rogres left the Chapter House, walking with purpose but no hint of flight; the central magistrate watched him go, saying, "He will not return."

"You do not know him," Saint-Germain said, "if you believe that." He went back to the dying man on the bench and began to loosen his clothing; the odor of his flesh was unmistakable, and his labored breath rustled with infection.

"He is dying," said the central magistrate, his eyes hollow as he faced what he knew would be his fate.

"Yes," said Saint-Germain, who considered a moment, then said, "I have a remedy—it is not a cure, but for those the Blood Roses have not yet found, it will afford some measure of protection. You may sicken, but unless you are very weak, you will not die." He saw that he had the magistrate's attention. "Will you take what I give you? I must warn you that the smell of one of them is vile and the taste as bad, but it will aid in protecting you. The second has little taste at all." He chided himself inwardly for making this offer, for it could as easily result in his condemnation as in his vindication: his overriding conviction was that he could not bear to watch both these men die.

"What will these . . . remedies do?" The magistrate was struggling not to hope, but he could not resist the offer. "I may burn in Hell for this."

"You may, but the medications will not be the cause," said Saint-Germain, looking up as Rogres returned with a small vial in his hands. "Thank you, old friend," he said, taking the vial and measuring out a small amount of it into the lid. As he went to administer this to the dying magistrate, he added, "Will you add to your kindness by fetching two jars of the wound powder, and pour off a double measure of the sovereign remedy for this man?"

The dying magistrate moaned as he swallowed; his head lolled back and then dropped back onto the bench.

"Will he return this time as well?" The central magistrate was staring at his stricken colleague as if in thrall.

"Yes; he will," Saint-Germain said, then added an acceptable fiction. "He has taken what I propose to give to you and has no fear of the Black Death." He watched the dying man for a moment in silence.

"The medicament has made him—and you—proof against it?" His face nearly shone.

Saint-Germain's response was as cautious as it was accurate. "Neither of us have succumbed to it, nor will we." He saw the brilliance of the magistrate's eyes and he went on, "Not everyone can benefit from this remedy. Failure to follow the procedure in every particular will render it useless." He hoped he had not committed a great folly as he began his instructions. "The first medicament is to be taken at once, in four equal doses at midday and midnight." He saw the doubt in the man's eyes, and added, "When you take it you will say the *Ave* three times and the *Pater* once, to give it strength. When that is done, you must wait three full days and then take all of the second preparation just after morning Mass." The time of day was not significant, but Saint-Germain knew the magistrate would not complete the remedy if he suspected there was any chance of damning himself by doing it; allying his treatment to Church ritual robbed it of its most sinister aspect.

By the time Rogres returned, the magistrate was reviewing the course of the remedy with a feverish intensity that clearly troubled Saint-Germain.

Text of an order sent to Valence from Vadim, Vidame de Silenrieux.

To the clergy and magistrates of Valence, the greetings of Vadim, Vidame de Silenrieux.

It has come to my attention that you have detained Francois de Saint-Germain, Sieur Ragoczy; this Sieur Ragoczy is a known healer of ills, as given in the testimony of my peer, Percevall de Saunt Joachim. I have need of his services, and command you to send him, and his manservant, to me at once. I am providing an armed escort to ensure his prompt arrival.

As you are aware, I and my household have adjourned to my country estate where we propose to wait for the worst of the Great Dying to end. The presence of Sieur Ragoczy will increase our chance of survival, and in the Name of God and Pope Clement VI, I order him to attend me at once.

May God watch over you and spare you from His Wrath.

Vadim, Vidame de Silenrieux
By my own hand

At Non Trouves, near Col des Fans, on the 11th day of May, in the 1348th Year of Man's Salvation.

6

Guards were posted at the gates of Non Trouve, all of them armed and prepared to do anything necessary to defend the remote villa; as Saint-Germain, with Rogres and their animals, were admitted, the guards watched them with fearful suspicion, as if any intrusion from beyond the villa invited disaster. As the guards stepped aside, the courtyard of Non Trouve was revealed, and the castle itself, with the stables, bake-house, bath-house, and kitchen-garden to the east of the rear of the bailey. The buildings inside the crenelated walls were no more than a hundred years old, the stones new enough that the marks of the masons were still visible on many of them. There were five turrets to the main building, all with tall, narrow windows; the whole impression was that of a miniature Samur, formidable and elegant at once, a place for privacy as well as defense. Banners hung on the quiet air but no clarion greeted their arrival.

"The fields are untilled beyond the monastery gardens," Rogres observed in Greek as they heard the portcullis come down behind them.

"I saw; the monks have not fled, but the peasants and serfs have, or they are sick," Saint-Germain said in the same language. He was taking close stock of their situation but without appearing to be anything more than mildly interested; only Rogres knew how keenly Saint-Germain inspected the world with his enigmatic gaze. "There are not very many men-at-arms, either."

"Then what do you think: the Plague has reached here?" Rogres asked as he dismounted and waited for one of the grooms to show him where the animals were to be stabled.

"Or fear of it," Saint-Germain agreed, still in the saddle as he waited for the master of the castle to approach him; as a man of rank equal or superior to his host, he had the right to remain mounted until after he was presented to the Vidame.

A page in fine livery of brocade silks came running up, pausing to drop to his knee before saying, "The Vidame bids you welcome, mon Sieur. If you will accept his apologies for not being able to receive you at this time, I will consider it an honor to bring you into the Great Hall where you will be welcomed with all courtesy."

"Is the Vidame or one of his guests ill?" Saint-Germain asked, concealing his apprehension with a touch of disdain. "Does he want to remain alone? If you would prefer we will depart." He did not like the thought of being abroad in the growing chaos but it would be preferable to remaining in a place where Plague had come, for although he could not catch it, he might easily be blamed for its presence.

"Oh, no," said the page hurriedly, his young face creased with alarm.

"If he is not ill, why does he remain within doors?" Saint-Germain asked as he swung down from his horse.

The page shook his head. "As to that, mon Sieur, I cannot say: it has been his custom since he and his guests came here. The Vidame may be willing to tell you himself if you will follow me." He bowed deeply enough to remove any slight from the Vidame's inattention. "Your animals will be fed and watered."

"And my manservant?" Saint-Germain asked as he entered the Great Hall of Non Trouve.

"He will be housed near you," said the page, and bowed again as if to introduce the marvelous room to which he had brought Saint-Germain.

The Great Hall had two vast fireplaces, one at each end of the room; the massive chimneys ran up to the ceiling, both decorated with heraldic banners and painted devices on wooden shields; the walls were hung with tapestries depicting the story of the Sangrail; the work was expertly done and the colors glowed as if to make the Great Hall come alive with the mythic scenes. A minstrel's gallery at the back of the Hall was fronted with a long screen of carved wood made to resemble a woodland glade, with vine-twined trees and forest animals worked in it. Below the gallery was an expanse of table laid out with an array of food, from roast swan to a partially-consumed subtiltie made to look like gold with a thick coat of saffron paste. Breads and cheeses were piled in baskets, with tubs of butter and meat drippings to lend flavor to them. A tun of old red wine was open at one end of the table, and a tun of new ale at the other. Chairs and hassocks wre clustered at one side of the table, where Vadim, the Vidame de Silenrieux sat with his favored guests; he held a chalice in one hand, and as Saint-Germain entered the room, he lifted it in salute.

"So you came," he said, enunciating so carefully that it was apparent he has half-drunk. "They got to you in time."

"In time?" Saint-Germain asked as he completed his bow.

"Before they burned you, of course; that would have happened next," said the Vidame, and laughed; he was echoed by five of his companions. Getting unsteadily to his feet, he returned the bow. "I welcome you to Non Trouve, and I thank you for coming so promptly." Everything he wore was new: his houppelande was of pale-green embroidered silk, the triangular dagged sleeves lined in deep, brilliant blue; his underhose were the same blue, and his solers were dun-colored. His fashionably cropped hair was russet, and his long face might have been handsome if he were sober; as it was, his eyes were puffy and his cheeks sallow: those around him were dressed with equal luxury, and comported themselves in the same indulgent manner.

"If they were planning to burn me, then I am in your debt for your summons," said Saint-Germain, none of his sudden dismay showing in his features. "I am somewhat at a loss as to why you did, Vidame."

"Ah," said de Silenrieux, nodding to his companions. "Ah. Well, you see, we have come here to wait out the Great Dying." He smiled. "We have the best food and wine, we talk only of pleasant things, we live joyously in comity with one another, and we are shriven every morning, so that we are not in perils for our souls." Again he looked to his companions: there were nine young men and six young women gathered around him. "I have been told you have astonishing skills as a physician, or so Percevall, Vidame de Saunt Joachim has informed me."

Saint-Germain thought that if the food and drink laid out were any indication of the way the Vidame and his companions had been living, they might well suffer for it. All he said was, "I will do what I can to treat you."

"We abide amiably together, all animosity forsaken," said the Vidame ritualistically, as if he had not heard Saint-Germain. "We hear sweet music, we discuss only gracious subjects, we gratify our senses in every delightful way so that the miasma will have no means to gain access to this place. We permit nothing of ugliness or brutality in our surroundings, so that we may remain tranquil. All our thoughts and all our actions are focused on insouciance and the felicity of life." He gestured and the others seconded him with a lifting of their chalices.

Saint-Germain did not speak at once. "Your companions are all young," he observed at last, knowing this prudent selection might have some benefit.

"So they are," said the Vidame. "We have seen that those who die first are old or infirm, or very young. We have done all we might to ensure the Great Dying will pass us by." His smile remained though his eyes were hard. "We can admit no one among us who might bring the Blood Roses to bloom in our flesh."

Saint-Germain wondered why the Vidame assumed that he would not, for physicians were dying of the Black Death as readily as any others. He kept this to himself, remarking only, "The miasma has found others in more protected places than this."

The Vidame frowned as he went to refill his chalice with wine. "The monks at Silenrieux are praying for us—I am their Vidame. And no one at their monastery has fallen so far. My pages call upon them once a day to fetch bread and cheese, and bring me word of how they go on."

"Perhaps the monastery is in God's favor," said one of the Vidame's companions, a hale, gangly fellow not quite yet grown; his beard was still wispy and his face had fresh scars of youthful eruption. His clothes were as fine as his host's, and he wore a badge on his sleeve which allied him to the Bearnaise House of Troisvilles. He had his arm around one of the women, an extravagantly pretty creature with high, exposed breasts and shaved eyebrows who fawned on him.

"Perhaps," Saint-Germain agreed, but without conviction.

"The monks have provided us with the bread and cheese you see here, and they send more daily," the Vidame boasted. "Their holiness saves us from all danger."

"Yet you sent for me." Saint-Germain could not decide what it was that the Vidame sought from him.

"Yes; the Blood Roses are not the only afflictions that may overtake us, and against that, and because I am not wholly well myself, I knew you would be able to preserve us from all those evils of the flesh that might weaken us. To that end, I charge you to do all you can to keep me from . . ." He smiled slightly. "I have a pain—here." He touched his chest low and on the right side.

"Before or after you eat?" Saint-Germain asked quickly; this seemed to be within his capabilities to treat. "Is the pain sharp or dull?"

"Generally before, occasionally it is worse after I eat; dull at first, then sharp." He made a gesture that might have been apologetic. "I cannot fast for a full day without suffering, though I know it is essential now to keep the fast days, and my failure to observe them exposes all of us to the possibility of bringing the miasma." His expression was at once demanding and beseeching. "You took away the venom of the spider for de Saunt Joachim; he said you did it with the help of God's good Angels. Can you not deliver me from this . . . this rat gnawing at me?"

Saint-Germain saw the expectant miens of the others, and he felt a touch of relief. "I have a preparation that may be palliative, I will treat you as best I can, with God's help," he said, thinking of all the medicaments he had brought with him in the red lacquer chest. "I will have to send for my manservant, and I would like to clean myself." It was dangerous to ask to bathe, for that was often seen as an admission of vanity and therefore sinful; he compromised by saying, "I would like to wash the dirt away, to ensure the miasma is not contained in it."

"Not contained in dirt?" a young man in a pourpoint of Florentine velvet repeated in disbelief.

"A miasma may come in many forms," Saint-Germain reminded them all. "I have to think that it is wise to be rid of such items as may contain the seeds of miasmic exhalations." This was sufficiently in accord with the current teaching accepted by the Church that Saint-Germain had no hesitation in offering it to account for his request.

"He has shown himself an able physician," said the Vidame, dismissing the doubts of the rest with a wave of his hand. "If you have reason to suppose that washing would lessen the chance of the miasma coming here, do whatever you must."

"If you have a bath-house, perhaps I should bathe," said Saint-Germain with a calmness that was more convincing to the others than to him.

The Vidame laughed wildly. "Bathe? Why not: let us all bathe." He clapped his hands, and as soon as a page appeared he said, "We are all going to bathe, to wash away the taints of illness." He glared at Saint-Germain suddenly. "Will that alleviate this pain I have?"

Saint-Germain had his answer ready. "It will prepare you for the medicament, which has its greatest virtue when the patient has bathed. Until then, you must take care, for the illness you describe—if it is as you tell me—grows worse with fretting." He added at once, "I must bathe apart from you, or the efficacy will be less than it could be."

"Then you shall not bathe with us. Hear that, Curtise?" He pointed to the page who stood in the nearest doorway. "Saint-Germain is not to bathe with the rest of us." He pondered the matter with a look of fierce concentration. "Do not let anyone get into the bath until he is finished."

This was more than Saint-Germain had hoped for. He tried not to look too satisfied as he bowed. "Thank you, good Vidame, for your consideration."

"The bath-house, Curtise. Take the Sieur there as soon as it has been heated, and perform any service he may require of you. His manservant is to be aided in readying the medicaments his master may require. Go. Tend to it now."

The page, who was no more than nine, bowed and hastened away.

The Vidame smiled at Saint-Germain. "All will be ready shortly. While you wait, have something to eat and drink." He made his smile more affable. "You may avail yourself of any pleasure offered here." The suggestive smiles of the women and a few of the men underscored the Vidame's intent. "No one will deny you."

"Then I must deny myself," said Saint-Germain with a short bow, going on with the readiness of long experience, "I do not disdain your hospitality, good Vidame: if I am to treat you successfully, I must abstain from food and drink as well as . . ." His gesture toward the Vidame's companions implied regret.

"I can see why de Saunt Joachim has such a high opinion of you," the Vidame declared. "Most physicians would seize on this opportunity."

The young man in russet laughed aloud. "He is either very capable or very clever." He gazed at the woman beside him. "What do you think, Nichon? You are such a fine judge of men."

Nichon gave Saint-Germain a direct, appraising stare. "He has the bearing of a proper man," she said after brief consideration. "I would assume he is worthy; if the Vidame remains ill, we will know him for a deceiver."

"Well said, well said," the Vidame exclaimed, overriding the remarks of the rest. "That is a most astute assessment." He drank more of his wine; his face was now pasty with ruddy spots on his cheeks and nose.

Realizing his situation was uncertain, Saint-Germain took a chance, saying, "If you will drink, have bread or cheese as well. The wine will not dull the pain as much as you hope unless there is something more taken with it."

The Vidame cocked his head. "Is it so?"

"If it is not, you will know soon enough," Saint-Germain said, his voice a trifle grim. "There is bread in front of you, fresh-made. Eat some now, and if you do not have less pain by the time you go to bathe, have me whipped from your gates." He reached out for the half-loaf at the top of the basket and handed it to the Vidame. "No wine without bread: re-member."

"A worldly Mass, do you think?" the young man with Nichon suggested, snickering.

"Why not?" Saint-Germain responded at once, crossing himself to make a point. "In these times it is necessary to have God put us all in His keeping."

"Listen to him, Rudrique," the Vidame said with authority. "You have reason to safeguard yourself as much as the rest of us."

Quickly Rudrique managed a sheepish smile, his demeanor that of a child caught in a prank. "Of course, Vidame. We will do as this . . . wise man says." He glanced angrily at Saint-Germain. "But I want none of his aus-terity for myself, if you don't mind. It would put me in a gloomy state of mind, and then who knows what would come?"

The Vidame glanced at Saint-Germain, who shrugged. "Live as you like; I am not your Confessor."

Laughing merrily, the Vidame took a bite out of the half-loaf Saint-Germain had given him. "You see?" he asked around his full mouth. "I comply with your orders."

Saint-Germain merely nodded to show his approval; he noticed that Rudrique was whispering to Nichon and whatever he said made her gig-gle. The exquisite behind them leaned forward in order to hear it repeated; he, too, found it amusing.

"So, Guillaume," the Vidame challenged suddenly. "You are amused?"

The most elaborately dressed of the lot looked confused; he glowered at Nichon. "No. Not amused. It was a foolish thing only, mon Vidame."

"Foolishness can bring trouble," the Vidame said darkly as he chewed off another hunk of bread. "It is right that we do gratifying things, that we allow no unhappiness to come here, but it is wrong to conduct ourselves like fools." He swallowed more wine with his bread. "We have to keep alert to all signs of decay, even the most minor of them."

"Yes, mon Vidame," said Guillaume, frowning to show he would not in-dulge in silliness again.

"All of you," the Vidame insisted, "are to treat the Sieur Ragoczy with respect. He has come here to save us, and we will not deserve his aid if we make mock of him."

Nichon smiled eagerly to show she had meant nothing impertinent by her remark, whatever it had been. "He is so . . . so grave, all in black, like an apothecary or a notary," she said boldly; one of the other women put her hand to her lips to suppress a smile.

"You; Rosalbe," said the Vidame, pointing to the woman. "You will have to beg your bread tonight like a novice. You are not to discredit this man."

Saint-Germain tried to think of an excuse to leave the Vidame and his guests to themselves; he said, "I would like to supervise the handling of my medicaments. My manservant is experienced, but I would feel more sanguine if I—"

"I know what servants are," said the Vidame with heavy humor. "Yes, by all means. Go. I will have Avelin escort you." He clapped, and a moment later another page came into the Great Hall. "Take this good man to his quarters. At once."

The page bowed to the Vidame and to Saint-Germain. "Mon Sieur?"

Saint-Germain gave his attention to the Vidame. "I thank you; when I have bathed I will be at your service."

"And my gut should feel better," said the Vidame, his wolfish smile not lessening the threat.

"As God wills," said Saint-Germain, and turned to follow Avelin out of the Great Hall.

The rest of the little castle was splendid. Tapestries hung in the corridors and in the stairwells, all of the finest quality, all new enough to be undulled by smoke. The sconces for torches were iron wrought in the lily-shape or the cross Moline, credit to the King of France and the Pope. The floors had been recently strewn with fresh rushes after the old had been swept out of the building.

"It is that third door, mon Sieur," said Avelin, pointing along the corridor to the only door standing open. "Your manservant is there already."

"Very good. Thank you." Saint-Germain said to the boy, and handed him a silver apostle for his trouble; the page took the coin with an expression of awe, then bowed and hurried away as if he feared Saint-Germain would take the money back.

As Avelin had said, Saint-Germain found Rogres waiting in the largest of three rooms beyond the door. "What do you think?" he asked as he closed the door behind him. His gaze flicked in what appeared to be a cursory look about but was actually a close inspection.

"Non Trouve is well-named," said Rogres said. "In these times, what man would not want to be lost in such a place."

"True enough," said Saint-Germain loudly enough to be readily overheard; he made a circuit of the room, taking care to admire the tapestries. "Such fine work, all of them."

"The Vidame is a man of substance," said Rogres, his tone as neutral as his faded-blue eyes were expressive.

"As are his friends," Saint-Germain said, listening for the sound of surreptitious footsteps in the corridor; he nodded as Rogres lifted a warning finger. "It would seem he and his guests have taken every precaution." He made a sign to change languages. "What is your impression?"

"This is not as safe as the Vidame would like to think," said Rogres, speaking in Greek once again.

"Obviously not," said Saint-Germain in the same tongue. "No place is."

"As we have reason to know," said Rogres, aware that Saint-Germain had more to tell him.

"For example, the Vidame's serenity is not as complete as he would like." He looked around their apartment with an inquisitive air. "How closely were we being watched?"

Rogres shrugged as he sat on the largest of the crates standing in the middle of the chamber. "Closely enough," he said. "There are a dozen pages in this place and they are everywhere. They're devoted to him; they're orphans. They may be slaves, but if they are, he branded them on their arms not their faces. I will find out." He indicated the tapestry on the opposite wall. "There is a peephole from the corridor."

"Is there." Saint-Germain went to his red lacquer chest that Rogers had moved apart from the rest of their belongings. "Well, let us be sure they make reports to our credit." He opened the chest and took one of the stoneware jars from its interior; he went back to Provencal French, but indicated that Rogres should continue in Greek. "The Vidame suffers from a raw stomach; his pain is worst when fasting, but flares when he eats certain foods."

"A raw stomach by the sound of it." Rogres agreed, paused, then said, "What has he done to alleviate it, do you know?"

Saint-Germain answered without inflection, "He has been drinking wine, in part to lessen the pain."

"How . . . distressing," said Rogres carefully.

"Yes," Saint-Germain agreed. "He is not beyond treatment, thank all the forgotten gods. I will need the usual herbs, with pansy for anodyne. Then I think some oil of sweet hyssop to soothe the rawness." He took out a small carnelian jar. "This should look impressive enough to persuade the Vidame to follow my instructions." As he handed this to Rogres, he said, "I have convinced the Vidame to let me bathe. I would like the black velvet amigaut ready when I return from the bath-house."

"With the white chamise?" Rogres asked, still in Greek.

"No, I think not. Let it be the dark-red samite." He slapped at the front of his Flemish houppelande, then waved at the dust that rose from it. "I do not want to give a shabby impression."

Rogres did not think the white linen chamise was shabby, but he said only, "Very well; the dark-red samite. Red underhose?"

"Of course," said Saint-Germain with a quick smile. He made another swift perusal of their quarters. "It could be worse."

"Certainly it could," said Rogres, this time in the dialect of the region. "We might still be in Valence."

✦   ✦   ✦

Text of a warrant issued by Eudoin Tissant for the execution of Francois de
Saint-Germain, Sieur Ragoczy; ten copies sent by courier to various cities
in the Kingdom of France and the Holy Roman Empire: the courier succumbed to the Black Death after leaving Chalon; four warrants still un-
delivered.

*By the authority of the office of Tax Collector and First Magistrate of
Orgon in the County of Provence in the Holy Roman Empire, I, Eudoin
Tissant, order the immediate arrest and execution of the perfidious al-
chemist calling himself Francois de Saint-Germain, Sieur Ragoczy.*

*It is the determination of Pare Herriot and myself, acting First Magis-
trate of Orgon, that this said Sieur Ragoczy brought the Great Dying to our
region through his nefarious practices. This accusation is not brought
lightly, for this said Sieur Ragoczy is a man of apparent high birth. It is
known that this said Sieur Ragoczy often visited Marsailla, and we have
such catastrophic reports of that great city that there can be no doubt that
the Black Death came there by conjuration, for no illness has ever been so
mortal as this one.*

*Through the execution of this most evil man we wish to redeem our-
selves in the eyes of God, and to save the souls of all who perished as a result of his damnable sorcery. We have learned that he frequently ordered his
villa filled with smoke, surely an homage to his Infernal Master. We have
also been told that he never ate any meat served to his guests, which is a sign
of poisoned food. Those who were his servants have said this Sieur Ragoczy
often kept to himself in a tower room devoted to all the Black Arts; it was in
this place he summoned up the miasma which has so preyed upon the people of this region that only one in six is alive to speak of it. We must expunge
the presence of this Sieur Ragoczy from the minds of men, or we may bring
greater calamity upon ourselves, our families, and our beloved Provence,
which has suffered most hideously as the result of the Great Dying.*

*To enable this warrant to be executed without error, the following de-
scription is appended to enable the man to be identified: he is of mature
years, elegant in his person which is of medium height, or a trifle taller,
with a deep chest and strengthy appearance. His hair is dark with ruddy
glints; his beard is also dark, curling slightly, as does his hair. His eyes are
like black coals lambent with Hell's fires. His hands are small and well-
shaped; likewise he has small feet. He is accompanied by his manservant,
a man of middle years or slightly more, a lean fellow with tawny hair turning white and light-blue eyes, a man of dignified comportment. Find the
servant and you will find the master; and kill him with his master or you
will leave yourself at the mercy of fiends.*

*This Sieur Ragoczy has already been tried and condemned so there is no
reason to subject him to further trials. Consign him to the flames and know
you are saving the souls of hundreds: fail to kill him and you will damn
thousands to perdition.*

With the prayers of all those still alive in Orgon, I commend myself to your good offices and the fulfillment of your duty in our name.

Eudoin Tissant
By the hand of Frer Silvain, novice Benedictine

In Orgon in the County of Provence in the Holy Roman Empire, on the 2nd day of June, in the 1348th Year of Grace.

7

Twisting the tuning peg with care, Saint-Germain tested the string for pitch a fourth time; of late the mandola had been increasingly difficult to keep in tune; the strings had been replaced before he left Clair dela Luna and should last for another few months, so it was the pegbox that was causing the trouble. He thumbed the strings; this time he was rewarded with harmony instead of dissonance. Picking out a melody, he strolled out of his sleeping chamber onto the bailey ramparts of Non Trouve and looked across the valley beneath them beyond the walls, enjoying the early-morning light as much as the cool breeze that would shortly be warm.

There were two men-at-arms near the turret, both of them doing their best to waken; neither paid any attention to the foreigner in the black-and-silver silken lucco, for in the month since Saint-Germain's arrival they had become used to his early-morning ambles along the decorative battlements of the bailey, and his presence no longer excited their suspicions.

Saint-Germain nodded to the men-at-arms and wished them a good morning as he continued on his way. With the sun just above the horizon its beams did not burn him as cruelly as they would later in the day, still he was grateful for the lining of his native earth in the soles of his heuze. He continued to amble, his attention apparently on nothing more than the beauty of the morning; he saw three of the pages leave Non Trouve by the eastern kitchen-gate and hurry along the track leading to the Silenrieux monastery, a bit more than a league away. He looked toward the southern horizon, and saw a large flock of birds gathering in the brightening sky, then he glanced westward toward the crest above the little castle as he went on walking, improvising a song. To the north there was a small hamlet, scarcely more than a collection of crofter's huts; a trail of smoke was rising from there, not sufficient to be alarming, but enough to draw Saint-Germain's swift scrutiny as he finished his morning reconnaissance.

"What did you see?" Rogres asked as Saint-Germain returned to his sleeping room.

"The pages are off to get the bread and cheese for today, Avelin and Pol, I think," said Saint-Germain as he put his mandola aside. "Morning haze covers Col des Fans; I could not make out anything about it. There are birds gathering in the south and a fire in the little village to the north." He fingered his well-trimmed beard. "What do the pages say?"

"The same as always: the monastery is doing well, and there has been no sign of anyone with Black Plague come there." He paused. "I am not so convinced of that as I was two weeks ago."

"No," said Saint-Germain. "Nor am I." He stared toward the window that gave access to the ramparts, and frowned. "I feel uneasy. It is one thing to treat a raw stomach; it is another to be surrounded by Blood Roses, and be able to help only a very few."

"Yes," said Rogres. "Do you think it will come to that?"

"I hope not, but I cannot be sure," said Saint-Germain quietly. "It would distress me to discover that the Vidame has been deceiving us; not you and me alone, but all his guests."

"I have heard the pages say that the fears are foolish," said Rogres in a neutral tone. "They have much to lose if the Vidame leaves this place."

"Then perhaps the Vidame is deceiving himself," Saint-Germain said with a small sigh of resignation. "The rest are not wholly confident: when I visited Rosalbe in her sleep, I was aware that she is very frightened and no longer feels safe; she is not the only one."

Rogres tapped his lean fingers as he thought. "The Vidame does not plan to leave this place."

At this, Saint-Germain nodded. "It is true. And he permits none of his guests to leave; only religious pilgrims and players are allowed to come and depart." His tone was remote but his dark eyes shone with intensity.

"Except the pages," Rogres said.

"Yes; except the pages. And they are slaves." He made a small gesture of distaste as he continued to stare at the window, musing. "Being slaves, why would the pages lie?"

"To please their master; they live only at his pleasure," Rogres said at once. "Not all slaves are as obstreperous as you were, my master. They are only boys and this is their haven as much as it is the Vidame's."

"They have chosen a strange way to protect it," said Saint-Germain, "if that is what they are doing. The pages are not providing the necessary intelligence the Vidame must have: they certainly provide an optimistic report on the monastery and the village, which I no longer find convincing. You may be right about them." He picked up his pectoral-and-chain from where Rogres had set it out for him on the stack of earth-filled chests; the silver links of the collar shone in the lucid morning light and the black sapphire that formed the disk of the eclipse flashed its star as Saint-Germain set it in place around his neck. "I can learn a great deal on the ramparts, but it is not enough, not now. We need specific information I cannot glean from here."

Rogres ducked his head in agreement. "You are troubled, are you not?"

"Very," said Saint-Germain with a lightness of tone that belied his word. "I must get outside these walls. Or you must." He regarded Rogres. "What do you think, old friend?"

There was no hesitation in his reply. "I will do what I can, if you arrange—"

"I think it may be possible," said Saint-Germain, seizing on the notion with a gesture of approbation. "For I must have new herbs for the tinctures I use in treating fevers; that is at least the truth." He pondered a moment. "Yes. Willow for fevers, of course; there must be willows growing somewhere in this valley. Tansy for the women, and pennyroyal. Then pansy, and monkshood for spasms. No doubt the Vidame will permit you to do this for me; I am certain he will not let me leave. So I will have to convince him that I must have these if I am to be able to . . . minister to injuries and sickness." He glanced toward the window again. "For once I must approve the Vidame's belief that he and his guests are safer from the miasma indoors than out: no one will notice what you do or where you go."

"The monastery, then, and where else?" Rogres went to the window, pointing at the road along the front of the castle. "Should I go as far as the crossroads? To Col des Fans?"

"As you think best," said Saint-Germain. "But do not go where the guards can see you; that would rouse their suspicions once more. Circle around by the stream; it will provide you some cover and it is not so obvious as walking the track to the monastery. You will be able to collect some herbs there, as you must if you are not to raise distrust in the minds of the guards." He gave a single, sardonic laugh. "This is not going to be easy; the guards are bored enough to overlook what they see daily, but they will make note of anything unfamiliar. Whatever lies beyond these walls, they know more of it than the Vidame does." He stared thoughtfully at one of the tapestries hanging in the room: it depicted a wounded knight being tended by two does. "The pages will not help you."

"No," said Rogres. "They would distrust me, if what we suspect is true."

Saint-Germain nodded. "They would, and they would hold it against you." Then he turned abruptly on his heel, exasperation in every lineament. "I no longer trust our refuge here. Pleasant as this place is, I am apprehensive: why do I feel we are at Mao-T'ou stronghold again, and the horsemen of Jenghiz Khan are coming?"

"If that is the case, why should we not leave? No one is keeping you here; the Vidame is not T'en Chi-Yu, nor are any of the women around him." Rogres saw the grief in Saint-Germain's eyes and was about to apologize.

Saint-Germain held up his hand; when he spoke, his tone was gently chagrined. "You are right. Nothing is keeping me here but the worry of what we will encounter outside."

"Is that all?" Rogres asked, sensing there was more.

It took a short moment for Saint-Germain to answer. "No; but it is a good portion of what keeps me here. I cannot be indifferent. It is hard to watch them die; when so many are stricken, it pains me more than the Emir's son's lance through my side did."

Rogres, who had remained with Saint-Germain through his long recovery, said, "You do not have to watch them. You could go . . . oh, to China again, or India, or Africa. Why should you stay if it causes you such anguish?"

"Why, indeed?" Saint-Germain considered his answer. "I served in the Temple of Imhotep for more than eight centuries; I find it difficult to turn away from all I learned there."

"You cannot save them all, my master," Rogres reminded him. "If you had oceans of the sovereign remedy, you could not save them all."

"No; but I can spare a few, and those who would not recover without help can be succored: some of them will survive." His dark eyes fixed on the distance in years as well as leagues. "What right have I to live long if I will not do what I can for those who do not? It is touching them that sustains me." His voice grew quiet and he spoke in the language of his long-vanished people. "When the god of my House made me one of his blood, I gave him my vow that I would honor and protect the lives of those who were wholly mortal; that I would value their brevity. Even now, after all the centuries that have passed, I cannot abjure my oath. I forgot it for a time, long ago, but no more, and not here." He came out of his reverie suddenly, and said pragmatically, "And who is to say, after all, that we would not find the Black Plague in those places as well?"

"But nothing like this," Rogres reminded him unnecessarily. "When we left Clair dela Luna you could not know how dire—"

Saint-Germain cut him off, saying gently, "All the more reason to do what I can. I have not the excuse of fear, since the Black Plague has no power to harm me."

"Not in your flesh, perhaps," Rogres said with an edge in his voice.

"Ah," Saint-Germain said without any change in his tone.

There was nothing more Rogres could do to persuade Saint-Germain to reconsider; he knew this of old. So he straightened his gippon and asked, "Very well. When do you want me to . . . search for herbs?"

Saint-Germain favored him with a rueful smile. "You are always wise, old friend. Yes, I will try to get the Vidame's permission for you to leave this morning, if that will suit you."

"It will." He indicated the ramparts beyond the windows. "Do you think the guards have overheard?"

"I doubt it," said Saint-Germain. "They have better things to think about than what I say to my servant." He picked up his mandola. "If this will only hold its tuning awhile . . ."

"Are you going to play for the Vidame?" Rogres asked, mildly surprised.

"Yes; and his guests. He will be more apt to grant my request if he is in a happy frame of mind; a few stirring tales of heros will make the Vidame feel braver." He reached the door. "Wait for me here. I will be back as soon as I can."

It was almost noon when Saint-Germain finally returned to his apartments; he found Rogres readying four sacks to take with him. "I apologize for the delay, but inducing our host to relent was more trying than I anticipated. The Vidame has consented, but only if you are back by sundown."

"That may be difficult," said Rogres, reckoning the distances in his head. "I may not be able to reach both the monastery and Col des Fans in that time, for all it is near the solstice. Perhaps I should try for the little village?"

"The monastery is the more important," said Saint-Germain, seeing Rogres' nod of consent. "Yesterday I noticed that the cheeses are less plentiful than two days ago and the loaves are smaller; there was no fresh butter brought yesterday, either, which may mean trouble." He put his mandola down. "I must fix this pegbox."

"Shall I look for wood as well?" Rogres suggested with a touch of amusement.

"No," Saint-Germain responded with a fading smile. "You have more important things to do." He became more somber. "You are to leave by the kitchen-gate and return by the same." He paused. "I wish I could go with you, but the Vidame will not have it. He was adamant."

"I will return before sundown," said Rogres, and picked up the sacks. "Willow, pansy, monkshood—what else? Comfrey? Cranesbill? Borage? Valerian?"

At this Saint-Germain chuckled. "You know my stock as well as I do: use your own judgment. I haven't been able to explore, so I am not certain what you will find. If there are nettles, bring them. I know my supply is low."

"Anything from the monastery?" Rogres asked.

"You mean holy water?" Saint-Germain countered. "I could not account for having it. If we need it, a monk will be summoned." He continued to worry the pegbox. "I will expect you before sundown."

"Well enough," said Rogres, and left Saint-Germain to repair his instrument while he made his way down the narrow stairs to the kitchen and from there out to the kitchen garden and its gate. The day was hot; the air smelled ripe with summer, and the running water chuckled to itself as it ran. The shade along the stream was filled with rustling leaves and the quick call of birds. Rogres went down to the bank and began picking nettles and putting them in the sack he carried; he added borage and a few branches from a young willow as he went, following the course along to the edge of the fields of the monastery.

Goats and sheep wandered in the far end of their pasture, and beyond, in a fenced-off portion, two spotted cows grazed, one with a calf at her side.

A novice monk stood at the junction of the two parts of the pasture, his habit pulled up to his knees to relieve him of the heat. Occasionally he swatted at flies, but otherwise he did not move more than absolutely necessary; the afternoon was too hot for anything more active.

Rogres kept in the shadow of the pasture wall and made his way toward the buildings on the monastery ground and while he made no obvious attempt to remain concealed he did nothing to draw attention to his presence, either; as he rounded the end of the pasture fence, the stench hit him: a large pit filled with lime was freshly dug and a dozen shrouded bodies waited to be interred; five of them had crucifixes painted on their chests, the rest did not. "So," Rogres murmured. "There have been travelers here, and the Great Dying has come." From the length of the pit, he assumed these were not the first corpses to be interred here.

Moving carefully and keeping to the shadows, Rogres made his way around to the front of the monastery; there he saw a number of carts and wagons drawn up, some pulled by donkeys, some by cattle, one by two large dogs. The monks had come out to greet the travelers and to determine which of them would be admitted: those who were obviously sick were given a loaf of bread and a skin of water and sent on their way; only those who looked healthy were allowed to enter. He paused to kneel and pray at the monastery gates, saying to the monk who approached him, "I have what I need, good Frer. Save what you have for those more in need than I."

The monk looked at him in some surprise. "God will bless you for your charity, my son," he said when he had recovered himself. He looked closely at Rogres. "You do not seem ill."

"Nor am I," said Rogres, "and I have many hours of sunlight to reach Col des Fans." He waited, hoping the monk would tell him of the town.

The monk studied the sky. "Col des Fans. The gates are barred there, and they have burned all the cats. You will have to look elsewhere for a bed tonight."

"No one is allowed in?" Rogres asked, trying to coax more from the monk without appearing to. "I am a servant who has lost a master and now must find other employment."

"If you were a pilgrim or a player they might open the gates to you, but a servant . . . no." He blessed Rogres automatically and turned away to deal with a family in the dog-drawn cart.

A peasant in one of the larger wagons leaned down from his seat. "Servant?" he said.

Rogres looked up at him. "God give you good day," he said, curious about what the man would tell him.

"If I were you, I would not go to Col des Fans. No one is welcome there, not even pilgrims unless they are in Holy Orders. Better to go north; the way is hard but there are fewer robbers." His accent was rough and hard to place, but his manner was respectful. He rubbed his chin.

"Why would you warn me in this way, good fellow?" Rogres inquired, smiling to show he was not unthankful for the words of caution.

"Because you do not want to stay here; I am mindful of kindly acts. And because my brother and his family were robbed at the gates of Col des Fans." He glowered at the memory.

"Then many thanks," said Rogres, and walked away from the monastery, going in the direction of the little village rather than toward Col des Fans. The road he took was not much wider than a cattle path, used by the peasants to bring their goods to market; usually at this time of year, the way would be busy, but now, with the fields untilled, there was grass springing up in the road.

Halfway between the monastery and the village, Rogres found a small flock of chickens wandering untended at the edge of the fields; since he was hungry, he took the time to catch one, skinned it, and ate it, sitting in the shade of a large tree. His meal finished, he tossed the bones into the brush, knowing they would provide food for other creatures, then he went on toward the village, walking quickly in spite of the drowsing heat; occasionally he stopped to cut herbs and to dig up roots for Saint-Germain's use. He saw that the wild berries had been eaten before they were ripe, which told him people and animals were hungry; if summer was lean, winter would be very hard. As he came up to the village, he could see one of the huts was afire, the people of the village standing around it with buckets of water, but making no effort to put it out.

A squint-eyed child with a dirty face gave the alarm of Rogres' approach. He screamed as if he had been struck with a stick, pointing at Rogres as if to keep away the Devil.

Rogres stopped at once. "I fear I have lost my way," he called out, hoping the villagers would understand him.

"Lost, are you?" scoffed one of the men, his dialect sounding archaic to Rogres' ears, like the language spoken here five hundred years ago.

"I fear I am," said Rogres, adjusting his speech. "I am from Cadiz," he went on. "I am bound for Nevers in the Seigniory of Bourbon. I must have been given poor directions." He gestured back over his shoulder in vague indication of where he had been misinformed.

The man who had spoken to him laughed. "In these times, you must take care; you will be sent astray purposefully, and you will come to harm."

"From Blood Roses, you mean," said Rogres, taking care to appear trusting of the villagers.

"Possibly. The lords of the earth are a plague in their own right." His laughter was nasty. "Here we know how to keep the Great Dying away." He nodded toward the fire. "That was the third house where it came. We are rid of the sickness and the house together."

"The sick are not left to spread their miasma," said one of the younger men, though his face was very white.

"They would have died anyway, Tipot. This is faster." The man who had spoken first swung around to Rogres again. "What else are we to do? A few can die, or many."

"Others have done worse," said Rogres. "Who is to say what is best, but God?"

"Amen," said the man. "Your road to Nevers lies back the way you came. When you reach the monastery, turn to the east, not the north." He folded his arms. "We answer to the Vidame de Silenrieux and he has not forbidden us to do what we are doing."

Rogres knew enough to seem unconcerned. "The Church will have his answer." In another voice, he said, "I thank you for setting me on the right road. May God protect you in these terrible days." He was about to leave when the younger man, Tipot, spoke to him.

"I had the Blood Roses, but I lived. They did not burn me." He sounded both proud and frightened of his admission.

"Then God must favor you above many," said Rogres. He crossed himself.

"As to that, who can tell?" said Tipot, waving Rogres on his way.

"Stay clear of the great lords," the village leader called after him.

The sun was a brazen smear low in the western sky by the time Rogres came back to the kitchen-gate, his sacks bulging with herbs and roots, his gippon dusty, his heuze muddy from the stream. His travels had left him tired but not exhausted, and he composed himself before entering the grounds of Non Trouve. He nodded to the cook's assistant and helped him bolt the gate before going into the kitchen.

"It is getting late," the cook pointed out unnecessarily as he cut up a mass of beef into collops; the spit over the fire turned and one of the scullions basted the two piglets with mustard mixed with beer and horseradish.

"But I am here before sundown," said Rogres hospitably. "And I thank you for sending your assistant to let me in."

The cook frowned. "You have herbs with you?"

"For my master." He held up the sacks. "These are for his medicaments, or I would leave you some for your work."

"Ha," said the cook, making it clear he would not accept anything from Rogres had it been offered. "The man you serve is a magician, so the pages say."

"He may seem so to them," said Rogres, preparing to leave the kitchen. "You have been good to him, and to me."

"It is the Vidame who is good," said the cook, and continued to hack at the meat. "All within these walls have reason to remember his goodness."

"As all here have cause to know." With that, Rogres left the kitchen, his attention already on what he would tell Saint-Germain. He was on the narrow stairs to the floors above when he saw Curtise standing at the top of the landing; he halted and looked at the boy. "Is there something you required of me?" he asked when Curtise did not speak.

"You will say nothing," the boy ordered, his young face set in an expression that did not belong to youth. "You will tell them *nothing.*"

Rogres shrugged. "What should I tell? That the fields are untilled? They can see for themselves. That there are travelers at the monastery? When have there not been?" He was about to continue his climb when Curtise blocked his way.

"No matter what you saw, *be silent.* If you do not, I will kill you." He touched the small dagger he carried in his belt and gave a single, emphatic nod. Then he very deliberately stepped aside. "Go to your master. Remember what I have said."

Rogres gazed at the boy. "Why should you care what I say? I am a foreigner's servant, you are the Vidame's page."

"I will kill you," Curtise said again. "Speak of anything, and you are dead."

"But why?" Rogres asked, knowing the page meant his threat; if he attempted to carry it out, he would find Rogres a more formidable target than he supposed.

Curtise spat a curse and left Rogres standing one step below the landing.

When Rogres reached Saint-Germain's apartments, he heard the mandola and the Italian song *"Laude Novella sia Cantata"* through the door.

> *Tu se' rosa tu se' gillio*
> *tu portasti el dolce fillio*
> *pero donna si m'enpillio*
> *de laudar te honorata:*
> *Laude novella sia cantata*
> *a l'alta donna encoronata . . .*

The rhythmic phrase broke off and Saint-Germain said, "I am glad you are back." He spoke in Greek; he opened the door for Rogres. "What is the matter?"

Rogres closed the door and handed the sacks of herbs to Saint-Germain, who set his mandola aside to take them. "I saw Curtise just now, on the landing of the back-stairs," he told Saint-Germain in the same language.

"And?" Saint-Germain prompted when Rogres faltered.

"And he said he would kill me if I said what I saw," he answered, shaking his head slowly. "He would not tell me why."

"Is it so bad?" Saint-Germain kept his tone level, but there was an urgency about him that Rogres recognized.

"It could be much worse; it is not Marsailla." He sat down. "There were bodies awaiting burial at the monastery." He reported all he had seen with careful precision while Saint-Germain listened in silence and used flint-and-steel to light the oil-lamps as sunset gave way to night.

When Rogres was finished, Saint-Germain waited a moment before he spoke. "Then we must leave. Not tomorrow, but the next day."

"Will the Vidame allow it?" Rogres asked, made circumspect by Curtise's commination. "If his pages are following his orders, my master, he may refuse."

"Probably he would; I am not planning to ask him." He touched his mandola, regret in his dark eyes. "And I have just repaired the pegbox."

Rogres said nothing; his silence was eloquent. Finally he rose. "I must hang the herbs in your red chest. We will have need of them in our travels." His reserve held no condemnation or disappointment, only a deep-seated concern.

"Thank you, old friend," said Saint-Germain, and both he and Rogres knew he was not referring to the herbs.

Text of an edict in the city of Bourges in the County of Barry in the Kingdom of France: posted at all churches in the city and at the city gates.

Be it known throughout the city of Bourges: These eighteen items now constitute the law:

1) that any who shall have intercourse of any nature whatsoever with anyone showing signs of the Black Plague shall immediately be branded and expelled from the city;

2) that anyone, whether child or parent, sister or brother, who shall discover the Black Plague within his family shall immediately report its presence and remove himself from the contagion at once without any attempt to aid said family; those who fail to do this will be put to death by fire;

3) that anyone entering the city will at once submit to a complete examination of his person, and should Blood Roses be found, that person shall immediately be put to death by fire;

4) that anyone who knows of Black Plague in the city and fails to report it shall immediately be branded and exiled from the city and the County of Barry, forfeiting all fortune and property;

5) that anyone who shall knowingly conceal any person suffering from the Black Plague will immediately be put to death by fire with any such afflicted persons as shall have sign of the illness;

6) that anyone who shall bring a priest to administer Extreme Unction to anyone dying of the Black Plague will, with the priest, immediately be branded and shut out of the city gates and will not be admitted again for any reason or upon any orders but those of the Pope;

7) that anyone found looting the houses of those who have died of the Black Plague will immediately be put to death by fire;

8) that all bodies in the city, whether dead of Black Plague or not, will be interred in the general grave, without any rites beyond those given at said general grave;

9) that any babe born to a mother showing signs of the Black Plague will be baptized with a long spoon and then laid with his mother until such time as God claims them or grants recovery and that any attempting to succor such mother and babe will immediately be branded and shut out of the city;

10) that anyone having shared the premises of a house where Black Plague is shall immediately be branded on the forehead to show the perfidy of the person, and then immediately thereafter be shut out of the city;

11) that anyone attending a banquet or a celebration where Black Plague is seen shall immediately be branded and expelled from the city;

12) that the Mass may be celebrated in the vernacular while the Black Plague is in the city, and that all rites conducted in the vernacular will be held as binding as any recited in Latin;

13) that all records of the city may be made in the vernacular rather than Latin for the duration of the visitation of the Black Plague;

14) that all those who bring damage to the city because of the Black Plague shall be held accountable for the damage they do when the Plague has passed;

15) that anyone who sins in the cause of the Black Plague shall be immediately put to death by fire;

16) that the terms of this edict will be binding for as long as the Black Plague is upon us;

17) that all the terms of this edict will be enforced no matter who among the leaders of the city fall to the Black Plague in this time of Great Dying;

18) and that any who fail to heed these items will be reckoned a traitor, branded for treason to the city and immediately exiled from the County of Barry with all his family and with none of their possessions or monies for as long as the traitor shall live.

The Magistrates and Bishop of the city of Bourges

In the County of Barry on the 16th day of July in the 1348th Year of Grace: may God have mercy on us.

8

There were a number of fresh graves at the crossroad; moonlight showed the turned earth as low hummocks where the roads met: these were the graves of those unentitled to Christian burial, or who were feared as unwilling to lie quiet until Judgment Day. The night was warm and the scent of thyme rode on the breeze from the hillsides to the south; it could not entirely mask the sweet-metallic odor of decaying flesh that came from the new graves. No wagons or carts were pulled to the side of the road here for fear of waking the spirits of the newly dead and no wanderers took shelter near the old shrine, as if the power of the Virgin might not be sufficient to hold the Great Dying at bay.

As Saint-Germain drew in his horse and two mules, Rogres, mounted behind him on a mule and leading the donkey, called out, "Which way?"

"To Nevers north or Chalon east," said Saint-Germain; it was the first time he had spoken since sunrise, and his voice was remote and preoccupied, as if his thoughts still held his attention more than the road they traveled. "The east is a better road, or it was: who is to say what it is now."

"North, then?" Rogres suggested.

"For the time being," Saint-Germain agreed. "In a day or two we may decide to go east." He was silent for a brief moment, then said something that had weighed on him for the last three days as they had left Non Trouve behind. "I wish we had not had to abandon so much: four chests of native earth and one of clothing." He looked over his shoulder at Rogres. "That is nothing to your discredit, old friend. The page discovered us too soon: we could not change that."

Rogres shifted uncomfortably in the saddle. "If we had had a little more time . . . As it was, I did not like to hurt the boy."

"No more did I," said Saint-Germain, "but he had an axe and he had already crippled one mule and was about to chop your ankles." He shook his head. "You did not kill him; he would have killed you."

"He was mad with rage," said Rogres as if trying to understand what he had done. He kicked his mule, clicking his tongue to encourage the animal to resume walking. "I recall my son once nearly had a fit from anger, but he was three or four at the time, and he did not try to kill anyone." Speaking of his long-ago family made him sad; he had seen them last while Nero ruled in Roma, and their images were no longer clear in his mind.

Saint-Germain called back to him, "Your child was not this child."

"No; no," Rogres said, and fell into a reverie that lasted for most of the night, ending only when they stopped to feed and rest their animals in the final dark of the night, when he said, "Those pages—why would they be so unwilling to let us go?" He was not expecting an answer, but Saint-Germain spoke anyway.

"They thought it was the Vidame's will, or so I infer," said Saint-Germain, his tone less certain than his words. "He gave orders that only religious and players could come and go, and we are neither. They have made it their work to carry out his orders to the letter, to make themselves valuable to him." He had dismounted beside an abandoned field with a herder's hut close at hand, and was loosening the girth on his saddle; the sky was still wrapped in night, but the early breeze had begun to stir, warning that dawn was not far off, promising the whole heat of summer. "Rosalbe said that one of the women had tried to leave before we came: the pages hanged her by her heels from the ramparts until the Vidame ordered her cut down."

"Did she tell you that when you visited her in sleep?" Rogres had secured his mule to an old gatepost and was tugging the donkey up to it; the gate was sagging off its hinges and could not be opened.

"No. She never wakened while I was with her for her dreams: I made sure of that. No; she told me one afternoon after I had been playing for the Vidame and his guests, and she became sad, I think because one of the songs reminded her of the woman—it was '*Lament deles Regines*'; you know, the old ballade from Rouen?—and she told me about the woman, then became frightened and asked that I say nothing of this to anyone. She said Pol watched her." He glanced back the way they had come. "I hope nothing happens to her." His expression clouded. "If the pages heard what she told me—" He did not go on.

"They watched everyone; who knows what they made of what they saw—they will tell the Vidame what they suppose he wants to hear," said Rogres, checking the pack-saddles on the donkey and mules for any shifting of their loads. "How long are we going to be here?" He indicated the herder's hut next to the gate.

"Until midmorning. The animals will be ready to travel then, and we will want to make the most of the day." He raised his head, staring into the sky. "There is a haze near the horizon and a heaviness slowing the wind. We may get a thunderstorm in the afternoon."

Rogres had seen Saint-Germain read the air enough times to trust his pronouncements. "I will go cut some hay for these animals." He was about to climb over the gate when he said, "We should be on guard. This road is traveled."

"Yes, we should," Saint-Germain said at once. He put his hand on his mount's breastplate, checking for any chafing the thick leather straps might have caused on their long night ride; the darkness did not hamper his vision as he examined his tack. When he was finished he straightened up, saying, "Bells will not be sufficient to alert us in time."

"I can remain awake," said Rogres, going over the gate.

"For half the span of our rest; then I'll relieve you. We must put more distance between us and Silenrieux. We do not want to be detained on the Vidame's orders." He frowned. "I would rather not take that gamble."

"Yes; I share your caution, my master," said Rogres as he set to cutting the wild hay in the pasture, pulling out the brambles and trailing weeds as he worked. When he had an armful he brought it back to the horse, mules, and donkey; they were already grazing on the grass growing in tufts along the gate, but began to eat the hay as soon as it was piled at their feet. Rogres went back to cut more while Saint-Germain entered the herder's hut.

"Nothing much to sleep on and the thatch is old and musty, but it is out of the sun," Saint-Germain reported as Rogres finished gathering hay for their animals. "I've swept out the worst of the refuse; we may have to be careful of rats."

"Rats are ever-present," said Rogres philosophically.

"There were none outside Baghdad," Saint-Germain reminded him with an ironic smile.

"The desert kept them away," said Rogres as he came toward the hut. "It was a small enough mercy, having no rats."

"Truly," Saint-Germain said as they stepped inside the hut, their entrance met by furtive scuttlings in the thatch overhead. "By the smell of the place, I surmise we have a nest of martens in the roof."

"Clever creatures, martens," said Rogres as he took stock of the interior: his eyes did not pierce the shadows as readily as Saint-Germain's, but he was less hampered than living men would be. He saw there was a single rough bench and an unsteady plank table, and a small hearth with a cracked chimney, which rendered it useless. "Well, it's shelter."

"And we have had worse, have we not, old friend," said Saint-Germain as he flung a small blanket down on the earthen floor; he was less remote than he had been, but a distance lingered about him, and Rogres knew Saint-Germain had not put Silenrieux entirely behind him.

Rogres did not answer as he looked around the hut. He noticed the door did not close properly, leaving a gap more than a handsbreadth wide. "This place has not been used in some time."

Saint-Germain spread out the blanket, saying, "Probably not since the winter at the latest, judging by the chimney."

Rogres made a gesture of agreement. "So it is at least three seasons since the place was used. Strange, to find it abandoned."

"I wonder why it is," said Saint-Germain. "Located so near a road, I would expect travelers to rest here." He shrugged, then said, "Unless lepers used it in years passed. That would account for its vacancy."

"The Black Plague may have done this," said Rogres. "If the herder had the Plague no one would stay here afterward."

"Three seasons since?" Saint-Germain asked; he expected no answer and got none. "Whatever the cause, it may be to our advantage."

"There aren't many lepers anymore," Rogres observed. "Fifty years ago, there were enough of them that every town had a place for them outside the gates; a century before everyone went in terror of it." He pressed his thin lips together. "I don't think I've seen a leper it in . . . thirty? thirty-five? years. The last was that old man at that shrine near Bruges: none since."

"The people still dread it, as if it continued to raven among them." Saint-Germain sighed. "Instead we have the Black Plague." He sank onto the blanket and lay back. "Waken me shortly after dawn, if you would."

"I will," said Rogres, taking his seat on the bench and preparing to keep watch through the end of the night.

By the time Saint-Germain awoke, birds were calling out in the fields and there was the distant sound of goats. He sat up with very little transition from sleeping to wakefulness, his face revealing no sign of fatigue after his short slumber. "Anything on the road?" he asked Rogres as he got to his feet and set to dusting off his linen cotehardie.

"Nothing so far." He made a gesture of bafflement. "I would have thought there would be some travelers by now, pilgrims if no others."

Saint-Germain nodded twice. "Odd," he concurred, but he did not pursue it. "Get some rest. We will have little enough of it for a while."

Rogres rubbed his chin, saying, "I must shave soon, and you must have your beard and hair trimmed." He went to the blanket Saint-Germain had just vacated; he sat down tailor-fashion and peered up into the thatch.

Saint-Germain sat down on the bench. "I'll cut some hay for the animals so we will be ready when you've slept."

"Remember the donkey is greedy," Rogres said as he prepared to lie back. "They'll need water again before we go much farther."

"I know," said Saint-Germain, and fell silent so that Rogres could get to sleep.

Afternoon found them under lowering clouds and thickening warm air at the crossroad to Bourbon; unlike the earlier one they had found, this place was busy; carts and wagons and mounted men clustered around a small shrine. As Saint-Germain and Rogres approached, they heard an angry shout.

"No. They are not letting anyone cross the Loire to Bourbon; they have barricaded the western end of the bridge and have threatened to take it down if we fight for it. They have men-at-arms posted to kill anyone who tries to get through." The man giving this unwelcome news was standing in the bed of a wagon used to haul sacks of grain; it was drawn by yoked oxen and filled with household goods and his family.

"They will not do it," called a man in an Austin's habit.

"I wouldn't put them to the test," yelled another.

This created a babel of arguments and protests that got louder and more heated as everyone strove to be heard.

A splinter of lightning lanced the sky, and a few heartbeats later, thunder thudded; among those drawn up at the crossroad there was a long, anxious stillness before the disputes erupted again, this time with an underlying urgency that had not been present before.

Suddenly a voice Saint-Germain recognized was raised above the others; it came from a cluster of wagons on the far side of the crossroads. "If you want to cross the river, make a ferry of your own. You do not need the bridge if Bourbon will not let you use it."

"Faustino," Saint-Germain said to Rogres, not quite smiling but with a sign of real satisfaction.

"Are you certain?" Rogres asked, searching the crowd for the source of the voice; in the confusion he could not single out any speaker with such confidence.

"After hearing him declaim that speech of Virgil's from *The Gates of Hell* for six rehearsals?" Saint-Germain asked. "I could not mistake him."

Rogres shrugged, not in doubt so much as in acceptance. "I will believe you, my master," he said, and held out his hand for the reins of Saint-Germain's horse. "You will do better looking for him on foot in this crowd."

"I agree," said Saint-Germain as he swung out of the saddle and began to press through the close-packed mass of vehicles, animals, and human beings; he paid little attention to the debate raging around him, concentrating on finding his way to the source of the voice he recognized: jostled by elbows and the flanks of animals, shoved by muddy wheels and anxious children, he did not let himself become caught up in disputes, though he was occasionally shouted at and once prodded with the handle of a hoe; one or two persons were impressed enough by Saint-Germain's clothing to give way to him in deference. Finally he reached a mule-drawn wagon he knew; the illustrations painted on the sides were faded and the mules showed ribs under their coat. Saint-Germain saw Faustino standing up on the driver's box, and he called out, "Good player!"

Faustino stared down into the milling confusion with sudden intensity. He frowned as if that would improve his vision. "Who calls me?"

"Francois de Saint-Germain," he answered. "Look down on the off-side of your mules."

The player did as he was told; his scowl turned at once to a smile. "God's Fishes, mon Sieur. I thought you were in prison for sure, or far away."

"In prison?" Saint-Germain laughed. "Now why would you think that?"

Instead of answering, Faustino gestured to him to climb onto the wagon, glancing around as if to assure himself they were not being too closely noticed. Only when Saint-Germain was next to him on the box did he say, as quietly as he could and still be heard over the noise, "There is a warrant out for your execution. Didn't you know?"

"No," said Saint-Germain, and realized he was not shocked by this revelation; he had been expecting something of the sort since he left Orgon. "On what authority am I condemned?"

"Some magistrate in the south, so I'm told. We were detained at Lyon, to answer questions about you." Faustino spat to show what he thought of this.

"That is unjust. I am sorry you have suffered on my account, my friend," Saint-Germain said at once with unmistakable sincerity.

Another bolt of lightning ricocheted through the clouds, pursued by thunder; the confusion at the crossroads increased: horses whinnied, mules and donkeys brayed, dogs barked, children shrieked, and men swore and prayed in the same breath.

"It is going to rain soon," said Faustino. "We will want to get under cover." He sat down and took the reins in his hands. "We will move back. Hang on, mon Sieur."

"You cannot back up in this crush," Saint-Germain said, knowing that general panic was not far off. "Let me get down and see what I can do to make some room for you to move."

"Mon Sieur!" Faustino protested.

Saint-Germain waved his objections away before Faustino could voice them. "How many wagons are yours?"

"Just this one," Faustino admitted, embarrassed to admit it. "And two carts behind, one mule, one donkey."

"Very well," said Saint-Germain, and began to make his way to the rear of the wagon.

Suddenly a cry arose, a high, frightened wail from somewhere in front of the players' wagon. *"Blood Roses!"*

The consternation caused by the thunder was nothing compared to the riot that surged from one end of the gathering to the next: shouts and imprecations were all but inaudible over the wailing and screams; men mounted or in wagons were the first to try to break out of the tangled knot of men and equipment. The minimal order gave way to chaos, with men and women striking out at those nearest to them with whatever came to hand. Animals became wild with fear and tried to escape only to be tangled in their harnesses or struck down by terrified humans; wagons overturned and carts were flung on end, as if the lightning had struck in their midst instead of half a league away.

Saint-Germain felt the players' wagon sway and begin to lean as a bullock-cart on the far side slammed into it; he braced himself and took the weight of the cart, straining to hold it up as Faustino dragged on the reins to back the mules away from the growing chaos; his shoulders shook with the effort as the wagon tilted more dangerously, and he felt his foot slipping as the weight continued to shift. The mules brayed and one of them kicked in alarm, knocking the wagon back an arm's length and canting it at a more precarious angle.

Then there was a sharp tug at the rear and the wagon began to move back, righting itself as it went; Rogres had come around the outside of the turmoil and was using the strength of their mules to extricate the players' wagon from the growing peril in the crowd. The wheels of the wagon slithered in the old ruts as it pulled away, and finally there was room enough for it to swing around and start along the road north to Nevers.

Walking beside the wagon and preparing to steady it if necessary, Saint-Germain shook out his arms; his tremendous strength had been tested as he held up the wagon and he knew he would be a bit stiff for the next day. If he had someone he could visit in sleep, he would be restored, but he did not hold out much hope for such an opportunity tonight, or the following night. He signaled to Rogres to bring his horse up, and when he did, Saint-Germain vaulted into the saddle and rode up beside Faustino. "Where are you bound?"

"Devil take me if I know," said Faustino grimly. "The Great Dying has made our old routes impossible." He looked up at Saint-Germain. "And not to be ungrateful, but you are a danger to us, with a death warrant issued for you."

Saint-Germain nodded. "I know; I will not foist my company on you much longer."

"Oh, not just you. They describe your manservant, too, and include him it in the execution order," said Faustino. "If I hadn't lost four players since I saw you last, I might want to defy them for their stupidity, but as it is, I cannot afford to be spoken against, or to lose another player." He coughed. "Timoteo had Blood Roses, as did his wife. She lived, but she will not travel with us again; she swore it on the altar. Palot's wife died of it, and so did Ettore."

"I am sorry to hear it," said Saint-Germain. "It is a terrible thing to lose old friends."

"That it is, that it is," said Faustino, ignoring the tear that ran down his lean cheek. "But they were spared much. We may yet find it in our hearts to envy them."

There was nothing Saint-Germain could say to that, for he agreed with Faustino's gloomy assessment. He rode without speaking until a new slash of lightning brought them all to a halt in the ground-shuddering thunder. "The rain is coming."

"We must find a place to shelter. This wagon won't keep all of us dry, and the mules are hungry," said Faustino, no emotion at all in his voice.

"If you will permit me, I will ride ahead and see if I can find anything that will serve as shelter for the night," Saint-Germain offered. He could feel the storm growing nearer and knew they would soon be drenched.

Faustino indicated the decision was Saint-Germain's, then said, "The carts cannot go over very rough road."

"I am aware of it," said Saint-Germain, dropping back to tell Rogres what he planned to do.

"I can come with you," Rogres offered.

"It would be wiser, I think, if you remained with Faustino and the players. Do not worry, old friend. I have my sword and my francisca." He was an expert with the little throwing-axe that lay against the small of his back under his belt. "I doubt any robbers will be waiting with the storm almost upon us." His heels urged his grey forward to a trot.

Less than two leagues along the road, he came upon an old turnpike-shed of considerable size where goods were kept in forfeit when the toll was not paid. The whole thing was deserted, other travelers having taken shelter before now in more hospitable places. Saint-Germain circled it twice before looking inside long enough to ascertain it was truly vacant; satisfied that it was empty—probably looted—he shut the double doors, hoping that would deter others from entering. Then he remounted; as he began to retrace his steps back to the players, the heavens opened: rain pelted him, and hail, and as the ruts filled with water, Saint-Germain had to fight the growing queasiness water always caused him.

By the time he reached the players, he was wet to the skin and the ache in his shoulders from holding the wagon was enough to hurt him. He rode directly up to Faustino, and, shouting to be heard, he described what he had found. "There is no hearth, but a small fire could be lit without burning the whole building down," he finished.

"I would be content with a cow's byre," Faustino growled, and slapped his driving whip on the mules' rumps to make them move more quickly; being mules, they did not alter their pace at all. He glowered down at them. "How far?"

His answer was accompanied by a roll of thunder pursuing lightning through the clouds. "More than a league, less than two. It is hard by the old tolling place. The door is on the north side, large enough for wagons. You will not find stalls, but there is plenty of room to tie your animals and have enough left for your company." Saint-Germain could feel the power of his native earth lessen as the soles of his heuze soaked through; at least the sun was not shining, he thought, and he was spared that added vitiation.

"Will you tell the others?" Faustino asked. "They will want to know."

"Of course," said Saint-Germain, welcoming the chance to speak to Rogres as well. He spoke first to Dormahn in the larger cart, and then to Palot, who glared at Saint-Germain as if he were responsible for their current fortunes.

Rogres greeted this news with careful consideration. "What shall I do with our animals?" he asked as he tugged on the leads to keep them all moving.

"We will be able to stable them with the players' stock," Saint-Germain replied, hoping that Faustino would agree when they arrived at the place.

"And then what?" Rogres asked as he tugged their pack-animals along.

"We will have to see," said Saint-Germain, deliberately oblique.

For once, Rogres was unwilling to be put off. "You have something in mind, my master."

Saint-Germain laughed once. "Yes; I do have something in mind. And since it will require persuasion, as you say, I will tell you when all can listen." Before Rogres could protest, he kicked his grey back into a trot so he could lead Faustino and his players to the shelter he had found.

Text of a letter from Sanct' Germain Franciscus to Atta Olivia Clemens; carried by Rogres in the company of the players.

My dearest Olivia;

First, do not be angry with Rogres; he tried to convince me to come with him and the players who accompany him, but I have refused; for you see, there is a warrant for the death of Francois de Saint-Germain, Sieur Ragoczy, and his manservant. It seems prudent for Rogres to travel apart from me until the danger of such a warrant is past, as it seems equally prudent for Francois de Saint-Germain to disappear.

I am continuing on to Bruges, to my holdings there, but not as Sieur Ragoczy. I will be safe enough, you need not fear. Rogres will explain all to you, and you are not to berate him for complying with my instructions, or for permitting me to continue my travels alone. I rely on you to honor my obligation to him. You will keep him safe for me until I come to claim him again; if I do not come, I commend him to your care. No doubt he and Niklos will manage well enough somehow; you will not lack for protection in their care.

As to these players: they are in need of a place to be safe while they wait for the Great Dying to end so that they may once again resume their travels to the market-towns and the castles where they have been welcome before. It is true that players and troubadors are not being turned away from as many places as other travelers are, but the Blood Roses may be more eager for them than a magistrate or a lord. They have lost some of their number already; let them be spared any greater loss. Their leader is Faustino and I have treated him for putrid lungs before he set out with his company. Rogres will have taken care of him during their travels. You will find them entertaining, and no doubt you will learn much from what they have to tell you.

Second, do not castigate me for what I am doing. It is only what I must do if I am to retain any trace of integrity. I know you would delight in hectoring me, but consider that I must do what my blood has bound me to do; you have experienced the strength of the bond.

If you are vexed with me, you may tell me so when next I see you. Content yourself for now with the certainty of my gratitude, and my undying love.

> By my own hand,
> Ragoczy Sanct' Germain Franciscus
> (his sigil, the eclipse)

On the 2nd day of August in the Christian year 1348.

PART III

HEUGENET DA BRABANT

*T*ext of a letter from Eudoin Tissant in Orgon, the County of Provence, in the Holy Roman Empire, to the Papal Court at Avignon; written in the Provencal vernacular.

To His Eminence, Baudiet, Cardinal Villesrouges, the greeting and prayers from the Tax Collector and Chief Magistrate of the town of Orgon, in the County of Provence, in the Holy Roman Empire, and to his successor if his Excellency has been called to God;

As the most senior member of the magisterial authorities of this town, it is my unfortunate duty to inform you that Pare Herriot has succumbed, not to the Black Death, but to the rigors of fasting and flagellation, which he offered up for the salvation of the souls of all who have died of Blood Roses. The occasion of his death has been marked by funereal observations, and in accordance with his wishes, he has been interred in the general grave of all who have perished in the Great Dying.

Our town is now hardly more than a village. The pestilence has not yet left us, and our numbers are reduced so greatly that many of the houses have no one to claim them, and the work that would have been done cannot be undertaken with so few skilled artisans left alive. One in four have died, and before the visitation is over, I fear it may be one in three. No child born to a woman of this place since the nativity was last celebrated has lived more than a month, and we begin to suspect that what the Blood Roses will not claim, old age will, until Orgon is nothing but a word over an unguarded gate to an empty town.

It was the belief of Pare Herriot that the dangerous foreign magician,

Francois de Saint-Germain, Sieur Ragoczy, had brought the Black Plague to us by his unholy arts; that is still the opinion of many, but as news of the deadly toll continues to increase, a few have said it would take a more malign power than said Sieur Ragoczy to cause so much dying; a few have said he is one of many servants of the Devil, who has been sent to show a foretaste of Judgment Day. I continue in my conviction that this Sieur Ragoczy is capable of any evil art, and I continue to ask that he be captured and put to death, along with his manservant, who must be as guilty as his master.

The warrant for their execution is not rescinded. Their deaths should be pleasing in the sight of God, Who seeks only for our perfection through Our Savior. Unfortunately, it would seem from the rare reports we receive that these men have vanished from the earth. If this means that the Great Dying has overtaken them, then we must thank God for ridding us of such iniquity; these men are better in their graves than in the world. We have no tortures severe enough to repay what their heinous deeds have brought to us, and I fear that the Devil would claim them before the boot had done its work, let alone the knotted cord or the red-hot pincers.

In that this Sieur Ragoczy cannot be found, and he is a known criminal who has committed the most unspeakable crimes which has placed him beyond the rights of his station in life, all his property is forfeit to the town and the Church; I have claimed his villa and estate, Clair dela Luna, which I will administer as my own until such time as the magistrates of the town, or the Papal Court, should decide otherwise. So many of our fields are fallow because the owners have died or fled, it is necessary that the lands in the best heart be kept under the plow, in order to make it possible for this village to survive beyond the fury of the Blood Roses. We are all agreed, the remaining authorities and I, that this decision is a prudent and righteous one. With the Black Plague still ravaging the region, I will abide at this estate in order to preserve my health and the record of my office. Any Will left by this pernicious foreigner must not be honored, for that would serve to reward those who have worked for the ruin of mankind.

It is possible that the civic records of Orgon may prove incomplete when the Great Dying ends, despite my efforts to preserve them, and for that reason I have taken it upon myself to send this to you in Avignon in the hope that God will preserve the affairs of the Pope more rigorously than He has seen fit to care for His most devout children in Provence. If what I have laid out here is not against the dictates of His Holiness, I beg you to tell the messenger who brings this so that he may inform us in Orgon that our work is recognized and we are not completely forgotten.

May God spare you, Your Eminence, and may He bring an end to our suffering when the world is sufficiently purged of evil. When we are restored to our former health and prosperity, I will be honored to show you true signs of gratitude for all you have done to aid the oppressed people of Orgon; we will have three or four more estates unclaimed which should rightly be in the hands of Godly men, such as yourself, to indicate that we have seen God's Hand in all these terrible things, and we know how to thank those who have delivered us from death and sin.

With the prayers of all those who live still in Orgon, and with our supplication to you to be remembered in your prayers: may God save you, and His Holiness the Pope from the Pit, and may you know the glory of Paradise when God summons you to the Mercy Seat.

Eudoin Tissant,
Chief Magistrate and Tax Collector of Orgon
by the hand of Frer Leopardi de Pisa, tertiary Franciscan

On the 29th day of August, the Feast of the Death of Jehan le Baptiste, in the 1348th year of man's Salvation.

1

In Sainte-Wilgefortis, those with Blood Roses on their flesh were sent out of the gates of the town to the old Lepers' House, which had been pressed into use without repairs, where the monks from Saint-Niere did what little they could to alleviate the agonies of the disease, and then sang the *Requiem* with Mass every morning; it was not on a main road, though it was the center for five small hamlets, and had been the market-place for them. It limped along in this capacity in spite of the Great Dying.

Germain le-Comte arrived in the village not long after dawn; a tired guard felt his neck, armpits, and groin before allowing him through the gates, for as a jongleur he was allowed access to the town if he was not diseased. He accepted this examination with good grace, having experienced worse; his appearance mitigated in his favor: he was dressed in jongleur-motley—a long gippon of red-and-black with open sleeves over a dark-red chamisa, and red-and-black particolored underhose—and led a shaggy donkey hitched to a small cart in which four large chests were stored, one being very old of red lacquer; it also contained two sacks of grain and farrier's tools, which made Germain le-Comte the object of mild curiosity for those few desperate families bringing goods and food to market-day: it should have been high harvest, with the bounty of the fields and orchards displayed in heaps, while the coopers readied barrels for new beer and wine; today only a dozen stalls were set up, with poor pickings for the small groups of peasants and servants that straggled in from the estates and crofts to try to find food for those who had survived the Black Plague in time to face winter, which was beginning to whisper in the wind and to leech the warmth from the day. All the signs were for cold, and everyone knew that the season would be hard had the Great Dying not come—as it was, the prospects for the dark of the year were grim enough to make even the most faithful doubt the Mercy of God.

"You!" shouted a monk in the Premonstratensian habit as he bustled out of the church of Sainte-Wilgefortis; the building was nearly as old as the legendary Portuguese saint herself. He flapped his hands in Germain le-Comte's direction.

Germain le-Comte turned and bowed to the monk in the lavish style of players. "God give you good day, mon Frer," he said, his voice musical, accented strangely, as was often the case with jongleurs and players. He opened the smallest of his cases and pulled out a mandola, handling it with expertise. "I trust you fare—"

"What brings you to this place?" He scowled forbiddingly, making no sign of encouragement or welcome.

"It is market-day, and I have a romance or two to sing." Germain le-Comte was also weary and hungry, but he said nothing of either as he shut the instrument's chest and lifted the mandola into position for playing.

"You see how we keep market-day in Sainte-Wilgefortis since the Great Dying began," the monk exclaimed with a wave of his hand at the near-empty square under the glare of high, thin clouds that provided more shine than light.

"All the more reason to welcome a song or two," said Germain le-Comte. He began to tune the strings of his mandola, apparently unaware of the attention his presence was attracting. "I know songs of faith as well as songs of love, mon Frer," he went on. "If you will tell me which Psalm you would like to hear, I will sing it for you, in the French or Italian style."

"You . . . you must leave at once," the monk declared. "This is no place for the likes of you."

"Your guards admitted me," said Germain le-Comte without any signs of distress at this inhospitable reception.

A child of eight or nine came running up to the stranger, his small hands held out as he shouted, "Carrots! Cabbage!"

"Go away, boy," said the monk. "He does not have such food to spare for you." The severity of his words was not present in his weathered features. "We will have charity later." He glanced at Germain le-Comte. "You are jongleur, or troubador? Well? What is your purpose here?"

"To answer your first question: in these times, I am some of both; village or court, old songs or new, it hardly matters now," said Germain le-Comte. He began to pluck out a melody. "To answer the second: I am a singer of songs." And he began, his voice rich and sweet.

> *Quant revient la sesons*
> *Que l'erbe reverdoie*
> *Que droiz est et resons*
> *Que l'en deduire doie,*
> *Seuls aloie*
> *Si pensoie*
> *As novaius sons.*

The child stared up at him. "But the plants are dying," he said in disappointment; his child's face looked prematurely ancient, blighted by tragedy. "Why should you want to see dead fields?"

"The song is about spring; when the flowers come back," Germain le-Comte said gently to the boy. "It is for after winter ends." He had seen too many neglected fields on his journey north, and with the year fading, the prospects for the spring were not encouraging.

"There will be no more spring," the child announced.

Frer Herebert looked down in shock. "You doubt the spring will come? Where did you hear such heresy?"

Germain le-Comte put out his hand. "He is too young to know heresy," he told the monk. "He repeats only what he has been told."

"My father died in the summer, and my mother died on the Feast of Saint Johan's Death. That was"—he screwed up his face with thought—"three weeks ago, almost. My brothers were sent to my uncle in the north, and only my gran' is left, and she's simple." He stood up very straight. "I was sick, but the Plague Virgin came and took my fever away."

"God spared you through His Grace," Frer Herebert corrected him.

"The Plague Virgin," the boy insisted. "I saw her. A pale lady all in white, with the Blood Roses in her arms. She came to me, wan as an angel, and she touched me."

"Heresy springs from such roots," the monk stated, looking at the boy. He shrugged suddenly, unwilling to pursue the question. "Plague Virgin, indeed! It is not surprising that the boy should listen to such tales; they are everywhere, and he has no one to guide him. His father was the miller. Those mills on the barges in the river you saw coming here—those are his."

"You assume I came from the south," said Germain le-Comte as he began to play another melody; he noticed that he had drawn more attention from those few who had come to market, but whether it was for a song or for news, he could not tell.

"Every stranger comes from the south since the Great Dying began," Frer Herebert said. "No one goes that way, they only leave, all those who can walk," He put his hand on the boy's matted hair. "There are scores of orphans, widows, and widowers in this region. It is no different than any other."

Germain le-Comte remembered what he had seen in Marsailla and he shook his head. "Some places are worse than what you have seen." He went on before the monk could rebuke him, "I do not make light of what you have endured, but I know that the burden has fallen more dreadfully on other places."

"It is not so," said the boy.

"For you, no, it is not," said Germain le-Comte with kindness. He bent down and looked at the child levelly. "You are fortunate to have survived. So few do, once they become ill."

The child smiled though he seemed about to cry. "The Plague Virgin told me I would live. She said my mother would die."

In his long, long life Germain le-Comte had learned not to question such assertions; when he had served in the Temple of Imhotep he had heard similar stories, and he no longer doubted that those in the throes of deadly illness occasionally learned remarkable things. "You will want to remember your mother, boy."

"I am Doonet," he announced, ducking his head to Germain le-Comte.

"And I am Germain le-Comte," was his answer.

Doonet grinned, looking truly young for the first time. "Germain le-Comte? Le-Comte? You are a nobleman's *bastard*? You? A jongleur?" He laughed once, the sound so unfamiliar to him that he stopped as soon as he heard himself.

"Does your father recognize you? In these days a living son might well become an heir," Frer Herebert said, referring to what had already happened in Artois.

"My father is dead, many years ago," said Germain le-Comte truthfully, reckoning the years in millennia; his words were neutral enough to discourage more inquiry; he began to pluck out a new tune, one intended for dancing.

"It is sad when a parent dies," Frer Herebert said solemnly, as much for Doonet's benefit as Germain le-Comte's. "But it is the way of the world. God does not intend that we should live forever but in His Kingdom." He crossed himself with automatic piety.

"You are going to entertain us?" Doonet asked abruptly, as if he hardly dared hope for such a treat.

"It is what jongleurs and troubadors do," German le-Comte said as his playing became more regular; his small hands moved expertly over the strings, pulling out melody that began to catch the attention of others in the market-place.

"You play very well," Frer Herebert approved with a scowl; he had no wish to have gaiety in his village while so many were falling under the scythe of the Black Death.

"I have played for years and years," said Germain le-Comte in rhythm with his musical cadence: he had not always played the mandola; he had begun with the Egyptian harp and had learned the Greek lyre and kythera, then the Roman hydraulic organ and bagpipes before he had come to the buisines and rebecs and psalstrires and gitterns and mandolas of the present age.

"Something done over time becomes mastery," the monk said, and gave a warning look to Doonet. "Think of this, my boy, when you come to apprentice yourself."

Doonet looked up at Germain le-Comte. "Do you have an apprentice?"

Germain le-Comte faltered in his playing. "No," he said after a brief hesitation. "Not many jongleurs do."

"Oh." He looked crestfallen; the aged cast to his features returned.

"Men without lords who travel their lives away are not good masters," said Frer Herebert, his rebuke softened by his next words, "And we of Sainte-Wilgefortis cannot lose another healthy child."

Doonet gave a wistful, little sigh. "I know." He did his best to look pleased. "And I will work my father's mills, when I am old enough."

"That you will," said the monk with false heartiness. "We will need our mills again, in days to come." He crossed himself again, as if to ensure the future.

"And when the fields are rich again, I will be rich, too," said Doonet, repeating what he had been told over the last several weeks. "I will not have to come for charity to get something to eat."

"Certainly not," said the monk with heavy optimism. "You will donate the bread we give to the hungry, and everyone will praise your name."

This innocent mention of food reminded Germain le-Comte how hungry he was. Since Rogres had left—protesting—with the players, Germain le-Comte had had only four occasions to visit women in sleep to gain sustenance; in the last seven days he had found no nourishment, for he would not prey upon those struck with illness; they were already weak and he would not deprive them of any strength they would need. He glanced with apparent mild curiosity around the market-place, and saw two women who might welcome the ephemeral fulfillment of dreams; he would learn more about them as the day wore on. "My donkey would be the better for some hay," he said. "And in a while he will need water." He saw Doonet begin to smile. "There will be a silver emperor for you if you will tend to my donkey and guard my cart."

"That I will," said Doonet, moving closer to the cart; he hesitated, his hand raised to touch the lead. "Does he have a name?"

"I call him Caesar, for like all donkeys, he thinks he can order the world to his liking," said Germain le-Comte as he patted the donkey; he was shaggier than ever, his winter coat growing in thick and long.

"A profane name," said Frer Herebert.

"He's a donkey," Germain le-Comte pointed out. "God cannot object to giving him the name of the emperors of Rome."

Frer Herebert pondered the problem, alert to any hint of heretical thought; finally he declared, "If Pare Bottegar were still alive, he would be able to say." He folded his hands as he studied the donkey. "Perhaps it is not very much of a sin to call a donkey Caesar."

Doonet patted Caesar's neck. "I'll keep you fed, boy," he promised the donkey. "And I'll bring you water."

Germain le-Comte put one hand on Doonet's shoulder. "Thank you. He ought to be grateful, but he will not be." Saying that, he bowed to the monk and began to stroll about the market-square, playing his mandola and exchanging banter with the few vendors in Sainte-Wilgefortis, as he had seen Faustino do while they had traveled together. His demeanor was easy, as if he did not notice the neglect or the dismay in the faces of those in the market-square.

> *Adieu vous di, tres doulce compaynie,*
> *Puis que de vous departir me convient*
> *Per fortune, qui per grant aramie*
> *A toute heure de moy grever souvient . . .*

"Have you gone to Paris, jongleur? since the Blood Roses bloomed." asked one old woman sitting with a small display of fresh-caught fish and two baskets of apples; she wore a stiffened widow's coif, and over her rusty-black brancs she had tied a threadbare apron.

"No, I have not," he said, interrupting the saltarello he had been playing. "I have not been there in several years."

"They say the Great Dying is very bad in Paris," she said, prompting him to tell her more. "We have heard that half the city is dead and the rest are too ill to bury them."

"It may be; the Great Dying is hard everywhere; the cities are most straitened." He picked up the melody again. "I pray God spares you any more grief."

She shook her head. "Oh, don't do that, jongleur; I will cease grieving only when I am dead. My family will end with me, for none of my children . . . lived long enough to have children, and my husband was killed by the English." The cold smile she gave him was so unhappy that he stayed beside her and played *"Jherusalem, grant damage me fais"* for her, letting the plaintive lament give her an excuse to weep; the music curled like smoke, twining and rising with the words. When he was done, she wiped her eyes with her apron, saying, "Such a pretty song, and so sad."

"Your monk does not think this is a time for levity," said Germain le-Comte without any trace of condemnation. He moved away from the woman's stall, now playing the estampie *"Bele li gossi"* as he went.

"I have heard there were more jongleurs, many years ago," remarked a brewer as he sat next to his barrel, ladling out beer for those who had the two copper roses to pay for it. "My grandfather said that they were once plentiful as rats."

"There were fewer players in those times," said Germain le-Comte, pausing to talk to the florid-faced man. "There had to be more jongleurs and troubadors."

The brewer laughed. "So you are traveling the road alone. Doesn't that worry you, with the Great Dying and the brigands?"

"Brigands find jongleurs poor picking," Germain le-Comte said, ignoring the rancor in the brewer's manner. "And I know of no place where Blood Roses cannot bloom, so I might as well travel."

"With winter coming, you will change your tune." He chuckled at his own witticism. "The wolves will be hungry, and the bears."

"And they will have enough to feed on without testing their teeth on me," said Germain le-Comte responded with the same bantering tone the brewer used. "I am only worried that I will not find men and women enough who want to find respite from their troubles for the length of a song or two." He patted his mandola as if it were a tame animal. "At least the instrument does not need to eat, unlike my donkey."

"A handsome beast," said the brewer. "You would not consider selling him?" He lifted one thick brow in speculation.

"Yes; a handsome beast, and no, I will not sell him." He began to play again, and knew that the brewer understood his meaning.

The brewer shrugged. "Well, in these times, I might find just such an animal wandering the roads and glad of a stall and an armload of hay." He made a gesture to show he did not resent Germain le-Comte's refusal to sell his donkey. "Do you know this region?"

"Somewhat," said Germain le-Comte. "I have not been here in . . . a while."

"Since the English came, no doubt," said the brewer, and spat to show his contempt. "Mad, reckless dogs, the English. May they all be swallowed up by the sea."

"Swallowed up," Germain le-Comte echoed, knowing that sentiments ran high in this part of the country, and that the English were despised foes.

"You're a good fellow, jongleur, for all you talk like a foreigner. May the English have Blood Roses for their pains in France." The brewer let out a sudden belch, laughed, and gave his attention to Germain le-Comte again. "You will need somewhere to winter, won't you?" Before Germain le-Comte could answer, he said, "In Hainaut you may find what you seek. They know how to welcome jongleurs and troubadors, and they said fewer of them have died than in the south. Go to Sant-Brede near Maissin: to the castle. The English have not sacked it yet. They will not turn you away, as many would. They like jongleurs and troubadors and players; you will not starve there."

"You are kind to suggest it; I may go there," Germain le-Comte said to the brewer.

"I hope you will think so when winter is over; that it is kind," said the brewer. "You might come back this way in the spring; if everyone has not left in fear, we may have markets again, and markets mean amusements. God willing, you will find more of us to listen to you and make merry." He drank another long sip of his own product. "We have not had much to lighten our days. When one in four dies, and one in three runs away, there is great suffering." He put his hands on his hips. "People drink more beer when they are happy."

"I will keep that in mind," said Germain le-Comte as he continued on around the market-square, playing dances and ballades as he went until he came back to the steps of Sainte-Wilgefortis where Doonet waited with Caesar.

"He is a good donkey," the boy approved as he finished smoothing the long hair on the donkey's neck.

"So I think," Germain le-Comte agreed. "And I thank you for tending him for me."

The boy grinned. "It pleases me, too."

"He has come many miles to be here," said Germaine le-Comte, glancing at the woman who emerged from the door of the one inn; the woman was moving hurriedly, trying to catch one of the ducks that wandered near the front of the building.

"That is Mère Patrice; she runs the inn now that her husband is dead," said Doonet, his young face wistful. "She gives me eggs, sometimes."

"You like her," said Germain le-Comte.

"She is a good woman. Not like some." His expression darkened, and he went on grudgingly, "Some will chase you away if you have been sick, no matter what the illness might be, even if it is nothing more than a dripping nose. Some will not let you sleep in their barns, though half the stalls are empty, and there is little hay in the loft." He angled his head toward the inn. "Mère Patrice will give me a place by the hearth when the frost comes. She said so."

"Then do you think she might have a place for a jongleur?" He asked it lightly enough, hiding his hunger with the ease of experience.

"If you have more coins, she will give you a good bed." Doonet made a face in the direction of the church. "She is better than the monks."

"Very likely," said Germain le-Comte.

"She'll feed you well," said Doonet. "Not just bread and soft cheese the monks give."

Germain le-Comte smiled briefly. "They give what they have," he said, reaching for the lead to Caesar's halter. "She will have a place in her barn for him?"

At this, Doonet put his hand on his chest in a show of pride. "I will look after him myself; I have a place in the barn, and have since . . . since my parents were buried with the others." He shot a single, defiant look in the direction of the church. "They said it was not wise to let anyone who had . . ." Seeing Frer Herebert he stopped himself from saying anything more. "Talk to Mère Patrice. She will be glad of a paying traveler."

"She has said so," Germain le-Comte guessed, smiling down at Doonet.

"Yes," the boy declared. "All the world is on the roads, but none of them stay at inns." He lifted his arms in imitation of what Mère Patrice had done many times. "A few coins would be useful."

"Fortunately, I have a few coins," said Germain le-Comte, who carried four large sacks of them hidden in his chests. "She will not have to let me have a bed for a song."

Doonet took hold of Germain le-Comte's long, dagged outer sleeve. "I will bring you. And I will take care of Caesar." He grinned with precarious happiness at these simple anticipations.

"Very well," said Germain le-Comte, allowing Doonet to lead him in the direction of the inn, saying as he went, "I am grateful to you, lad."

The child beamed. "You will like Mère Patrice," he promised as he tugged on Caesar's lead with one hand, and on Germain le-Comte's sleeve with the other.

A slight smile pulled at the corner of Germain le-Comte's mouth. "I do hope so," he said, and followed the boy to the door of the inn.

Text of a letter from Josue Roebertis in Constanz in the Duchy of Swabia to Fabrice Rocene in Pont Sant-Pierre in the County of Hainaut; carried by pilgrims returning from the Holy Land to Antwerp on the road from Venezia, delivered 19 October, 1348.

To the esteemed kinsman of my late brother-in-law, the greetings of one whom God has favored to another who has been spared the pains of death in this dreadful time; this brings my prayers for your well-being and the health of your family, including that of Jenfra, whom this message concerns:

I apologize that this is written in the language of the Swabian Duchy and not in the Latin tongue, as is proper, but so many have succumbed to the Great Dying that few remain who are trained in Latin, and so I must address you in the Swabian vernacular, and hope that you will have someone who can read it for you.

I received your gracious letter on the 19th day of July, and went at once to church to give thanks for the many benefices of the Holy Spirit which has so moved my late sister's stepdaughter to decide to enter the cloister; I am overcome with joy that God should find her so to His liking that He should move her to this vocation in so desperate a time as ours. The honor of providing her dowry to her convent is one I welcome with all humility and thanksgiving; it is entrusted to these pilgrims, and once it is in your hands, I pray you will convey it to the Superior of the convent without delay, for I know how eager Jenfra must be to begin embracing the duties of her vocation, and the sweet joys of the contemplative and humble life of service it is the privilege of the Brides of Christ to render in His Name to all those caught in the trials of the world. I pray most devoutly that the convent will value the worth of this girl.

My notary has recorded this dowry, along with the transfer of titles and inheritance rights to me. I am certain the bona fide copy that accompanies this letter will be wanted at the convent where Jenfra will serve. I know that in these times such records are not as rigorously maintained as the Church instructs, but as long as I am able, I will do all within my power to maintain those documents that the laws of Emperor and Church demand; in times to come, I would like to spare my heirs, and those of Hue d'Ormonde, any difficulties arising out of disputes caused by the lack of records kept in these times. I have sent word to the magistrates of Marsailla, if any such be living still, of all that has transpired in regard to Jenfra. You may wish to send confirmation: I leave that up to you.

Let me implore you to give that blessed young woman my greetings and tell her that she is always in my thoughts and prayers, not only to esteem her virtues, but to remember her father and all he has given to our House.

Her prayers on behalf of those of us lingering in this dreadful world will surely aid us and add to her sanctity.

Send me word when this is in your hands, that I may again thank God for His protection and goodness. I am deeply obliged to you for all you have done to help that orphan child who has now chosen a parent greater than any the world may provide. May God spare her any more suffering in this world and welcome her to His Glory in the world that is to come.

With my most sincere blessings for your many kindnesses and goodness, I commend myself to you, and thank you again for all you have done on behalf of Jenfra.

Josue Roebertis
by the hand of the Lay Brother Baude

At Constanz in the Duchy of Swabia, on this 29th day of August, in the Lord's Year 1348.

2

Around him the trees were bare, not from winter, but from the cruelty of war: English soldiers had chopped the branches from the trees not only to provide fuel for their fires, but to get rid of any hiding places the forest might provide their opponents. Under the leaden sky, the wind evoked no rustling as it passed, only a strange humming sound as the trunks quivered. Germain le-Comte lowered his head and raised the hood of his balandras against the coming storm while he pulled on the lead, feeling Caesar's protestation in the resistance on the rope. To provide some sense of companionship, he spoke to the donkey. "You want to be out of this place as much as I do; you are holding back only because you cannot believe it will ever end."

The shaggy donkey brayed in distress but began to walk more willingly. His long ears angled about as he struggled to catch every sound on the wind.

Germain le-Comte could feel the storm rising as he walked, and he was aware that Caesar sensed it, too. "We will find shelter tonight. You and I will not have to brave the gale as sailors must at sea." He recalled the shipwreck that had left him stranded on the shores of the Baltic, four centuries ago, and he grieved anew for Ranegonda, who had succored him; his failure to protect her in battle still rankled with him.

It was raining heavily and night was almost upon them when Germain le-Comte and his donkey finally reached the edge of the stripped forest;

they found themselves on the banks of a swollen river with a ruined bridge to mock them; on the far side was a small village, its houses closed against the night and the recollection of the English.

Germain le-Comte went up to the edge of the river, the vitiating might of its rising waters increasing his hunger. It would not be possible to cross the river tonight, or any time soon; he had no doubt that the villagers had isolated themselves in order to keep the Great Dying from reaching them.

"We will have to look further," said Germain le-Comte, feeling worn-out by this admission. He tugged on the lead, and, after a perfunctory resistance, the shaggy donkey went along with him, the cart he pulled groaned as the mud around its wheels became deeper.

A short while later they came upon a large, partially covered communal grave. Germain le-Comte stopped beside it. "Well, there must be survivors not far from here, and empty houses to stay in." The last he said with sadness, no touch of irony in his words. "It won't be much longer, Caesar, before you are warm and resting." He did not mention food, for he realized he might have to forage for the donkey; when villages were fled, those leaving often took everything with them, and food for dray animals was a necessity. The night was dark, with the rain clouds blotting out the stars and the blowing rain itself obscuring the shapes in the night around them; even Germain le-Comte's eyes, which were not often troubled by darkness, could not easily pierce the obumbration: he could make out the road ahead and the blowing trees and undergrowth, but he could achieve no sharply defined sight. "We'll find what we're seeking soon enough," he said to the donkey.

Some short distance onward, they came to a shrine marking a crossroad; there were graves here, too, four of them, where criminals and the ungodly were buried face-down to ensure they would not be called to Heaven when the Last Judgment sounded. Germain le-Comte paused to peer along the roadways and saw in the distance the outlines of a small fortress, possibly a border post or supply station for soldiers. "Come along, Caesar." He could feel his own weariness in each step; the next day he would have to rest on one of the crates of his native earth to restore himself, for it was highly unlikely he would find anyone he could rouse in dreams to assuage his esurience, not in that place, not in this night.

The door of the fortress was barred; Germain le-Comte hoped this was a favorable sign as he reached for the bell-rope to summon the keepers within; he would not let himself think they had died, or were so gone in fever they would not hear or answer any summons but Death's. Listening to the harsh clang, he put his attention on moving Caesar and the cart into the lee of the gate, beneath the broad crenelated overhead. Then he pulled the bell-rope again, doing his utmost not to be discouraged.

Beyond the planks of the gate, there was a sound, a rattle and a curse, which were more welcome than a consort of musicians playing in harmony. "It's the dead of night!" came a harsh voice from the gate-house window; the speaker was a mature man by the sound of his voice, one who often shouted orders. "Who comes?"

"I am Germain le-Comte," he said, continuing in the accent of the region. "I am a troubador seeking a place to rest myself and my donkey for a day or two."

"And a little occasion to sing," was the quick response. "We can't turn a troubador away, not yet, in any case." The speaker sighed noisily. "Our sergeant will have to make sure you bring no Blood Roses."

"Fair enough," said Germain le-Comte.

"And you'll have to sing for your supper, but you're used to that, I suppose." Chuckling to himself, the speaker began to work the noisy crank that opened the gate. "Stand clear, troubador."

Germain le-Comte stepped back and was rewarded with a steady trickle of cold water on his shoulder. He waited patiently until the opening was wide enough to admit him, Caesar, and the cart.

The courtyard inside the gate was stone-paved and small; the single largest part of the enclosure was a series of box stalls along one side of the open area. This was a remount station, then, where fresh horses and supplies could be had. It was at least two centuries old, but its location must have made it useful during the recent English wars; Germain le-Comte stopped in the middle of the courtyard, Caesar beside him, the cart far enough forward to allow the gate to be closed behind it.

As soon as the gate was shut, a man of middle years in an old acton came out of the gate-house, a torch in one hand, a sword in the other. "So, Germain le-Comte, if that is your name—"

"It is," he answered, thinking it was as good as any other he might claim. "I am bound to the north."

"I should think so," said the man. "They are all dying in the south." He looked over Germain le-Comte. "Well, you're dressed like a troubador, right enough, and that donkey cart is fitting to the work." He gestured with the sword-point. "Get on with you."

Germain le-Comte paused. "If you would allow me to stable and feed my animal first, I would be grateful. He has covered many leagues and deserves—"

"Yes, yes, all right," said the man. "Take the fifth stall along. Leave the cart outside the stall. No one will touch it, and no one will bother your donkey. There is fodder in the manger and a pail of water. When you are done, come to the hall opposite the gate. If you fail to come, I will find you, which will be unfortunate for you."

"I will come when the donkey is groomed enough to be left," said Germain le-Comte.

"You are the guest of Armandal d'Ais, Duc de Verviers; his lady-wife and his second son are in this fortress. You will owe your thanks to them." He made another movement of his sword. "Go about your chores, troubador," he ordered.

"That I will," said Germain le-Comte, and led Caesar toward the stall; the donkey swiveled his huge ears and gave a single bray; he was answered with whinnies, which seemed to satisfy him. He went willingly to the stall, pausing only to make a single, long inhale as he crossed the threshold. Germain le-Comte stopped Caesar and unhitched the cart as quickly as he could; he backed the cart out of the stall, took out the small tackbox in the cart, then came back, where Caesar was already munching on the hay in the manger; ordinarily the donkey would have been reprimanded for eating without permission, but tonight all Germain le-Comte did was give him a cuff on the neck before he began to comb the shaggy animal. "This is going to be cursory at best," he apologized as he worked. "I will groom you properly tomorrow."

The donkey whuffled and went on eating; he was warm and fed and not neglected, which satisfied him down to his hooves.

When Germain le-Comte emerged from the stall, he went where he had been told to go, and found himself in a square stone room with shuttered windows and a big fireplace with a length of log aflame in it. There were four long, plank tables set up, benches on either side of the tables; near the fireplace was a smaller table with chairs, clearly intended for the commanding officer of the fortress. The man who had admitted Germain le-Comte was standing before that table, half-blocking the woman who sat in one of the chairs. "I am at your disposal, wife of Armandal d'Ais," Germain le-Comte said as he came forward and went down on his knee to the woman.

She half-rose as she turned tired, sea-green eyes on him, her gorget and wimple framing her face in white; the goffering of her wimple was limp as was the collar of her beluque of boiled wool with triangular French sleeves over the chemise of simple linen; she had too much chin and too strong a brow for beauty in the current mode, but Germain le-Comte knew she would have been thought stunning in the Rome of Julius and Vespasianus Caesar; no older than thirty, her body was unfashionably voluptuous, with full breasts and a neat waist: she had the bearing of privilege and maturity as well as the burdens of her position which marked her demeanor. She nudged the sleeve of the soldier, murmuring, "Oh; the troubador. Give me a moment with him, Villard. And tell me how Sergeant Michonet is doing. I am grieved to learn he is ill."

"No reason to fret; he has no Blood Roses. His fever brings neither raving nor dancing." The man bowed. "There are other maladies than the Plague." He nodded toward the door, "I will be just outside, my lady." He gave a warning glance to Germain le-Comte as if he expected this late arrival to attempt something desperate.

"As you wish, Villard; I will call if I require your help. A pity Michonet is ill, and the priest left us yesterday, but I know what must be done," she said with quiet authority, and looked at Germain le-Comte, showing real attention for the first time. "You may rise, troubador," she said to Germain le-Comte as Villard passed him on his way to the door.

Germain le-Comte got to his feet and waited for her to signal permission to approach.

"Oh, for God's Nails," she said with an impatient shake of her head. "We are not at court; you need not maintain such ceremony with me, troubador, not in this place." She made a wan smile. "I may ask you to sing for me: tomorrow, not tonight; you will want to rest from your travels."

Germain le-Comte gave her a short bow as he came to the table; the heat from the fire was welcome and made his hands tingle as warmth returned. "It will be my pleasure, my lady—?"

"I am Heugenet da Brabant. My husband is Armandal d'Ais, Duc de Verviers. His mother is still alive; I am not the Ducesse." She recited this without any inflection; she had either said it often or she had her mind on other things; at least that was what Germain le-Comte assumed as he bent to kiss her fingertips with the gallantry of the Tuscan or Roman courts.

"I am Germain le-Comte; I have come from the south in the company of players; they are bound for other regions now." He looked directly into her eyes, although it was socially audacious to do so. "Thank you for receiving a traveler on this night."

Heugenet did not reprimand him for his stare. "It would be a poor Christian who would turn away a traveler."

"In these times, it is more the rule, Christian or not," said Germain le-Comte. "And I know in these times you will have to assure yourself that I do not bring Blood Roses."

"You will have to undress completely," she said brusquely. "I will be as swift as I can."

"I understand," Germain le-Comte told her, doing his best to make the trial less uncomfortable for them both. "Circumstances impose on us all."

"Yes; as you may have heard, I have no priest with me here to attend to it, and my Sergeant is ill, so . . ." She finished her thought with a turn of her hand. "Villard will preserve our modesty."

Germain le-Comte nodded twice. "I should warn you I have scars."

"What man does not?" she responded, unimpressed. "Troubadours and jongleurs have their battles as knights and soldiers do." She made a point of staring at the far wall with an air of complete fascination.

As he unfastened his clothes and climbed out of them, Germain le-Comte noticed again how cold the room was where the heat of the fire did not reach. He was down to his chamisa—his last item of clothing—before he spoke again. "I will remove this now."

Heugenet blinked as if recalled from deep thought. "Very well." She rose and came toward him, standing an arm's length away as he lifted his chamisa. She made a point of looking past him so that she would do nothing more than touch him, which was difficult enough; she could not entirely ignore his physical presence which confused her.

Tossing the chamisa aside, Germain le-Comte remained with his arms lifted so that as she came up to him she could touch his armpits to be certain there were no swellings there. Her fingers were firm and her examination was quick and thorough; armpits, neck, behind his ears. She extended her exploration to his chest; he could feel her sudden expulsion of breath on his skin. "I told you I was scarred," he said quietly, for she had faltered at the wide swath of white tissue that began at the base of his ribs and continued down the width of his abdomen to his groin.

She swallowed. "I will have to touch the scars. I pray I will not pain you."

"They are very old," he said, adding inwardly, thirty-three centuries old.

"Then you will have forgiven the wretch who did this to you," she said, a suggestion of uncertainty in her statement. "Haven't you?" she prompted when he did not answer at once.

He gave a swift, bemused smile. "I suppose I have. I was much younger when it was done." He regarded her with new interest. "Why should it matter to you?"

She shook her head. "Only that the sin against you was very great. And for the sake of your soul, you should not harbor hatred in your heart."

This unanticipated reply held his attention. "I do not," he assured her.

"They are . . . very bad." Then recalling her purpose, she added, "And they are not all I will have to touch—" She glanced at his penis. "To be sure you have no—"

"Blood Roses," he finished for her. "I understand."

"Then you will not—" Whatever it was she feared she might do she did not express; instead she continued with her inspection impersonally; she touched him without any hint of titillation, but was shamed that she did so as an act of will, not a matter of virtue. When she stepped back, she said, as if to account for her response to him, "Your height is not great; your bearing is straight and your shoulders have good breadth. You have a deep chest and well-muscled legs. That must come from walking."

"Troubadors and jongleurs walk many leagues," he said. "May I put my clothes on?"

Her cheeks turned scarlet. "Yes. I will not watch."

Under the circumstances this seemed unnecessary, but he realized she was eager to reestablish the barriers between them, so he said, "You are kind to a stranger; I am grateful to you." He picked up his chamisa and pulled it over his head and reached for the rest of his clothes in the untidy heap where he had dropped them.

Although she did not look at him, she said, "You must have seen much, coming here from the south." She ought to put more space between them, she knew, but it was an effort to move beyond the unexpected comfort of his nearness.

"Yes." He continued to dress.

"They say it is very bad in the south." She did not have to specify what "it" was.

"Bad enough," he said quietly. "The cities fare worst of all, but it is hard everywhere. And it will get harder. The sickness ravages now, famine will come after."

"Many have come here, trying to escape the Great Dying. Not only peasants, but any who could escape. You would travel, in any case— troubadors do, don't they?—but for others, who have never been more than two leagues from their own doorway—" She paused as if uncertain how to continue. "You . . . have lost . . ."

"Friends," he responded when she did not go on. It was a safe answer, and accurate.

"I see," she said in some confusion. "You did not—"

"I have neither wife nor children, good lady: those who live as I do rarely do; my father and mother died long ago. And in these dreadful times, I have been glad of it." He spoke levelly without displaying grief or anger.

There was real relief in Heugenet's voice. "They have been spared this terrible . . . I have four sons and my husband alive still; I fear for them and my daughters every day. My brother died two months ago, with two of his daughters and one son, and my mother is ill. My youngest brother is in Holy Orders and so far he has been spared, as have two of my nephews and a niece, though my sister has . . . I have been thankful that my father died in battle at Cresy, that he did not live to see what has become of us all." She crossed herself. "I pray for them, all of them, but God will do His Will."

Germain le-Comte felt a pang of sympathy; he finished dressing and turned toward her. "May He be merciful."

"Amen, troubador," she said with feeling. Her voice dropped. "Though His Mercy may mean a swift death instead of life." She stared past his shoulder. "I do not know why I tell you these things."

"I hope you do not say such things to your Confessor," Germain le-Comte said with a quick, ironic smile.

"It is heretical, I know. But when so many die and die and die, what can I think?" She returned to her chair. "I don't know what made me say that. It must be the lateness of the hour." Her faint laughter was unconvincing. "One cannot answer for thoughts that come when one should be asleep, for they are the stuff of dreams."

"So they are." He watched her in silence, then said, "I will not speak of it; nor of any other thing you would rather I would not."

She blinked at him as if he had said something remarkable. "A trouba-dor—and a bastard—with honor." Germain le-Comte offered her an old-fashioned reverence but said nothing to her; she regarded him with curiosity. "Is it hard, to be a troubador?"

"Easier than some things I have done, more demanding than others," he answered, deeply aware of her scrutiny.

"So you have not always been a troubador?" She could not look away from him.

"No; not always," he answered honestly.

Other questions awakened in her, but she suppressed them; this man was a stranger and his connections might be noble enough, but they were not legitimate, and she could not assume he would keep his word, no matter how courteously given. Yet his dark eyes were fascinating and his presence impressed her as few men had; this recognition troubled her and she told herself it was the precarious world in which they found themselves that made her want to know more about him. Her gaze wavered; she vowed she would not let herself be drawn to him.

"Is something the matter, Heugenet da Brabant?" He was standing just across the table from her, his features set in an expression of concern.

"Nothing," she lied. "I am very tired and Sergeant Michonet's condition worries me," she went on. "You cannot be surprised that this should be so."

"No, I cannot be," he agreed as he thought back to all he had seen since he left Clair dela Luna, and of the devastation he had encountered in other places over the centuries.

In spite of her resolve not to she looked at him directly. "If Sergeant Michonet is unable to travel, I will have to resume my journey without him the day after tomorrow; I cannot delay for longer than that." She found it impossible to listen to herself, for she could not be proposing such a thing to this troubador with a bastard's name. "I do not know where you are bound, but I can see you have a place to winter if you would join the escort for me and my son. If," she added carefully, "Sergeant Michonet is unable to travel."

"Is he your only escort? What of Villard?" Germain le-Comte asked, masking his surprise at her suggestion; he did not know why she was making such a suggestion.

"Villard mans this place for my husband; he will not leave with us. He has two men to remain here with him. There were ten last year, but our ranks are much reduced and my husband cannot spare more men for these outposts—" She stopped, reminding herself she need provide no explanations to this stranger with the compelling eyes. "I have an escort of four for my second son and me."

"The four includes Sergeant Michonet?" Germain le-Comte guessed.

"Yes." She studied the grain of the wood of the table. "I am told you have a donkey and a cart. Can you ride a horse?"

"Yes, I can ride," he said without pride.

"Then will you—" She stared up at him and chided herself for being intrigued by him.

"I will come with you, but I will bring my donkey and the cart he pulls. My instruments and clothes are in that cart and I cannot leave them behind." There were also chests filled with his native earth and the red lacquer chest containing his medicaments, which he refused to leave here. He studied the angle of her head. "If you will allow that, you may command me if you have need of me."

"How do you mean?" she challenged, feeling the heat rise in her face.

"Only that Sergeant Michonet may recover and you will not require my escort," he said, the kindness in his voice taking away any sting his words might have had.

Heugenet did what she could to restore her composure, puzzled why this troubador was so disconcerting: she had seen attractive men before, and known those with inherent authority, but this Germain le-Comte was different; she had never met anyone with such self-composure who was not also indifferent to the world around him, yet Germain le-Comte had none of that aloofness. She decided she must not think about him. "Yes; he may recover. His fever will break and his pain will ease." She glanced at the fire which was no longer as fine as it had been. "The fire is dying. This room will be cold soon."

"Then you will want to seek your bed," Germain le-Comte said, and saw her head come up and her mouth turn down indignantly.

"What do you mean?" she demanded, her posture very straight. She could not allow him such liberty, even in jest; she put her hands flat on the table and prepared to rise. "How am I to take such license? What do you intend by such—"

He stepped back and reverenced her again. "Why, that it is cold and I, for one, am weary from the road. I would not demean your consideration with any compromise: believe this."

"But you said—" She broke off. "No, I cannot lay the blame on you," she told him.

"If I gave you any cause for offense, I apologize," he said. "I would not want you to think I have no regard for you; that would be fine thanks for your hospitality."

She made a sudden gesture as if to wipe away a stain. "It is for me to ask your pardon," she said with meticulous courtesy. "I fear the demands of our travels have left me uncivil."

"Where there is no injury pardon is not necessary," Germain le-Comte said, and prepared to leave the room.

"Tomorrow I will tell you when we will leave. It will be the day after, but I have not yet decided upon the time." She was saying things to keep him in the room with her; she recognized this and was powerless to stop herself.

"As you wish," said Germain le-Comte. "I fear I will not rise early tomorrow."

"No. It is late and you have traveled far." She continued to stare at him, many questions in her sea-green eyes.

He dropped to his knee again. "You have done me much courtesy, Heugenet da Brabant; I am truly grateful."

"So you have told me," she said, her voice catching in her throat.

"And I am at your service." He rose. "You have but to name my task."

It took her a moment to answer. "For now, I wish God will send you a pleasant sleep and a healthy waking."

He put his hand on the latch. "May your dreams be sweet." Then he let himself out before she could find another excuse for him to linger. He nodded to Villard.

"No Blood Roses?" the soldier asked.

"None were found," Germain le-Comte said carefully, then added, "I will sleep in the stall with my donkey and my cart. There is ample room for all."

Villard shrugged. "If you would like that better than a cot in the barracks, well enough. Will you need bedding?"

"I carry what I need for rest," said Germain le-Comte, who did not want to take the risk of sleeping in a room with soldiers where his chests might give rise to questions he would prefer not to answer; a night spent on the chests filled with his native earth would do much to restore him, and Caesar would not mind the company.

"I suppose wanderers like you must do," Villard said without much interest. "Then I wish you a good night, troubador."

"And I you, soldier," was his quick response before he strode away across the courtyard to the safety of the box-stall, the warmth of Caesar and the protection of his native earth.

Text of two letters from Germain le-Comte to Atta Olivia Clemens and his manservant Rogres, both in Latin, written in multiple copies on linen and dispatched with various carriers; the letter to Olivia was delivered in January of 1349; the letter to Rogres was delivered in March and May of 1349.

To my treasured Olivia, my greetings from the north of France, fourfold. I trust one of the quartet of copies I am sending by various messengers will reach you; in these days, I cannot believe it will be possible that all four will reach you.

So that you will not fret, I am in the north of France, still bound for the Low Countries, although I may winter near Maissin, for I have received an invitation from Armandal d'Ais, Duc de Verviers and his wife Heugenet da Brabant to be one of their company at the castle of Sant-Brede; the castle was not sacked by the English and many of the nobles in the region are going to gather there for strategy and what they hope is safety.

You must know the Black Plague continues its advance. Although I have seen nothing to equal what I found in Marsailla, the loss of life is staggering. The Plague has not claimed them all—starvation, exhaustion, fanaticism, and despair have taken their tolls as well, and will continue to do so as the Plague recedes.

I thank you for sheltering Rogerian for me; no doubt you will have excoriated my character between you by now, and not without cause:

nonetheless with warrants out for our deaths I know we both have a bet-ter chance of surviving apart, and where would he find a finer haven than with you? The warrant for our deaths does stipulate man and servant; so long as we were together, our danger was greater: apart, we have much greater safety, each of us. And before you chide me for being separated from the world, let me assure you that I have not held myself isolated as much as I might have. In the midst of this catastrophe, I discover I am drawn to Heugenet da Brabant and she to me. I had not anticipated this would happen, but since it has, I will not turn away from it.

With that for what consolation it may be, I send you my continuing love and my vow by all the forgotten gods that I will come to you as soon as my work here is done and the danger to my life and Rogerian's is past.

Know this carries my fondest love and my gratitude.

Sanct' Germain
(his sigil, the eclipse)

By my own hand, four copies, on the 29th day of October, 1348, on the road to Sant-Brede.

and

To Rogerian, with the assurance that I know your fealty is beyond what I deserve, my greetings;

As the winter closes in I can find it in my heart to covet your place with Olivia; cold as it has been in Provence it is colder here in the north. If you are still vexed with me, mitigate your exasperation with the knowledge that you will not have to wade through snows in a month or so, and con-tinue wading for three months at least.

It is possible that the severity of the winter will slow down the progress of the Plague; you and I have seen such things before. But I am not san-guine, for the people do not want to take the measures needed to rid their houses of vermin, and that may be the only means of arresting the out-breaks, for where there are vermin, there is pestilence also.

I will be in the Lowlands in the spring, and from there I will inform you when I plan to come south and east to join you at Olivia's estate. By that time, I will certainly long for respite from all I have seen. You need not be semi-immortal, as you and those of my blood are, to feel compassion for the suffering of those besieged by the Plague, or to feel helpless in the face of their plight. As you have reminded me many times, I have an obligation to life; all of my blood do.

As you and Olivia will undoubtedly compare what I have told you, I will add that while I am at Sant-Brede I will be there at the behest of Arman-dal d'Ais and his wife Heugenet da Brabant. They are at Sant-Brede with their second son, who has spasms of the lungs and for whom his mother is very worried, fearing, and not without cause, that the Plague might more easily claim him than some others of more hale constitutions.

The warrant for our execution is still in effect, but you and I are no longer the primary enemy, though I have no reservation in saying that we would be rigorously hunted were we to be discovered; I have witnessed the ferocity of what passes for justice now; I have no wish to tempt fate by being apprehended as Sieur Ragoczy.

With my thanks and commending myself to your and Olivia's good opinions once again,

Ragoczy Saint-Germain
(his sigil, the eclipse)

By my own hand on the 29th day of October, 1348, on the road to Sant-Brede.

3

Grinning wickedly, Armandal d'Ais reached for a wedge of cheese and threw it at the juggler who was striving to keep two tankards, a dagger, and a pewter platter in the air; the cheese struck him in the small of the back and he dropped the dagger while all the guests at the dinner tables laughed as they had not laughed for the sharp-tongued jester who had come before the juggler. Of the forty-three guests at table, only eleven were above the salt; the rest were below, making do with ale where the eleven drank wine, and with pea-and-onion soup while the eleven had fish and venison in their chicken broth.

A shout of approval went up for Armandal d'Ais, who acknowledged this with drinking the general health of the company. "And to our hosts, our heartfelt gratitude. For those of us who have lost so much to the English, this visitation of Blood Roses has made the assistance of our peers a necessity instead of a courtesy. I give you Yves Roueleur, Comte de Sant-Brede."

"Sant-Brede," the rest echoed before drinking.

From his place in the minstrels' gallery, Germain le-Comte watched these antics without much humor; he had spoken to the juggler earlier and knew the man had wrenched his shoulder two days ago and was trying not to succumb to the pain of it; while Armandal d'Ais knew nothing of this injury, Germain le-Comte supposed that if he had, it would have made no difference to him. He touched the strings of his mandola very lightly to be certain they were holding pitch: when the meat was brought in, he had been ordered to begin his songs.

Yves Roueleur threw back his head and bellowed laughter. "You have a way, d'Ais," he declared, finding it difficult to speak through his mirth. He was somewhat younger than Armandal d'Ais—in his mid-thirties, showing signs of hard fighting—but he had amassed sufficient wealth, even in time of war, to make his castle as luxurious as any in the north of Europe, and his wardrobe elegant beyond what his rank would usually display. He clearly relished being able to entertain in a manner beyond what those of higher position could afford.

As a woman of noble birth, Heugenet da Brabant was allowed to sit with her husband in spite of her lack of the title held by his mother; she was one of three women at the high table and she felt conspicuous. She had put on her best cotehardie—vine-embroidered over bronze-and-copper brocade with grapes worked in green and gold—and the small jeweled crucifix that her husband had given her after the birth of their oldest son; she was nowhere near as grand as the Comtesse de Sant-Brede, who was a lovely girl half the age of her husband, in a magnificent houppelande of dark-peach-colored samite with vast, dagged sleeves lined in red fox-fur. She was awkward with her advanced pregnancy. Heugenet smiled automatically as Armandal tossed a small, hard roll to the juggler; she could think of nothing to say; a year ago she would have found this as funny as the rest, but now she was unable to laugh at what seemed petty and thoughtless. She drank more of the wine that had been poured for her, hoping her heart would lighten.

The juggler recovered and added the roll to the other items he was juggling; only the sheen of sweat on his face revealed that this was not just another game to him.

"Very good, very good," said the old priest who was serving as bishop in the region; after years in humble service, his advancement was going to his head. His lean cheeks were flushed with wine and his every move and statement was exaggerated. Seated beside Yves Roueleur, he was basking in the distinction of the occasion. "The juggler is accomplished."

"That he is," said Yves Roueleur. He clapped his hands and the steward came to refill the wine goblets. "Where is the meat?" he asked in a furious whisper.

"Shortly, mon Comte," said the steward. "We must do what we can to present it as you would wish. Two boars and three goats are not easily carried." He endured the box on his ear with the stoic air of one who has had much worse done to him.

"I want them served as soon as possible. Do you understand me?" Yves Roueleur glared at the steward. "My guests should not be made to wait for their food."

"We can bring out the baked cheeses now," the steward suggested, managing not to cringe while he waited for the Comte de Sant-Brede to make up his mind.

"Oh, very well; the cheese it will be," Yves Roueleur decided aloud. He reached for his goblet, which was larger than the others, with jewels in the base; he drank deeply while the steward retreated.

The juggler was visibly tiring now; he dropped the platter and was hooted at for clumsiness.

"D'Ais," called out Yves Roueleur, "is that troubador of yours ready to sing? I don't want this oaf to cut off his toes, which he may do if he goes on." His words were a bit too crisp.

"I am sure he is," said Armandal d'Ais, glancing toward the gallery. "I can have him begin whenever you like."

"Well enough," said the host. "Let him begin now, and for Marie's Tits, let him sing something spritely. I am tired of all these plaints and laments and dirges." He motioned to Germain le-Comte in the gallery. "Tell me you know such a song."

From his place above the diners, Germain le-Comte answered. "I do. But two are in the Tuscan dialect and one is in English." It was a bold move, to say this among these people who had battled the English and who distrusted the Italian peoples almost as much as they distrusted the Germans.

"Let's have the English first. We know how to deal with them," the priest called out, and laughed more energetically than the others who had fought them.

This was met with a roar of endorsement, as well as a few derisive whistles; Yves Roueleur slapped the table with his hand. "Yes. The English, and then the Tuscan."

Germain le-Comte inclined his head and set his fingers to the strings of his mandola. "The song is in praise of Our Lady," he said. The melody was limpid and sweet, almost a love-song. It was the second verse that was the most courtly, having more to do with homage to the old goddess of spring:

> *Thu asteye so the daiy-rewe*
> *The deleth from the derke nicht.*
> *Of thee sprong a leome newe*
> *That al this world ilicht.*
> *Nis no maide of thine hewe*
> *So fair, so scheene, so rudi, so bricht,*
> *Mi swete levdi of me thu rewe*
> *And have merci of thi knicht.*

As he sang, Germain le-Comte looked at Heugenet da Brabant, catching her eyes at the last two lines of the verse which he addressed to her: *my sweet lady, show me compassion and have mercy on thy knight.* The end of the next verse he also directed to her:

> *Levdi milde, soft and swoot,*
> *Ich crie thi merci, ich am thi mon*

Bothen to honde and to foot
On alle wise that ich kon.

Kind and gentle lady, I beg thee pity me, I am thy man, hand and foot,
every way I can be. He finished the next two verses without glancing at her
again. There was grudging approval of the song, the reservation coming
from it being English and not Germain le-Comte's performance.

"Just what we wanted. Sweet," Yves Roueleur approved, his slight frown
fading from his forehead. "No gloom, no complaining about anything."
He clapped twice. "This time choose something more amusing. Something not English."

"Yes. Don't you know anything merry in French?" Armandal d'Ais asked
loudly, wanting to show his command over the troubador he had brought
to Sant-Brede.

"I know a song, an old one, that might suffice," Germain le-Comte
answered, thinking back almost a century to the first time he had heard
the song, far away from France, sung by a merchant traveling to Constantinople.

"Let's have it, then, so long as it's French," Yves Roueleur ordered, emphasizing his demand by banging his goblet down on the table. "Old, new,
it hardly matters."

Germain le-Comte chose a brisker pace than the music originally called
for, and began:

> *Le mont Aon de Thrace, doulz pais*
> *Ou resonnent les doucours d'armonie,*
> *A en sa court nuef dames de haut pris*
> *Qui de beaute tiennent la seygnourie . . .*

He improvised variations on the melody between each verse while the
guests below him were served baked cheese and more wine and ale were
poured. Occasionally he gave Heugenet a swift perusal, seeing she was
worried and preoccupied, disinclined to lose herself in the revels as so
many of the others were.

When, a short while later, a number of scullions and footmen staggered
in bearing spits supported between them on their shoulders on which
whole boars and goats had been roasted; the goats were for those below the
salt, the boars for those above. Setting up iron holders for the spits, the servants made way for three cooks whose job it was to slice off meat for the
guests; they looked shiny and hot as the meat they were serving. In good
times this would have been extravagant fare, but now, with the English so
recently fled and the Great Dying spreading everywhere, a lavish meal
like this was as astonishing as it was rare. The boars had been basted in
pepper and saffron, a gesture intended to reveal wealth as much as the nature of the meal, and the smell of the meat and spices filled the hall,

reawakening appetites and luring the hunting dogs who lay in the shadows out to beg.

There was a scramble as scullions and footmen tried to get the meat out to the diners as quickly as possible. Occasionally one of the dogs would make a snap at the roast carcasses and earn a kick for his attempt.

"Well, go on, troubador," called out Armandal d'Ais. "The meat is here, and you are supposed to show it honor. Sing something grand."

So while the diners fed on boar and goat, Germain le-Comte sang in strophic Latin about the fall of Troy, amusing himself with the knowledge that only he knew this was what Nero had sung—in classic Greek—to Rome while the city burned. When the next course was brought in—stew that was mostly onions and cabbage for those below the salt, braised venison with leeks garnished with crab apples above—he stopped playing and watched the tumblers who were next to entertain.

The meal was almost finished when a servant went to Heugenet and said something to her that made her turn pale. She spoke hurriedly to her husband, then rose and left the banquet; from his place in the minstrels' gallery, Germain le-Comte watched her with growing concern. Whatever the servant had told Heugenet had been troubling enough to take her out of the hall without ceremony, circumstances that must be unusual to cause her to risk offending the host by her departure.

Knowing that speculation accomplished nothing, he decided to leave the gallery—he was not expected to sing again that evening—and made his way down to the main floor, hoping to find where Heugenet had gone. The servants of the castle were busy with their chores; few noticed him as he continued his search. Finally, more by accident than design, he came upon a small room in the wing of the castle where the guests were housed; he heard Heugenet's voice and stopped to listen.

". . . he is so weak. To take more blood might—" she was saying, her voice low and distressed.

"The child must be bled. If he is not, the poisonous humors will accumulate in him and he will be carried off." The speaker's accent was rough and uneducated, but very determined.

"How much blood will you have to take to end his coughing?" Heugenet asked with difficulty.

There was a pause and then the man said, "I will not know until I see the color of it."

To underscore the urgency, there was a muffled eruption of coughing, followed by a brief, exhausted moan.

Whatever the churigeon would have responded was silenced by Germain le-Comte's quick rap on the door. "Lady Heugenet," he said. "It's—"

"I know who it is," she said, coming to open the door; she peered out at him. "What do you want?"

He had not decided how he would explain himself, or his purpose. "I saw you leave the hall and I was concerned for you." He knew she wanted him to go away, but he remained. "If there is anything I might do to help?"

"Can songs stop coughing?" she asked, curt without apology.

"No," said Germain le-Comte. "But I have come upon some compounds during my travels that can be of use." Now that he had hit upon the means to deal with this problem, he went on, "Those who live by their voices quickly learn how to treat coughs."

This remark was sensible enough to command Heugenet's attention. She stared at him. "Yes." Her interest increased. "Do you mean you may have something that could help my son?"

He saw how desperate she was to have any remedy offered to her on the boy's behalf; this made his response more cautious than it might have been at another time. "I have something that may ease his breathing: I have known it to succeed in similar cases," he told her gently. "If he does not improve, the churigeon can always bleed him again."

"Yes, yes. But this might be tried first and spare him bleeding?" She opened the door a bit wider. "What do you require?"

"The compound is with my cart. I will go fetch it, and return as quickly as I am able." This was not quite the truth; he was capable of moving at speeds that would attract more attention than he wanted and lead to questions he would not be able to answer. "Do not let him be bled, not yet." He looked directly into her eyes.

"No. I will wait." Her face, tight with anxiety, softened as she returned his stare. "This is very kind of you."

"No, Heugenet," he said. "Not kind." He turned away and hastened down the corridor to the staircase that would take him down to the level of the stable. Once he found Caesar's stall where the cart as well as the donkey had been put, he unloaded the red lacquer chest and took out a small ceramic flask and a sachet of mugwort and valerian. With a fleeting pat to the donkey, he left the stall, taking care to close it. He shoved the sachet into the base of his big, square sleeve and put the flask into the leather wallet that hung on his belt, then made for the stairs at a jog.

The churigeon was glowering at Heugenet when Germain le-Comte returned to the room. "He's a mountebank, I tell you. You'll do the boy more harm than good letting that one at him."

"I said I would permit—" She broke off as Germain le-Comte closed the door behind him. "Saint Agatha, you startled me."

"I've brought what may help your boy." He held out the two things he carried. "If you will take me to him?"

"Poisons and potions, poisons and potions," muttered the churigeon, holding up his basin as if it were a shield. "You abuse this good lady, you scoundrel."

Germain le-Comte looked at the lumpy, red-face fellow and felt a mix of pity and contempt for him. "If I fail, you may denounce me," he said, his air of quiet authority silencing the churigeon and bringing a look of dawning esteem to Heugenet's face. "Where is the boy?"

"In the alcove by the fire; he has been cold," she said quietly. "You have not met him, though you have seen him," she went on as she led him toward the fireplace.

"Yes. But he knows who I am," said Germain le-Comte. "That is not important now." The bed on which the boy lay was small and narrow, squeezed in next to the side of the fireplace. The corner was dark which did not hamper Germain le-Comte's vision; he saw the boy under a heap of fur rugs, his face pinched with the effort to exhale. It was precisely the malady Germain le-Comte had supposed it was, and he knew the medicaments he carried would treat it if the boy had not developed an inflammation of the lungs. He approached the boy as best he could, leaning down toward the bed to inspect his face. "I will need a basin of hot water and a cup of wine," he said over his shoulder.

"Wine?" the churigeon scoffed. "How do you think to use wine on such a boy?"

"I intend I should put a tincture in it and that he should drink it," said Germain le-Comte calmly as if this treatment, and not the churigeon's, was the standard one. "Then I want him to inhale the steam of hot herbs." He glanced at Heugenet. "Send a servant for these things, if you will."

She moved slowly, as if emerging from sleep. "A cup of wine and a basin of hot water?"

"Yes." He was studying the boy, listening to his labored breathing; he could sense the rapid beat of his heart. Though the light was low, he could see the pasty color of the child's skin, and touched his hand, finding it too cool and the palm clammy. "Have patience, boy," he said, realizing he had not been told the child's name.

The boy tried to say something and fell to coughing again; he fought the spasm, tears in his eyes from the effort.

"He has his mother's eyes," Germain le-Comte said in an undervoice.

"That he does, woe betide him," said the churigeon, who had taken it upon himself to watch the troubador while Heugenet summoned the servant. "It is ever unlucky for a boy to have women's eyes."

"Do you think so?" Germain le-Comte asked.

"It is known by everyone, and you may see it borne out often." He folded his arms and stared hard at Germain le-Comte's back.

The boy twisted in the bed trying to find a position in which he could breathe more easily. He managed to gasp out, "No Blood Roses."

"I know," said Germain le-Comte at his most soothing. "What bothers you is not Plague, it is another ailment."

The churigeon laughed once, the sound like the bark of a dog. "What do you think will become of him? He will be in the pits with the rest of the dead unless the poison is drained from his blood."

Germain le-Comte turned around and regarded the churigeon steadily.

"There is nothing wrong with his blood, but that you have taken too much of it already." He spoke quietly, his expression not quite angry. Then he gave his attention to the boy again.

"I was shriven . . . this morning," he said to Germain le-Comte. "If I die . . . God will . . . not refuse . . . to let . . ." His breathing became more strenuous.

"Do not fret," said Germain le-Comte, leaning forward to help steady the boy. "God always welcomes the innocent, which you surely are. I am going to treat you, and you will recover from your malady." He brushed the boy's lank hair back from his brow; as he did he realized he had never seen Heugenet's hair, though he supposed it must be mouse-colored, for her plucked eyebrows were that shade.

There was sudden activity behind them as two servants arrived with the wine and the basin of hot water; Heugenet admitted them and pointed them toward the fireplace which the servants were reluctant to approach.

"Tell them to put them down. I will want to work with them," said Germain le-Comte, and was rewarded with a quick smile from Heugenet, who came toward him, holding out the wine. "Would you rather have the basin first?" she asked as she did her best not to look worried.

"No; the wine first." He ignored the other man's glare.

"If you think best," she said, scrutinizing his actions as he took the flask out of his wallet, opened it with care and tipped half its contents into the wine, then stoppered the bottle and returned it to his wallet. "This should stop the coughing," he said, ignoring the snort of contempt from the churigeon.

"His name is Armand; he is twelve," she said quickly. "My oldest, who is being trained for fighting, is Bernard. He is currently in Trier." This confidence was welcome but unexpected; the names of noble male children were often kept secret until the child came of age or advanced to his father's dignities.

"Named for your husband's father, no doubt," said Germain le-Comte, his voice warm; he hoped she understood how he valued what she told him.

"Yes," she said, startled that he would know such a thing: she remembered then that his name implied his father was a noble, and she supposed even a bastard would know the traditions of names in noble families.

"Well, then, Armand," said Germain le-Comte, bending over and lifting the boy toward the cup, "if you will drink this, you will soon be over this spate of coughing." He tilted the cup to the boy's mouth and held him until most of the wine had been drunk. As he straightened up he handed the cup to Heugenet. "It should take effect shortly. When his coughing abates, take this sachet"—he retrieved it from his sleeve and pressed it into her hand—"and put it in the water; make sure it is still hot. When the steam begins to smell of the herbs, then have him sit over it with a cloth over his head so he will inhale all the virtue of the herbs."

"Yes. Very well. I will see to it," she said, concentrating on his instructions.

"He will be dead by tomorrow night," the churigeon predicted with a satisfaction that was out of place in the sickroom. "And he will have Blood Roses; you will see."

"No, he will not," said Germain le-Comte, and directed his next remarks to Heugenet. "He is ill; I will not deny that, but the ailment is not Black Plague. I would guess he has had this trouble for some time, perhaps even years?"

She nodded. "It began when he was in leading strings," she said, relieved that someone seemed to know what disease had taken hold of her son. "It has been getting worse of late. His Confessor said it showed weakness and has advised flagellation to drive out the Devil."

Germain le-Comte said nothing about this treatment, though his mouth thinned; he met her gaze steadily. "He will improve now, if he is strong enough."

Her eyes brimmed with tears. "Thank you, thank you."

The churigeon laughed unpleasantly. "Oh yes, thank him. For sending the boy to his grave."

Germain le-Comte directed his compelling gaze on the man. "If the boy dies, you may accuse me." As he turned back to Heugenet, it was as if the churigeon had been banished. "I will come again later, to see how he is doing."

"I will sit up with him," said Heugenet. "If he does not improve, or he becomes worse—?" The worry was back in her eyes even as she wiped them.

"I'll be in the stable, tending to Caesar," he said. "Any servant will find me there."

Her laughter was shaky. "Your ridiculous donkey. Of course."

His old-fashioned reverence earned another bark of laughter from the churigeon, though neither Germain le-Comte nor Heugenet heeded him. "I will return by midnight," he promised, reminding himself that he would have to visit one of the women in the castle in her sleep; he was briefly saddened that it would not be Heugenet.

"I will be waiting," she said, apprehension and hope warring in her face.

"So will I," the churigeon told them both.

Text of a letter from Eudoin Tissant to the Holy See at Avignon; carried by a procession of Weepers and delivered after High Mass ten days after it was written.

To the most august and worthy servants of His Holiness, this most humble of petitioners presents his pleas, wholly aware that they have the guidance of God and His Angels in this time of devastation, when the rest of Christianity is faltering on the brink of apostacy.

This village is insignificant, but the souls of those who still live here must be as precious to God as any in the Kingdom of France or the Holy Roman Empire, and it is on their behalf that I appeal to you to come to our aid in any manner that you can: we have lost many of our people to the Great Dying, which must be so throughout the whole of the world. Some of the peasants have run away, thinking to escape from the Plague in this way.

Of late, however, we have been subjected to the depredations of bands of wandering men who come with whips and flails to scourge the people of the village and to beat our few remaining priests and monks to death. We must have help if we are to keep these terrible marauders from coming again, and it is for this reason that I appeal to you, as the acting leader of the village, to succor us. If you could send us two or three armed knights, they would certainly be able to hold off anything the men with whips might attempt.

We are also now without anyone to celebrate Mass or to pray for those who have died. The people of the village are in despair and I can do little or nothing to assure them they have not been forgotten. I have explained that their harboring of that vile sorcerer, Francois de Saint-Germain, the so-called Sieur Ragoczy, has put them beyond most help, but I have promised them I would throw myself on your mercy on their behalf in the hope that you will find it within your Godly souls to send us your help, unworthy though the people have shown themselves to be. This pernicious foreigner has been gone for many months now, and the village has more than paid for the sin of receiving him into their midst. Those of us who warned them of the danger have been vindicated, and now it is fitting that the people of the village be shown pity.

The Weepers who carry this to you have already demonstrated their compassion by praying at the edge of the burial pit we have had to dig at the edge of the village. They have traveled far to show their grief and contrition to God, and we honor their piety. If any travelers should come here again, let it be more Weepers, not those processions of men scourging themselves and anyone who is ill-fated enough to encounter them in their wanderings. I beseech you to be moved by their devotion if not by my paltry words, to provide us some protection in this world and the next. We have come to know our sins and we repent them most sincerely; the contrition felt here should make the village an example to all those afflicted by the pestilence that has been visited upon us as well as renewing our dedication to God's Will.

I assure you that any act to guard us will not go unrewarded by those of us left in this village. The estate of the execrable Sieur Ragoczy has been seized and I am certain that the remaining authorities—led by me—would be pleased to dedicate the estate, which I have been tending, to the use of the Pope or any of his Court.

With my prayers that our plaints will not go unanswered, I sign myself, beneath the writing of my clerk, Egide the apothecary,

Eudoin Tissant
Village leader, Orgon

In Provence, of the Holy Roman Empire on the 10th day of November in the 1348th Year of Grace.

4

There was ice in the ruts of the road when Armandal d'Ais rode out with his men to patrol the countryside. Wind that raked the world with frigid tines made the brightness of the sky a mockery. The few birds that remained in this wintry place shot noisily into the sky as the hunters went into the woods.

Watching them from the window of her son's room, Heugenet da Brabant gave an affectionate shake to her head, and turned to Germain le-Comte, who stood behind her. "I am so grateful that my father chose Armandal d'Ais for me. He is a good man; he shows me respect. He only beats me when the priest tells him to—sometimes not even then."

"High praise," said Germain le-Comte, his sardonic intent lost on Heugenet; in these times he realized Armandal's forbearance was exemplary, for most men of rank treated their horses better than they treated their wives.

"Yes," she said, her smile remaining. "He has never slighted me with his mistresses, or tried to use my portion for his own gain. He is a good father, too. He has refused to send Armand to a monastery simply because he is not as strong as his brothers. He has never castigated him for his curiosity as most others would, or forbidden him to study. If he were not the man I know him to be, I would think him indifferent to Armand's life, but that is not so. Our two youngest sons are still with their nurses, with my aunt in the north, but when the Great Dying is over, they will come back to us. And our two daughters are safe. How many men do you know who are so well-disposed to their children?" She glanced over her shoulder toward the window where the hunt could still be discerned going deeper into the woods. "He would like to be fighting again."

"No doubt he will have his chance," said Germain le-Comte with flat conviction; no matter what tragedies were visited on men by nature, Germain le-Comte had been staggered by the capacity of men to add to their calamities with war.

"Troubadors do not like war, do they?" Heugenet said, being deliberately provocative.

"Only to sing about, and then long after the war is over, so everyone has forgot the horror of it," he said, something haunted at the back of his eyes. He deliberately lightened his tone. "And I am as much at fault as any: to this day I would fight to defend my native earth."

"Of course," Heugenet responded with a nod. "What man of honor would not? My husband has and every nobleman staying here this winter has done the same. You may be a Comte's bastard, but you know what is due your blood, don't you?" She did not see his quick, one-sided smile as she touched his sleeve, her fingers rubbing the fabric as if to remove some blemish only she could see; her voice dropped so that it was hard for Germain le-Comte to hear what she was saying. "Why should I forget him so much in my heart when you are by? I am a fortunate woman. Why am I not satisfied with my lot when you are near me?" It was not an accusation, but her revelation was not given without distress. "Am I so fallen that I am one with Eve?"

"You have done nothing to deserve censure," Germain le-Comte pointed out to her.

"Perhaps not, but my soul has not been faithful," she said, her mouth turning down at the corners. "I should pray for grace."

"Because you like me?" he asked, the question calm.

"And I should not." She nodded. "My chastity should be more dear to me."

Germain le-Comte touched her chin with one finger to turn her face to his. "Have I done anything to compromise your chastity?"

"You have been all that is honorable; more honorable than I have been in my soul. I should confess it, but I could not repent, and so . . . I will tell you what has become of me and trust I may continue to rely upon your honor," she told him, her brows coming together in a frown. "Pray do not tell me that troubadors are without honor."

"Some do have honor, I will allow," he replied, smiling at her. He laid his small hand over hers, and might have done more but Armand came into the room, beaming and restless; Germain le-Comte stepped back from Heugenet without awkwardness as the boy hurried to the warmth of the fireplace.

"It was above anything I hoped for," he enthused. "Oh, ma Mère, you should have seen it; the cannon-ball went just where I intended it should. The door burst into pieces on the first strike." He hit his fist into his open hand to demonstrate the success.

"Very impressive," said Heugenet, going to stand beside her second son, though she tried not to hover over him; it was difficult, for he had been fragile for so long she could not completely believe he was finally going to improve.

"I should say," he declared. "I did not aim so high that it did not cover the distance, nor too low so that the impact was wasted. It struck the oast-house door squarely, and smashed it into kindling." He could not have been more proud if he had rousted the English.

"And luckily Yves Roueleur does not mind," said Heugenet, fondly indulgent; just to see Armand out of his bed and active was a delight to her: if he wanted to demolish every door on Roueleur's estate, she would not chide him for it. She could not keep from asking, "You have been . . . well?"

He stared at her, resentment in his young eyes. "Mère, do not fuss. There is no need to worry. Look at me: I am perfectly stout. That concoction that he"—he nodded to Germain le-Comte—"has given me is magic."

"Hardly that," said Germain le-Comte, knowing how easily magic could become sorcery in retelling. "I have followed the teachings of men more knowledgeable than I." That was less than the truth, but he saw no advantage in admitting the long centuries he had served in the Temple of Imhotep.

"And we give thanks to God and Sant Lucas that you have," said Heugenet, her eyes shining with gratitude and something more. She made herself look away from Germain le-Comte, afraid she might say more than was wise.

"I would have liked to go hunting," Armand said suddenly. "You say I am not ready yet, but I think I could do it." He glanced at Germain le-Comte, a challenge in his young face that might have amused the troubador at another time.

"Perhaps you could," he agreed. "But if you will wait a little longer, you will be certain. That will make your venturing out better for everyone." He saw Heugenet give a tiny nod, and added, "You may not worry, but others do."

"I know that," Armand said impatiently. "It is because I have been ill. But I am not ill now."

Germain le-Comte did not dispute this. "You will have to give your family time to get used to it," he recommended. "They have had many years of anxiety on your behalf; they will not lose it in a few days."

"The priest says I should devote my life to God because in this time of Plague, I have been delivered, as if I am improved only for a life of prayer, which I would have done had the affliction continued." He glowered at the fire to show he had no intention of following the priest's advice. "You told me, troubador, that I have not been delivered from the Great Dying, only from the affliction I have known since I was young."

"And you are still young," said his mother. She watched as he flopped into the old chair near the fire. "Armand, you must not tax your strength now, when you are still recovering from the long malady you have endured."

He shook his head, his impatience increasing. "I have been drinking that tinctured wine morning and night and I have had no more trouble. I know I am recovered, and if you do not—"

Germain le-Comte came up to him. "You are improved," he said with firmness and kindness. "But you are not yet recovered. That will take time." And he would have to make more of the tincture before spring if the boy was going to continue to improve; he would need his athanor to do the work properly, and that seemed impossible to acquire. He would think of something, he vowed, for Heugenet as much as for Armand.

Armand kicked out to show his exasperation. "How much time?"

"We will have to see how you are in the spring," said Germain le-Comte. He realized he might not remain in this place after winter was over, but he made no mention of it; he knew it would cause Heugenet distress to think he might leave before her boy was quite well.

"The *spring*?" Armand repeated incredulously. "But that is months away. The Nativity is still two weeks . . . Why should I have to wait so long?"

Germain le-Comte laid his forearms on the back of Armand's chair. "Well, you have had this affliction since you were little more than a baby, and that is years, not months, ago. Do you think it is unreasonable to require some time to be sure the affliction is routed?"

"Miracles happen at once," muttered Armand. He looked darkly at his mother. "You said this was like a miracle."

"But it was not a miracle," Germain le-Comte reminded him; it could be troublesome to have such praise heaped upon him in this desperate time. "This was only the work of medicinal tinctures and herbs. Such treatments take longer than miracles." He glanced at Heugenet. "Your mother is concerned for you, Armand. She does not wish to see a return of your . . . condition. For her sake, as well as your own, wait until spring to test your prowess in the field." Knowing it was unwise to press for other concessions just now, Germain le-Comte gave a single nod of approval. "You show prudence as well as mettle, which are not often found in so young a man."

Armand flushed and squirmed in his chair, looking at his mother. "I still would like to hunt."

"And so you shall," she promised him. "When you are in no danger of suffering another spasm. Your father will require it of you when he sees that you are no longer prey to such troubles." She went up to him and, to his intense embarrassment, kissed his forehead.

"Someday," said Germain le-Comte, "you will know how fortunate you are."

Now it was Heugenet who blushed. She shot a single look, not as angry as she would have liked, at him. "The troubador is making a jest, Armand. Do not heed him."

"I am not; I am paying a compliment," said Germain le-Comte without apology.

"Troubadors are supposed to do that, aren't they?" Armand asked as if relieved that someone other than he would undertake that onerous task.

He fussed at his mother's nearness. "Do you think I might be allowed to ride?"

Germain le-Comte answered for her. "Not with the weather so raw. When the days are milder, then it would probably benefit you to get out. There is little enjoyment in dashing across the barren fields into the leaf-less forest. The spring will be better." By then, Armand would be stronger, and he would not need the careful and constant observation to which he was now subjected. "It is a while to wait, but think of the horses, if not of yourself; they deserve a chance to stay out of the cold, don't you think?"

"Not if we must ride them; they must do what we need of them. God put them on earth to serve our will," said Armand, repeating what his Con-fessor had taught him. "As He appointed every man to his place in the world."

Heugenet did not respond to this announcement, saying instead, "You will be called to dine soon after the hunt returns. You may think that is far off, but the time will pass quickly, and you will not want to be laggard. You will want to put on more suitable garments, since Yves Roueleur has hon-ored you with a place at the high table tonight. You will want to do your fa-ther proud."

"Oh, all right," said Armand, his manner sulky but his smile secretly pleased. "I will wear the cotehardie you had made for me three months ago; it is the fanciest clothing I own and I have only worn it twice, and once was at home."

"A very good choice," his mother approved. She signaled to Germain le-Comte. "Since you must dress, we will leave you to it. Remember to wash your face. There are smirches from firing the cannon on your skin. It would be unsuitable to present yourself to your host as if you had been defend-ing the castle." She smiled to show this was not a serious failing. "You will soon be old enough to be included in feasts all the time."

Armand shook his head. "I will have to show I am worthy." He looked at Germain le-Comte. "You will not dine, will you?"

"No; not while you do," he agreed as if there were nothing more to it. "I will play for your entertainment." As he straightened up he added, "I will try to sing something you will like."

The laughter with which Armand approved of this offer ended in a sin-gle cough, but it was enough to quiet the boy. "I will lie down, Mère; you do not have to tell me I should."

Heugenet had gone pale, but she made herself say, "A short rest will re-store you."

"Ma Mère, I will cough from time to time. Everyone does," he said, doing his best to make a joke of her worry. "Even your troubador must cough now and again."

"And so I do," Germain le-Comte said at once. "It is inconvenient to one who makes his living with his voice." He made an encouraging gesture to Armand. "Go have your lie-down," he recommended, knowing the boy would bridle at the notion of a nap. "You will be glad of a little quiet by the time the banquet is over."

Armand chuckled. "You will more than I."

"Armand," Heugenet said to reprimand him. "It is not fitting for you to—"

"He's right," Germain le-Comte interrupted. "I will welcome silence long before you will." He started toward the door. "And if I do not leave, you will not rest at all. Until this evening." His bow was respectful and included Heugenet as well as her son.

"If you will wait a moment, I will join you, Germain le-Comte," said Heugenet, and without waiting for an answer addressed her son. "Do not let yourself be chilled."

"No, ma Mère," he replied with the patience of one much put-upon.

She hesitated as if she wanted to say more; then she turned away from him and went to the door, leaving it with Germain le-Comte. "I know it is not wise, but I do fret when he . . ." She could not find the words to finish.

"You are his mother," Germain le-Comte reminded her as they went along the corridor; it was wide enough to allow them to walk side by side, another of the luxuries of the castle. Torches blazed in sconces even now when daylight filtered in.

"My husband says I have remained too close to my children, especially to Armand. He wanted me to turn them over to nurses and Confessors to teach them, but I could not." She put her hand to her mouth as if ashamed of speaking of such a failing. "I know they say that it is not fitting for any but peasants to tend their own children, but I am not able to convince myself of this. My mother took very good care of me when my nurse died of the bending sickness, and I have remembered those years with gratitude." She stopped and looked at Germain le-Comte. "You make me speak of the most . . . the most private things."

"What can I be but honored," he responded.

Her laughter was self-mocking. "You might be disgusted, or shocked, or disapprov—"

He stopped her, his finger barely touching her lips. "Not I."

She saw something in his dark eyes then that she had never noticed before, and it flustered her more than any other attention he had shown her. She felt her pulse rush. "You should not," she admonished him obscurely.

A thousand years ago he would have challenged her, asked her to explain what he should not do and why he should not do it; he had learned over time not to make such demands, so he only said, "You have nothing to fear from me, Heugenet da Brabant."

Her expression changed subtly. "How can you say so?" She wanted an answer from him and would not be satisfied with courtesy.

He held her with his steady gaze. "Because I would never do anything that would displease you: believe this."

A household slave appeared at the end of the corridor and with averted face hurried past them; this was enough to break her fascination. She took a deep breath. "I believe you," she said, as if surprised at herself for this admission. She cocked her head. "What if what I required displeased *you*: would you do it still?"

"If you asked, I would." He paused and added, watching her closely, "If it did not also displease you to have me do it."

"Dear me, how absolute you are," she said, escaping behind a shield of banter. "You are like one of those fine knights you sing about." She resumed walking. "I am going to have to consider all you have said."

Germain le-Comte walked with her, a step behind her to permit her to ignore him without being rude. He had not visited her in dreams, and now he decided he would not; if he could become her lover it would be with her full knowledge. There were many women at this castle who would be glad of a fulfilled dream, and although this would suffice, he would not be nourished as shared passion with Heugenet would be. It was something to hope for, he reminded himself as he watched her straight back and quick stride. He could sense her ambivalence in every aspect of her comportment; he shared it to a greater extent than he liked, for he knew his own esurience could not be mitigated as long as she was unprepared to do more than chide herself for her strong attraction to him. They reached the end of the corridor and had to descend the narrow stairs. This time she let him go ahead of her as politeness required, so that if she should trip, he could break her fall.

When they were both on the main floor, Heugenet turned to Germain le-Comte and said, "It is the Great Dying. It's all around us; it hasn't come here yet, but we all know that it will; we don't speak of it, but we're all waiting. I think it makes us all wish for things that would be impossible if not—" She met his gaze without apology. "Who has not been touched by the presence of Death?"

"Is that all it is?" he responded, his voice deep and gentle. "The fear of death?"

"Isn't that sufficient?" She heard the wistful note in her words and felt abashed for what she had just told him. She would have backed away had there been room.

"No; not for me," he replied. "Nor for you, I surmise; or you would not be saying any of this."

There was silence between them more laden with meaning than any words they had spoken. He had seen more of pestilence than she could comprehend, but he had never become inured to the suffering it brought; when he cared for one in the path of that invisible destruction, his sense of danger was as keen as any of the living, though he had nothing to fear from this or any other disease. He would have liked to convey this to her, but was not prepared to answer her questions that must accompany any revelation he might make. He was aware of her yearning as much as he was of her equivocalness and very nearly set his reserve aside in spite of her contradictory emotions. Then he inclined his head. "What would you like me to sing tonight? I have Armand's request already: what would please you?"

"Does that matter?" She faced him but her eyes were looking at something far away.

"It does, to me." He waited while her attention returned to him. "If there is nothing you would like to hear, tell me."

"There is nothing I can think of. Choose what you think I would like," she said, recovering her hauteur. "I will claim your third song, whatever it may be."

"As you wish." He moved so that she could slip past him without touching him, then watched her as she hurried across the courtyard to the main hall where the other women staying here at Sant-Brede gathered to prepare for the evening festivities and to share what news they had heard of the world beyond the gates. He did not follow her; he turned and went in the direction of the stable to see how Caesar was doing—it was time to file his hooves—after three days in a box-stall.

The donkey was restless, his ears moving nervously as Germain le-Comte came into his stall, speaking a greeting before he patted the donkey's rump; Caesar twitched and shook his head to show he was itching to be outside.

"All right. I will turn you out in the foaling-pen. It's large enough to let you get the fidgets out of your feet." Germain le-Comte took down the halter and fitted it over the donkey's head, secured it with a knot over Caesar's cheek, then tied the lead to the halter. The donkey responded to the tug on his head with alacrity, wanting for once to be moving.

The foaling-pen stood empty, its wooden walls stout enough to withstand a direct kick from a full-sized mare. The pen was empty as Germain le-Comte had known it would be. He released the donkey inside and stepped out to close the gate.

"The boy is doing well," said Père Herve; he held his breviary and he sketched a blessing in Germain le-Comte's direction.

Germain le-Comte paused in securing the gate-latch to cross himself. "He has been favored at last," he said; he heard Caesar begin to trot about the interior of the pen.

"They are saying that you cured him," the priest went on; he held himself very straight. "What have you to say to that?"

"I?" Germain le-Comte responded, taking care to maintain an air of respect toward the priest. "I have learned a few ways to deal with coughs. Fortunately one of them was what the boy needed."

The priest smiled, self-satisfaction and suspicion mixed in his stance. "And you claim no credit for yourself?"

Now Germain le-Comte was on the alert. "Beyond knowing a few nostrums: no. Why should I?" He knew he would have to answer his own question or Père Herve would invent one. "I am thankful that God put me here when Armand needed my knowledge."

"Armandal d'Ais will be beholden to you for saving his son." Père Herve's eyes narrowed as he said this.

"A Duc indebted to a troubador? I think not," Germain le-Comte said with a hint of laughter. "If anything, I am obliged to him for the protection he has given me."

"Which you repay by curing his son." The priest nodded grandly.

"Or in any other manner that comes my way," Germain le-Comte agreed. "This is not a time to be wandering the world alone."

"True enough," said Père Herve. "A donkey cart is not as safe as castle walls."

Germain le-Comte laughed aloud as if the priest had said something witty. "Amen to that, mon Père." He saw some of the distrust in Père Herve's eyes begin to fade; he had not realized until then how much he had dreaded incurring wariness in Père Herve; wariness could lead to scrutiny and that would result in more trouble than Germain le-Comte was prepared to handle.

"Your donkey is very active," Père Herve said, changing the subject gracelessly.

"Yes; he is used to walking long distances most days; a stall is a luxury, but one that palls on him, after a day or two." Germain le-Comte indicated the foaling-pen. "I wanted him to shake his heels before he starts kicking the walls." The distant sound of a horn gave the news that game had been killed; Germain le-Comte listened to the call, making the most of its interruption. "Deer or boar: what do you think?"

"Either will be welcome, and we will thank God for it," said Père Herve austerely. He studied Germain le-Comte for a moment, and then went his way.

Germain le-Comte looked after the priest, consoled for once that those of his blood did not sweat; he would have to be more careful while he remained at Sant-Brede, for he was convinced that Père Herve was unwilling to accept their brief conversation as adequate response to the questions that had been raised in the priest's mind regarding Armand's improvement.

Text of a letter to Armandal d'Ais, Duc de Verviers at Sant-Brede, from Tancred Liesomme, Baron de Sant-Aube, carried in triplicate by baronial couriers; delivered 10 January, and 2 March 1349.

To the most puissant Armandal d'Ais, Duc de Verviers, the greetings and condolences of Tancred Liesomme, at Trier.

It is with heavy heart that I dictate these words to my clerk, Frer Dominique, who will have the lamentable task of copying the sad news twice more before entrusting the letters to my couriers. It is my most ardent hope that two of them will arrive; I dare not hope all three will, not in these desperate times.

Surely you must know the purpose of my letter, for in this time of Great Dying, what letter brings news other than of death? I must inform you that your son, Bernard, whom you entrusted to me to train as a knight to take the field in our war with the English, has died, two weeks since. He did not succumb to Plague, but to the rocks and scourges of the peasants, who have risen in revolt because we have been unable to feed them in this harsh winter. They have done little growing or planting, so it ought to have been expected that they would go hungry: we have all been hungry this winter. Such is the nature of peasants that they banded together and tried to storm my fortress, for the purpose of seizing what little is left in our larder. The walls and gates were manned to put down this insurrection, and all who were capable of wielding a weapon in our defense were given posts to stand; your son was one of the first to face these furious peasants, and he stood his ground as well as any belted and spurred knight would.

If it will ease your pain, I will tell you that Bernard fought valiantly, defending the creamery with one of my guards; he accounted for eight of the attackers and by his action allowed my men-at-arms to repel the peasants and drive them from our gates. His death was the result of a pitchfork being plunged into his chest and neck; the tines sunk too deep for him to be saved. It is to his honor that he killed the peasant who killed him. We have buried him in the churchyard, not in the Plague pit, to show him distinction which he earned so bravely.

What a Nativity was ours. The assault on the fortress left it much damaged; I have removed my household to Trier until spring when the walls may be rebuilt. We may risk acquiring Blood Roses, but were we to remain at the fortress, we would surely starve or freeze. That we were able to salvage half of our food was due to the courage of your son; the peasants took our swine and sheep and by now will have eaten them.

To lose a son is hard; I know for I have lost three. To lose an heir is more terrible still, and I pray that God will ease your hours of grief with the knowledge that He gave up His only Son for our salvation; in battling to preserve the fortress, your son died that others might live, showing an example that is worthy of any good Christian.

I pray this finds you well, and that God has not set His Hand too punishingly upon you. He has your oldest son; may He make no greater claim upon you. May He Who lifts up and casts down nations give you peace; may He protect you from harm and from the Peste Maiden; may He restore you as He restored Job after his tribulations; may He shine His Face upon you.

Tancred Liesomme,
Baron de Sant-Aube
by the hand of Frer Dominique

From Trier on the 5th day of January in the 1349th Year of Grace.

5

Weepers lined the avenue leading from the castle to the four-hundred-year-old church at Sant-Brede; their black habits reminiscent of cerements, their hoods drawn down to cover their faces, they wept as they walked ahead of the guests of Yves Roueleur, following his carved wooden coffin to its resting place beneath the floor in front of the altar. As if in mockery of the mourners, the sky was polished blue and the sun off the mantle of snow made the whole world glisten. The funeral procession was not as grand as it would have been before the Great Dying, but it was much finer than any of the obsequies of those who succumbed to Blood Roses beyond the castle walls.

The *Requiem* was as short as the liturgy and the dead Comte's position would allow; Père Herve, still unused to his advancement, went through the rite with nervous haste, staying as far away from the coffin as he legitimately could as he consigned the soul of Yves Roueleur, Comte de Sant-Brede, to God's care. Out of respect for Sant-Brede none of the mourners rode their horses into the church, and no talking was allowed during the Mass. The milky light from the windows of thin ivory-colored alabaster made the whole interior look as if it were a vast, drowned ship, under water. The chanting of the Weepers, low and deliberately muffled, created a quiet tide, adding to the illusion; the joy of Epiphany, only a fortnight past, seemed remote as the fabled cities of the Great Khan.

At the rear of the church, next to a stone baptismal font carved with the heads of monsters, Germain le-Comte watched the Mass impassively; he realized already what the rest of the mourners were only beginning to grasp—that Sant-Brede was no longer safe and that the hospitality they had come to expect was at an end. He was aware that many of those in the church were numbed by Yves Roueleur's death: they had supposed they could remain untouched by Blood Roses while at the castle; now their faith was betrayed.

When the Mass was over, those who had been Sant-Brede's guests gathered in front of the church; Germain le-Comte stayed outside this knot of unhappy people, knowing they would resent a troubador intruding on their misery. Along the avenue, the Weepers went their way, going toward Maissin where the Blood Roses had begun to flourish among the townspeople.

Armand moved away from the other guests and approached Germain le-Comte; his young face was pinched with cold. "My father says we will have to go home."

"So will all the rest, I would suppose," Germain le-Comte said. "I am sorry about your brother."

"My father says it's God's Will." He shrugged to show he had not made up his mind. "My other brothers won't like it; they think I am a weakling."

"You and I know you are not," Germain le-Comte reminded him, glancing at the mourners as a few of them began to straggle back to the castle; Armandal d'Ais and his wife were not yet among them, staying with the larger number of guests to condole with them. "Your mother knows it as well. Your father will come to believe it."

"He will have to, now that Bernard is dead. He used to pay no notice of me, for he thought he would never have need of me," Armand said darkly. "But my brothers might want to put me to the test before I am much older."

"If they do, you will know how to deal with them." He was not as certain of this as he sounded, but Germain le-Comte knew the boy was looking for encouragement. "Consider a moment; you have an advantage because they are likely to underestimate you. You are intelligent, and intelligence will prevail against brute force." He had seen just the opposite more times than he cared to remember, but he had also come to realize that intelligence had very real advantages over press of arms; he hoped Armand would learn this for himself, and quickly.

"A troubador would believe that," said Armand with world-weary cynicism.

"Troubadors and Julius Caesar," said Germain le-Comte, recalling the clever Roman with more respect than he had felt for him when, as Franciscus Germanicus, he had followed the Roman troops to Gaul and Britain fourteen centuries earlier.

Armand laughed sarcastically. "You have read Caesar, then? Or do you mean your donkey?"

"What do you think?" Germain le-Comte replied, deliberately leaving the boy's question unanswered.

This time Armand's laughter sounded like a child's; his mirth was stopped by a quelling glance from his father. "I . . . forgot," he muttered by way of apology.

Heugenet put her hand on her husband's arm. "He has had little to laugh about; let him find what amusement he can in these trying days."

Armandal grunted. "A boy in his position should show respect to those who are due it. Pray God no one laughs when you are buried."

Armand's answer was quick and sharp. "I pray God someone does. When I am gone, I want singing and dancing to mark my passing."

"That would not be suitable," said Armandal austerely. "You will come to great power and that power must be respected." He glanced at Germain le-Comte. "We will have to depart this place soon. I will not wait here to shame the widow, and I must make my provisions quickly. My wife has said that you have some skill as a tutor, and that Armand seems to hold you in some regard." His demeanor was authoritative, and it was apparent he did not expect Germain le-Comte to refuse his offer of employment. "I would like you to undertake schooling Armand. The boy will require instruction, as well as your efforts to keep him in health. You may be a bastard, but you know what is due my son. If things were different, Père Larent would teach him, but he died in the autumn, and we have no time to send about the country for other priests. There are not enough of them to spare for Masses, and the rest are not able to tell my son what he must know." He waited a moment. "Well?"

Germain le-Comte paused long enough to make his consideration plausible. "In these uncertain times," he said thoughtfully, "I would have to be a very great fool to turn away from a secure place." It was not so long ago, he recalled, that he had taught Gaspard Estin; what had happened to that merchant's son from Orgon, he did not want to consider. Clair dela Luna now seemed as far away as China and as long ago as the battle at Leosan Fortress. Out of the tail of his eye he could see color mount in Heugenet's face; he hoped that Armandal had not noticed it.

"A sensible man," approved Armandal. "Be ready to depart when I leave. You will travel with us, you and your donkey."

"Caesar," Armand interjected, trying to hide the amusement that threatened to overcome him again. He turned chagrined eyes on his father. "I didn't mean to laugh again."

Rather than remonstrate with his son once more, Armandal turned his back. "Tomorrow or the day after, we will go. If the snows come tonight, we will have to wait until the weather clears." He signaled to Heugenet. "You will hold yourself ready, as well."

"Of course," she said, so promptly that Armandal gave her a nod of approval.

"We must go back to the castle. The funeral feast will be set out," Armandal announced. He paid no attention to either his son or his wife as he started off; he assumed they would follow him.

Heugenet motioned to Armand. "Come. And you as well, Germain le-Comte." This last was added in a rush, as if it were a lapse in conduct for her to give him an order.

Germain le-Comte inclined his head and fell in behind the others as they began the walk that would take them back to the castle. He felt more than saw the eyes of the remaining villagers upon him. With their seigneur gone, their lives were far more precarious than they had been, Germain le-Comte knew with far more certainty than they did. When he reached the side gate of the castle, he turned and looked back at Sant-Brede, hoping the village would not have to endure more than it already had.

The two main halls of the castle were draped in red and black for mourning; the servants all wore black cowls to show their grief as they went about their duties; the steward muttered prayers as he supervised the transition of power in the household, although no one was certain who would inherit his title, since many of his relatives had died in the last year and no direct claimant had been determined. Yves Roueleur's dazed and pregnant widow was left to the care of her weeping women.

"The poor child," Heugenet said to Germain le-Comte as they stood aside to make room for the young woman to pass; Armandal had gone off to the castle's herald to arrange for their departure, for the herald was serving as Yves Roueleur's deputy until an heir was installed. "I pray nothing terrible will become of her. She has no family nearby, and the convent is unable to take her in."

"The nuns have the poor and the orphaned and the mad to care for," said Germain le-Comte. "Now, between the war and Blood Roses, they must be overwhelmed."

"So I think," said Heugenet. "They have their obligations to God, and that demands they offer all Christian charity, but—"

"Yes: but," Germain le-Comte agreed. He noticed one of the cooks staggering under the weight of a huge tureen of thick soup. "Is there no one to help that man?"

Heugenet shook her head. "They say the scullions ran away last night. They fear the Blood Roses as much as anyone."

Germain le-Comte murmured a word of excuse then went to help the cook with his burden. "Here," he said, coming to the man's side. "I will take one handle; you hold on to the other."

The cook was so startled he almost dropped the tureen. "God send you good cess for this, troubador," he said as he let Germain le-Comte take one handle.

When the tureen was set in place at the end of the long table below the salt, the cook indicated his gratitude with a nervous gesture, then hurried away to complete his work in the kitchen; Germain le-Comte returned to Heugenet da Brabant's side.

"Why did you do that?" she asked, her curiosity making her features sharpen.

"The man was overburdened," said Germain le-Comte.

"But he is a cook," Heugenet reminded him. "He has his work to do."

"That he does," Germain le-Comte agreed at once. "He also has scullions to help him, or he did have until last night."

She studied him as if trying to fathom his meaning. Finally she said, "You are a most perplexing man, Germain le-Comte," she said.

"Why is that?" he asked. He waited for her answer, listening closely to what she told him, for he knew what she said now might shape his hopes for her.

"Such vanity," she chided him lightly, retreating from the compelling light of his dark eyes by turning to jests. "I will not flatter you, much as you might like me to." She was able to smile, but there was an ardor in her green eyes that the smile did not mitigate. "You know you are a puzzle: how can you not?" She turned away, smiling slightly, unwilling to say anything more; after a moment, Germain le-Comte accompanied her as if he were her page. They paused in a window embrasure that overlooked the bakehouse and the creamery.

He gazed out at the sky, studying it for signs of change; then he gave his whole attention to her. "Gracious Heugenet," he began, his manner as respectful as society demanded, "why do you want me to teach your son?"

She had an answer for him. "Who else is there? Any tutor who could leave has done so, and those who are left will not venture where Blood Roses bloom. No priest is ready to undertake his education; you may not be legitimate, but I know you have some learning yourself—I have seen you read from that book of songs you carry in your cart. My husband is satisfied that you are capable of the task, as he told you himself. You see how much he respects me: he consults me in these things and heeds what I tell him. I am a fortunate wife, that my husband attends to what I say. For that alone, I am thankful for what I have been given by God and my father." She glanced at Germain le-Comte, then looked away as if she needed to impose a distance upon them in order to maintain her composure. "Most important of all, Armand will listen to you." She faltered before saying the last. "If he should have more . . . trouble, you will be able to help him. That pleases me, your concern in this dreadful time."

Germain le-Comte was not surprised by any of this, but he did not speak too quickly. "You are kind to me; I am yours to command." He felt her presence as powerfully as he felt his native earth; he knew she had the same response to him, for his came from her.

She gave her head a tiny shake. "I wonder," she said softly, addressing the air instead of him.

By nightfall the wind had picked up and the first streamers of clouds were reaching out across the sky; in the castle of Sant-Brede more than half the guests were finishing preparations for their departures. The shine of lamps held the most pervasive dark at bay, but the somberness that had engulfed the castle could not be so readily banished. The funeral feast went on into the night, accompanied by prayers from Père Herve instead of songs and entertainers; Germain le-Comte sat in the minstrels' gallery and watched the guests consume the meal laid out for them. He realized that they would probably not have many occasions to feast again for some time, and he saw in their apparent gluttony the spectre of looming famine.

The following morning thin snow was blowing across the countryside, leaving gossamer shrouds behind; the guests at Sant-Brede postponed their departures, a few with obvious relief. Understewards were sent out to help the woodmen gather more logs to fuel the castle's fireplaces. The bustle that had been the usual state in the castle only a few days ago was now replaced with sporadic flurries of activities carried out almost furtively, as if everyone feared a superior enemy just beyond the walls.

"I don't want to study Latin today," Armand told Germain le-Comte when he came to the boy's room shortly after noon.

"Of course you don't," Germain le-Comte said affably. "You were planning to be on the road today, not maundering about the castle with nothing to do." He smiled. "Which is why I thought it would be a good time to get started on your studies. You will be bored and surly by evening if you do nothing to occupy yourself."

"My mother sent you, didn't she?" he challenged, his face set in uncompromising lines.

"Not specifically, no," Germain le-Comte replied, infuriatingly unruffled. "Time can hang as heavily on my hands as on yours, and I have practiced for the day already."

"So you are amusing yourself?" His indignation was mixed with doubt. "You would like me to entertain you?"

"Not exactly," said Germain le-Comte; he strolled nearer to the fire and held out his small hands to warm them. When he spoke he managed to sound as if he wanted to relieve his own boredom. "But I did think we would both be the better for an afternoon of thought."

Armand glared, torn between the annoyance of being made to study and the flattery of doing something with a man of some learning, though he was only a troubador: as a boy with an infirmity, too often he had done things for those instructing him. Finally he hitched up his shoulders. "Perhaps for a while." It was an enormous concession, he told himself as he dragged his stool nearer to the fireplace. "I've already packed my tablets and stylus away."

"As have I," Germain le-Comte agreed. "So we will have to study by speaking."

"Is that possible?" Armand marveled, the potentials of such instruction exciting him in spite of himself.

"It was how the ancients taught," said Germain le-Comte, who had heard Socrates and Aristotle in Athens long ago. "Their students listened and learned." It saddened him to think of how most young men of noble family were taught in these stifling times: given lists of questions to memorize to put to a Church-affiliated tutor, who would respond with memorized answers. The impact upon the intellectual life of Europe was devastating; Germain le-Comte despaired of any change in this stringency.

"Then I will listen, too: the way the ancients did." The notion of studying this way was continuing to spark more curiosity in the boy. "I will show you how well I remember. You may question me about anything you teach. And you cannot beat me unless my father permits it," Armand warned hastily.

"I would not beat you," Germain le-Comte said. "Learning enforced with a rod is always hated."

Armand laughed. "Why else would anyone learn?" It was the question he had heard repeated by his father and brothers so many times that he no longer thought about it.

"Why, for curiosity, for adventure, for love," came the answer; Germain le-Comte's demeanor was so candid that Armand was impressed.

"Love?" He tasted the word, finding it strange. "Curiosity?"

"Yes," said Germain le-Comte. "Learning acquired this way is never lost." He reflected that one of the most subtle, pernicious things the Church had done in its bid for control of Christian world was to make all learning but religion dangerous and odious; he also knew that to voice such an opinion would expose him, and Armand as well, to the most rigorous censure of the Church.

After a moment of contemplation, Armand nodded. "All right. You have had to learn—you are a bastard and you have had to fend for yourself—but I am going to inherit my father's position."

Germain le-Comte held up one hand. "You suppose you will. It may not turn out that you do, for in these hard times, fortunes rise and fall with caprice. You may find that everything is much different when the Great Dying ends." He saw dismay in Armand's face and changed his tone to a brisker one. "Still, you must prepare to fill your father's place. You have seen what has happened to men of rank who have relied on their priests and clerks, haven't you?"

"Who has not? The English would never have dared to come here but for the cowardice of priests." He folded his arms. "My father told me that Bernard would not have let priests turn him from the defense of his lands, or making him delay until the English had established their hold."

"It may be so," Germain le-Comte said, aware that Bernard was already being invested with the perfection of intent only death could provide: for as long as Armandal lived, Bernard's flawlessness would continue to escalate, and Armand, by comparison, would be found wanting. "But he will not be able to do so now, will he?" He saw the shock in Armand's young face. "What you will do is the thing we must deal with," he went on, his tone deliberately gentler than before.

"Yes," said Armand slowly. "So it is." He looked up at Germain le-Comte. "You are very persuasive."

"And you are very astute," Germain le-Comte countered. "It is a trait you would do well to cultivate." He sank down on the bearskin before the fire. "You may begin by learning from what other men—wise and foolish—have done before you."

"A man who learns from fools is one himself," said Armand, repeating the lesson he had been taught since early childhood.

"Only if he repeats the errors of the fool," Germain le-Comte said quietly. He gave the boy a little time to think about this, then said in the Latin of the Church, "Shall we begin with the fools?"

Armand grinned, and answered, his Latin poorly constructed, "I could like that."

Germain le-Comte corrected his usage to *would*. "I think that was your meaning."

"Yes," Armand said quickly as color mounted in his face. "You're right."

For most of the afternoon, the two sat together, speaking in occasionally clumsy Latin, about the wisdom and folly of the past; the time sped away until the summons to evening prayers and supper intruded on their discussion and a short while later, Heugenet came to take Armand with her to the hall.

"Thank you," she said to Germain le-Comte as she left the room.

He smiled at her. "It was what you have asked me to do."

"Yes," she said. "But I had not supposed you would begin while we were here." She motioned to her son to follow her, saying as he did, "Your father may have entrusted you to me because he feared for your health, but now he will have to let me guide you."

"Yes, ma Mère," he said, trying to sound burdened.

As she reached the door, she turned back. "I thank the storm that brought you to us."

Germain le-Comte stood alone after the door was closed, his expression enigmatic, masking the surge of hope that welled within him. He left the chamber a short while later and made his way down to the stable where he occupied his time readying his donkey and cart for travel; as he went about these routine tasks, he found himself missing Rogres, not for his service but for his company. He longed for someone to talk to openly, someone with whom he need not dissemble, someone who understood his nature without dismay. He was aware that both he and Rogres were safer this way, but that did not diminish his sense of lack with Rogres gone, who had shared much of his life for hundreds of years. "That's nothing against you, Caesar," he told the donkey in the language of his long-vanished people. "You are a very worthy companion. And the women I visit in sleep are enough to sustain me. But isolated amid such dread and suffering, without another who knows the centuries, loneliness becomes—" He stopped himself from saying anything more, as if hearing the word aloud would make it impossible to accommodate. Silently he took a comb and began to work on the donkey's mane.

Text of a letter from Fabrice Rocene in Pont Sant-Pierre in the County of Hainaut to Josue Roebertis in the Duchy of Swabia. The messenger carrying the letter froze to death outside the city of Besancon.

To our kinsman-in-law, the good merchant Josue Roebertis, Fabrice Rocene sends his greetings and the pious hope that it may find you alive and well in this time of suffering and lamentation. Your goodness toward our family has been one of the few sources of joy in our travail and grief.

It is my hope that you have been spared, and that you have not buried all your family; we have lost two of our children, but five still remain alive, may God be thanked. They are saying that one in four in Hainaut have died from Blood Roses, and if this is so, I cannot help but pray that no heavier hand is laid upon us even as I offer up Psalms for those who have died.

I must suppose you wish to know what has become of Jenfra now that she has become a novice: she began at a convent close by, but Flagellants attacked it some two months since, and with the aid of some of the peasants who had abandoned their fields; as a result the convent was razed and those nuns who escaped the flames and the madness of their attackers have been sent to another convent, one some distance from here, at Sante-Amienne, where it is hoped they will all be safe. The Sante-Amienne convent is the parent house for her Order in Hainaut and as such has the obligation to protect all the nuns of the Order. The convent there has stout walls and can summon aid from the garrison of the Duc de Verviers. When the Duc himself returns to his seat, the convent will officially be placed under his protection.

This, I fear, is the most I can do for Jenfra. Without your generosity, I do not like to think what might have become of her. She has told us that all she lived for in the world is gone, and a curse has taken the place of the favor of those who loved her. It is apparent that she has determined to devote her life to prayer and penitence, for she said to us that she had almost been lured from Grace by a foreigner who had made himself odious to her through his unwanted attentions. She knows that the foreigner was sent to test her devotion; so accomplished a seducer was he that he nearly succeeded in causing her to forsake her faith and her family.

Her convent has not asked for any more dowries for those nuns who have come there as Jenfra has, as one displaced from her worldly home, but of course, with so much calamity around them, they seek donations to continue their good works for the sake of Heaven. I have sent ten golden apostles in the name of my dead children, and I urge you to extend your generosity once more. The nuns at Sante-Amienne are worthy of your help, and all monies given to God's Church will surely be remembered before the Mercy Seat.

I pray my messenger reaches you in safety and finds you well.

Fabrice Rocene
by the hand of the clerk Amies

In the County of Hainaut in the Holy Roman Empire on the 30th day of January in the 1350th Year of Grace.

6

When they had almost reached Cascade-en-Foudre, the Sergeant commanding their escort declared they would have to stop; the sun was almost down and the moon would rise late. He indicated the sorry state of the men-at-arms and the mud on the wheels of the carts and wagons as he told Armandal d'Ais of his decision. "I would not defy you in anything, mon Duc, but I must put your safety and the safety of the men ahead of your order to enter your gates tonight. If we were halted for any reason, we might well be attacked by desperate men."

Armandal looked thunderous, his arms folded as he sat upon his big bay horse, his head down, the collar of his mantel up against the cutting wind. "It *is* late, and we are still some distance from Mon Gardien," he conceded, using his castle's name with real affection. "And there is an inn hard by the waterfall. If the landlord has not fled, we may find shelter there for the night."

The Sergeant touched his forehead as if to raise an invisible visor. "Thank you, mon Duc. The men will be grateful."

"And well they should be," Armandal grumbled. "My wife and . . . heir should be protected. It will not take us long to reach the inn." He said this as if reciting by rote. "Cascade-en-Foudre is near enough, I suppose. We need not fear marauders in this stretch of road. The turning for the inn is a lane to the right."

"Yes," said the Sergeant as if he had not known this; he pulled his horse around then rode to his men to announce their change in plans.

In the curtained wagon behind Armandal, Heugenet sat wrapped in a bear-skin cloak; her back and legs ached from the long hours of being jostled while crouched in the low seat provided for her. Armand lay at her feet, snuggled into a mantel with a wolf-skin lining, a sign of his position as his father's heir. He had slept fitfully for part of the journey, as much from boredom as fatigue.

Walking beside Caesar, his cart at the rear of the little train—a wagon carrying supplies, provisions, and crated belongings was between him and the wagon where Heugenet rode—Germain le-Comte could only agree with the decision to stop; the whole of their journey had been hazardous: bridges were in poor repair or cut down completely, towns were barricaded and farms were looted or turned into improvised fortresses, even monasteries and nunneries which usually extended spartan hospitality to travelers now stalwartly refused to admit anyone who might bring Blood Roses to bloom among their numbers. The few inns that remained open were not quite so picky as many other places and were considered dangerous by their very liberality.

At the turn for the inn the second wagon bogged down on the shoulder of the icy road, canted at a tricky angle, and the men-at-arms had to struggle for some time to haul it out without tipping it over. By the time they had finished it was full dark and lanthorns had to be lit to show them the way to the inn.

The landlord was a macilent fellow, all angles and knobs; he was waiting in front of his inn, a pike in one hand and a lanthorn in the other, ready to greet or repel as necessary. He achieved a rictus smile as he saw the arrivals.

"Landlord!" the Sergeant bellowed as he drew in his horse. "The Duc de Verviers, his lady-wife, his heir, and his entourage seek room for the night."

"I have room," the landlord declared, leaning the pike against the wall of the inn. "The stable is all but empty; I have no ostlers or grooms to assist you, but the cook's-girl will help you." He clapped his hands and shouted into the inn. "Service for the Duc de Verviers. At once!" Then he turned back to the Sergeant. "You come in a good hour. How many rooms will you need? I have no guests at the inn tonight, and none expected tomorrow. You may command the whole place if the Duc would—"

"Done," said Armandal. "My men-at-arms will take care of the horses. And the troubador will tend to his donkey." He said this loudly enough for Germain le-Comte to hear. "What have you to eat, landlord?"

The landlord's face did not change but something in his expression soured. "I have half a pig and a lamb to cook. There is a pottage of onions and yellow peas." He held up his hands to show he could not change this. "The harvest was . . . was small, and we have only our kitchen-garden to keep us. There has been no market held since August." He offered another gesture of apology.

Armandal came down from his horse and faced the landlord. "We have seen as much for ourselves. Whatever you can prepare will suffice." He handed his reins to the nearest man-at-arms. "If you would tend to him for me?"

"At once," the man declared, and looked about the innyard for the stable.

"Over there," the landlord said, pointing to a building with a hanging door. "There was a small fire two months ago. I have not had time to order repairs. The roof is sound enough, and the door may be dragged closed." He sounded more resentful than sorry.

"We will manage," said the Sergeant, and signaled his men to begin unhitching the horses from the wagons; they paid no attention to Germain le-

Comte and his donkey-cart as they went about their chores with the steady determination of fatigue.

Armandal went to the first wagon, saying, "You may come down now." He stood waiting, prepared to help his wife descend as modestly as possible from the wagon.

Heugenet reluctantly set the bear-skin aside and rose unsteadily to a half-crouching posture. "Come, Armand. Get up, my boy." She leaned over to shake his shoulder.

"Are we—?" he muttered as he sat up.

"We are at an inn for the night." She urged him to his feet. "Descend."

"I'm hungry," Armand complained as he made his way to the edge of the wagon and lifted the flap of heavy cloth that enclosed them.

"There is food waiting," said Armandal, helping his son get out of the wagon.

As he led Caesar and the cart toward the stable, Germain le-Comte paused to watch Heugenet come down from the wagon. He could see how exhausted she was by the way she moved and he decided he would keep his entertaining brief that night so that she could have an opportunity to rest. He would sing while the meat was cooking but would not continue after the meal was done. He went on to the stable to tend to Caesar and secure his cart.

The Sergeant commandeered the largest of the open stalls for the horses, pointing Germain le-Comte to a small corner stall near the tackroom. "Your donkey will do well enough there."

The stable smelled of hay and something less wholesome; Caesar balked at going near the second smell, as if he could sense trouble. Germain le-Comte recognized it at once: the odor of old decay. Whatever had died here had been dead since autumn.

"What do you think it is?" the Sergeant asked the air.

"Something dead in the loft, I would suppose," Germain le-Comte answered laconically, concealing the apprehension he felt growing within him.

"Dead in the loft," the Sergeant repeated. "Go look."

Germain le-Comte was under no constraints to obey the Sergeant, but he shrugged. "When my donkey is unhitched and fed, I will."

This was not the answer the Sergeant wanted. He glowered and bristled, but did not force the matter. "Well, be quick about it," he growled, and went to tend to Armandal's horse before the rest of them; the troubador remained unfazed as he stowed his cart and brushed down Caesar's shaggy coat.

A short while later, Germain le-Comte climbed up the rickety ladder into the loft; he went with every sign of reluctance and when he reached the stored hay, he began to poke about although he could have gone directly to the source of the offensive stench. He allowed himself to find the desiccated body after a brief search; judging from the size of the skeleton, this was a child, probably no more than nine or ten. Bits of blackened flesh clung to the bones where insects and rats had not entirely stripped the carcass clean. A few shreds of cloth were all that remained of the garments. Germain le-Comte looked down at the body and could not keep from sighing. How young the dead were! He dropped to one knee and called down to the Sergeant, "We will need a grave."

The Sergeant's voice was five tones higher than its usual pitch when he replied. "Was it Blood Roses?"

"I don't know," Germain le-Comte answered truthfully. "It could have been. It might have been cold or starvation as well." He heard the mutters of alarm from the men-at-arms. "You have nothing to fear."

"I will order a grave be dug. Behind this building." The Sergeant had found his tone again and he issued terse orders to his men. "Montcerry, you and Biebart will go and dig a shallow grave near the midden. You will not be fed until the task is done."

There was mumbled assent, and a moment later the rear door groaned on its hinges as the men went out to begin their work.

"You will have to bring the body down," the Sergeant informed Germain le-Comte. "The ladder isn't strong enough to hold the body and two men."

Germain le-Comte did not challenge this. He composed himself and said, "I will attend to it." As he spoke, he told himself he would have to be careful or the remnants of the body would fall apart when he moved it. "I will need a sheet to wrap it."

"Very well," the Sergeant allowed and went to the wagon carrying supplies to find one.

When he had wrapped the small bones and bits of flesh in the old sheet, Germain le-Comte secured it over his shoulder with his right arm and began the descent down the ladder; when he was halfway to the stable floor, the rung he was standing on broke. He hung on for a moment with his left hand, then dropped to the floor, landing lightly and steadily.

The Sergeant was staring at him. "You are stronger than you look," he said at last.

"I was lucky," Germain le-Comte said, deliberately breathing faster. "I was sure I was going to land in a heap."

One of the other men-at-arms studied him but said nothing; Germain le-Comte knew the incident would not be forgotten. He glanced toward the rear of the stable. "The grave?"

"It will be ready shortly." He paused in fussing with the tack he was stowing for the night. "What will you say to the landlord?"

"Very little," Germain le-Comte replied as he made for the door.

The Sergeant looked mildly disgusted. "No prayers? No marker?"

"I will pray for him, and make a marker," Germain le-Comte said quietly. He was puzzled by the Sergeant, who boasted of the stacks of bodies he had seen in war, yet now balked at one skeleton found in a hayloft.

"Very good," said the Sergeant, satisfied by this assurance. He went back to inspecting the breastplate, holding the metal-studded leather near to the lanthorn to see it clearly. The other men-at-arms ignored him completely, as if to save themselves from the presence of death.

Germain le-Comte let himself out the rear door and stood in the spill of light from the door while Montcerry and Biebart dug in the frozen ground to make a place for the body. The night was turning fiercely cold and the men sweated and shivered while they worked. Had he not attracted the Sergeant's suspicion, he might have offered to dig the grave, but he was sure two feats of strength would bring unwanted scrutiny.

When at last the men were finished, Germain le-Comte laid the bones, close-wrapped in the sheet, deep in the grave. "I will finish," he said to the men-at-arms. "You have earned your supper, and more." Montcerry and Biebart needed no other recommendation. As they hastened away, Biebart called over his shoulder, "We are much obliged."

Germain le-Comte nodded as he picked up a shovel and commenced to cover the pathetic remains. With the men-at-arms out of sight he worked swiftly and with a stamina that would have amazed the men-at-arms; when he was done he stood over the newly-turned earth and spoke a few words in the language of his long-vanished people. Then he walked toward the inn, brushing the soil off his hands as he went.

Armandal d'Ais was seated in front of the hearth drinking the last of the hot wine when Germain le-Comte came through the door; the rest of his men sat about on benches, some of them half-asleep already. On a table near the taps the last of the supper waited for the kitchen-servants to collect it; only a crock of baked cheese remained unfinished—all the rest had been picked clean. A pitcher stood by Armandal's elbow, its dark contents giving off a pungent steam. "Troubador," he exclaimed as he caught sight of Germain le-Comte. "Have some of the wine."

Germain le-Comte lowered his head in respect. "Thank you, mon Duc, but I do not drink wine."

"Suit yourself," said Armandal with a shrug. "You want a clear head and a nimble tongue for your work, don't you? You might want the wine tonight, though. There isn't much left for you to eat." For a man of his position, Armandal was being most accommodating to a troubador. The explanation was not long in coming. "Sergeant Naceon told me what you did, out in the stable. A most charitable act."

"I would like to think someone might do the same for me, one day," Germain le-Comte responded in a level voice. "Is there a ewer in the kitchen? I would like to clean my hands."

"So fastidious," said one of the men-at-arms, amused but not contemptuous.

"Troubadors look after their hands," said Biebart, taking the last of the baked cheese.

"My lady-wife asked me to tell you that she would like a song tonight. She and Armand are in the parlor." He shook his head. "Women. Wanting music and amusement every day." He made a sign to Germain le-Comte not to leave yet. "You must talk to her and the boy. Make him ready for what is coming."

"The lad should be with us," Montcerry said, ending on a belch loud enough to make all his companions laugh.

"Time enough for that once we reach Mon Gardien; my wife will have him with her until then." Armandal's expression darkened.

Two of the men laughed, one of them adding a wink. "He's been with his mother so long, he may not like what you teach him."

"God has chosen him to be my heir," said Armandal sullenly as he drank the last of his hot wine and signaled for more. "I will not question God's ways, but I doubt my lands will be safe in his hands. Be certain you teach him of these things, troubador, along with Latin and numbers." He shook his head. "To lose Bernard for Armand!"

"God will reward you," said Montcerry. "What He has taken He will not leave you without recompense." He crossed himself to show his remarks were meant to be pious, not sarcastic.

"You may think He will," said one of the others. "God does not always do what we wish. We have all seen the pits where we may lie." He lowered his eyes. "God has called so many to Judgment, what can He expect of those left behind?"

"If the Great Dying is not the work of the Devil, what else can it be?" Biebart demanded suddenly. "The priests are right. The Devil has sent this to us, to turn us away from salvation." He stamped his foot. "What man could think otherwise?"

Germain le-Comte listened to the men-at-arms with growing apprehension. If these men were convinced that the Devil brought the Plague, then no one would be safe from the fear that had worked so many into a frenzy greater than the fever of Blood Roses. He began to consider how he would address these matters with Armand, for the boy would have to face them soon enough. "Mon Duc—?"

Armandal looked at him, blinked once as if trying to remind himself of why Germain le-Comte should still be there. "Oh, yes. You have leave to go to my wife and son." His wave was negligent and he drank some more wine as Biebart refilled his cup.

Germain le-Comte went to the kitchen first, taking a moment to wash his hands in the tub of brackish water kept for that purpose. The cook was sitting in the corner, already half-asleep; the landlord was in the pantry door, shaking his head. "What is the matter?" the troubador asked as he studied the landlord. "Trouble?"

The landlord concealed his surprise at Germain le-Comte's presence. "Rats," he replied succinctly. "In the bread and the cheese." He crossed his arms over his chest. "And there aren't many eggs. I don't know how we will feed the Duc's party for another day." He closed the pantry door.

"There are no farms nearby?" Germain le-Comte asked.

"Oh, there are farms. Most of them are abandoned, and those that are not have been raided and plundered." He shook his head slowly. "My own stock is depleted, and I cannot replenish it soon, not without a market or a festival. What festival could we hold now?"

"Surely that will change when the Plague passes?" Germain le-Comte said, thinking of the many, many times he had seen sickness devastate a place only to flourish again when the illness was gone; he did not know how to convey this hope to the landlord.

"If the Plague passes, you mean," he corrected sourly. "In time it will be gone; pray God we have not all gone with it."

Germain le-Comte nodded as he tried to summon the words that would provide some relief to the landlord. "Each day you live is a victory over death."

The landlord listened; then he crossed himself. "Amen."

As Germain le-Comte entered the parlor where Heugenet and Armand were spending the evening he noticed that the fire was burning very low and only half the lamps had been lit. He paused to bow in the Italian manner, then went to the long settle where Heugenet and Armand huddled together against the encroaching cold.

Heugenet watched Germain le-Comte with an emotion she did not recognize; her smile was more revealing than anything she might have said. "Finally. The evening has been interminable." She held out her hand to him and was unnerved as he kissed her hand as if she, and not her husband, were the seigneur Germain le-Comte served.

"You wanted some entertainment?" He paused long enough for her to nod. "My mandola is still in my donkey-cart, in its case. I can sing without it, or tell you fables, or recite poetry." He glanced at Armand. "If you would like to hear something, my student, you have only to tell me."

Armand blinked sleepily at Germain le-Comte, dark circles under his eyes and his face a bit pale. "I'm tired," he announced.

"Then you would rather I tell you a story," said Germain le-Comte as he drew a stool up to the settle. "Your mother may choose what the story is about."

Heugenet frowned a little. "What would be appropriate for Armand? I am sure his father has told you what he wants the boy to hear."

"He does not want the boy coddled," said Germain le-Comte, his tone carefully neutral.

"Not he," said Heugenet with sharp pride. "He has endured poor health and has not been overcome by it."

"Do you know who Hannibal is?" Armand asked suddenly. "I want to know about Hannibal. Can you tell me?"

Germain le-Comte smiled slightly; he had had but one encounter with the ambitious Cartheginian general, several years after his defeat at the hands of the Romans; then the man had been caustic and world-weary: that was not the story Armand wanted to hear. "You want to know about the elephants, is that it?"

"Yes," said the boy, his expression brightening. "I've never seen an elephant. Are they really so big that they have houses on their backs?"

"They are more like small tents, for two or three people," Germain le-Comte said, and saw the boy's face fall. "The elephants are still much larger than any warhorse or miller's ox you could find. They are very tall, and their hide is wrinkled grey."

"What color is their fur?" Armand asked, trying to keep his disappointment from showing.

"They haven't got a pelt," Germain le-Comte told him. "There are a few coarse black hairs growing out of their shoulders, but for the most part their hide is hairless. They live in such hot places that they have no need of fur."

Armand scowled, trying to imagine the creatures, and failing. "I saw a picture of one, once. The monks had it in a book. It had a long nose, a very long nose."

"Yes," said Germain le-Comte. "It is longer than a man's arm, and it is strong and very supple. They use it to grab food, and to bathe with."

The boy squirmed, unsure whether he ought to believe this or not. "How do they bathe with their noses?" he asked after a short while.

"They suck water into their noses and blow it out over their shoulders and flanks." He saw Heugenet smile. "I've seen them." It was an incautious remark, offered in answer to her kindness.

"Have you? Really?" Armand pushed himself onto his elbow. "Where?" He was awake now and his curiosity made him impatient.

Now Germain le-Comte realized he was in a dangerous position here. "My wandering has taken me to many distant shores," he answered obliquely. "Troubadors, jongleurs, and players, we often find ourselves in far-away climes."

"But elephants—*elephants*," Armand marveled. "Tell me about them."

Heugenet nodded her approval, saying for her son's benefit. "Nothing too long or too fantastical. Armand must rest tonight." She laid her hand on Armand's shoulder. "Remember it is your tutor who tells you these things."

Recognizing the warning for what it was, Germain le-Comte began to speak, mixing the story of Hannibal's campaign against the burgeoning Roman Empire with his own recollections from his travels, describing the long trek through the Alps; his narrative was engaging, but after a while Armand began to doze and shortly he was wholly asleep.

Heugenet shifted her position on the settle to make her son more comfortable. "You have been very good to him," she whispered.

"This?" Germain le-Comte responded in an under-voice. "This was the amusement of an evening. It was no more than any other would do."

She was staring into the darkness of his eyes. "But no other did," she breathed.

He said nothing for a short while. Then: "Would you like me to carry him to his room?"

She touched Armand's hair lightly. "If you would? I do not want to wake him."

Germain le-Comte ducked his head to show his intent; he helped Heugenet to rise without disturbing her son, then he reached down and lifted the boy. "Which room?"

"The one at the right at the top of the stairs. My husband will post a guard there for the night," she answered barely above the sound of breathing. "I will be in the room next to his." As she said this, she wondered why she had revealed this to him.

"If you will hold the door?" Germain le-Comte asked as he reached it. "If I bend to the latch, he may waken."

She opened the latch and held the door for him as he carried her son out of the parlor and down the corridor toward the stairs. After a brief hesitation she followed after them, moving as lightly as she could as if afraid of waking her son. When they reached the door of the room assigned to Armand, she slipped past Germain le-Comte to open it for him. On impulse, she glanced at him. "Where did you see elephants? Tell me again."

The smile he offered her was at once tantalizing and sad. "If I told you that," he murmured as he carried her son into his chamber, "you would not believe me."

Text of a letter from Armandal d'Ais, Duc de Verviers, to Carles IV, Luxembourg, Holy Roman Empire; four copies were dispatched and three were delivered, in April, May, and July of 1350.

To the most puissant, most reverend Carles IV in his seat at Luxembourg, Armandal d'Ais, Duc de Verviers, sends his most humble assurance of fealty in accordance with the vows of vassalage given by my ancestor to Otto the Great in the time of his triumph. I anticipate with joy the day of your coronation, and I vow to be present at that splendid celebration, if God so wills.

I have just returned to my seat at Mon Gardien, and I regret to inform you I found it badly damaged. I have therefore put my family into my mother's house, which has suffered only minor damage, and will, at the first improvement in the weather, begin the necessary repairs in order to make it habitable once more.

Half my garrison is gone, and of that number, more than half of them have been laid in the common grave for those with Blood Roses on their corpses. This has put the castle at its lowest complement since the days of Robert Curthose, and I cannot spare one of these loyal men for any purpose whatsoever. I have given orders to my remaining men to be diligent in their duties, but I fear it will be many months before they are prepared to mount a defense of Mon Gardien, let alone enter into any battle beyond these walls.

I write this to you in the hope that you will be able to send a few men to me to bolster the garrison here. My plight is no worse than that of many others; I bow to your judgment whether it favors me or another even as I remind you that Mon Gardien is in a disputed region, and the Ducs de Verviers have bent the knee to French Kings as well as to your predecessors. In a time of great turmoil, surely it is wise to keep the borders armed and ready against those who might seek to press their advantage while all is in disarray.

I await your response with the certainty that God will not desert those who remain true to their sacred vows, and the firm conviction that you know the worth of Verviers, small and old though this Duchy may be.

May God make His face to shine upon you, may He give you many long years and many loyal sons, may He confound your enemies and strengthen your right hand in His cause. May you never battle but for His righteous purpose. May He keep the Peste Maiden from your door and the Blood Roses away from your flesh. May He lift you up to glory.

> *Armandal d'Ais,*
> *Duc de Verviers*
> *by the hand of Germain le-Comte, troubador*

At Mon Gardien, near the County of Hainaut, on the Feast of Sante Scholastice, on the 10th day of February, in the 1350th Year of Grace.

7

Germain le-Comte was seated by the window in the attic room of the dowager Ducesse's house that had been allocated for his use; it was long and narrow with a steeply pitched ceiling, but large enough to accommodate his chests of earth as well as his other belongings and still leave room for his narrow bed, a tall stool, and high table; a small fireplace supplied what little heat he had; he had unrolled a dark-red Armenian carpet in front of it. Beyond the open shutters he could hear the sound of sawing and hammering as the men made the most of the break in the weather. On his lap he held an old book, the pages showing ghosts of previous writing beneath the emphatic black text, long ago washed off to provide parchment for newer authors. He was attempting to read the earlier work, an effort that taxed even his remarkable eyes.

A knock on the door disrupted his concentration; he frowned as he called out, "Come in."

The door remained closed a bit longer; then Heugenet stepped through. She was wearing an old cotehardie of faded bronze-green wool with substantial sleeves and a heavy pleated skirt, clearly a garment that had been retired from her current wardrobe and kept for housework and gardening. Her gorget was wilted and her wimple askew so that tendrils of hair framed her face with the linen, and there was an oil smudge on the collar of her touret-de-col. "I didn't mean to interrupt."

"No matter," he said, rising and setting the book aside. "What may I do for you?"

"So formal," she said, her lightness forced. "I've been working to put the pantry—"

"I assumed you must have been busy with some task," he interjected, indicating the slight disarray of her clothes.

"And you are very grand," she countered at once, indicating the eclipse-embroidered black huque he wore.

Germain le-Comte cursed himself inwardly for donning this garment from Clair dela Luna but answered her implied question. "Patrons do not always pay in coin and keep."

"It becomes you," she said, her sea-green eyes troubled. She gave herself a little shake and went on more distantly. "You told me you would need herbs and honey to make more of the remedies for Armand. I am reviewing the stores now, and thought you would want to see what we have on hand. The Ducesse is there, but you need not heed her; age has made her simple." There was no trace of rancor in this remark, for Heugenet held her husband's mother in genuine affection.

"Is she working with you?" Germain le-Comte asked, preparing to go with her.

"She is where there are women doing their work: the cook and a kitchen-maid. She finds such companions comforting, and I have no wish to deny her any consolation she may find." She smiled at Germain le-Comte, her expression softening.

"Since the Great Dying, or before?" Germain le-Comte closed his shutters and set the brace to lock them, then turned back to Heugenet.

"My husband has treated her well—better than many other sons might have done. She saw eight of her children to their graves before her husband died." She crossed herself. "For her, there has been great dying all her life."

Germain le-Comte held the door for Heugenet, his face revealing his quick concern. "How many of her children survived?" He shut the door behind them, set the lock, and fell in behind Heugenet.

"Four. One died of Blood Roses last autumn; a daughter in the Church." She sighed. "She was a stranger to her mother when she died. She was thirty-two, as I recall; a year younger than I am." Her expression became more thoughtful. "It is worse than the Great Dying; everyone is touched by Blood Roses. I cannot think how it must be to lose so many children. If God sent me so heavy a burden, I would not be able to sustain myself under it."

"Do you think so." A pang of sympathy went through him, and he had to hold back his desire to comfort her; it struck him that she was now the same age he had been when he was killed more than thirty-three centuries ago. He said to her, "Did the daughter have a vocation, or was this a different kind of calling?" It was a common-enough bargain struck with the Church, Germain le-Comte knew, and one that had proved useful to the nobility and wealthy merchants who sent their children into Holy Orders, but the arrangement rankled with him, so he added, "A heavy burden for a child to bear, whatever the circumstances."

Heugenet surprised him by saying, "So I think. To pray for all the sins of your blood! I have not allowed Armandal to force our children into the Church. He would have done so with Armand had I not insisted he refrain." She was too well-mannered to take pride in her victory, but a smile flickered at her mouth.

"And in the event, you have been proven wise in your circumspection." They had reached the steep, narrow stairs and began their descent.

"We have other children. Four— Three," she corrected herself, "sons living and two daughters. I do not know how our daughters have fared in these times." She glanced back over her shoulder, a slight frown showing between her brows. "Now we are returned here, I will ask my husband to discover how our daughters are."

"They have been affianced?" Germain le-Comte inquired.

"Marinelle is at the court of the uncrowned Emperor to wait upon his sister; she is now eleven. Joachime is with her affianced husband's family. She is just nine. She was sent to her bridegroom's family as soon as the wedding contract was signed two years ago." She did her best to smile. "It is wrong to want to keep them with me, I know, but it pains me to have them so far away from me." Her voice lowered as if she feared being overheard. "I know Armand is better suited to the cloister than the world, but I could not give him to God while he was so young. Many another would, but I could not."

"And now he is the heir," said Germain le-Comte. "Is the Duc grateful to you for your perspicacity?"

"I don't know," she answered. They were almost to the bottom of the stairs now, and she stopped for a few precious heartbeats. "He may think so, one day. But for now, I suppose he would prefer Ignace were the heir, though he is ten and cannot be named yet. Durand is only six, and his character is not formed yet, according to my husband's kinsman. I am relying on you to help change my husband's favor to Armand."

He read her recklessness in her stance. "I will do what I can, Heugenet," he promised.

"I pray you do, Germain le-Comte," she said, and resumed the last of her downward climb. As she reached the bottom, she paused to wait for him. Finally she looked directly at him and said, "I suppose it is my failing, and I know the wisdom of keeping children far from danger, but I do miss them, Joachime and Durand more than the others, probably because they are youngest and were with me until two years ago. When the war with the English became heated in the north, my husband made sure our children were far from the fighting."

"But Hainaut is not in France," Germain le-Comte pointed out, aware that the borders of France and Hainaut as well as Brabant had changed many times in the last few centuries and could shift again. "What quarrel can the English have with you?"

"We are near enough, and the ties are old ones; the English will hold their conquests in any way they can. Even one fief in Hainaut would secure them in France." She nodded once for emphasis. "You came from the south. You know what they are capable of doing."

"They are no worse and no better than any army on enemy ground," said Germain le-Comte. "French soldiers—or German or Lowlanders— would do the same in England." As they had done, almost three centuries earlier, he thought, when Norman William had crossed the Channel to become the sovereign lord of the English; Germain le-Comte had been in Persia practicing alchemy and developing pigments for the artists who had flourished then in that country while William was making England a Plantagenet fiefdom.

"The English are . . ." She could not find words to express her contempt for them. "Come. Let us see what I have that you need." She started toward the kitchen, motioning to Germain le-Comte to follow her.

He obeyed, glancing around as he trailed Heugenet; the kitchen was a single, vaulted cave of a room with three open fireplaces at one end, each with an array of kettles and spits in front of it. Next to the fireplaces were stone ovens, large structures with metal doors that could accommodate a whole goat or pig. Four chopping-blocks stood in the middle of the room, with pots stacked beside them and an array of knives and cleavers stuck in slots on the sides of the blocks. A rack of wicker trays showed where vegetables were usually kept; they were empty just now but for onions and a few turnips. The kitchen was lit by the fireplaces and by a functional hanging array of oil-lamps, two of which were sputtering from untrimmed wicks.

One woman bustled about the kitchen, taking millet from a bin by the pantry and putting it in a kettle half-filled with water; she was no older than Heugenet, a woman who had once been portly but was now rawboned and loose-fleshed; she had an economy of movement that showed her long experience in her work. She ducked her head to Heugenet and murmured some respectful phrases.

"That is our cook. She was the baxter for five years, but when the cook died she took over the whole of the kitchen. There is a kitchen-maid some-where. All the scullions are gone." Heugenet opened the pantry door and clicked her tongue. "Ma Mère," she said to the woman who puttered among the shelves. "You should not be in here by yourself."

The Ducesse de Verviers turned pale, dazed eyes on her son's wife. "Oh. Dulcine. I didn't see you."

Heugenet turned to Germain le-Comte. "Dulcine was her sister. She died twenty years ago, but sometimes the Ducesse does not remember," she whispered and gave her attention to the Ducesse again. "It would be better if you went into the kitchen. Perside would be glad of your com-pany."

"Perside?" the Ducesse repeated. "How . . ." She looked at Heugenet and smiled. "You're a good girl."

Heugenet's smile lost some of its warmth. "You are tired, ma Mère," she said firmly as if dealing with a stubborn child. "Perside will give you a cup of ale and bake an egg for you." She took the Ducesse by the shoulder and started to guide her out of the pantry.

The old woman wrenched herself free, her mouth becoming a single, obstinate line. "I have to wait here."

"Here?" Heugenet gestured to the shelves with their bins and crocks. "Who will look for you in this place, ma Mère? Why not go into the kitchen—it is warmer and there are stools to sit upon."

The Ducesse blinked once; gradually her face changed and an uncer-tain expression of goodwill returned. "It is a fine day today; so bright," she said as if in the middle of a conversation.

Germain le-Comte stepped to the side, not wanting to provide a dis-traction for the Ducesse; he sensed the dismay that Heugenet concealed, and wished he could alleviate it.

"Yes," Heugenet said patiently. "And Perside has a cup of ale waiting for you." She gave a swift look of apology to Germain le-Comte. "Come, ma Mère. You will be tired soon and you do not want to tax yourself."

The old woman allowed herself to be led out of the pantry and given over to Perside's care. As she drank the proffered cup of ale, she said ab-stractedly, "You're a good girl," to no one in particular.

Perside cocked her head toward the pantry, indicating Heugenet should return to her tasks. "Ducesse," she said, speaking loudly enough to com-mand the woman's attention, "I have a goose here that wants plucking. You like plucking fowl, don't you?"

With a grateful nod to the cook, Heugenet slipped away, going back into the pantry and closing the door behind her. She put her hand to her brow as if to gather her thoughts together as she went up to Germain le-Comte. "She does not know—" Then she fell silent as she went into his arms, rest-ing against him; she slid her arms around him, doubling her safety. She was half a head shorter than he and their closeness was suddenly the most nat-ural, comfortable thing she could want for herself.

Germain le-Comte stood very still, feeling the rigidity go out of her; only then did he kiss her brow and her closed eyes. He did not speak while she released the strict composure she had maintained for so long. When she tilted her face a little upward he kissed her mouth, very softly at first, but with increasing ardor as her close-commanded passion stirred within her. When she broke their kiss, it was with a quiet, reluctant sigh; her hands fell away, and she moved back a step and was remotely disappointed when he did not cling to her. "I wanted that," she said, explaining her lapse to herself.

"I know," said Germain le-Comte, his voice deep and tranquil.

She shook her head. "I . . . I was weak." As if this confession horrified her, she turned away from him. "I am not wanton."

He did not go after her. "Yes, I know."

"But I *am* grateful," she went on, erecting barriers between them, using words to hold him off from her. "What you have done for Armand deserves my thanks. He could not be heir had you not restored him."

"You have nothing to thank me for; Armand is a promising boy, but anything I did was for your sake," he told her, and the defenses she strove to shore up crumbled.

Tears shone in her eyes; she daubed at them brusquely with the hem of her outer sleeve. "I don't know why I should do this," she said, making her tone gruff.

"Perhaps you are tired," Germain le-Comte suggested. There was no condescension in his manner; his dark eyes were filled with concern.

"Perhaps," she allowed, sniffing. She had to fight the impulse to rush back to the shelter of his arms, to the solace of his strength. "It will pass."

He took his tone from her. "In the meantime there is work to do." He indicated the hanging bundles of dried herbs. "Is this all you have?"

"There are some bundles hanging in the stables, but yes, this is all we have within the castle. What is in the stable is used to treat the horses for worms and wounds and rot. If you think any of them would suit your purpose, you may take half of what is there." She managed to regain her briskness; the disastrous urge deep within her quieted. "If there is any herb you need that is not here, and that we may find in this region, then you have only to ask for it; I will dispatch a servant to harvest them in season."

There were two plants Germain le-Comte knew he would have to find on his own: monkshood and hawthorn—monkshood was known to be poisonous and hawthorn was considered the Devil's plant though Germain le-Comte had used it medicinally for nearly three millennia. "I will look over your stores."

She came nearer to him, but was very careful to stay an arm's length away so that she would not be tempted to touch him. "I fear our herbs are sadly depleted."

"As are many other things since the Blood Roses came," Germain le-Comte said. "I am surprised you have so much left."

This minor compliment brought color to her cheeks. "That is more to Perside's credit than mine; she had maintained the kitchen."

"And done so very well," he agreed as he took a bunch of dried lavender and sniffed. "Last year's."

"We have much to do," she said, and lifted a crock down from its place on the shelves. "This honey is gone to granules. We will have to heat it if we are to use it."

"Mix it with a little wine," Germain le-Comte recommended; the Romans had done that with old honey.

She made a gesture to show she had heard him. "We used to have branches of rosemary and thyme, but they're almost gone. Thyme doesn't grow well here; it's too cold." Her self-discipline was taking hold again and she felt less fragile.

"Which accounts for the high price for herbs and spices," Germain le-Comte agreed, recalling the many times he had traded profitably in pepper as well as other spices.

Heugenet took down another crock, opened it and made a face. "The oil is—"

"—rancid," he finished for her. "You'll have to scour the crock with dry sand to get rid of it all." He took a step closer to her to claim the vessel. "I'll put it out."

She backed away from him. "No," she said, color mounting in her face again. "I will tend to it." As she hurried to the door, she offered a kind of explanation. "Perside will not take orders from you. She will listen to me."

"Of course," Germain le-Comte said as if this made sense, and moved away from the place Heugenet had been working.

When she came back, she left the door to the pantry open wide, and busied herself with her inventory, leaving him to select those dried herbs he could use. She looked up only once, and then it was to say, "I am sorry we have so little. I hoped more might have been salvaged, but . . ."

"You have nothing to apologize for," he said kindly. "Those who ransacked the castle are responsible, not you."

She shook her head and murmured a few disjointed phrases as she continued diligently to work.

It was almost sundown when they left the pantry. By then Perside was bustling in the kitchen preparing a hearty stew for the men who had been working through the day; she had set the Ducesse to gathering up the feathers of the goose she had plucked, an occupation that had kept the old woman amused for a good portion of the afternoon. Heugenet stopped to leave her orders in regard to supper for her and Armand, and was about to go on when Germain le-Comte stopped her.

"Will you and your husband want me to play for you this evening?" It was a reasonable question, yet she blushed as if he had proposed something scandalous.

"My husband is with his mistress tonight, and will be for several days,"

she said. "If my son would like songs or stories, we will send word to you."
The stiffness of her response troubled her and she tried to lessen its impact. "I would like to hear a song, but Armand has been at his books all day
and he may not—" She stopped herself.

"I will be happy to serve you in whatever capacity you deem suitable,"
Germain le-Comte said courteously. He nodded to the cook and gave
Heugenet an old-fashioned reverence.

"Such pretty manners," the Ducesse approved, her attention keen for
a moment.

Germain le-Comte reverenced her as well, then left the kitchen, climb-
ing back up the narrow stairs to his room under the eaves. He had two
bundles of herbs in cloth bags, and these he put down on the long table he
had been given; as the light faded from the sky, he began to sort the herbs.
He worked without haste, weighing and bagging, keeping notes on a sheet
of vellum he took from his red lacquer chest. As he continued his self-
appointed labors, he found himself fighting off a fit of melancholy. He was
certain it originated with the Plague, but it had sharpened with his growing concern for Heugenet; the intensity of her need that he had felt in the
pantry only served to increase his despondency, for he was aware that all
the passion he had sensed in her was as genuine as she was hopeless of daring to express it more fully. That puzzled him; she was a woman of purpose
and a great deal of courage, but she regarded both these qualities with suspicion, and he knew that the more she recognized her strength, the more
she would be troubled by it: the Church had taught her she was the weaker
vessel, prey to frenzy and madness, and she had never questioned the wisdom of the teaching, which also assured her that the world was fixed by
God's Will which only the minions of the Devil would seek to disrupt. He
put aside the pennyroyal he had weighed and reached for flint-and-steel
to light a second oil-lamp; his room was sunk in darkness but for the single wisp of flame that illuminated the end of his table. Yet what others
could not see in such gloom, he could, and he was stilled by what he saw.

Heugenet stood in the doorway, a bear-skin rug pulled around her
shoulders over her chamise. Her uncovered hair fell in a single braid over
her shoulder and she moved as if she had just wakened from sleep.
She started as his dark eyes met hers in the gloom. "I . . . I have to speak
to you."

His dejection vanished as if taken away by a conjurer. "Come in," he invited, wondering how long she had been standing there watching him
measure and weigh herbs, and what had brought her here. "There isn't
much—"

She closed the door behind her. "I didn't come for that," she said, the
breath catching in her throat as she went on as if she had already spoken
her thoughts. "But if my thoughts damn me, then I will have the deeds as
well."

He regarded her in silence for a long moment, perceiving her desire and her dread. When he spoke, his voice was gentle. "I am yours to command, Heugenet."

Her laughter was nervous. "It has been almost six years since Armandal has touched me as my husband." This confession made her face flame. "When our youngest was stillborn, he swore he would have no more children, and put me away from him." She was beginning to shiver in spite of the heavy bear-skin. "He has maintained me well, and shown me great respect, but—" She silenced herself by hurling herself into his embrace and pressing her lips to his; the bear-skin fell to her feet in an untidy pile.

Germain le-Comte held her, his ardor answering hers, and he encompassed the tumult of her soul with his love. Gradually he began to caress her through the linen of her chamise, his small hands soothing and arousing at once, evoking her joy as well as her long-pent tears. His kisses were long and deep, and they moved from her mouth to her neck and then, as he opened the pleated collar of her chamise, to the rise of her breasts.

She gasped as his tongue touched her nipple; according to her Confessor, such ministrations were sinful: she reminded herself she was here for sin and abandoned herself to the kindling heat in her flesh. Let her Confessor beat her, she told herself as Germain le-Comte's hands opened her chamise completely. That would pay for her rapture now: this was what she had yearned for and never known, and she was resolved to make the most of it. Her skin had never been so sensitive; every touch, every pressure, every nuance of motion brought increased frissons of excitement. As his lips traced her body from breast to belly to the apex of her thighs, she began to tremble; only by taking hold of his shoulders was she able to remain standing.

He rose at once and drew her to him, cradling her in his arms until she no longer shook. "There is no hurry," he whispered to her.

Recalling her nights with Armandal, she shot him a look of sudden qualms. "What man does not want his pleasure taken quickly?"

"This man, for one," Germain le-Comte said serenely; he would tell her why later, if it became necessary. His esurience flared as he responded to her yearning "Since my pleasure comes from yours, and yours will increase with prolonging. Come. Let me make us a place to lie." Without waiting for her to protest, he bent down and took the bear-skin, and flung it not on his narrow, austere bed, but on the small carpet he had placed before the little fireplace; a few thick branches smoldered in its interior and Germain le-Comte prodded them to sparks as he put another pair of cut branches on the embers. The wood was from pear trees and its smoke was fragrant as incense.

Watching him with apolaustic intensity, Heugenet once again stilled the voice of her Confessor that promised shame and more dire consequences to her for this lascivious debauch. All she would let herself know was that she had never before experienced any pleasure like Germain le-Comte's touch; she refused to relinquish this chance to the strictures of the

Church. For this night, he was all her world; she decided she had never seen a man so graceful and so powerful.

He reclined on the bear-skin and reached up his hand to her. "Come," he repeated softly. "Let me warm you."

She dropped to her knees beside him, her chamise flapping open as she did; it was an effort of will not to hold it closed. "Take what you will," she murmured, and waited as if in prayer.

"Ah, no, Heugenet. You have been taken from enough. Give me what you want me to have," he said as his fingers lingered on the curve of her breast.

"I have forgotten how." His touch ignited her desire more fully, making her bold. She leaned down above him. "Show me how you want me," she said, astonished at her certainty. "Do what you think will gratify me."

He raised himself enough to kiss her mouth as he recommenced his persuasive exploration of her body and slowly she sank down beside him, lying supine as he lavished attention on every part of her flesh that responded to him: hands, lips, even his breath worked enchantment upon her until she was caught up in transports that began in the sea-scented folds at the top of her thighs, expanding through her with such force that she believed she might faint; only Germain le-Comte's head bent to the curve of her neck seemed real.

When she could find words, she whispered, "What have you done to me?"

He raised himself on his elbow and leaned down to kiss the corner of her mouth. "I have loved you." He traced the line of her cheek and brow with one finger.

Her smile was tentative. "But you—? You did not tup me. And you . . . you are still clothed." She searched his face. "I have seen you naked, and there is nothing to—"

He touched her lips lightly to silence her. "If you are satisfied, I am, as well." He knew there would be more questions later; for now she was content to lie in the haven of his arms and drift into sleep. He pulled the edge of the bear-skin over her to keep her warm as the fire died; until the first bird calls he held her beside him, treasuring the revelation of her passion.

Text of a decree from the Bishop of Reims, posted throughout the city and on its gates.

In the Name of God, His Son and the Holy Spirit, amen.
All those who are found with Blood Roses on their flesh, living or dead, shall be taken to the peste-houses beyond the city walls and when they are buried, it will be in the pits dug for that purpose. No victim of this Plague will be buried within the city walls.
All those poisoning wells will be taken outside the city walls and burned.
All those stealing from the dead and dying will be set to work in the peste-

houses where God will judge their repentance and heal or strike them down for their sins.

All those who commit sins against God will be taken from the city and burned as an act of faith. Any who protect or shelter such miscreants will be hanged from the city walls as an example to others.

All those wandering the roads of the region with the intention of doing ill to others, of stealing land and possessions will be put to work in peste-houses. Those who ally themselves with Flagellants will be burned for their crimes and sins against Holy Church.

All those spreading lies and sedition will be taken from the city and burned at the stake.

All those living in faith are enjoined to pray four times every day for the salvation of mankind and the souls of those who have been called to the Mercy Seat. On those true followers of Christ, the Church extends blessings and the promise of interment in Church grounds when the Great Dying is over.

All those remaining at their work in the world are promised the favor of the Church for their devotion to the Will of God, and the prayers of monks and nuns from now until the end of the world. God has taken one in four of our people in this city, and for this loss we have much to attone.

In the absence of the ministers of the King of France, I set my seal of command upon this.

Aloys, Bishop
by my own hand

On the 5th day of March, the feast of Saint Gerasimus, in the 1350th Year of Our Lord.

8

Three peasants bore a fourth on a litter up to the gates of Mon Gardien. The spring rain muddied the road and left tracks on their weathered faces as they approached the warder, averting their eyes in respect. Their bowl-cut, shaggy hair and spatulate fingers showed them to be more than farmers: smiths or carpenters, judging from their shoulders and forearms.

"Well?" the warder asked; he had been watching the peasants approach for a while and had decided they had not brought Blood Roses to the castle: that was a hanging offense. Already three bodies of those foolish enough to attempt such a heinous act hung over the gates from the battlement above; the odor of decay clung to the entrance.

"The man has a fever but no Blood Roses. He has not danced and he does not cough." The oldest peasant acted as their leader, but as he spoke, his courage failed him.

"Tell him, Tros," urged the man behind him. "Tell him."

Tros cleared his throat. "They say the new heir is cured of coughing. They said there was a foreigner who treated him and the coughing stopped. We were told the foreigner is still with the boy, so we brought—" He pointed to the litter. "We hoped this man could be cured, too."

The warder opened his grille a little wider to try to see the man on the litter. "What is wrong with him?" he asked when he could not discern that for himself.

"He has pains in the belly. He shits himself all the time. He burns with fever." Tros recited the symptoms carefully. "We have inspected him; there are no Blood Roses."

"Bring him a bit nearer," said the warder reluctantly; it was the duty of the seigneur of the castle to offer succor to vassals in need and as warder he did not have the authority to turn these men away unless the stricken peasant had contracted the Black Plague.

The peasants obeyed with alacrity, the gratitude in their faces almost painful. "We would not bring him if it were Blood Roses," Tros assured the warder as the litter was put down in front of the portcullis.

"Wise of you," muttered the warder as he tried to inspect the man on the litter. He noticed the sufferer lay on his side, not his back, and that his knees were drawn up against his abdomen; he stank of feces. "How long has he been like this?"

"It struck him last night," said one of the other peasants. "He had gone to his house and closed the door. He went to the midden some time later. He was moaning, so my woman and I went to see what his trouble was." He did not add that they had carried a club to beat him with in case he had been taken by the dancing frenzy that sometimes heralded Blood Roses. "He was white and weak and his wits were wandering."

"We made him drink urine, to drive out the fever, but he did not improve," said Tros. He looked directly at the warder. "He must be taken in."

The warder frowned. "It is a good thing, to show charity to the sick," he said at last, as if giving himself permission to allow the peasants to bring the sufferer inside the walls of Mon Gardien. He left his post and went to open the small gate set in the portcullis. "Bear him into the courtyard." As he said this, he was thinking of all he would have to do now; he would have to send one of the men-at-arms to summon Heugenet da Brabant since Armandal d'Ais was gone from the castle and the Ducesse was beyond understanding. Once that was done, he would have to see that the peasants who brought him were given food and drink before they were sent back to their hamlet. He went after the men with the litter, almost forgetting to secure the door in the gate before he left his post. "You peasants," he called to them. "Don't go any farther. Stay where you are."

The men turned to face him, one of them clearly frightened. "What have we done wrong?" Tros asked, doing his best to present himself well to this man of authority.

"I must find out where this man is to be taken," said the warder. "Stay where you are until I return." He shouted over his shoulder, "Hannes, man the gate for me."

From somewhere behind him, a shout of compliance came; the warder did not wait to see the man-at-arms take up his post. He went past the keep to the dowager's house, his heart loud in his ears for no reason he could determine. As he scratched on the door for admittance, he squared his shoulders and set his face to impassivity. When Remi, the understeward, opened the door, the warder was almost ready for him; he took his damp woolen cap off in respect. "There is a sick man. Not Blood Roses. The peasants brought him. They're in the main courtyard. They want—"

Remi, who was twenty-three, sighed heavily. "They want succor for him, I suppose." He indicated the warder should step inside. "I will fetch Heugenet da Brabant; she is with her son. He is having lessons."

"I will wait," the warder assured him, and took up his place next to the door as if he planned to continue his gate-keeping here.

The room set aside for lessons was on the second floor, a good-sized chamber with a worn tapestry on one wall opposite the fireplace. Two benches and a table had been moved in, and Armand was seated on one of them, his mother on the other, while Germain le-Comte walked the length of the room and back while explaining the military campaigns during the reign of Diocletian; Heugenet was sewing while Armand scribbled notes with a stylus on a wax tablet. "—on the Dalmatian coast, where the Emperor maintained a palace and an extensive estate—" He stopped as Remi tapped on the door.

Heugenet looked up, mildly annoyed at the interruption. "Yes? What is it?" She motioned to Germain le-Comte to resume, and went to the door to speak with Remi.

Germain le-Comte remained silent while Heugenet and Remi spoke softly in the door. "Is something wrong?" he asked as she turned away.

She shrugged in exasperation. "I don't know. Some peasants have brought a sick man here. With my husband gone to Luxembourg, I cannot refuse to take him in if he does not have Blood Roses." She glanced at Armand. "If you come with me, it may be best. Your father is not here to decide; they will like it better if his heir tends to the matter." Her eyes softened as she turned to Germain le-Comte. "I am sorry to stop the lesson."

"You have no reason to apologize," Germain le-Comte said to her. "If my assistance is needed, you have only to tell me."

Armand had set his tablet and stylus aside and now rose from the bench. "Yes. He must come. If anyone can treat the man's ills, it is Germain le-

Comte." He did not notice the quick look of alarm Heugenet exchanged with Germain le-Comte.

"But it isn't fitting for him to wait on vassals," Heugenet reminded Armand. "He is not a vassal himself; we will send for him when the——"

Heugenet watched as Armand left the room in disgust, ordering Remi to follow him. "Do you mind?" she asked Germain le-Comte. "He's right, you know. We have no herb-woman to care for him; she died last year."

Although he had strong misgivings, Germain le-Comte said, "If you request it, how can I refuse?" There was a trace of irony in his bow, at odds with the warmth of his dark eyes.

She whispered thank-you and hurried out of the room, saying, "He will come," to Armand as he started down the stairs.

Taking the time to close the schoolroom door, Germain le-Comte had a brief while to chide himself for his folly: treating a sick man would bring him precisely the attention he had hoped to avoid. But he had promised to help Heugenet and he would not renege on that pledge.

Remi was with the warder when Germain le-Comte joined Armand and Heugenet by the door. "He cannot be brought under this roof," he was insisting. "The Ducesse cannot be exposed to any illness; she has no protection against miasmas, or the corruption of her soul."

"Then we will put him somewhere that will not endanger her; that is not a difficult precaution," said Heugenet with decision; she had already given the matter some thought. "There is a place in the stables, an old feed room; it is empty now." She glanced at Germain le-Comte. "Will you be able to work there?"

"As well as anywhere," he answered, not quite candidly; the conditions he would have liked to have had not been available in Gaul for centuries: the Moors in Spain practiced medicine more wholesomely than their Christian counterparts, but neither of them maintained the standards of the old Romans, whose pursuit of cleanliness had advanced their physicians as well as their architects. "I will need a soldier's stove and a cask of fresh water. They must be taken to the room where the peasant is to be treated." He would supply the rest of his materials from the contents of his red lacquer chest. "It may be well to keep him apart from the rest."

"Is there danger?" Remi asked, suddenly worried. He shot a look toward the litter and the peasants standing guard around it. "If this is not Blood Roses, could it be something worse?" He was scaring himself and troubling the others as he voiced his apprehension.

"Germain le-Comte will discover that for us," said Armand unexpectedly; he stood a bit straighter and spoke with a confidence he had not shown before. "Will you not?"

The troubador inclined his head. "I will do my utmost." He thought briefly of his laboratory at Clair dela Luna, but quickly put it from his mind; he was as far from that as if it were in China. "If you have hyssop among your herbs stored in the stable, that could be helpful." Had Rogres been with him, he would have sent him to find it in the forest, along with nettles and wild garlic. Again he shut such useless thoughts away; had Rogres been with him, he would not have been accepted as a troubador.

"Thank you," said Heugenet; she wanted to touch him, to embrace him, but that would lead to the exposure that could send them both to early graves.

"And I thank you, too," said Armand quickly, determined to make the most of his new-found sense of prestige. "You helped me. You will help the peasant."

Remi nodded in approval of Armand's order. "My father has told me I am obliged to protect my vassals. The Great Dying has not changed that."

"No; I suppose not," said Heugenet, and put her hand on her son's arm. "You will honor your name."

Germain le-Comte was aware that Remi did not want to go near the peasant, and that Heugenet was concerned; with a half-reverence, he said, "It will probably be more prudent if I examined the man alone." He indicated the warder, standing within earshot. "This good man will take me. You need not come any farther."

Heugenet studied his face a moment, then said, "That may be the best way." With that she nodded to the warder. "See the sufferer is put in the room in the stable and make sure the men who brought him have food and drink before they leave."

"Yes, my lady," said the warder, motioning to Germain le-Comte to follow him. As they began to walk toward the peasants, he pointed. "There they are."

"So I supposed," Germain le-Comte said, his sardonic note lost on the warder.

Tros watched the warder approach with the man in troubador's motley with misgiving. "Who is this? Why do you bring him?"

The warder ignored the insolence in the question. "This is Germain le-Comte. It is he who has cured the heir of his coughing. Armand has ordered that he inspect your—"

The other two peasants were staring at Germain le-Comte in unabashed curiosity; one of them crossed himself, watching the stranger closely to see if he would flinch at this act of protection.

Germain le-Comte crossed himself as if to answer a challenge. "May God guide me to do well by your companion," he said, and went down on one knee beside the litter. "How long has he been like this?" The man had a fever; he was hollow-eyed and he had the taut look of thirst: Germain le-Comte knew he would have to salt the water he gave to the man.

"Since late in the night," said Tros. "He has no Blood Roses. We looked." He spoke as if he expected praise.

"A wise precaution," said Germain le-Comte automatically. "How do you think he has come to have this . . . trouble?"

Tros shrugged. "The Devil, a miasma, some unknown sin."

"Or the disfavor of the old gods, perhaps?" Germain le-Comte added. "I will do what I can to make him well again." He rose. "The room in the stable will do."

Relieved, Tros nodded his approval to Germain le-Comte; he swung around to his companions. "This man has been appointed." He spoke over his shoulder to Germain le-Comte. "We will pray for you, and for Pieret."

"Is that his name?" Germain le-Comte saw the nod. "It will be easier to speak with him if I know his name. Pieret. Good." He gave his attention to the warder, his manner authoritative without being overbearing. "Have him borne to the room and have the stove and water put there. I will attend him shortly." He made a gesture of respect to the peasants who had brought him. "If he lives, it will be more from your care than my skill."

Tros stepped back. "We will want to know what becomes of him."

"God willing, he will come back to you whole," said Germain le-Comte, knowing he was being tested. "He is not improving while we stand here in the rain." There was not enough water to make him uncomfortable; he was concerned for Pieret.

"Certainly," said the warder, and shouted to the men-at-arms across the courtyard near the smithy. "Montcerry! Damolin! Come here."

The two men-at-arms responded without haste; they had been watching what was going on and they had no wish to have any contact with a sick peasant, but they were not willing to risk punishment for defiance. "What?" Montcerry asked as they came up to the group around the litter; the peasants moved farther away.

"You know the empty feedroom in the stable? Take this man there. Put the litter up, on one of the old trestle-beds, so that he will not leave his miasma in the floor." The warder rapped out his orders as much to command the cooperation of the men-at-arms as to impress the peasants with his importance. "When you have done, report to me."

Germain le-Comte could see the reluctance in the men's stride, and could not blame them for their hesitation: with so much sickness abroad in the world, all ills were suspect. "Do not touch him any more than you must," he recommended.

Damolin made a face, but went to the head of the litter and took one of the two pulls in his hands. "Montcerry. Let's get this done."

Montcerry took the other pull, saying, "The old feed-room. Very good."

The two men set off as if they were horses in harness; neither would look back at the peasant on the litter. They worked quickly, as if haste would lessen their risk.

As they reached the door of the stable, Germain le-Comte called after them, "Wash your hands in wine and water when you are done." It was little enough, but men-at-arms would consider anything more than that effeminate and unworthy of them. He saw Montcerry cock his head but could not tell if this meant assent or defiance.

"Well?" The warder looked directly at Germain le-Comte. "What more are my men to do?"

"The peasant is to have a blanket, and fresh straw in his mattress if it is permitted." He swung around to look at the dowager's house. "The understeward should be able to provide that. I must go get my supplies."

The warder watched him narrowly. "How is it that a troubador knows such things?"

Germain le-Comte gave him the same answer that he had given Heugenet: one who travels as a troubador must, must also learn to care for himself and for all manner of ills. Then he added, "I have been in many foreign places and everywhere I have gone, I have learned something of value." With that explanation, he went off toward the dowager's house. He was admitted by Remi who was still flustered.

"It is not Blood Roses, is it?" the understeward asked in a rush, peering out toward the stable door. "He looks so . . . so sick."

"One can be sick, even to death, without Blood Roses," Germain le-Comte reminded him. "I have seen this illness before." He knew it usually came from eating rotten meat or fowl, and he recalled that those who contracted the disease often died from it; he knew it would not be wise to say so. "I must get my medicaments if I am to do anything for him."

Remi stood aside, saying as he did, "Heugenet da Brabant wants to speak to you before you treat that peasant."

"I will wait upon her now," said Germain le-Comte as he went for the stairs.

He found Heugenet in the schoolroom; she was pacing, her face pale with dismay. "I didn't know what else to do," she exclaimed as she caught sight of him. "I could not order the farrier to treat him; the men would not tolerate that. But I . . . If I have put you in danger, I cannot bear it."

"I am not in danger," said Germain le-Comte quietly, making a swift perusal of the room to be certain Armand was not there.

Guessing his intent, Heugenet said, "He has gone into the keep, to locate some books that the men salvaged." She came close to him. "How can you not be in danger? The peasant is near dying—anyone can see that."

"Those of my blood have nothing to fear from disease," he said, hoping to soothe her. "Not this, not the bending-sickness, not Blood Roses: none of them can touch me."

She crossed herself. "Do not lie to reassure me," she said, angry with herself and vexed with him. "How can you lie to me?" Tears filled her eyes as she closed the distance between them. "You must not lie to me."

He kissed her brow, the linen of her coif stiff against his upper lip. "I am not lying, Heugenet." He took her face in his hands. "Look at me; I am not lying."

She turned her eyes toward his and gradually the frightened accusation in hers turned to astonishment. "You are not lying," she breathed. She shook her head, the motions so tiny that if he were not touching her, he might not have seen them. "How can that be?"

"It is my nature," he told her gently and felt her shake.

"Your nature—what nature does not fear sickness?" The fear was back in her eyes again, this time less urgent than before, but still potent.

He would have to give her some explanation; he could not offer her half-truths or facile accommodation to religion or superstition. "Death— death from illness—cannot touch me." He moved his hands to her shoulders. "Oh, I can die. Fire, beheading, breaking my spine, all those are as fatal to me as to you. But no disease can touch me. Believe this."

She was staring now, her face all but blank as she took two steps back from him. "Those scars . . . I remember them." She stretched out her hand and touched him just above his waist, as if feeling his skin and not cloth. "The scars were . . ." Finding no words, she shook her head. He said nothing; he waited for her to decide what would be next between them. His dark eyes never wavered from hers. Finally she gave a short little sigh and came back to him, wrapping her arms around his waist. "Whatever it is, I don't care." When they kissed this time there was a change in the quality of it, as if an ephemeral barrier had been penetrated or an invisible chain had been broken. As she ended their kiss she smiled at him. "Go. Tend to the peasant."

"I will do what I can for him," Germain le-Comte promised her, releasing her slowly.

"If there is cause for alarm, you will tell me," she requested as he started for the door.

"From his sickness?" he asked, going on without waiting for an answer. "If I am right, he has eaten tainted meat or fowl. Make sure Perside cooks all her dishes thoroughly and serves nothing that has sat for more than a day, or that smells metallic."

"Metallic?" Heugenet wanted him to remain with her as much as she wanted an answer for her question. "What is the danger in that?"

"Food that has become tainted sometimes smells metallic," he said, and shook his head. "I must go; the man is suffering."

"And I am cruel to keep you here," she said, waving him away. "Come to me when you can. I have missed you since—" The color that mounted in her face made her meaning plain.

"And I you," he said. He stepped out into the corridor and went to the stairs leading up to his quarters, wondering as he went if he should tell her the whole of it: that disclosure was not yet necessary, but he disliked misleading her.

He reached his room and took his red lacquer chest, lifting with an ease that would have astonished anyone who knew how heavy the chest was. Maneuvering with care, he got the chest down the two flights of stairs and out into the side courtyard; he was stymied by the presence of the men-at-arms, Montcerry among them, who waited in the stable door. Pretending to stagger, he called out, "Will one of you men lend a hand?" This was less than the truth but it would postpone suspicion.

Montcerry grinned. "Too much for a troubador?" His expression said that he would not be hampered by the burden. Swaggering a bit he came up to Germain le-Comte. "Let me carry it." Smiling a little he wrapped his arms around the chest and lifted, grunted, and tightened his grip.

"Do you want me to help," Germain le-Comte offered, slightly amused at Montcerry's efforts.

"I'll . . . manage," he hissed through his teeth. He tottered along, panting. Making his way into the stable, he put the chest down and shoved it the rest of the way to the open door of the empty room. His only concession to Germain le-Comte was a muttered, "Weighs more than it looks."

Germain le-Comte made a gesture of agreement as Montcerry swung away from the door. "I will take care of it from here." He could see how this release pleased the man-at-arms. "Thank you for helping me."

Montcerry made no response as he continued on his way toward the stable-door and the rain that was now hardly more than a mist that shone beyond.

The men-at-arms had brought the stove and the cask of water as well as a small scuttle of wood; they were just inside the door, obviously left in haste; Germain le-Comte nodded slowly and began to arrange the stone room for the work he would have to do. As soon as his materials were in place, he stripped off his houppelande, remaining in his dark-red chamisa over braise of fine black wool and knee-length ritter-hose of heavy black Antioch silk. Rolling up his sleeves, he went to examine Pieret, removing his garments and putting him in a loose Egyptian robe of cream-colored cotton, taking note as he did this of the odor of the peasant's flesh and breath as well as the heat of the fever in him. "Tainted food," he said to himself, his assumptions confirmed; the man was thin, and probably could not bring himself to waste one scrap of food, no matter how old it was. "Listen to me, Pieret. If you will fight the sickness, so will I."

Through the afternoon he forced the sick man to drink salted water as well as a purgative tincture to rid his body of the poisons from the meat; every time the peasant vomited or passed urine or feces, Germain le-Comte would make him drink more before going about cleaning him. He worked methodically with the economy of long practice: the treatment was an old one, learned in the Temple of Imhotep, more than two thousand years ago; over the centuries Germain le-Comte had modified it a little, but not so drastically that Sehet-ptenh would not recognize it even now. Soon after sundown, he began to hope his patient could recover. He took another tincture from his chest, this one a preparation of strengthening herbs and honey to shore up what little strength Pieret had left. He wanted to use his most sovereign remedy, but worried that Pieret was too weak. Finally he mixed some of the clear liquid in the salted water and gave it to the peasant.

"No . . . no more," Pieret gasped as more of the mixture was tilted down his throat. He coughed twice and tried to spit the water out of his mouth, sputtering with effort.

"You must. The virtue will not be present if you do not drink it all," Germain le-Comte said, his voice level, his small hands firm.

"It is not Blood Roses, then?" Pieret's words came shakily, but with growing purpose. "I thought . . . it had to be . . . Blood Roses."

"No." Germain le-Comte wiped Pieret's brow with a small linen cloth. "Don't waste your strength talking. Rest. There will be plenty of time to talk later."

Pieret made a gesture that might have been gratitude or might have been protest as he lay back. Only then did he become aware of his unfamiliar garment. "What . . ."

"It is something for you to wear while you are recovering," Germain le-Comte said.

"It looks like a shroud." Pieret managed to cross himself to ward off the ill-omen.

"It also looks like the robes of angels," Germain le-Comte pointed out, hoping the peasant had seen pictures in church.

Apparently this answer was acceptable; Pieret sighed and pulled the blanket up to his chin, lapsing into a half-sleep at once.

Some time later that night, Germain le-Comte went to the deserted kitchen and made a pot of strong broth of goat-meat and bones; from his own stores he added ginger, hyssop, and comfrey root. When this was ready, he took it back to the stable to feed to Pieret, thinking to himself as his patient drank the broth that the man's hunger and thirst were ending: his own were increasing.

Text of a letter from Armandal d'Ais, Duc de Verviers, at the stronghold of Luxembourg, to his wife, Heugenet da Brabant, at Mon Gardien in Hainaut.

To my most esteemed wife, greetings from the court of our Emperor. May God guard and protect our son and you while I am away, and may no harm come to Mon Gardien.

It will be some time before I will be at liberty to leave the Emperor's company, three more months at the least; I and many of my peers have been ordered to remain here at the Emperor's pleasure, and I am obedient to his order in this and all things but those of God.

I have your letter of a fortnight since, and I am pleased to know that the deaths from the Black Plague have been declining. May we have an end to the Great Dying at last. I have informed the Emperor and the Archbishop of this and they have rejoiced and thanked God for His Mercy.

I am authorizing you to spend ten golden crowns to pay for such food as you may need to keep my household for the months of April and May. At that time, I will know how much longer I will be remaining here and will provide you with the funds you will need then if my absence is to continue. You are not to squander the money on anything for fancy; demand full value for your gold. If Perside accompanies you, you will not be tempted by frivolous luxuries or inferior goods. I will keep my steward Pinceau with me still; Remi will be able to manage for you a while longer, and be proud of his opportunity. My man-at-arms, Biebart, will carry this to you and will bring your reply back to me. I hope that over the next two months the Emperor will garrison more men to Mon Gardien and my fortresses, which protect the Emperor as much as they protect my holdings.

Before I return home, I plan to inspect all the forts that guard my lands. This review is long overdue, and I cannot hope to enforce my claims with my borders unprotected; the fortresses are crucial to maintaining the fiefdom. I will send you word when I depart this place that I am coming, and by what route. If I am delayed along the way, I will try to inform you of it.

In your reply, stipulate the depletion of stores of weapons and any repairs that must be attended to at Mon Gardien, so that I may authorize their replacement and restocking to meet any threat to the castle. There are many dangers I anticipate may arise when the Blood Roses have passed. I do not want the castle to be left vulnerable when there is so much that might yet lead to disaster. We have not seen the rebellions that have sprung up in France and Lorraine and the Low Countries as well as in Brabant; that does not mean we will not have to contend with them. I expect an account of our arms and their conditions to be a part of your reply.

May God keep you and my heir, and may He protect Verviers from all harm.

In show of respect and affection, I sign myself,

> *Armandal d'Ais,*
> *Duc de Verviers*
> *by the hand of Frer Paulot*

At Luxembourg on the second day of April, in the 1350th Year of Grace.

Post Scriptum: I have seen our daughter, Marinelle, on two occasions now. She conducts herself with modesty and shows herself devoted to the Emperor's sister, who tells me that she is a very pleasing companion. This should bode well for my interests here at court.

PART IV

GERMAIN LE-COMTE

*T*ext of a letter from Atta Olivia Clemens to Sanct' Germain Franciscus written in the Latin of Imperial Rome; never sent.

To my dearest, oldest, most vexatious of friends, my greetings from Trieste.
  Since I haven't a notion where you are, or what name you may be using, or if you can be found, I do not know how I will get this to you, yet I must write to you: you worry me with this long silence, or what I assume is long silence, since nothing sent later than last winter has reached me. For all I know, you have been dispatching letters to me every fortnight, and none of them have found their way here, which is hardly surprising, given what has become of the world.
  I am pleased to tell you that the Black Plague seems to be passing at last. The number of deaths has dropped in the last month and some are beginning to say that it is possible that we will see the end of it before summer. I am not as convinced as many of them are, but I would be happy to be wrong in my fears. I cannot remember such profligate dying as I have witnessed in the last year. It is astonishing how many people can suddenly disappear from the face of the earth. I know I said much the same thing when the malaria of Rome was at its worst, but I confess I erred.
  Unfortunately we have not been wholly unscathed; three of my servants died from the Plague, and one of the drayers who brought food to my villa. Your old friend Faustino took ill and died six weeks since; it was not Blood Roses that killed him but a corruption of the lungs. He fought the illness long and hard, but it conquered him in the end, nothing Rogerian or Niklos could do would stem that tide. The local monks were unwilling to bury

him because he was a player, and therefore they considered him unworthy of their prayers. Never mind. We made him a grave in the center of my courtyard at Il Capolavoro, where he rehearsed with his troupe, and where we are certain he will rest peacefully. We have marked the place with a stone carved with the masks of comedy and tragedy with his name beneath. The troupe remains at Il Capolavoro while I am here in Trieste; I will be returning there in a few days, as soon as I have received word from Rome: I do not want to return to the city while it is still in the throes of the disease, or another civil rebellion. Yet I do miss it: it is my native earth.

And you, my friend, what of you? Are you still taking on the burdens of the living? How much longer do you intend to continue to work to save them? Do you do this to expiate your longevity, I wonder? Or is it something more than that, some roundabout apology for living as you do? If that is the case, then you little appreciate how much you give when you bestow your love, and I do not mean the pleasure you impart, I mean the strength of your cherishing, and the revelation that comes with your intimacy. I realize you do not perceive yourself in this way, but as one who has received your deliverance, I comprehend your gifts more truly than you do.

If you have, in all this death, found living passion, I rejoice for you. This is no time to deny yourself the joys you can offer. Let your call to life serve to assuage the grief of those whom you treasure, and spare the recipients of your love the finality of the grave. I know you, Sanct' Germain, and I know how obdurate you can be, no matter how you claim it is not so; I have reason to thank all your forgotten gods for your obduracy. I would never have achieved my advanced years had you not insisted that you were bound to me until the True Death itself.

How bothersome it is not to be able to hand this to a courier and send him off to you. I suppose I shall have to keep it until you deign to come and claim it for yourself. You had better do that before too long; Niklos and Rogerian are looking after me far too well to be good for me.

With my everlasting—or very nearly everlasting—love, as well as my continuing exasperation, I sign myself,

Olivia

At Trieste, on the Feast of Saint Mark the Evangelist, the 25th day of April, 1350 Christian Years.

1

Long into the night, Germain le-Comte sat in his room and picked out melodies on his mandola; some were familiar songs, others were foreign, coming from China, from India, from Egypt, fashioned from scales and harmonies unknown in the West. His playing was desultory, more part of his thoughts than a performance, and he had a great deal to think about; another family had brought a sick youngster to Mon Gardien, asking for his help in saving the boy. He had agreed to try, for he saw that the illness was not so dire that the child could not recover, but he was uncomfortably aware that for everyone he treated, five more would come, hoping to be cured: their numbers had been increasing, from two and three in a week to more than ten in the last six days. Heugenet had encouraged him to accept these patients, for such charity enhanced the reputation of Armand as the next seigneur; she was aware that her son needed the support of the peasants to ensure his position. Germain le-Comte did not like refusing her any more than he wanted to turn away those he could help, but he could not forget how dangerous a thing fame could be for him and he was already seeing proof of his spreading reputation as a healer: Pieret had spent the first market-day of spring regaling anyone who would listen with a harrowing account of his sickness and miraculous recovery—which grew more extraordinary with every retelling, and which was being repeated and embroidered throughout Verviers.

As Germain le-Comte's patients recovered and left, a shift took place among the residents of Mon Gardien; in the last two days the castle servants had begun to avoid him, taking pains to be very courteous when they had to deal with him, and grateful when he went to his room or left the dowager's house to treat a new patient. He had experienced this partial invisibility many times before, and he told himself he should be used to it, and thankful for the privacy it assured him; but he also knew that the more foreign he became, the greater the suspicions were that would be visited upon him. Eventually it would be easy to assign malefic purposes to his actions, and then to make those assumptions reason enough to find fault with everything he had done.

There was also the death warrant that had been issued for Francois Saint-Germain, Sieur Ragoczy; he had been careful, but it was still possible he might be identified as the man they sought, and then what might become of him? He hoped that Heugenet would try to protect him, but he was sure she would do so only if her protection did not endanger her son. He set the mandola aside and nearly sighed. "I will have to tell her," he remarked to the night. "If she understands, she can prepare."

If Rogres were with him, he would have discussed these things at length; he had concealed his true nature for longer periods many times before, but now, with the presence of the Plague all around him, he felt a double demand upon him. He knew this was an extension of his isolation, as unrelenting as his hunger for touching and the intimacy of his esurience; he was bound to life, Rogres would tell him, and sometimes the bond was as much shackle as vow.

Shortly before dawn he went down to the paddock behind the stable to check on Caesar; the donkey had been enjoying his rest from travels and had gained weight as he shed the heaviest part of his shaggy coat. At Germain le-Comte's call, he ambled over to the fence and butted his nose against the troubador's small hand. Germain le-Comte obliged with scratching him between the ears while the donkey craned his neck in ecstasy.

Before he went back to the dowager's house, Germain le-Comte stopped in the stable: four stalls and the feedroom had been transformed into an infirmary for the sick and injured who had come to be tended to. Making his rounds as he did every night at this time, his next-to-last stop was by the makeshift bed of a ten-year-old boy whose foot had been badly hurt: Germain le-Comte had set the broken bones and packed the lacerations with spirits of moldy bread; so far there was very little infection and the cuts and scrapes were beginning to mend.

"Will I have to use a crutch?" the boy asked suddenly, opening his candid blue eyes so easily that Germain le-Comte knew he had not been fully asleep.

"I don't know," Germain le-Comte answered, keeping his voice low so as not to wake the others. He continued his perusal of the wrappings on the child's foot.

"They let my sisters die, all of them," he said in a rush. "They're all gone."

"Yes," said Germain le-Comte, his tone steady; of all those he had treated, only one had been a woman, and she had been pregnant; she had recovered without miscarrying, which had earned Germain le-Comte the gratitude of her man and her father. He realized his attention had wandered from the boy; he resumed his observations.

Watching him, the child began to frown. He swallowed hard. "I'm not going to die, am I?"

"Yes," said Germain le-Comte calmly. "When you are an old man." He laid his hand on the boy's forehead. "Everyone dies: you, everyone you know. Even I will die, in time."

The boy crossed himself. "But not now?"

"Not from your injuries; no," he replied carefully as he completed his examination.

"Doesn't it scare you?" the boy asked, peering up at Germain le-Comte's face.

"Death?" He saw the child nod. "No; death does not scare me. I am troubled for those I will leave behind, but for myself—" He got to his feet. "I have seen death far too often to fear it." His execution had left him enraged, but that had been thirty-three centuries ago.

The child blinked. "Oh. Yes. I guess you must have." The tension eased from his features. "I've been trying to stay awake, so I will know I'm alive. But if I don't have to—"

"Sleep is more a healer than anything I can do for you," Germain le-Comte said, his dark eyes gentle and enigmatic.

As if in agreement the boy yawned. "It's very late, isn't it?"

"Very early is more like it. Go on. Rest now," Germain le-Comte said as he passed on to the last of his patients.

The last man was not doing as well as the boy; he was a stonemason, accustomed to working naked to the waist, he had an ugly canker on his shoulder that had been growing and was now a spiderlike shape about the size of a silver royal perched like a malevolent ornament on his skin. Germain le-Comte had given the man pansy and syrup of poppies to lessen the pain; if the mason had come sooner, there might have been some hope of saving him, but that was no longer possible: all he could do now was lessen the man's suffering.

The man moaned in his stuporous sleep; his body stank with the rot of his canker and his flesh was wasted so that his bones strained against his skin.

"Two more days," said Germain le-Comte. Then it would be over; the mason would be free of the burden his life had become. He touched the mason's brow, his eyes half-closed in concentration; he could feel the life in the man waning, slipping away like morning mist. Carefully he made the sign of the cross on the mason's forehead and recited a few of the prayers he had heard so many times; perhaps the mason was still cognizant enough to find the ritual comforting. Rising, he went to the door of the stable and looked out into the lightening sky where the morning star burned. The sun was a palpable presence to him, looming just out of sight; an urtication that reminded him he would have to refill the soles of his solers with his native earth or risk being burned. He strode away from the stable to the kitchen door of the dowager's house. As he closed the door, he saw Heugenet standing by the window.

"I've been watching for you," she said quietly, and jumped as a cock bawled a welcome to the morning; other birds called out their tributes in echo of the cock.

He stood very still. "Is that wise?" He asked at last, when he had satisfied himself that they were alone.

"Don't fret: I have kept myself out of the sight of the sentries—not that they pay any attention to this house; there is no trouble here. I am not going to compromise myself, or you." She had dressed in a dark cote-hardie—he assumed it was deep-green or -blue—with tippet-sleeves that allowed her to show off the fine linen of her chamise; she wore neither gorget nor wimple, leaving her hair in a single plait down her back, and her brow encircled with a coronet of braided ribbands. "But I long for you."

"And I for you," he responded, her vitality touching all his senses. He took a step toward her, holding his hands out to her. "Come away from the window."

She put her hands in his and allowed him to draw her into the shadows. "How can I do this?" she asked herself just before she kissed him.

Their silence was long, complex and complicated, their flesh responding to more than need or simple desire: the kiss was a quest in which both sought to claim the ineffable heart of the other. As she ended the kiss, she held him more tightly, as if she were suddenly on unsteady ground. He did not release her. "Heugenet, Heugenet, what do you seek in me?"

She shook her head. "I don't know," she whispered, as if to speak more loudly would require more of an answer from her. She huddled against him, finding solace in his nearness and his steadfast calm. "I am *so lonely*," she confessed in a rush. "And everyone is dying." Her soft cry struck him to the core; for millennia he had endured what she had been forced to experience in little more than a year. Her emotion echoed his own. She put her hand to his mouth. "You are true. You are here." She kissed his hands, trying to express her gratitude. "You are not imprisoned by fear. I see that in your eyes—you grieve yet you are not afraid." The intensity of his response grew; the kitchen, the castle around them now as unreal as the cloud-castle of the Danish heros; there was only the ignited yearning they shared, and the fulfillment they sought. Abruptly she pushed his shoulder as the first pink light of dawn sent streamers across the sky. "Not here," she breathed. "We must not . . . be discovered."

"Where?" he murmured, stroking her uncovered hair; he removed the coronet and kissed her brow where it had rested.

"In the keep," she said suddenly. "The repairs are nearly finished; no one will look for us there. We will be alone. The workers are on the roof and the top story." A brief, mischievous smile flicked over her features. "We can go there and no one will know. They will not even think to look for us." She pulled at his arm, her urgency making her brusque. "Come. The workers will be gathering for prayers shortly."

He followed her out of the dowager's house into the courtyard; the brightening day made everything seem new. Along the rooftops and highest battlements the brilliant light made the stones glow, and the call of birds joined in unruly chorus. As they reached the door at the rear of the keep, a sleepy goatherd wandered into the courtyard they had just crossed; he was eating a wedge of cheese and noticed nothing beyond his breakfast.

Heugenet closed the door carefully and stared into the corridor. "Not here," she said in an undervoice that trembled a little with excitement and apprehension. "On the floor above. There is a room where I keep my regal and my organ. I used to play them . . . every day, before the Blood Roses bloomed." The sadness was back in her voice and she shook her head to ward it off. "No one would go there." Her tug on his hand was more insistent. "Hurry."

He wanted to know what she had played on those instruments before the Great Dying came; he would learn that later, he supposed, as they made their way up the narrow stairs to the floor above, and along the twilight corridors to the room she had chosen.

It was a small six-sided room with two windows, one facing south, the other southeast, which lent the room a little of the pale morning-blush. The small fireplace was cold, but a rug of marten-fur lay before it, new enough to show only minor wear and damage from moths and mice. The musical instruments stood in a slat-fronted cabinet on the wall opposite the fireplace, their shapes like sketches beyond the slats. Heugenet pulled Germain le-Comte toward the fur rug after she had closed the door; her eagerness had turned to something more serious. "This is where we . . . we will not be found, or disturbed." She dropped to her knees, holding his hand to draw him down before her. "Guilty lovers: what will become of us?"

"We will love each other." He knelt before her, his compelling eyes never leaving hers. He touched her face, his fingers light as down; he followed the line of her brow, her cheek, her lips, her chin, fixing every nuance of her countenance in his memory. He would not be rushed, savoring her desire as it enhanced his own.

"Though I am damned for it," she declared softly, and reached for him so impetuously that they might have toppled if he had not been as strong as he was; he held them both with deceptive ease while she pressed her mouth to his as if summoning his soul. She sank back on her heels and began to loosen her clothes, her haste making her clumsy.

"Here," he offered gently. "Let me." His small hands took over working out the knots in the tie at the neck of her chamise, then the lacing in the front of her cotehardie, so that when she wriggled out of the outer garment, her chamise fell open; she would have skinned out of it at once, but he stopped her. "Let me," he repeated, stilling her frantic rush to undress with slow kisses to the palms of her hands before he resumed her undressing. He took his time sliding the chamise off her shoulders, making it an act of reverence as much as an erotic invitation. When she began to tremble, he drew her into his arms once again, his hands caressing her back while they kissed again.

"You are . . ." She shook her head, unable to tell him.

"Ssh," he murmured as he bent to kiss her where her jaw made a tantalizing angle with her neck.

Heat mounted in her body, though she trembled; she clung to him as sensations went through her in waves, stirring her flesh and her emotions in a welcome dazzle. She could feel the life within her in a way that was new, as if she had heard an old tune set to new words, or played in a different mode. The passion he aroused in her elated her to the point of frenzy and she wondered fleetingly if this was what the saints felt in their divine transports that could not be described. Every place he touched her with hands or mouth, her body seemed transformed, every movement he made brought new and unexpected exultation to her; she swayed, the muscles in her legs quivering from kneeling, but she dared not speak for fear of ending the enormity of her pleasure. She held his shoulders to keep herself upright, and found herself held close to him, supported entirely by his encircling arms.

Tenderly, luxuriously, he eased her down onto the rug, stretching her out beneath him as he continued his awakening of her undiscovered sensuality: there were sensations she had never imagined she possessed that he brought forth from her breasts, her flanks, her abdomen, her thighs, and the secret recesses between them that subsumed her completely. This was greater than anything he had offered her before, and she reveled in it, encouraging him with little gasps of delight. He lingered over each attention that evoked a sigh of pleasure or a yielding of her flesh, summoning the whole of her being to one pellucid, encompassing revelation that united them in a consummate moment that approached transfiguration. Nothing in her life had prepared her for this, not even her two previous intimate encounters with Germain le-Comte; she had not supposed there was such rapture this side of Paradise: she had thought it impossible to find so much fulfillment in the midst of so much suffering. Gradually her joy became ephemeral, and she sighed for the loss of it.

Some time later, the sounds of hammering and shouting became noticeable, and a sliver of sunlight made a shining smear on the far wall; Heugenet rolled onto her side, lying close against Germain le-Comte so that the black linen of his chamisa pressed its texture into her skin. "How do you know?" she asked, her voice slow and musical. "Everything that gives me pleasure, you know to do." She touched her lips with her tongue as she smiled.

"I know because I know you," he said, the depth of his emotion in his voice.

"How can you know me so?" She kissed his jaw and his chin.

He spoke very carefully. "I know it from your blood, which is the essence of you."

She put her hand on his chest, over the place she knew he was scarred. "Is that so important to you?"

"The blood?" He felt her nod as a movement on his upper arm. "Yes, because it brings all of you to me." He turned his head to kiss her brow. "I know the whole of you, through the blood."

"Is that possible?" She raised herself so that she was looking down on him. "Other men do not know women this way."

"I am not like other men," he said, his words caressing her.

"That I have discerned," she said, smiling. "You do not take my body."

"There is no need." He raised himself enough to kiss her lightly. "I have the whole of you in what you give me."

Her eyes shone. "Is that the purpose of the blood?—knowing?"

His gaze grew more profound. "The knowing sustains me." He waited for her to flinch, and was more relieved than he wanted to admit when she did not.

She took a long, deep breath. "Then what are you?" As soon as she asked, she realized it was a question that had burned in her since she had first laid eyes on him, months ago, in the cold fortress. "What are you, that you do not rut with me? What are you, that you do not fear illness?"

He had planned for this moment, prepared for it, yet now that it had come he felt unready. He put his arm around her, holding her against his chest. "You would be distressed to learn," he said, his voice remote. He had told himself he was ready for this; now that it was upon him, he discovered he was not: he dreaded the prospect of her loathing.

"You have saved my son and you have given me such . . ." To explain, she kissed him. "Though you were a Fallen Angel, I could not be distressed."

"I am not that," he said with a trace of sardonic amusement. "Not that your priests would agree with me."

"Tell me," she insisted, giving his hair a playful tweak. "I'll get it out of you somehow."

He caught her hand in his and kissed each finger once. "Very well. But hear me out before you judge me."

"How can I judge you anything but my friend?" she asked, her body languid and replete; nothing he could say would take that from her.

He perused her face, searching for any hidden sign of dismay, no matter how small or unacknowledged. "There are tales of those who do not lie easy in their graves, who walk the night to prey upon the living. You have heard them, haven't you: those legends of the undead? You have heard them and thought the undead monstrous."

She crossed herself. "God between us and evil."

"Amen," he said at once.

Her eyes widened. "You are not such a . . . creature. You cannot be."

His voice softened. "No, I am not; there are those who would consider me one." He wrapped her in his arms and held her, his lips brushing her brow. "But I did die and rise afterward."

"So did Our Lord," said Heugenet, and put her hand to her mouth for uttering such blasphemy. "I didn't mean . . . It was . . . There is no . . ." She fell silent, suddenly watchful as if she expected an angel or a devil to appear and demand an explanation.

Only Germain le-Comte replied. "So He did." He stroked her hair, quieting the turmoil within her. "And you drink His blood to honor Him."

She shivered a little. "Yes."

"Flesh and blood are the means of Communion," he whispered.

"And of damnation," she said, but without conviction. "This is not damnation. My adultery may be, but not this."

"What adultery?" He asked it almost lightly. "I have done nothing to defile you, and you have not betrayed your husband, not in any way the law would see it. You have not compromised his children, or his House." He knew he was suggesting a sop to her conscience, but it was an acceptable one, in accord with what the law and the Church taught. "Had I used you as most men would, it would be another matter."

She considered what he said, grateful for the protection of his embrace. "You . . . could not impregnate me, could you?"

"No; I cannot," he said.

"You cannot cause me to conceive? If you are not like other men, you may be capable of—of bringing me to bed of your child." She shook her head. "There are those who quicken by a look."

"No, Heugenet," he said more kindly than before. "I cannot. No one can, no matter what the priests may tell you." Using one hand he turned her face to his. "You have nothing to fear from me on that account. Those of my blood have no children of the body."

She blinked as she strove to comprehend him. "But . . . surely you must . . . How do you continue your line?"

He hesitated before answering her. "We bring those who seek our life to our nature. If you and I express our love three or four more times, you, too, will rise when you die. If you taste my blood as I have yours, you will become as I am." He saw her frown deepen. "You are in no danger from me yet: my Word on it."

The creaking sound of pulleys came through the windows, and the occasional bump of something heavy against the side of the building as it was raised.

"Are there many of your . . . line?" She stared down at him. "Tell me."

"No. We are few." There was a sadness in his tone that caught her attention.

"What is it?" she asked, her apprehension fading; she studied him, her expression acute as she persisted. "Why are you few?"

"We are not invulnerable. I told you we can die the True Death, and how." He looked past her shoulder into imponderable distances. "Mankind fears us. When we are known, we are hunted." His face changed, grief visible in his attractive, irregular features.

"Have you been?" She did not let him answer. "Of course you have," she said. "You must have been."

"More times than I care to recall," he told her, although each instance was etched indelibly in his memory. He fingered a wisp of her hair. "Don't fret. You are safe from me still."

"And Armand? Is he safe?" She bit her lip as she waited to hear what he would say.

"I could not do so unworthy a thing," he said, indignation sharpening his voice. "Your son is a child; I do not—" He broke off, then went on more quietly, "I would never impose myself on one unwilling, or unready." He did not add that few adults were so prepared, that most of those who provided sustenance to him did so in dreams.

For a long moment she remained caught up in thought, then she regarded him with new curiosity. "You said you rose from the dead. When did you do that?"

It was the one question he had dreaded, the one that would fix the seal on his alienness. "A very long time ago," he said, and knew she would not be satisfied with that.

"More than a century? More than two?" She was fully alert now, and no longer content to lie in his arms; she sat up and looked down at him, her features keen with interest. She pulled on his shoulder as if to tug words out of him. "How long ago?"

Shouts from the men working on the roof were punctuated with a loud crash in the courtyard beneath, followed by fulsome curses and laughter.

"Many centuries ago," he said, his dark, enigmatic eyes on hers. "Too many to want to number them." He did not add that he remembered each year of his life with a clarity that was occasionally too acute; he had long ago lost the talent of forgetfulness.

She considered his answer; then, apparently satisfied, she bent down and kissed him, murmuring when she was done, "I don't care." For the present, she meant it.

Text of a letter from the Superior of the convent at Sante-Amienne to Josue Roebertis, written in Latin and delivered in August.

To the most generous patron of our convent, Josue Roebertis, Mère Lucille of Sant-Amienne sends her most grateful, humble thanks, and prays that God will spare you and yours in this time of Great Dying.

I ask your forgiveness in my tardiness acknowledging the gift you have provided; the Black Plague is very much with us, and I have only recently come to my position in this convent. May you be alive to read these words when Frer Barnaba brings them to you.

Your money has reached our convent with good speed and without hazard, and we all praise your generosity in Seur Jenfra's name. How good of God and Mère Marie to inspire you with such grace: we see by what example Seur Jenfra has come to her piety. We will put the money to good use, never fear. There is great need in Sant-Amienne and throughout Hainaut, Brabant, and Flanders, and the price of necessities is high through scarcity and lack of sound labor. Your donation will supply some of those things we must have in order to do our work in the world.

To reply to your question regarding Seur Jenfra, I am pleased to inform you that she is well. One in four of our Sisters has fallen to Blood Roses, but through Grace and the gift of prayer, Seur Jenfra continues to serve God with humility and devotion. She has said she would like to make herself an example of Christian faith, and demonstrate to the world how a soul may be made a worthy gift to the God Who made it. She does not refuse to succor anyone, no matter how afflicted they may be, or how sunk in sin. She shines in her goodness, and were she not a nun, her name would be known everywhere for her many Christian acts.

I have charged our mason to cut your name in the stones of our chapel, to remind us of your worthiness. In addition, your name will be spoken in our prayers of thanksgiving, our gratitude will assail Heaven on your behalf and we will honor Seur Jenfra for your care of her, and of all the nuns here. Be assured that we will not forget you for as long as Christian worship prevails, even to the Last Judgment.

May God spare you pain in this world and welcome you to His everlasting Glory in the life that is to come, when those who have served Him best will be nearest His Throne.

Mère Lucille
by the hand of Frer Anselm

On the 4th day of May, the eve of the Feast of Sant Hilarie of Arles, in the Lord's Year 1350.

2

While the workers on the roof unfurled their banner of the d'Ais arms, the household cheered; the repairs on the keep were finished at last, and this splendid May morning gave everyone occasion to celebrate. The workers whooped in triumph and prepared to descend to the makeshift festivities waiting below in the front and side courtyards of Mon Gardien. The weather was mild, the sun was bright, and it was almost possible to believe the last year had been nothing more than a nightmare, banished by the dawn, so long as no one mentioned the dead.

"In the name of my father, I thank you for your labor and your duty," Armand shouted up to them, and held out a purse. "You shall share in this equally, and know my gratitude." His stance was too awkward to be arrogant, and the household liked him better because he was not yet so sure of his position that he assumed the airs of a lord.

As the noise increased Heugenet put her hand on her son's shoulder. "Well done. Your father would be proud of you."

"He might not want to spend the money, not when everything is so dear," said Armand, just loudly enough for Heugenet to hear him.

"Your father ordered the keep repaired; he knows that requires money, little though he may want to spend it." Heugenet gave her son an encouraging smile. "You have followed his orders; if he is displeased, he has only himself to blame." As she said this, she knew Armandal would complain when he found out how much they had had to spend.

Armand waved to the workmen, motioning for them to come down. "You have earned your reward!" he shouted up to them, and pointed to the two spits where whole goats stuffed with millet and green peas in onion gravy were turning.

The servants gathered in the courtyards applauded energetically as the workers left the scaffolding for the last time, making their way down the ladders to the third-story walkway, and from there down through the keep to emerge at the main door, grinning in anticipation of the meal that was waiting, along with two barrels of ale which had been broached for the occasion; trenchers and tankards waited to be filled.

"They are good men, and you must show them you appreciate their loyalty," said Heugenet to Armand. "They could have run away, as many others did, but they stayed here."

Armand gave an impatient shrug. "I know what is expected of me, ma Mère." In the last few weeks, his voice had begun to deepen, and now it cracked, going from the low tones of maturity to treble without warning. He glowered at himself, muttering in irritation.

"Good." She let him move ahead of her so that he would not be encumbered with her presence; she watched him with glowing approval, a half-smile hovering about her mouth. She had dressed for the occasion, not in the grand style of the Emperor's Court, but in reasonable finery: a cotehardie of fine green wool embroidered with the arms of Verviers and Brabant; her coif was goffered and her gorget did not have a single wrinkle in its white linen. Her chamise, of pale blue silk, was a glossy contrast to the wool of her cotehardie. She was sensible enough to wear clogs on her feet, for the courtyard was littered with bits of wood and stone that made walking a challenge in less sturdy footwear.

The dowager Ducesse had been brought outside for this occasion; she sat on a stool working a churn and humming to herself. Her smile was dreamy and remote, as if she were being entertained by unseen creatures. As Remi hurried to join the throng waiting for a slice of goat, she called out to him, "You're a clever child, Armandal. You will do your father much honor one day."

Remi had been around the dowager Ducesse far too long to find anything strange in her remarks. He swung around and bowed to her, not wanting to cause her any upset on so happy an occasion.

"Make sure you save some of the meat for the invalids in the stable," Armand called out to the servants pressed into service as assistant cooks. "They are not to go hungry while we feast."

There was a general shout of approval as the first slices were laid on the platters; Perside supervised the cutting and helped to remove the stuffing into huge stoneware bowls, beaming at the fragrant steam that rose from the stuffing. Tubs of soft cheese stood near the spits, along with baskets of bread. It was the grandest meal served at Mon Gardien in more than a year.

"They had better enjoy this," Heugenet said quietly to Germain le-Comte, who had come to stand behind her. "It will be the last we can offer until harvest—if there *is* a harvest."

"Why should there not be?" Germain le-Comte asked, reassuring her. "Your peasants are planting. There will be some food coming from that, surely."

"Yes, but the year will be lean, and we may still have losses," she said, and they both knew it was the truth. She continued to watch Armand as he went among the workers, giving each of them two silver apostles in appreciation of their labor. "He is doing all he can. They will accept him in time."

"He is a capable boy," said Germain le-Comte, smiling at her, though she did not see it. "And he is getting stronger with every passing day."

"That he is," she said, and turned to him at last. "Thanks to you."

He shook his head. "You have no reason to thank me."

"But I do thank you," she said, her expression serious. "Without your help, he would not be able to conduct himself as the Duc de Verviers must. This may be a minor Dukedom in these days, but it is still a responsibility to maintain it." She cocked her head. "You have changed him, and you have changed me. Are you angel or devil, that you change us so?"

"You know what I am," Germain le-Comte answered, his curtness deliberate.

She studied him, then said, "If we are as God made us to be, do you serve Him or the Devil?" Noticing his frown, she went on, "No one is listening. Look around you: they care nothing about you, or me. Should anyone notice that you and I are talking, I will say you are reporting on the men you are treating, as you ought. Now, tell me how you have wrought these changes."

"The change is within you." He spoke softly but with purpose. "That may be heresy, but it is the truth. You are the source of your changing." Ten centuries ago, he might have tried to prove his point to her, but he had learned that such disputes were folly, as he had learned to his despair in Spain; he tried to put the issue aside. "Do not fear, Heugenet," he said as his eyes softened. "You do not err, or sin in your changing: no one does."

"But—" She did not know how to go on; she shook her head. "God or the Devil works changes within us."

"Look around you, Heugenet. You must know that no one has come through the last year without having to change." He made himself stop. "We have no reason to argue."

"Those who died were called of God to answer for their lives; we who remain have not yet fulfilled God's Work for Him. There is some purpose to our living; we must pray that God will reveal it." She crossed herself, sorry now that no priest or monk resided at Mon Gardien, who could explain this better than she.

Germain le-Comte looked at her, his dark eyes intent; he chided himself inwardly even as he spoke. "You are not a pawn, made to carry out the whims of God or the Devil like some weaver's engine for a pattern. God would be nothing more than a capricious child if that were the case, and the Devil only a petulant younger brother. You do not thrive or fail by their eccentricity; you confront the difficulties you find, or you avoid them. If that were not the case, no one of my nature would exist."

"God gives us life," said Heugenet indignantly. "Without Him, there is nothing."

"If He does, He is like a bird, who feeds its young until they are fledged and then pushes them out of the nest." He glanced toward the lines for food, and changed the subject. "You had better get yourself something to eat; I will fetch my mandola."

She raised her chin in a display of stubbornness. "So you will be a troubador for me now?" Her expression was not humorless, but there were uncertainties pulling at the corners of her mouth, keeping her from grinning at him. "Another display of your generosity of spirit?"

His smile matched the ironic tone of his voice. "It will make my failure to eat less obvious."

"So it will," she said, and turned away from him, her shoulders stiff with unresolved conflicts. She heard him walk away from her and had to control a surge of panic that threatened to take hold of her: she was not losing him: he was only going to get his mandola. Repeating that inwardly, she went to take up her place at the end of the serving-line, making sure that all the workers had been given food before she would allow any meat to be cut for her. "Remember the men in the stable; they will need their food as well."

Perside pointed to a small platter set aside. "There is their portion. I will send Remi to give it to them." She handed a wooden trencher to Heugenet. "This is for you, my lady."

"It smells delicious," said Heugenet, and nodded in the direction of Armand. "Has he taken his portion yet?"

"Yes; I reminded him his men would not eat until he began, so he took a trencher and cut a slice of goat with good speed. He has a tankard of the ale, as well."

"Then he will manage well enough, I pray," she said, her eyes never leaving her son as he made his way through the crowd, thinking it was smaller than the last such gathering at Mon Gardien. She received the greetings of her household with the ease of long practice, and reminded herself that this would have to suffice until harvest time. She noticed the oldest builder had a crude set of jangling sistra set in a double rack which he shook in time to the beat, emphasizing the double time on the second count of the measure. There was an open space between the portcullis and the entrance to the keep and the drummers set themselves at the edge of this area, making a space for others to dance.

"It is unfortunate that Charmot isn't here anymore," said Perside to Heugenet; the bagpiper had died in the winter and none of his family had taken his place. "We need someone to play tunes for us, or the dancing will become a rout."

"Germain le-Comte is bringing his mandola. It isn't as loud as the bag-pipes, but it is better than no melody at all." She managed to smile enough to convince Perside that this would be a satisfactory compromise.

"Germain le-Comte playing with Hannes le-Duc," said Perside with a slight chuckle as she cocked her head toward the youngster with the tabor.

"Yes," said Heugenet, meaning nothing beyond an acknowledgment; she was often confronted with Armandal's bastards and had managed to maintain her demeanor in their company.

Perside made a face at the nearer of the two youngsters turning the spits. "Not so fast, boy. Steady and slow; steady and slow. You don't want bits flying off."

The child blushed furiously and reduced his turning speed by more than half. As he continued with his task, he scowled at the goat as if the an-imal had been to blame for his mistake.

"He is trying to do the thing right," said Heugenet.

"I know," said Perside. "But in cooking, too much is too much, no mat-ter what the thing may be: speed or pepper or hanging, too much is too much." She rubbed her hands on her grease-spotted surcote, and poked straggling hair back under her padded coif. "You will not want to wait here too long; once the dancing begins, it will be rowdy."

"I will see that the Ducesse is taken inside," said Heugenet, anticipat-ing the old woman's complaints at being denied the pleasure of the day's celebration.

"Once she finishes her second cup of ale, she will sleep until evening. The Sisters at Sant-Amienne should be given the care of her," said Perside. "It is part of their duty to care for those afflicted in their wits."

"My husband would forbid it," said Heugenet, "and the Sisters have more than enough to do with the peste-house they keep." She sighed.

Perside shrugged. "God made her as she is; let His servants care for her in His Name." With that she went back to supervising the last of the serv-ing; she gave Heugenet a quick look of sympathy before she counted the last of the breads.

Heugenet was staring at the keep, pleased that the banner of d'Ais was flying over it once again. She would be expected to sleep inside it tonight, and she hoped her servants would not become so drunk that they could not carry her things from the dowager's house to the keep. She decided she would have to say something about it to Remi before the carousing became too great. She sighed once and went to find her mother-in-law, hoping that nothing had become of her since the revels began.

"Philomiele," the Ducesse said, her greeting as happy as it was remote. "I didn't know you were here." She held up an arm to try to embrace Heugenet.

Heugenet had never heard of Philomiele before; she supposed it was someone remembered from the Ducesse's childhood. As she held out her arms to help the Ducesse up, she saw that there was a tub of new butter waiting next to the churn; it was one less task for her to face that day, and she could not keep from feeling a twinge of gratitude for the old woman's labor. "Come; Remi is bringing you another cup of ale, and then you should lie down."

"Lie down?" The Ducesse was as quarrelsome as a sleepy baby. "It isn't . . . They aren't dancing yet, just playing the drums." She pulled in her elbows and turned away, huffy at being deprived of a treat.

"It will be workers dancing, Ducesse," said Heugenet patiently. "They will do peasant dances, not the ones you do at Court." She put her arm around the old woman's shoulder. "You know that peasant dances are—"

"Rough and lewd," the Ducesse cackled, her face crinkling with mirth. "Yes. We're not supposed to watch," she went on confidentially, "but we watch, my brothers and I."

"That's very clever of you," said Heugenet, trying to keep her voice level. "You will have to go there now if you want to see the dancing, won't you?"

"You'll tell Nurse," the Ducesse complained. "She'll stop us."

"I promise I will not tell Nurse," said Heugenet with great sincerity; the Ducesse blinked at her, her expression clearing as she did. "Come, let me take you in."

"Heugenet, dear child; I didn't see you," said the Ducesse. "How good of you to think of me. I am a little tired." She leaned on Heugenet's arm and allowed herself to be led to her house.

As he came out of the dowager's house, Germain le-Comte paused to hold the door open for Heugenet and the Ducesse, exchanging little more than a quick glance with Heugenet, then continued on his way to where the drummers were setting to work in earnest. He approached them respectfully, for as an outsider he knew his welcome was far from certain. By way of introduction he picked out the familiar tune of the *"Ballade du Nord,"* which gave a garbled account of long-ago Viking attacks; he hoped this would serve as sufficient credential to place him among their company.

"God give you good strings, foreigner," said the drummer nearest him; he was a young man with a strong resemblance to Armand, surely one of Armandal's bastards. "You'll need them before this day is through." It was all the concession the drummers would give, but it was enough. "Better stand in front of us. We'll drown you out if you're behind."

Relieved, Germain le-Comte moved closer to the drummers, playing the melody in octaves to get the most volume he could from his mandola; the older worker with the sistra shook his instrument energetically as if determined to overwhelm the sound of the mandola. By the time they finished that *"Ballade,"* a dozen revelers were dancing; they demanded more as soon as the music stopped.

Hannes le-Duc was considered the player in charge, as much for his illegitimacy as for his drumming. He listened to the shouted requests, then turned to German le-Comte. "Do you know *'Por Coi me Bait mes Maris?'* troubador?"

"Yes. Well enough to play it," said Germain le-Comte, plucking the first few measures in demonstration.

"Don't bother with the words, or you'll have no voice by the end of the day." He struck up a rhythm, a little fast for the meaning of the song, but spritely enough for dancing. "Keep the pace, troubador, and we'll be grateful."

They filled the midday with dances, their performance more energetic than aesthetic; the number of dancers grew until almost all the household had joined with the workers to celebrate. They drank ale when they were not dancing, and sang along with the melodies.

Finally Hannes le-Duc called a halt, complaining that he needed a rest and more ale; he was sweating freely and his face was ruddy from effort and drink. As he put his drum aside, he looked at Germain le-Comte. "Are you tired, troubador?"

"Not yet," said Germain le-Comte as he slung his mandola across his back. "Those of us who travel from market-town to market-town have to be able to sing and play the day through." It was true enough that the answer raised no suspicions. He saw the other drummers hold out their tankards and cups for more ale, and said, "While you are resting, I have men I am treating I should visit. I will try not to be long."

"Not thirsty?" Hannes le-Duc asked skeptically.

"Oh, yes; I am thirsty," Germain le-Comte replied. "But I will drink later." He nodded to Hannes le-Duc and went off toward the stable, his head lowered in thought.

Remi was sitting with the men, an empty platter on the floor beside him. "They have all eaten," he said as he got to his feet, an anxious look in his eyes.

"Good," Germain le-Comte approved. "How are they otherwise?"

"The music and all the rest makes them . . . troubled," Remi told him, looking about uneasily. "They fret."

"As well they might," said Germain le-Comte. "Well, I will speak with them; you will make sure each has water to drink." He hung his mandola on a bridle-peg and set about his task, beginning with the shepherd who had come with a broken arm.

The shepherd watched Germain le-Comte with narrowed eyes, being careful not to show him disrespect. He indicated the splint on his arm, saying quietly, "I am much better, Magister."

The honorific caught Germain le-Comte's attention. "You do me too much honor," he protested, his tone kindly.

"No," said the shepherd. "Others may believe that, I know you are not what you seem." He made the sign against the Evil Eye because with his arm in the splint he could not cross himself.

Germain le-Comte made the blessing for them both. "You have nothing to fear from me," he said, and went on to the next stall. He noticed this man was feverish and decided he would have to approach Heugenet about building an athanor; he was running low on his sovereign remedy and would not be able to replenish it without an athanor. He promised the man willow-bark tea for the interim, and hoped he could save the man. When the dancing resumed outside, he continued to tend to the sufferers in the stable.

By the time he was through, the afternoon shadows had extended all the way to the far walls leaving no sunlight to brighten the dancers; he left his patients in Remi's care and strolled out into the courtyard, his mandola slung across his back. He saw that several couples were still dancing to the beat of the drums, though most of the celebrants were too worn-out or too gone in drink to do more than cheer them on; the barrels of ale were empty and the two spitted goats were nothing more than skeletons, hardly enough meat left on them for soup.

"There you are," called Hannes le-Duc, his voice hoarse with over-use. "They said you were with the invalids."

"And so I was," said Germain le-Comte as he swung his mandola to the ready. "Would you like to rest and let me beguile the time with a romance or two?" He worked the pegs in their box, returning the instrument. "You look tired."

"Drumming is thirsty work. They'll have to find some ale for us if we're to keep on." He winked broadly at Germain le-Comte. "And a sweet song earns fine rewards, doesn't it?"

Germain le-Comte went cold, but managed an affable smile. "What do you mean?"

"Only that many girls have their heads turned by sweet tunes and grand tales," said Hannes le-Duc, his face stiffening. "What else should I mean?"

Alleviation of his worst anxiety made laughter easy for Germain le-Comte. "Oh, that I would try to gain favor from the well-born; it is often said that troubadors cater to the wishes of their patrons."

"And don't you?" Hannes le-Duc challenged, his eyes shiny with drink.

"Only when necessary; only when necessary," Germain le-Comte assured him as he took his place in front of the drums and sounded his first chord. "This is a legend of Spain in the time of the Caesars," he explained, "and of a sorceress who brought shame upon her blood relatives, and how she fled the world in expiation." He doubted Csimenae would recognize herself in the story his account told, for which he was pleased; her rejection of her bond with him still rankled, in spite of the passage of time. He saw most of the dancers nod in anticipation as he played the first measures of the romance he had written three hundred years before. "I will sing it in the language of Spain, and tell you the meaning between stanzas."

"Old Spain," said the nearest dancer, half-drunk and impertinent. "How shall we know it means what you tell us?"

"Because I say it; what reason would I have for prevarication?" He launched into the tale at once, concentrating on the complex rhyme-scheme of the words while his fingers picked the melody from the strings of his mandola. The revelers fell silent to listen to him, a few of them reclining against the stones of the keep while Germain le-Comte continued to play. Only when he was finished did noise break out once more.

"They are bringing a cask of wine," Perside told him in an undervoice as she came up behind him. "The Lady Heugenet has ordered it."

"That is generous of her," said Germain le-Comte. "I know these people will be pleased." He strummed an easy dancing-song. "And while the wine is being readied, it may be well to amuse ourselves with—" To complete his thought, he plucked the rest of the melodic phrase.

Hannes le-Duc chuckled. "You've been around the mighty so long you have caught their airs, le-Comte." With that he ambled off to where the wine cask was being tapped, whistling as he went.

Looking about the courtyard, Germain le-Comte felt himself an intruder; loneliness went through him like a sword of ice. To assuage his desolation, he began to play again, very softly, this time choosing a song he had first learned on an Egyptian harp in the Temple of Imhotep that told the story of Anubis and Thoth, and of the Feather weighed against the heart of everyone who died; for once he was glad that no one heard but himself.

Text of a letter from Curtise, servant of the Vidame de Silenrieux, to Eudoin Tissant, Magistrate of Orgon in Provence.

To the most honored First Magistrate of Orgon, the worthy Eudoin Tissant, the humble page called Curtise sends his respectful greetings from Non Trouves near Col des Fans. This letter is being given into the care of Frer Thomas, an English Austin who is journeying to Tuscany; he will vouch for its authenticity, having taken the dictation himself in the presence of the Vidame de Silenrieux.

I am a page to Vadim, Vidame de Silenrieux, who bought me from my parents when I was six, and who has housed and fed me from that day. In the performance of my duties, and in accordance with my fealty to my master, I tender this account.

When Vadim, Vidame de Silenrieux, ordered the foreigner called Francois de Saint-Germain, Sieur Ragoczy, to attend him here at Non Trouves,

he did so on the recommendation of Percevall, Vidame de Saunt Joachim,
who claimed that the Sieur Ragoczy had delivered him from death through
a practice of his Great Arts, and with such hope welcomed him here.

I now confess to killing the Sieur Ragoczy, and present myself for your
judgment.

From his arrival here, I suspected the Sieur Ragoczy was inappropri-
ately the recipient of the high regard my master reposed in him; I discov-
ered that he was often gone from Non Trouves for hours on errands no one
could explain, least of all his manservant, who proved to be as sly and un-
trustworthy as the man he served. I became suspicious of both men and
took it upon myself to observe them.

I saw that the master was determined to maintain himself in the Vi-
dame's esteem, and to that end began to comport himself to conform with
the Vidame's expectations, but all the while he was lying in wait to bring
calamity upon us. While he professed to be saving the guests of my master,
he was working to bring Blood Roses to this place, and to carry the souls
of all who live here to Hell.

When I was convinced of his intent, I made plans of my own: I ascer-
tained that Sieur Ragoczy intended to flee, leaving the guests of the Vidame
to die. I vowed I would not allow this to happen, and so I followed him and
his servant, taking a broadaxe with me for my own protection. When the
two had entered a defile not more than two leagues from Non Trouves, I
struck. My first blow cleaved the skull of Sieur Ragoczy, who fell dead at
once, a foul stench coming from him as if he had been dead for many weeks.
His manservant was so aghast at what I had done that he was unable to act;
I hacked his arms from his body and questioned him while he bled to death.

His Confession revealed that he had sold his soul to the Devil, who had
made him servant to Sieur Ragoczy and who had sent them into the world
to spread the Great Dying as far as could be done. He predicted that Blood
Roses would come to Non Trouves and that many of those living within its
walls would die there, but that some would sicken and recover, which has
been the case: the Vidame is one who has lived, may God be thanked for His
goodness forever and ever.

When the servant was dead, I cut the bodies into parts with the broad-
axe and buried them in diverse places beyond the walls of Non Trouves so
that they could not rise at Judgment Day, but would forever be lost to
Grace. I made no marking of those places, and will not reveal them to any-
one. I saved one finger of Sieur Ragoczy, which I have entrusted to Frer
Thomas' care, and which he will present to you as proof of my deed, which
I swear upon my salvation is rightly recounted here.

Your death warrant has been fulfilled, and I hope this will spare me suf-
fering the fate of homicides: if you have not paid the reward for his death,
I submit I have earned it, and I ask that you send it by messenger to Non
Trouves where I will gladly share it with my master, in gratitude for his
buying me when my family would have left me in the marketplace of their

village. It is fitting that I be awarded the sums in the name of my master.

I pray every night for the souls of the men I killed, but I know their deaths were necessary to spare those living here at Non Trouves. Now that justice has been served, I beseech you to bestow the money in token and recognition of my act, which I implore you to record in the annals of Orgon.

Curtise (his mark)
Frer Thomas, scribe

At Non Trouves, on the 23rd day of May in the 1350th Year of Grace.

3

Perside sat rocking, caught in a rapture of fear as she pressed her hands into her armpits in a futile attempt to hide the inflammations there; she could feel the swellings straining against her chamise. She repeated the *Ave Maria* over and over, their recitation was a way to keep from admitting that Blood Roses had taken root in her flesh. Her whole body felt tainted to her, and she was unable to stop the tears that ran down her face. She had been so *sure* that the Peste Maiden would not touch her; when others fell, she had remained clean; she had kept to her devotions without fail, no matter how great the temptation was to abandon them might be, and she had thanked God and Mère Marie day and night for her deliverance. But now this: she would not be able to conceal her affliction for long, and then she would be taken out of Mon Gardien to Sant-Amienne to be tended by the nuns until she died.

The kitchen in the restored keep was vast, with sufficient room to prepare whole cattle for roasting; there was a bank of ovens next to the open hearths; warmth held in their bricks could still be felt where Perside sat— either that, or the fever was already upon her. She could not see the distant wall clearly; her vision swayed, spun, and fuzzed as she attempted to make out where she was. In former times, half a dozen cooks and twenty scullions would be bustling through the kitchen, but now only she held sway here; she thought it was hideously funny that she should rise so far only to have her accomplishments be struck down by Blood Roses.

She forced herself to be still: the rocking was making her nauseated. She steadied herself with one hand and shoved, striving to get to her feet, reeling as her aching muscles protested. Her breath was thick in her lungs and she coughed without finding relief. Her headache brought spangles to her eyes as she started across the kitchen, only to collapse in a heap between the chopping-table and the butcher's-rack. The cold stones were pleasant against her cheek; in her dazed state she thought she had fallen into a stream. As she struggled to breathe, she wondered if she might be drowning, and recalled she had been told it was an easy way to die.

There were sounds, shrill and high, that might be nothing more than the ringing in her ears; she tried to put her hands over her ears to stop it, but instead felt herself rolled onto her side, exclamations of horror and dread echoing with the ringing in her ears. Then she was alone again, her body so sore that she could find no position that afforded her any comfort. Twitching uncontrollably, she tried to pray for deliverance once again; her teeth chattered so badly that none of the sacred words escaped her lips. The swellings in her armpits grew hotter and larger; she supposed they were the red-black color of diseased blood, and heralded her death.

"Oh. Oh. Lord Jesus between us and danger," said Heugenet da Brabant when she came into the kitchen in answer to the serving-maid's screams. "Go, girl. Fetch Germain le-Comte at once."

"Where shall I—" The question was unfinished; the maid wanted to run away.

"He is either in the music room with my son or with the injured men in the stable. Try the music room first. Go. Go, go." She all but thrust the maid out of the kitchen, then steadied her nerves to deal with Perside. The stench of the cook's flesh was enough to make Heugenet want to retch; she steadied herself and raised her gorget, retying it over her nose and mouth to lessen the miasma she might inhale, as Germain le-Comte had instructed her. "Perside. Perside. I am going to have to examine you."

Perside tried unsuccessfully to answer; her moan was eloquent.

Steeling herself, Heugenet bent down and opened the neck of Perside's sorquenie, pulling out the laces so that she could unfasten her chamise; the skin beneath was hot, and the swellings were large and dark. "God have mercy upon us," Heugenet whispered, hoping that Perside did not hear her. She stood up, mentally ordering herself to think. Perside could not remain at Mon Gardien, but she could not decide who should take her to Sant-Amienne.

On the floor at Heugenet's feet, Perside flung her arms out and rolled prone, her face once again pressed to the cool stones. To bring Blood Roses here! What would she say to God when He demanded to know how she had lived? She knew she was crying, and was unable to stop her despicable tears.

Knowing she was a coward for her actions, Heugenet moved away from Perside toward the door leading to the dining-hall. She watched Perside, aghast at the cook's suffering. She had been so careful, and the worst of the Great Dying was said to be past. Yet here was Perside, with Blood Roses in her flesh, and the stamp of death upon her. If only there were still a priest at Mon Gardien, or even a monk, she would be less afraid. She knelt and pressed her hands together in prayerful contrition.

"What is the matter?" Germain le-Comte's sharp question cut into her orison. "That poor girl you sent was beside herself." He looked past her into the kitchen and saw Perside. "The Plague," he said with complete certainty.

"She has Blood Roses. I saw them." Heugenet crossed herself and got to her feet. "What am I to do?"

"You will do nothing beyond ordering the kitchen scrubbed thoroughly and rinsed with boiling water," he told her decisively. "You and all your household will bathe in camphor water and burn the clothes you have been wearing. Is that clear?"

"Bathing is vanity," said Heugenet automatically.

"Not in camphor water," said Germain le-Comte in grim amusement. "Go. All your household must do this before nightfall."

"But Perside—" said Heugenet, about to take the gorget from over her face.

Germain le-Comte stopped her. "Leave that where it is until you are ready to bathe. I will give you sufficient camphor for all of you in this castle." He kissed her forehead. "Go on; give your orders. I'll hitch up Caesar to his cart and take Perside to Sant-Amienne. It isn't more than four leagues, is it?"

"Four leagues. Yes." She moved blindly toward the hall. "What about Armand?" she whispered. "If he should . . ."

"Keep him away from the kitchen and see that he bathes first," Germain le-Comte told her, and recognized the shock that had taken hold of her. "I will fetch the camphor for you now, so you may begin to tend to your household." He knew he would not be able to do much for Perside but give her a palliative tincture of pansy and willow to ease her discomfort, and he would have to get that from his red lacquer chest where the camphor was kept in his new room two floors above. "Come, Heugenet. Find your understeward and have him fire up the bath-house furnace."

She shook herself visibly. "Yes; yes. I must find him." She was about to move when something more occurred to her. "What of the men-at-arms? What of your patients?" Her hands knotted together and tears stood in her eyes; she had resisted fear for so long that now when she tried to draw upon the courage that had sustained her, she discovered she had lost the knack of it.

Germain le-Comte rested his small hand on her shoulder and directed the full force of his dark gaze into her eyes; his voice was low and tranquil. "I will tend to my patients. The men-at-arms must bathe in camphor water like everyone else." He paused, and regarded her steadily once more. "You know how to deal with your household. Do not let your doubts keep you from action."

"No. You are right," she said distantly. "If God did not intend us to survive, He would not have sent you to us." She crossed herself. "I will ask everyone to pray."

He did not like the acquiescent manner she had assumed, but he did not want to encourage her resistance. "Pray while you bathe, then."

She looked around the kitchen blankly. "We will pray," she said.

"Good. But for the sake of your son, do not tarry here where the miasma may linger." He was relieved to see her shake her head sharply at his remark; he was aware she would need to be encouraged to keep functioning. "You will serve him best if you will move your household to action now." He was already going toward the stairs. "Hurry, my lady."

"Hurry," she repeated, and made herself walk along the corridor toward the servants' room where the understeward should be. As she walked, her thoughts began to stir and she wondered how he came to have such quantities of camphor that he could give them enough to bathe in. She could not ponder the matter now, but decided that one day she would have to demand an answer from him. Her pace quickened as she shook off the last of her terror-spawned lethargy.

Germain le-Comte made sure Heugenet was not watching him, then he sprinted up the stairs at a pace that would have amazed her had she seen him. In his room he opened his red lacquer chest and took out a good-sized earthenware jar and a much smaller glass vial. With these in hand, he closed the chest and sped down to the kitchen corridor once again. He found Guillem, the understeward of the keep, standing in the door of the kitchen and staring at Perside; he spoke quietly so as not to alarm the younger man. "Your mistress has given you orders?"

"Something about starting a fire in the bath-house furnace," said Guillem as if he could not have understood the instructions correctly.

"You had best be about it," said Germain le-Comte; he was sorry that Remi had remained in charge of the dowager's house, for Remi was more inclined to trust him than Guillem was. "Here is the camphor." He handed Guillem the earthenware jar. "You are to put all its contents—*all*, mind you—in the central bath. It has a strong odor to keep the miasma away." He did not believe that, but he knew Guillem would.

The understeward stared at the jar. "All of this in the central bath."

"Yes. The sooner the work is done, the sooner you will be protected," he said impatiently. "I am going to tend to Perside."

Guillem blanched. "She has Blood Roses."

Germain le-Comte regarded the understeward a moment. "If you would rather, I will defer to you."

Now Guillem retreated half a dozen paces. "No. No, no; you may tend to her, foreigner." With that assurance, he rushed off, leaving Germain le-Comte alone in the corridor.

Perside was lifted in strong arms, her head tilted back and an acrid liquid tipped down her throat; she coughed as she tried to swallow the stuff, then she peered upward and was reassured to see Germain le-Comte's kindly face. "You should not," she muttered.

"Better me than another," he told her as he carried her easily out of the kitchen, down the walkway that led to the stable. "I am going to put you down outside the stable," he said just before he lowered her to the flagstones. "The injured men—"

"Blood Roses; I know," she whispered, doing her best not to cough. She huddled against the stones and waited, aware that the worst of her aches had begun to ease. She tried again to pray, and to thank Germain le-Comte for caring for her, but she became lost in the words and drifted into a half-sleep that only ended when Germain le-Comte came out of the stable leading his donkey and cart.

"It will take awhile to reach Sant-Amienne," said Germain le-Comte as he lifted Perside into the cart and wrapped an old blanket around her, making sure to secure her in place with a wide leather strap that crossed her chest and buckled behind the rear slats of the cart. "The day is warm, which will give you comfort. If you need water or you are hurt, you have only to call out."

She mumbled disjointed bits of phrases to show that she understood him.

"We will leave through the rear gate," said Germain le-Comte as he started Caesar moving forward. "There are fewer men-at-arms there, and you will attract less notice." He hoped this would also lessen the apprehension that would be spreading throughout Mon Gardien, no matter how carefully he planned against it. He talked to Caesar as he went. "Steady, my long-eared friend. You will have to go gently for the sake of Perside."

The two men-at-arms on the rear gate gave the donkey-cart a wide birth as Germain le-Comte left Mon Gardien; they knew already that Perside was bound for Sant-Amienne, and the large common grave the nuns maintained for those claimed by Blood Roses.

He took the path that led around the small village below Mon Gardien; the peasants would not allow them to pass through their one street, but would fight them off with rocks and pitchforks and whips. There were few other travelers about; a merchant on a stolid palfrey went past them, the merchant facing away from the donkey-cart; a goatherd with his flock kept a good distance behind them for almost a league before he turned off on a track that led to a walled hamlet in the distance; a pair of monks in Carmelite habits muttered a blessing as they hurried by; and an old soldier with a missing arm trudged along next to them just as they approached the convent at Sant-Amienne.

It was large as the whole of Mon Gardien, its walls stout as any fortress, enclosing half a dozen buildings, including dormitories for travelers and extensive barns; in the center of the enclosure was a large well, still clear-flowing and once said to be miraculous, which had caused the founding of the convent. At one time it had housed more than two hundred nuns; now their numbers were reduced and there were signs of neglect in- and outside of the walls; there were slates missing from the roofs of the convent buildings and many of the windows were unshuttered. Weeds were as profuse as vegetables in the garden next to the bake-house and untended rabbits nibbled the leaves of everything they could find. The peste-house was beyond the convent walls: a low, makeshift place with covered windows and a smell of putrescence that hung on the air like a stain.

Germain le-Comte led Caesar toward the peste-house in spite of the donkey's fretting. He reached the open area in front of the entrance, and stopped, waiting for a while in the hope that someone would come; when no one did, he tied Caesar to a pole supporting a shrine to Sant Andre, and went in search of one of the Sisters.

Conditions inside the peste-house were appalling: pallets were set down for beds, all laid so close together that the Plague-stricken lay like stacked logs. The few blankets were filthy, and the pallets were stiff with old blood and other excretions. Brackish water stood in wooden pails near the heads of the pallets. Nuns moved along the narrow passages left at the foot of the pallets, most of them clearly exhausted, and a few dazed with fever themselves; the air was thick with the odors of contagion, and cries and moans echoed like the waves on the shore. At the far end of the peste-house a nun sat with a ledger open before her, a pen in hand to enter the names of the dead as their bodies were stacked near her for removal to the burial pit.

A Sister with a haggard face and a habit unlike most of the others came up to Germain le-Comte. "You don't look ill. You have to leave. We take only the sick here." When he did not budge, she took a gentler tone. "If you're looking for someone, ask Seur Minelle; she will know when your person was buried."

Germain le-Comte did not move. "I have someone for you to tend," he said, hating himself for agreeing to bring Perside to this place; it was intolerable to think that this was the best care available. He told the nun what she would need to know. "She has been the cook at Mon Gardien. She has Blood Roses on her flesh now."

The Sister took a long breath of the foetid air. "Where is she?"

"I have her in a donkey-cart outside," he said, gesturing toward the door. He could not help but add, "You have so many here."

"Yes. They bring them for ten leagues around. It was worse last autumn." Her weariness made her voice flat. "Show me this cook from Mon Gardien."

As they stepped out into the sunlight, Germain le-Comte saw that another two persons had arrived—a middle-aged man in stained apothecary's robes and a female child of about five or six whom he carried in his arms. The man stumbled and nearly fell; Germain le-Comte went to his side to steady him.

"Aren't you afraid of the Plague?" the man asked in a cracked voice.

"When Death has touched you once, you need no longer fear it," Germain le-Comte replied, for it was now generally understood that those few who recovered from Blood Roses could not suffer it again, just as those who lived through the Great Pox could face it with impunity; that he had another meaning would not be noticed. "The Plague reached the south before it came here; I left Provence more than a year ago." He saw the nun nod, little emotion in her face.

"A few do live; what he says is true." She was torn between assisting Perside and giving her attention to the apothecary and the child. "I must get some help."

"I'll carry the cook inside," said Germain le-Comte, shuddering inwardly at the prospect of leaving Perside here, although he knew he could not take her back to Mon Gardien.

The nun followed him, half-carrying the man and child. As soon as they were inside, other nuns came forward to take charge of the new arrivals, working in the gloom to find a sliver of space for these new sufferers.

"Tell the Duc that we will do all we can for his cook; it is in the hands of God now," said the nun, pausing to cross herself as a bell sounded from inside the convent walls.

"Amen," Germain le-Comte said.

As if to excuse conditions in the peste-house the nun went on, "We are sadly reduced in our numbers, and each of us must husband what strength we have, that we may serve Our Lord as He requires. In this dreadful time, Sant-Amienne has taken in Sisters from many Orders so that we are able to continue our devotion to Him. I, myself, began with the Redemptionists"—she indicated her blue-and-white habit—"as many of those here now did. We have Claires and Ambrosians and Assumptionists and Servites among our numbers here, and each keeps to her Rule when it is possible." She gave Germain le-Comte a serious stare, considering his motley for the first time. "You are the troubador they're all talking about, aren't you? The one at Mon Gardien. The one they say has mended so many hurts."

"I do not know what 'they' you mean, but I am a troubador," Germain le-Comte answered more guardedly than his affable demeanor implied. "And just at present, I come from Mon Gardien."

"We have seen only those with Blood Roses here since the Lady Heugenet and her son returned to Mon Gardien. We have been told that you treat those who are injured or ill. May God smile upon you for your charity."

"You have the more arduous task here," Germain le-Comte said quickly, noticing that the other nuns in the peste-house were gathering near the door in anticipation of leaving. "Tending those stricken with Blood Roses is sacrifice beyond all charity."

"We can do no less for Our Lord," said the nun, turning away to join her Sisters.

Germain le-Comte watched them step out of the door, then moved to follow them; a lingering despair possessed him, and an abiding sense of failure. So many times in the past he had seen disease scythe down vast numbers in terrible harvest, but this was beyond the catastrophes of the past: until now he had thought one in six an untenable scale of loss—now he saw Blood Roses strike down one in four, and of those stricken, fewer than one in ten survived them. He reached the door just as the new company of nuns arrived; stepping aside to allow them to pass, he lowered his head in respect for these women and the unfortunates they nursed. All the centuries he had spent in the Temple of Imhotep had not been enough to harden him to the agony of others and now he felt a renewed receptiveness to the plight of the nuns as well as those in their charge. He waited until all the nuns were past before he went to untie Caesar to begin the long walk back to Mon Gardien. He was so caught up in his reflections that he did not notice when one of the nuns toward the end of the line turned suddenly and stared in his direction, disbelief in her pinched, youthful visage; she crossed herself and murmured a prayer of protection from spectres and demons before she continued on into the peste-house.

Walking into the slanting sunlight, Germain le-Comte realized he would need to change his native earth in his soles, for he was enervated and the peste-house was not wholly the cause. He climbed into the donkey-cart and used his lead-rope as a rein, determined to conserve his strength on his way back to the castle. The disgrace of riding in a cart would not be as great for a troubador and bastard as it would be for anyone of more legitimate position in the world. Only one person passed him on the road: a herald wearing the tabbard of Flanders spurred by him just as the sun was setting. In the long dusk of June their return provided a respite from all the turmoil that had become so much a part of his life. When Caesar slowed to a shuffle and bent to snatch mouthfuls of grass from the verge, Germain le-Comte reluctantly called him to order, climbed out of the cart and set a brisk pace for the final league to Mon Gardien.

Text of a letter from Heugenet da Brabant at Mon Gardien in Verviers, to her husband, Armandal d'Ais, Duc de Verviers, at the Imperial Court in Luxembourg.

To my dear husband, my thankful greetings on this Solstice eve; I am grateful to you for sending your messenger to me in good time, and I ask God to look over you, and our daughter, in the Emperor's Court.

Montcerry and Biebart will carry this to you, along with the weapons you have asked for. I regret to tell you that the armorer, Philippe, has died; he is the third of the household to be taken with Blood Roses since you left for the Court. All our efforts to keep the miasma outside the walls of Mon Gardien have not been able to protect the household completely. Perside and Alfre, the old watchman, have also gone to Grace with the black blooms in their flesh. The precautions of the past have been kept, as well as those recommended by Germain le-Comte, whose methods have done some good, I believe. In the countryside the dying goes on, though not so fiercely as it did last autumn; some of those who have taken the disease have lived through it, though their numbers are few. Still we pray for an end to the Great Dying, and the recovery of those who suffer. As we still have no priest here, we care for the dead as best we can; those who have Blood Roses upon them we send to Sant-Amienne for the nuns to tend, but the rest we must hope our prayers will guard.

Your son Armand is showing himself a capable administrator here. His conduct has been all that you could want, for prudence and faith have been more required now than force of arms, and in these things, Armand excels. I know, my husband, that you have often regarded your heir with doubts, but I implore you to look upon his strengths, not his weaknesses.

It pains me to have to petition you for more money. I realize your lands here are not in good heart: no land in our world can be in these times. A third of the fields of Verviers are planted, and some are being tended with as much care as can be given, but most are being left to grow or fail as they may. The orchards are promising, but the fruit is not yet ready to pick; our hives are flourishing, but thieves often take honey, and we have not guards enough to keep watch over all the orchards and hives. The flocks of goats and sheep are not as disappointing as they were, but still many of their numbers are being carried off by thieves and wanderers, so we will have another thin year of meat. Our sheep yielded a fair amount of wool, but most of it will go to your vassals as the weavers of Liege and Ghent are not taking wool for their looms, so severely have the Blood Roses struck them; we have few spinning wheels, as you know, and cannot spin enough to provide a tempting amount of yarn to offer other weavers. If we had more spinning wheels, then the situation might be better, but as it is, I have set the women to simple weaving for our own uses, and I will hope that when markets are held again, that some of what they have made will fetch good prices and thus support their industry as well as my concessions to them. Those pigs that have not run wild are breeding well enough, but it is another matter with the cattle: we have lost several calves to wolves, which now are so daring that they snatch the calves from the peasants' fields. Of the two mares you left here, both have foaled, and one filly is doing well; the other mare had twins, one of which perished: the other, a colt, is thriving, but is terribly small and may not be of a size to work. With all these burdens placed upon this fief, I cannot demand higher rents from your dependants nor can I order new taxes, for that would impose suffering beyond that which God has sent.

We still have no kennel-boy to be with the dogs, and only old Rollo to tend the mews; I do not think we will find new servants for those positions until the Blood Roses are gone, unless you find some at the Imperial Court and send them here; our vassals need every sound hand to work the fields and crofts. We have less than ten woodmen now, and so the cutting of wood will have to be curtailed to all needs but our immediate ones. There are two widows in the village who are willing to take up the tasks of their herdsmen husbands, and one has taken in the orphans of her sister and will train them to tend the cattle. The beekeeper is dead, and his son has taken over the task, although he is only nine and is living with the smith's family, having no other family remaining to take him in.

If we were fighting enemies of flesh and blood, I would act in your name, and demand that Armand take money and goods from all your vassals, but as we are struck by the Hand of God, it is not fitting for any of us to impose requisitions that could not be met and would only increase the misery we see around us. The very depletions of the Great Dying have made many simple things dear, and I must meet the price. It is possible new taxation would be enough to drive away those vassals who have been faithful to d'Ais and Verviers, leaving us in more desperate straits than we are already.

Surely the Emperor is aware that many of his nobles labor under such circumstances, and he must be willing to extend his hand to those who serve him dutifully. If I were not needed here, I would come myself to plead with you and the Emperor to grant us those sums we must have if we are to continue to maintain your Dukedom. Nothing capricious or luxurious has been done here, nor will it be until the lands are in good heart once more. Yet that day will not come if no aid is given to the vassals of the fief, and in order for that to happen, I must have another purse; you need not send much, but I am now almost wholly without money of any kind, and with the harvest still to come, I have little to serve in lieu of silver and gold, nor would I want to promise your shares of stock and harvest when both are uncertain.

I vow to you, my husband, that the need here is genuine; I am no greedy woman seeking to plunder the fortunes of her husband's House. Our children have need of your support, and I cannot dispute their claims upon you, nor would I if I had grievances. In order to acquit myself honorably of the trust you repose in me, I must ask for gold and silver to meet the needs of your household. You may question anyone you choose: you will learn nothing to discredit my diligence on your behalf. I must be granted some measure of autonomy in regard to monies, or we will not prevail here as you would wish. I am also fearful of what may happen to us if the men-at-arms who guard us remain unpaid much longer. They understand the magnitude of the suffering in the world, and they remember the oath they took, but neither understanding nor oaths will fill their bellies or keep them at their posts if no effort is made to pay them for their loyalty. This fief could be forfeit to the demands of the men-at-arms should they turn against us.

Your son continues in excellent health, and I am well enough. Your mother has not lost her strength though her mind wanders more and more with each day, and Remi tells me she has taken to wandering off on her own, her person at the mercy of the vassals and the creatures of forest and field, and I, alas, can do nothing more than ask Remi to quit his post here to find the Ducesse. God has blasted her wits and we must bow to His Will, but it is a hard duty to care for her when she is so much lost to us. I

*have had no word from our sons, nor from our daughters; I have wanted
to believe that this is to the good, and that any news must be sent to you: I
pray when you have word of our other children you will inform me of how
they are fairing. In this regard, I am truly sorry to have to tell you that
word has come from Sant-Amienne that Janon le-Duc, Ancet le-Duc,
Marie-Anne le-Duc, and Eteniet le-Duc have all succumbed to Blood Roses:
Hannes le-Duc and Ninnel le-Duc have survived them, but Ninnel le-Duc
remains unwell and continues in the care of the Sisters; two of the moth-
ers of your children have perished as well; one of Blood Roses and one of
starvation.*

*May God protect and shelter you, my husband, and may He cause the
Emperor to show you distinction and favor. May your fortunes increase,
may your reputation be of the highest, may you never know disgrace, may
your name be held in honor. I ask you to tell our daughter that I keep her
in my prayers and that I hope she may grow in grace and worthiness, and
that she will ever be a credit to you, my husband.*

Heugenet da Brabant
(by her hand)
recorded to her dictation by Germain le-Comte

*At Mon Gardien of Verviers on the Feast of Saints Peter and Paul in the
1350th Year of Grace.*

4

"You are fond of my mother," Armand said to Germain le-Comte on a lazy
afternoon in mid-July; they had been discussing the forms of verse from
the time of the Romans to modern applications, and Armand was beginning to be agitated at the continuing demands of scholarship. Outside the
air was warm and the sounds of sheep below the castle in the fields provided as pleasant a counterpoint to Armand's lessons as the sound of water
in a fountain. "You must tell me; I am heir here, and you are my vassal."

"No: I am a troubador and no lord's vassal." Germain le-Comte looked
up from the volume of Latin poetry, marking his place with his finger.

"You are my tutor and I house and keep you," said Armand. "You must
answer me when I require you to answer." He was enjoying this first show
of authority, and was determined to make the most of it.

Germain le-Comte did not give a direct reply. "What makes you say
that?—about your mother." His inquiry was unhurried and without challenge.

"You are, aren't you? Fond of her?" Armand asked as he turned away from the open window that overlooked the western side of the walls and the fields beyond. He was showing the first signs of a beard and his voice was now lower more often than not.

"Of course I am. I admire her profoundly; it would be inexcusable if I did not. A hundred years ago, she would have been praised as a chatelaine. I have seen enough of the world to know how rare a woman she is. Your father has every reason to be proud of her." He was about to resume his discussion of poetry when he saw that Armand was frowning. "I know she is a married woman, and I know I would not be worthy of her if she were not." He waited, not wanting to force anything from Armand before he was ready to reveal it.

"She is fond of you," said Armand at last.

"Then what can I be but grateful for such tribute?" Germain le-Comte bowed slightly as if to acknowledge Heugenet's presence.

"You must not make light of her regard," Armand snapped. "She bestows her good opinion rarely; those who receive her esteem should . . . should be . . . They should appreciate . . . what she has . . . and . . . and . . ." He lost his intention in embarrassment.

Germain le-Comte regarded his pupil gravely. "Rest assured that I value your mother's good opinion above all others in Verviers: yours included, Heir d'Ais."

"As well you should. She is better than any of us," said Armand as if daring Germain le-Comte to contradict him. "My father has entrusted Mon Gardien to her care."

"And he has entrusted you, as well," said Germain le-Comte. "You have more value than his fiefdom."

Armand shook his head. "No. If we were peasants, that would be true, but not for us, who are sworn to maintain the land of our House. We d'Ais are accountable for Verviers," he said. He had reached the X-shaped chair and dropped into it. "It has already been reduced, to our disgrace. Any lessening of its place can only slight d'Ais."

"You had no part in that," said Germain le-Comte, aware that Armand felt chagrined by this ancient insult.

"It remains a continuing indignity to our House," he said darkly. "It will be a long time before we can regain what we have lost."

"That may be so, but this is not the time to concern yourself with such long-ago misfortunes. You have too many things to contend with at present to be distracted by the rashness of your ancestors, or the policies of Flanders and Brabant." He set the volume of poetry aside. "I had not intended to speak of this with you yet, but clearly it is appropriate that I do: listen, Armand, and use what you learn; you will need decades of purposeful industry if you are to come through the Great Dying without greater calamity than you have experienced already. You know how depleted your stores are, and how reduced your numbers in Verviers are. It is so everywhere, which only compounds the problems you will face." His voice dropped, and his dark eyes grew haunted. "The Blood Roses will not bloom forever, but if you live, you will have to maintain order and activity with fewer vassals to support your work. Everyone in France, everyone in the Holy Roman Empire, everyone in Spain and England and the Lowlands will face the harvest the Blood Roses have planted."

"Then we will share our adversities and offer up the pains we endure." Armand spoke by rote and then shook his head. "No, I do not suppose it will be so . . . so easy. God has not made all men of equal quality, and some will be moved by the Devil to compound the upheaval of the Great Dying, to use in the service of sin."

"And some will be desperate, or displaced, or mad. The reasons are not important, but how you manage Verviers will be." He saw a lost look flicker across Armand's countenance. "You have much to learn, and in a very short time. Your father may defend Verviers at Court, but you must maintain it as well as you can in this place."

Much as he hated the question, he asked, "What would you do?"

Germain le-Comte folded his arms, the dags on his triangular sleeves standing out from this pull on the fabric. "I would determine how much land my serfs could keep in good heart and let the rest go fallow. If the forest encroached on those fallow lands, I would not clear it, for the trees are as useful a crop as wheat and millet. They take longer to grow, but their worth is beyond doubt. I would make ponds in the river where fish would gather, and I would make sure any child in the village has permission to fish, for the flesh of fish is wholesome and strengthening. Then I would increase my flocks of sheep and goats—they produce milk, wool, hides, and meat, and do not need the kind of constant labor that fields do. I would also increase my orchards for the same reason, and put in more hives. Anything that would increase food and goods that could be used here or sold, I would encourage, be it weaving, leatherworking, copperage, or herding. I would put priorities on foods that can be stored, such as cheeses, so that the smaller harvests would not lead to famine. I would start breeding mules, for they are strong and useful; they keep lightly, and they are long-lived. That would leave horses for hunting and defending the castle, so that fewer horses would be needed without compromising the work they do. I would garrison the castle with men-at-arms with their families. It is an extra burden to house, feed, and clothe them, but it will serve to ensure the fealty of the men-at-arms as well as lessen the chance of their turning on you when money is in short supply—as it is now." He recalled the constant shortages at Leosan Fortress, four centuries ago, and knew the same scarcities could arise here, with the desperation that he had seen then as well.

Armand was listening with more interest than he had thought he would have for anything a troubador said. "So, Germain *le-Comte*, you learned a few things in spite of your bastardy."

"I know the value of my native earth," said Germain le-Comte. "And in my time I have defended it." That his defense had begun more than thirty-three centuries ago he kept to himself.

"Is there more?" He was still curious, his eyes alert and his manner attentive.

"Yes, there is more," said Germain le-Comte, wondering if it was prudent to tell the young man so much at one time. "I would send peasants to the fortresses that guard your frontiers, and I would grant them a greater share of their crops and slaughter than is usually given so long as they maintain the garrison at the fortress. I would also offer the chance for one of each family's sons to train to be a man-at-arms, which all serfs would welcome."

"But God did not make serfs to be soldiers." Armand crossed himself to show his observation was pious.

"If God has claimed a quarter of your men-at-arms, He will have to accept your replacement of them." Germain le-Comte said this lightly but with purpose. "Would He object if you required herdsmen to help build barriers to stop a flood? The flood is faster than the Plague, I grant you; it is just as damaging."

Armand took a long, careful breath, as if he stood on the edge of a chasm. "I wish we had a priest here, so that I could ask guidance of him."

"If God wants you to have a priest's guidance, let Him send you one," said Germain le-Comte, chuckling to mute the heresy he had spoken.

Shocked, Armand stared at his tutor in silence. "Pray God to forgive you for that," he said at last, and looked away toward the window.

"I ask your pardon, Heir d'Ais," said Germain le-Comte at once.

"Better to beg it of God than of me," said Armand, turning abruptly toward the door. "Our lessons are done for today, troubador. I will consider what you've told me—*all* of what you have told me." He stalked to the door and was gone.

Germain le-Comte studied the closed door for a short time; he had not been able to address the two most crucial issues for him. Preparing himself to continue the discussion that evening, he left the room, going first to the stable to visit his patients, assuring them he would bring them medicaments shortly after sundown, and then to the two narrow rooms on the third floor that had been assigned to him. He had made a kind of bed for himself atop the chests of his native earth; he removed his troubador's houppelande, setting it in one of his chests—this one was made of cedar—where he kept his clothes, then took off his chamisa and dropped it into a bucket of water mixed with rosemary. These minor chores done, he went to his bed, lay down on its uncompromising surface and was at once in a stupor-like sleep. He awakened, revived and restored, as the sun began to sink behind the hills in the west. Mindful of his promise to the men in the stable, he went to his red lacquer chest and took out the tinctures and unguents he would need, setting them in a small basket before he went to take out a clean chamisa of black linen and his haincelin of black, silver-shot silk, its hanging sleeves lined in dark-red silk; the standing collar had a narrow ruff of silver lace. These were finer garments than any he had allowed himself to wear since he had assumed his role as Germain le-Comte and he reckoned they ought to be sufficient to the task he intended they perform; he hoped his clothes might reinforce the suggestions he had made to Armand, for they implied a greater social position than he had claimed since he and Rogres had parted company so many months ago.

He completed his treatment of his patients and had informed one of the men that if he had no fever in the morning, he would be able to return to his family the next day. If any of the men noticed his finery, none of them spoke of it. As he crossed the courtyard, he saw Montcerry watching him from his post.

"You're as fine as anyone at the Emperor's Court," said the man-at-arms, who had returned two days ago from delivering Heugenet's report to her husband. "How came you by those garments? They are very grand."

"I wear them by right," said Germain le-Comte, keeping his voice neutral so that Montcerry could not construe his reaction as a challenge.

Montcerry laughed. "So your father recognized you, did he? No hope of succession, I suppose, until now. Perhaps the Great Dying will grant you a County."

"Perhaps," said Germain le-Comte, and continued on his way into the keep. He went to the dining-hall, pausing in the arched doorway to bow to Armand, who sat alone at the table; his mother dined alone in the gallery above.

Armand glanced up, then stared again at Germain le-Comte. "What on earth—?"

"May God send you a good night, Heir d'Ais," said Germain le-Comte formally; he waited to be invited into the dining-hall, aware that Heugenet was watching him as well as her son. His demeanor was appropriate to his clothes, and that alone made his appearance surprising.

"And to you, Germain le-Comte," said Armand after a moment when he had masked his incredulity to his satisfaction. "We have simple fare tonight: mutton-and-onions with berries-in-wine. There must be some left in the kitchen."

"I have not come to command a place at your table, Armand," said Germain le-Comte. "I have come with the purpose of discussing what you are planning to do to protect Verviers. We did not finish this afternoon."

"This is not a time for instruction, nor is your conduct that of the schoolroom," said Armand, his face fixed in an expression of determination. He reached out for his tankard of wine.

"That may be," said Germain le-Comte, making an elegant gesture of concession. "Yet I fear that it may not be possible to select a time more appropriate than this." He inclined his head again. "I have also come to ask a favor of you."

Armand stiffened and drank more of the wine than he had intended. "What favor?" His voice was wary and he scrutinized Germain le-Comte over the rim of his tankard.

"As you have noticed, I brought with me many healing potions and other healthful concoctions which I have used to benefit your household and peasants—"

"And I have said I am grateful," Armand interrupted.

"Many thanks," said Germain le-Comte automatically. "That does not concern me now: what I have come to ask you has nothing to do with gratitude, but is more to do with discretion and anticipation of need. I am troubled in that I am not going to be able to continue to administer these medicaments if I cannot establish some means of making more of them." He paused. "If you would allow me to construct an athanor, I could—"

Again Armand interrupted. "What is that? An athanor?"

"It is a kind of oven," said Germain le-Comte. "If I were to make one, I could replenish a number of my tinctures and salves—"

"Does that include the tincture you have given to me?" He could not wholly conceal his anxiety as he asked.

"That is one of many things that I need an athanor to prepare," Germain le-Comte said. "If you will grant me permission, I will—" He resumed his petition: "If you will grant permission, I will do all the labor myself. I will take no laborer from your fief." This was more to avert any more suspicion than had already fallen upon him, but he kept that to himself.

"Alchemy is Godless work," Armand declared.

As if he had not heard this last, Germain le-Comte went on, "And to show my gratitude, I will make gold for you."

The silence between them was sudden. Then Armand took another long draught of wine and said, "You can make gold."

"Not vast quantities, but I can make some, yes," Germain le-Comte answered. "Do not deny you have need of it."

"My mother told my father in her dispatch," said Armand, confirming his knowledge of Germain le-Comte's information. "When did you decide to make this offer: before or after you learned of our need for money?"

"I would have asked to build the athanor in any case; I offer to make the gold because I know how small your reserves are." His voice was steady and respectful.

Armand leaned back in his chair as he had so often seen his father do. "In essence, you are proposing to pay me for permission to build this athanor."

"In essence, yes," said Germain le-Comte quietly.

"You don't deny it?" Armand challenged him.

"No," Germain le-Comte replied.

For a long moment Armand sat very still, jaw angled up, his hand on his empty tankard of wine. Abruptly he tapped the tankard on the table, signaling for more wine and indicating he had made up his mind. "There is a room above your rooms. It has one window facing to the north. If that is large enough for your purposes, you may use it."

"Then I thank you, Heir d'Ais, and I pledge my Word to provide gold to you as soon as the athanor is built." This time he bowed in the Italian manner.

"You have very grand manners when you choose to," said Armand, a trace of envy in his tone.

"Ah, but I have been a troubador for some time, and I have learned many things in my travels," Germain le-Comte allowed. "Your decision is a wise one, for your own sake and the sake of Verviers, Armand. I thank you for what you have granted me." He began to withdraw from the dining-hall, but paused as he reached the door. "The athanor can also be used to make metal for swords, quarrels for crossbows, heads for axes."

"So you think we may have to fight for Mon Gardien?" Armand asked, glancing at the servant who brought his wine.

"I think any castle that has been sacked, as this one was, should be ready for attacks," Germain le-Comte said, remembering that fortress where he and Niklos Aulirios had been reduced to propping their frozen comrades in defensive positions and throwing stones at the Huns. "Your smith can shape the weapons, if you like, but I have some skill in armory; all students of the Great Art do."

Armand pretended to think it over. "What would that mean in terms of the gold?"

"You will have the gold; this would be another such gift. Since I am living within these walls, it is in my interest to see them defended," said Germain le-Comte. He bowed once more and turned to leave.

"Germain le-Comte," called Armand. "I accept your gift on behalf of Mon Gardien, and I thank you in the name of d'Ais."

From the ambulatory to the Great Hall, Germain le-Comte heard this with more comfort than satisfaction. He did not stop, but continued on to the staircase that led upward; his thoughts were on plans for his athanor.

"Germain le-Comte," said Heugenet stepping out of the door to the dining-gallery where she had taken her meal. She stood very straight, taking her position directly in his path, a step nearer to him than was wholly correct.

He stopped, his expression no longer preoccupied. "Lady Heugenet."

"Is everything you told my son true?" Her face revealed more fear than she knew.

"Which part of what I said concerns you?" he asked, his attention now completely on her. "I do not want to distress you with things that do not worry you."

She glanced about as if she thought they might be observed. "I know that thing you asked for—the athanor?—would trouble a priest, but it has no terror for me. My apprehension is for other things: do you think he will have to defend Mon Gardien?"

"I think it is possible," said Germain le-Comte quietly, his voice low and penetrating. "And so do you, or you would not ask me."

She nodded twice, her sea-green eyes a little too bright. "There have been peasant uprisings; I would like to think we would not see such a terrible thing, but I would be deceiving myself."

He brushed the backs of his fingers against her cheek. "You are a woman of sense, Heugenet, little though you may believe it, and you are wise enough to know that the aftermath of the Great Dying will be as disruptive as the Blood Roses themselves."

"I . . . I pray it will not be, but I know I must consider what may come." She lowered her head so that all he could see was her wimple. "I have no right to ask anything of you."

He turned her face upward again. "You have every claim upon me, Heugenet." His words were more of a caress than his hand laid along her jaw.

Tears welled in her eyes and one hand lifted to touch him. A sudden noise from the foot of the stairs recalled her to her situation and she broke away from him. "I think," she said crisply, "that it would be best if you would be ready to make steel for our weapons. You *can* make steel, can't you?"

"Yes, Lady Heugenet; I can make steel," Germain le-Comte replied, bowing elegantly to her as she hurried back to her place in the dining-gallery; the door closed behind her with a snap of the latch sharp as the champing of teeth.

Text of a letter from Josue Roebertis in Trier to Hilaire d'Ormonde in Toulouse; carried by messenger and delivered four months after it was written.

To my sole surviving relative, the son of my sister, Hilaire, my heartfelt greetings from my new house in Trier, with my prayers of consolation in this time of Great Dying.

You cannot know with what emotion I greeted the news that you had survived the Great Dying. How wise of your master to remove to Toulouse when the Blood Roses came to Marsailla. God preserve you from harm, dear nephew, and keep you in His favor.

When your mother's second husband agreed to make you his heir, I thought it was a generous gesture from one man to his new wife. Step-children are often left with short shrift in these marriages, and you cannot know what satisfaction I had in knowing that Hue d'Ormande had decided to invest his estate in you, preferring you to any husband he might have chosen for his own daughter. The point is moot since she has entered the convent, but when the contracts were signed, his concessions to my sister's children was most commendable. I mention this because you, as the only survivor beyond the nun, now have claim on his estate; as soon as the Plague subsides, I urge you to petition for your inheritance before some eager charlatan can ask the court to assign it to him in lieu of your claim.

I will, of course, act for you on your behalf. I am certain that the magistrates will have to be pressed to settle the question, for many inheritances may go begging for some time to come, and the courts will be filled with many seeking to have their claims verified. You and I should be able to persuade the magistrates to turn over all that Hue d'Ormonde left to you along with all estates left to him. You must not be lax in these dealings, for you deserve all that your step-father intended you to have. I put my experience and acumen at your disposal, out of consideration for the family, and I ask you to be willing to be guided by me until you have gained enough experience to manage the dealings yourself. As one who has been trained as a notary, you will have some understanding of contracts and courts, so you most certainly can comprehend my urging you to haste.

If the Blood Roses are declining, as it is said they are, I propose to visit you at the close of the year, to help you to prepare for your presentation to the courts. I will send word from Troyes when I reach that place, to tell you when I will arrive. In the meantime I will also review all the papers Hue d'Ormande left in my keeping so that I can show you what claims are due to you. Since you have not yet achieved your majority, you will need to have me, or some other man beyond legal age, to take charge of your inheritance until you do. As your uncle, I will be more than acceptable to the magistrates at Marsailla, or wherever we must go to deal with the estates of Marsailla.

May God spare you from all mischance, my dear nephew, and may He favor our mutual endeavors.

Josue Roebertis
witnessed by Gregorin Weisspherd, innkeeper

In Trier, Duchy of Lorraine, Kingdom of Germany, the Holy Roman Empire, on the 1st day of August in the 1350th Year of Man's Salvation.

5

Although it was nearly midnight, the little room Armand had given Germain le-Comte for his studies was still stifling; the heat from the new-made athanor permeated everything, eclipsing the heat of the day, so that even the flames on the cluster of oil-lamps seemed to shine with their own sweat. Germain le-Comte stood over his improvised crucible, carefully measuring shredded willow bark and a very few torn monkshood petals into it where they would combine with spirits of wine and a tincture of pansy-and-ginger to make the remedy he used for pain and fever. Because of the heat, he was working in a black linen kalasiris, made to the same pattern as the ones he had worn in the Temple of Imhotep; his concentration was so great that he did not hear footsteps on the narrow stairs, nor the opening of the door behind him.

"So this is the athanor," said Heugenet da Brabant when she had watched him work for a short while; she had waited to speak until she saw him set his materials aside and straighten up. The strangeness of his garb made him more foreign than his troubador's motley had done, and she did not know how to comport herself in his presence; her own chamise seemed painfully ordinary and vastly inappropriate.

He showed mild surprise as he swung around to face her. "Yes, this is the athanor. Have you been there long?"

"Not very long, no," she answered as if she were apologizing. "I did not want to interrupt you or I would have spoken . . ." Before she was aware she was doing it, she completed her thought by going to him, taking his head with both hands and kissing him full on the mouth.

Slowly he wrapped her in his arms, holding her close to him, her passion summoning up the whole of his ardor; he could feel her skin through her chamise, warm and eager. The complexity of her need awakened his sympathy as well as his desire, and he sought to keep her safe as much as he wanted to give her the fulfillment she longed for. As she released him, she started to pull away, her color heightened, he caught her hands and bent to kiss them on the palms. "You surprise and delight me, Heugenet," he said quietly.

"I don't know why I . . ." Her hands quivered at his kisses; the sensation went up her arms like rapturous fire.

"You have given me a great gift," he said, his voice as deep and sweet as the lowest notes on her portative organ, and just as palpable.

"I . . . I . . . should not have . . . it wasn't . . ." She did not want to look at him, as if seeing him would make it impossible to deny the yearning in her soul. Much as she knew she must, she could not bring herself to pull her hands away from him, for the sensations his kisses brought were too evocative and she was parched for want of them.

He rose and looked steadily into her eyes. "I have hoped you would come." His admission was so simple, so guileless that it shook her determination.

She shook her head, feeling as if she were trampling on flowers. "That was a lapse, the Devil twisting my—"

"You do me honor when you seek me out, Heugenet," he said, cutting short her castigation. "I have too high regard for you to think you are subject to unworthy lusts. You have other flames within you." He let her move away from him; he had no wish to coerce her into accepting him.

"To aspire to embraces instead of Salvation is sin; to succumb to temptation is the heritage of Eve," she said, crossing herself; the lessons of her childhood rang in her ears and she listened desperately to them, hoping she would not weaken again.

Taking up her tone, he said, "To be lonely is human, even for one like me. To want comfort is human, though you find it in a creature like me. To seek touching and tenderness is so human that even a vampire like me is sustained by it." He watched her as she began to pace.

"I hate that word," she said, her mouth showing her contempt.

"What word: 'vampire'?" he asked without any outward sign of distress.

She made a gesture of endorsement. "It sticks in my ears like a sore. I cannot think of you and that word, not together." She continued pacing, her contending desires lending strength to her movements. Deliberately she sought to hold him at bay, to blot out her hunger for him. "In times like these, I would have thought you would have not bothered with me; there are so many you could choose from, without risk. The Blood Roses provide you a feast—so many are dying."

Instead of answering her attack with one of his own, he shook his head. "No. Not now. Your lives pass so swiftly without diseases to hurry you along, and I have said good-bye so many times: I have seen enough of sickness and dying, I have felt the anger and fear of it more times than I can reckon. What began as consolation became far more in time, when I stopped resenting the brevity of your lives, and learned to cherish each moment you live. If the only contact I am able to have is the anguish of dying . . ." His voice softened to nothing; he inhaled sharply. "When I was much younger, perhaps I would have . . . taken what I could, and fed myself on misery and despair—but no more." He looked toward her, his dark eyes fixed in the distance, and filled with such sorrow that Heugenet stopped still. "It took me many years—centuries—to learn the folly of it. Without the knowing, the touching, there is nothing but surrender to wretchedness as the price of survival; the pain of loss is a lesser burden: believe this."

She found his haunted eyes more frightening than spite would have been. "Germain le-Comte," she cried out to recall him from his memories, and against her resolution, went to his side.

He regarded her with composure. "If you come to me, you come because it is what you want. You have chosen—not I, not the Devil, not God: you." His fingers touched her face so softly that they might have been petals.

She jumped as if stung, so great was her response to him. Her pulse began to race and her eyes filled with tears; she could not name the turmoil within her for that would lead to things she dared not hope for. "You have promised you will not disgrace me."

"Nor will I," he assured her. "Those of my blood have no children of their flesh." He understood her terror, for an adulterous woman could be treated with utmost barbarity if she had a child her husband would not acknowledge as his own.

"You have said so," she responded dubiously; she broke away from him again. "What are you making in the athanor?"

His answer astonished her. "Jewels."

She stared at him. "Jewels?" she repeated, and felt her face go pale.

"Rubies, sapphires, and diamonds, to be precise." He read astonishment in her features and went on, "That is why the athanor is so hot. When I prepare my medicaments, it will not be necessary to have such heat."

"But why jewels?" she persisted. "You spoke only of gold."

"And gold you shall have, in a day or two," he vowed. "But jewels are not as heavy as gold, and their value is greater. A handful of jewels is worth more than a bushel of gold. Jewels are more easily hidden and carried than gold is." His smile was quick, gone even as she saw it.

She could not speak: the enormity of his offering staggered her and she could not pretend she was not moved by it. Finally she whispered, "How many?"

"Probably a dozen or so, of each." He was puzzled by her dismay. "Does that make them unacceptable? What troubles you about them?"

Nervously she wiped the sweat from her face. "A single jewel, or two, I could claim were inherited. Perhaps as many as five, if I were clever. But three dozen?—when no such treasure were part of our marriage contract—how will I explain them to Armandal?"

"I should think the tangle of estates after the Great Dying will have stranger legacies than this. If you must have an explanation, let it be the generosity of kin." His suggestion was sharpened with exasperation. He had not often encountered a woman who was reluctant to receive jewels, or who worried about how to account for them; yet he realized Heugenet's discomfort was genuine, and had strong foundations. "If you are uneasy taking them, I will present them to Armand."

She considered this for a long moment. "It would be wiser if you give them to me. Some would question his right to have them before he is Duc. Then, too, Armand is young and he might boast of how he came by them. That would not be sensible of him; it would be difficult for you, as well." She nodded to Germain le-Comte; she had convinced herself. "Yes. Give them to me. That would be best. I will hold them for him, as a bequest of an uncle or . . . grandmother."

"As you wish. The jewels are yours, whatever you decide to do with them." There had been a time when a preference of this kind would have offended him, but no longer; he had seen gifts become traps for the unwary, the greedy, the naive.

"You can say that? What if I were to present them to the Church or throw them under the wheels of a cart?" Her indignation troubled her as much as it perplexed her, but she could not stem her outburst.

"They are yours, Heugenet; you may do with them what you will. I do not intend them as a bribe." He did not let himself get caught up in her conflict. "I am not some suitor you must put to the test. I am one who loves you."

Gladness and guilt knotted hot and cold within her; she took a hasty step toward the door, then turned toward Germain le-Comte. "You say that easily," she accused; the heat of the athanor had given her face a sheen of moisture that shone where the lamplight struck it.

"Easily, yes, because it is true; but not lightly." His self-possession was kind and his voice gentle which unnerved her more than vigorous protestations would have done.

"But how? A man loves when a woman lures him." She glanced down at her chamise; her cry was of condemnation. "I have caused this, haven't I?"

He laughed softly, no trace of mockery in him. "Of course you did, but not by artifice or seduction. My love for you came from knowing you, not from your devices to enthrall me, had you used any. If you had not been who you are, you might dress in Gates of Hell and perfumed your thighs without moving me." The open-sided fashion was not much seen these days, but he did not doubt Heugenet was familiar with the style.

"But I come here—like this." She took hold of the soft fabric of her chamise and pulled on it with disgust. "What man would not think I wished him to . . . to possess me."

"This one," he replied. "It is late and you could not sleep. What else would you wear but your chamise? If you had put on your cotehardie or some other grand attire, then I might think you were attempting to gain my adoration." He knew she was poised to flee; he went on as if he had not noticed her state of mind. "Were I the kind of man who supposes he has conquered a woman because he has compelled her to lie with him, then you might have reason for apprehension."

"God made me to be loyal," she whispered, more to herself than him.

"And you are," he said to her. "You have done everything your husband has required of you. The rest is inconsequential." He took a step nearer to her. "You have guarded your son as fiercely as a wolf guards her cubs; he will be Duc because of you, not because of anything Armandal has done."

Heugenet waved her hand before her face, the palm toward Germain le-Comte. "I must not listen to you."

"Very well," he said, not moving.

She retreated a little way; she was breathing quickly and told herself it was because the little room was so hot. Sweat ran between her breasts and slid down her belly, making her chamise stick to her skin. The sensation aroused her, making her keenly aware of her flesh. Her carnality appalled her: she was a woman, not a mad girl. She had borne children. She knew God had intended her for her role in life. But then Germain le-Comte had come, and none of the rest of it mattered. She was shameless, she accused herself, and all the while she was staring at him with an ache that seemed to consume her vitals. "What will happen if I stay?" she asked.

"Whatever you wish to happen," he answered; he waited calmly, his dark eyes holding her as surely as if they had the power of fascination that subdued tigers.

"What if I agree to . . . to be bedded and then change my mind?" She was amazed at how composed she sounded, as if she were purchasing chickens for the kitchen.

"You will leave as you like, when you like," he promised her.

She lifted her hands in capitulation. "I burn," she murmured. "There is fire within me. I cannot quench it, though I have tried." This confession shocked her more than him. "You have won."

This time his smile lasted longer. "Ah, no, Heugenet. This is not a contest. If you want the love I offer, it is yours. If you do not want it, I will not impose it, for there would be no . . . no benefit in theft."

"You tell me and tell me and I cannot understand," she said, walking toward him, all her attention on him. "You are unlike anyone I have ever known."

"Does that trouble you?" he asked as she came up to him. His hands brushed her arms through her chamise.

"Yes," she said, tilting her head so he could kiss her. Their mouths met tentatively at first, she testing him, he preparing to be rebuffed; her need intensified and she pressed against him, deepening their embrace and kiss at the same time. She could not draw a breath without sensing him the length of her body. As she broke the kiss, she whispered, "I will not deny you anything."

Almost without effort he lifted her into his arms. "Nor I you, but one," he answered as he bore her to the door and carried her down the stairs to his two rooms below; he moved as if she weighed no more than a little child, and she began to realize that he was truly all that he claimed to be. He brought her to a pile of bear- and wolf-skins that he had purchased from the huntsmen in the village. Lowering her onto the luxurious furs, he knelt down beside her, his dark eyes intent on her.

"Will anyone come?" She knew they would not, but could not keep from asking, her voice hushed; she listened for any sound of approaching footsteps.

"Not at this hour," he replied, just above a whisper. "The servants avoid my quarters during the day: why should that change at night?"

She nodded, reassured enough for her longing to heighten. Taking hold of the fluted linen of his kalasiris, she drew him down next to her. "You are . . ." She could not find words to express it; she showed him with her body. Of its own volition it moved to fill his hands wherever they went, and responded to his questing. Never before had she known the texture and weight of her breasts as she did now, as his fingers and lips worked a magic upon her that was beyond her imagining. Never had she realized the delight that could be found in the bend of her elbow or the nape of her neck. Never had she believed that her body could quiver as with music in answer to the easing open of her thighs.

From her head to her feet, Germain le-Comte caressed and fondled and kissed, summoning more pleasure than she had ever experienced; she closed her eyes the better to perceive the tremendous sensations coursing through her, and as she did, she was nearly overwhelmed by the myriad responses coursing through her, carried on a heat that had nothing to do with the athanor, or summer. His invention was never intrusive, always evocative, never demanding. When he discovered a new enjoyment, he dwelled on it, letting his esurience build with her ecstasy, paying homage to her with every motion, every word, every breath, until she could contain her fulfillment no longer and they lay clasped in each other's arms, replete and triumphant.

When Heugenet woke, it was to find herself alone in the pre-dawn gloom; annoyance and then disappointment went through her as she pulled her chamise on and sat with her knees drawn up to her chin, wondering what she had done. That they could share so much fired her longing once again and made his absence more painful. Had she been mistaken, and he had wanted nothing more than blood from her, after all? Had his protestations been a ruse? These glum thoughts leached the joy out of her. She was about to rise and return stealthily to her room when the door opened and Germain le-Comte stepped through it, carrying a magnificent cotehardie in his hands. As she regarded him with confusion he went down on his knee beside her and kissed her. "I thought . . . I was alone," she said.

"You need something more than your chamise to wear," he said, putting the lovely garment in her hands. "No one is stirring yet; I think the sentries are dozing. I doubt anyone would notice if you went naked through the Great Hall. But you must not be suspected." He gathered her close to him.

"It is wrong to be deceitful," said Heugenet, but with enough humor to show that it did not trouble her, at least not for this moment.

"The only alternative is to be open about our love," he said as he looked into her face, nothing but admiration in his eyes.

She smiled at him. "But that isn't possible," she said resignedly. "You know it as well as I."

"Yes," he admitted as he released her. "It will be growing light soon, and the servants will begin to stir. Go back to your room by way of the chapel, so that no one will remark on your being up so early." He kissed her brow without otherwise touching her.

She nodded as he helped her to her feet; she stood unmoving for a moment and then shook out the gold-embroidered cotehardie. "Where did you get this?"

"I brought it with me," he said, not answering her. "It was made in Genova." He had intended to present it to Dona Esterre as a parting gift, forty years ago in Bruges, but she had refused it when made his offer. He had kept the splendid garment in his largest clothing-chest without knowing why he had bothered; now he was glad he had.

"Do you always carry women's clothing with you?" she asked archly, all the while running her hands over the rich fabric.

"I have traveled with players in my time," he replied. "Players carry everything with them: crowns, sceptres, daggers, chalices, and clothes of all sorts. They even carry tables and chairs and painted trees for their performances."

She accepted this without too many reservations as she prepared to put the cotehardie on. "Will you help me put it on?" There was no coquetry in her question, only an eagerness to wear the lovely thing.

"Certainly," he said, and lifted the hem over her head, lowering it slowly enough for her to adjust her chamise at the arms.

She smoothed the front of it when it was on. "How is it? Do you have a mirror? I want to see how I look."

"There I cannot help you," he said drily. "Mirrors have no use for me." He stood back and admired her, then walked completely around her, pausing once to adjust the hang of the skirt in the back. "You will have to take my word for it that you look magnificent."

"So magnificent that the servants will stare," she said, suddenly struck with a new difficulty. "What am I to say?"

"The style is a trifle out-moded," Germain le-Comte pointed out. "Possibly it is a legacy from a female relative? Why not claim this as a remembrance?"

She rounded on him. "Because I would rather tell everyone that this is the gift given to me for the sake of love. I cannot let anyone know that this came from you, for that would ruin everything."

He went to her and touched her hair. "You and I know the truth; does it truly matter that no one else does?"

"Yes. It troubles me that I must hide my love of you, and you must do the same. In songs it seems gallant to have such love, but I do not think it is gallant any longer." Now that she had admitted so much she stared at him as if she had not seen him clearly until now. "I want to show everyone that we are lovers. And it rankles that I cannot."

Taking Heugenet in his arms for a moment, Germain le-Comte held her, stroking her hair. "The first birds are singing."

"I can hear them," she murmured. "We cannot be found together; you are right." She stepped back from him. "While I wear this, I will praise my aunt and think only of you."

Amusement smoldered in his dark eyes. "Be very kind to your aunt's memory."

She preened, glancing self-consciously at him. "You do not have to give me this."

"No, I do not," he said, bowing to her. "It pleases me to do it, nonetheless." He watched her as she fussed with the dropped waist and fingered the amber studs down the front.

"These are very fine. Such dark amber isn't often come-by. And there are sixteen studs on the front. Did you make them, too?" Her question was light, concealing a sense of awe at his unexpected generosity; she was still curious how he came to have it, for a Prince might give his mistress such a garment, not the illegitimate son of a Comte.

"No; those came from Poland, many years ago." He did not add that he had purchased the amber six hundred years ago, or that it had nearly cost him his life.

"Poland," she marveled. "They say the Poles are very fierce in battle."

Germain le-Comte made a gesture of concession. "They have that reputation."

There were dozens of questions she wanted to ask him, all of them excuses not to leave; she made herself forget them as she put her arms around him. "I will go pray for the repose of my aunt's soul and ask her to forgive me for making such use of her."

"I am certain she will not mind," Germain le-Comte said kissing her one last time before she slipped away from him, letting herself out of his door so quietly that no one could hear her go. Left alone, he went to rearrange the bear- and wolf-skins so that no impression of their bodies remained in the fur. Satisfied that there was nothing that would catch the attention of any of the servants—should any venture into his quarters—he slowly removed his kalasiris and began to wash, using a rag and a bucket of water. When he was clean, he once again donned his troubador's motley before going to the room above to gather up his new-made jewels, anticipating the moment when he would give them to Heugenet.

Text of a letter to Armandal d'Ais, Duc de Verviers, at the Court of the Holy Roman Emperor from Heugenet da Brabant at Mon Gardien. Carried by Biebart and delivered ten days after it was written.

To my husband, Armandal d'Ais, Duc de Verviers, the dutiful greetings of his wife, Heugenet de Brabant; may God keep you, my husband, and protect you from all ills, and so we all pray.

It is difficult for me to tell you this, for I know it will bring you distress in a time when there has been too much distress already, and I am loath to add to the pains you have borne thus far. Biebart will carry it back to me, as I have instructed him to do, and I ask you not to deal harshly with him for being the one to bring this news to you.

As you are aware, your mother has not kept her wits into old age; her forgetfulness has sometimes been a blessing, without doubt, and it is true that she is one who has remained benign in spite of her affliction. But of late she has taken to wandering off, and I have not enough servants to keep one tending to her day and night, for which I will answer to God when the Last Judgment comes. It happened this way: a tinker had come to the village and was mending pots and pans and other such when your mother decided she must go and see, thinking he was some friend from long past. Remi could not be spared, nor could Guillem, so Mauvra, the daughter of the old ferryman, was given the task of looking after her, and she was most attentive until one of her children fell out of a tree and broke his arm, at which point she gave her full concentration to her child. She left the Ducesse sitting at the spinning wheel, busy with yarn-making while she brought her son to Mon Gardien to Germain le-Comte, so that the bone could be set and spare the child from becoming a cripple.

When Mauvra returned, the Ducesse was not at the spinning wheel. She had told the bee-keeper that she was going home, which the bee-keeper took to mean that she was returning to Mon Gardien. But apparently she wandered off to wherever her addled wits led her. When Mauvra came to me, she had already searched the village and set a dozen children to scouring the countryside for her. I ordered five of the men-at-arms to join the search, and when they returned at nightfall, they had nothing to report beyond one or two peasants who said they might have seen her, but at a distance. I instructed the men-at-arms to carry word of the Ducesse's disappearance to all the towns for five leagues around, hoping that someone might have come upon her. By the next morning, when they returned, they brought no news of her, nor any other report that indicated where she might have gone. I ordered the churchbell in the village to be rung several times a day, so that if the Ducesse was nearby she might hear it and come toward it, but that was five days ago, and in spite of constant searching, we cannot find her.

I have asked all the household and all the villagers to pray for your mother, for her safe return or her Christian burial. I confess I am at a loss as to what more I should do. Armand has promised to pay a reward for her return, in case she is being held by those who want more than God's approbation for charity. You left her in my care and I have not been able to guard her; had we a larger household this would not have happened, my husband, and I beg you will remember that when you decide what is to be done.

I ask you to tell our daughter of this as gently as you can, for she will be distressed by the news. Forgive me for informing you so hastily, but I must return to searching, and I have paused in my efforts only long enough to put this into Biebart's hands. I do not like to spare him when he might be of use in searching, but I have deemed it necessary to let you know what has transpired.

May God keep you from all harm, and may He send His Angels to watch over the Ducesse. I ask you to pardon me for failing to keep your mother safe.

Heugenet de Brabant (by her hand)
Written to her dictation by Germain le-Comte

At Mon Gardien in Verviers on the 12th day of August in the 1350th Year of Grace.

6

Sunset was fading to twilight as Germain le-Comte rode up to the peste-house at Sant-Amienne, Heugenet beside him; this was the last, and most dreaded stop in their day-long search for the missing Ducesse. The horses were tired, but still they balked at the ghastly odor that hung around the whole of the convent.

"Let me go in to look for her," Germain le-Comte said quietly to Heugenet. "You should not go into the peste-house. I have nothing to fear from the place."

She nodded her consent, fatigue making her feel stupid. "Very well," she agreed, her back and shoulders aching from long hours in the saddle and her spirit so downcast that she could not summon up any token objection. She took the reins he handed to her and pulled the horses back a few paces, watching with tired eyes as he strode across the packed earth to the open doorway.

"Good Sister," Germain le-Comte said to the first nun he encountered, a middle-aged woman who was serving as warder at the entrance.

She began to speak with automatic grief that showed how great a toll this work had taken on her; her words tumbled out without inflection, and might have been a market-day tally for all the impact they had on her. "I regret we have no more beds. You will have to put your—" The nun stopped as she looked more closely at Germain le-Comte.

"I bring no one to you, Sister, as you see," he said as gently as he could. "I am here to ask if anyone has seen the Ducesse de Verviers. She is an old woman, no longer capable of fending for herself; she is easily distracted and her thoughts are not always of this world."

The nun crossed herself. "Addled from age, they say," she told him. "No, she is not here. Nor have we heard of her from anyone who has brought the afflicted to us."

Germain le-Comte ducked his head respectfully. "I have no cause to doubt you, Sister, but would you mind if I look for myself? The Ducesse has been gone for nine days now, and it may be that she has not been identified. She might not look like a well-born woman at all, not after having been lost for so long."

The nun shrugged. "If you think she may be with the abandoned ones, then look among them for yourself," she offered in a voice that cracked with exhaustion. She stood aside to let him enter the peste-house.

It was worse than before; there were as many sufferers and less to offer them; bedding had not been changed and with fewer nuns to nurse them, the sick groaned and thrashed and died with no one to assuage their agonies. Germain le-Comte made his way down the narrow aisle, peering at the faces of the patients; the gloom did not hamper his vision as it might another's, and he went from one victim to the next and the next without having to pause for too long. There were times he was grateful that he only needed breath to speak, for he was convinced that the Black Plague could be inhaled when it was as concentrated as it was here, and although he was not able to take infection himself, he did not want to be the inadvertent cause of bringing Blood Roses to someone else.

Seventy-one faces later he came upon a nun who was bending over a sick child, trying to hold on to him while he fussed and coughed. Realizing that the boy was about to break out of the nun's arms, Germain le-Comte went up to the two of them. "Here, my Sister," he offered, taking hold of the boy and steadying him so that the nun could bathe the child's face before looking at how large the Blood Roses had grown.

"Thank you," she muttered, turning slightly to look at her unexpected assistant. She went white as her habit. "You!" Color mounted in her sunken cheeks. "I saw you before, and I wasn't sure. Your hair is different and you have no beard. But I was not mistaken."

His first reaction was dismay, and then an emotion between gladness and anxiety came over him. He held the boy for her as he made out her thin features in the wan light. "Jenfra?" he exclaimed. "Jenfra d'Ormonde?"

"Seur Jenfra," she said austerely. "Francois de Saint-Germain. I wasn't sure until I heard you speak. Francois de Saint-Germain." She repeated his name as if it had its own vitality and would fortify her against this place where her faith had brought her.

"Germain le-Comte," he corrected her gently. Then he decided to try to explain his astonished response to finding her here, as much in the hope that he would understand it better than that she would. "I was told you had died; indeed, I had no reason to think otherwise," he went on. "When I went to your house in Marsailla, after the dying began, I was told you were dead."

"And so I am, to the world," she said, taking the boy from him and putting him down on the filthy straw that served as a mattress. "So you fled and became Germain le-Comte. You came to Mon Gardien." Her single bark of laughter was shocking to him. "From Sieur Ragoczy to le-Comte.

A considerable fall," she remarked as she reached for the pail of water. If she had intended this as an ironic observation there was no trace of it in her voice or her manner.

He handed it to her and watched while she ministered to the boy. "Have you any hope for him?" From long experience, he saw that the child was beyond help, but he could not bring himself to say so; he was still trying to comprehend what had happened to her. He had reconciled himself to the loss of all the d'Ormondes along with his loss of Clair dela Luna and his quiet life in the hills of Provence. Now to find her here: there were many questions he wanted to put to her, but knew this was not the place to do it, nor the time.

"Until yesterday I did," she said in an undervoice. "But look how the Blood Roses flourish." She pulled back the boy's chamise, revealing red-black swellings like blisters in his armpits. "They are in his groin as well." As she closed the chamise, she said, "It is hard to have hope when so many die. Yesterday a woman of twenty improved enough to be sent back to her husband, and two days before that, a carpenter from Cascade-en-Foudre left here on his own two feet, but no Blood Roses had bloomed on his flesh. I have seen hundreds die, and only a handful recover, and never one who was stricken as this child is. Look at him. He is too weak and the Blood Roses are too many; they will overwhelm him. In a day he will have them on his chest and neck, and then he will be gone, returned to God."

"If I had known you were alive, I would have—" He did not know what he might have done with that intelligence.

"What would a foreigner like you do for d'Ormonde?" she challenged him. "Once my father sent me away from Marsailla, I was lost to my family. I was grateful when my cousins agreed to let me enter the convent. When the Great Dying came, claiming all my father's family but me, I realized that God intended that I serve Him. All sorrow will be burned away in the fires of Hell, and all anguish annealed before God." She crossed herself. "I am in God's Hands."

"Jenfra, I grieve for your family; it is a welcome thing in these terrible days to know you have been spared." He could not read the expression in her face and could not tell if he had succeeded in providing her a little comfort. His demeanor was kind as he held out his hand to her. "Is there anything more you can do for the boy?" He knew the answer already.

"No. I know it is nearly over for him." She sketched the sign of the cross on the boy's forehead. "In case the priest does not come in time. God will understand that we cannot shrive them all. We only have two priests to help us now; a while ago there were five. The Angelus isn't over yet."

He helped her to rise. "There is nothing I can say to console you for so great a loss as you have endured; I wish it were otherwise," he said.

"Yes. God alone has any answer for this calamity, and He has not—" She made herself be silent, crossing herself to keep from the danger of blasphemy. "I cannot talk to you; it isn't suitable, and I have many who need me." She turned away and was about to continue her assigned tasks when he asked, "Have you anyone here who is an old woman, thin, with white hair?"

She glanced back at him. "We have many such."

"This woman would be simple, age having turned her thoughts to other times." He looked more closely at her; gone was the flirtatious child with the capricious will; in her place was a rail-thin nun who had put all womanhood behind her.

"No, I do not recall one like that." She started to move away, pausing to peer into the face of the next patient in line.

"She would have come here no more than nine days ago," he persisted, not following her but holding her attention with his voice.

"The only old woman with failed wits we have seen here died a fortnight ago." She turned her back on him, her shoulders stiff with determination.

"Seur Jenfra, I am so—" He was certain that nothing he said would be anodyne to the pain of her losses. He was about leave when she spoke to him without looking at him.

"Why did you come? I had put so much behind me. I had made myself content. You have brought it all back." The last was an accusation and they both realized it.

He had no answer for her. "If I have added to your grief, I apologize; I did not intend to—"

"Why did you not stay in Provence?" Her back was still turned to him; she was rigid as she continued to upbraid him. "You are a rich man. If you left, you could have gone anywhere. You did not have to go into the world where everyone is dying at all. You could have walled yourself up inside Clair dela Luna, and kept the Blood Roses from reaching you. Francois de Saint-Germain: why did you leave?" She swung around to face him at last; her mouth was square with fury. "Why did you have to come here?"

For a long moment he said nothing. "I could not . . ." Then he saw that she did not want an answer from him. Defeated, he lowered his head. "I apologize for adding to your grief, ma Seur."

"Go away," she told him, returning to her duties with such purpose that he made no more attempt to speak to her. As he left the peste-house he saw that night had taken hold of the sky but for a faint afterglow in the west. He paused to look up, then went to Heugenet, taking the reins from her hand in silence before swinging into the saddle.

"You were gone longer than I thought you'd be," she said speculatively as they started their horses back toward the road that led to Mon Gardien; with their mounts worn-out, they let the animals set the pace: a slow walk. "It was horrible in there, I can hardly guess how horrible. Yet you stayed. Why?"

He considered his answer. "One of the nuns spoke to me. I knew her in the south, nearly three years ago, when she was not much more than a child: before she took the veil. She has lost her family to Blood Roses," he said, hoping it would be enough.

"Did her family give you patronage?" she asked, letting him take the lead.

"No," he said, and after a short while relented. "I have not always been a troubador."

"So I have surmised," she said, and managed not to demand explanations. Watching him riding ahead of her she sensed his remoteness and did her best not to disturb it. A bit later she asked, "Did you find the Ducesse?"

"No. She was not there today, and has not been there," he replied. He could feel his mount's tiredness through the flaps of the saddle, and he shared the enervation; he had been riding for many hours on a bright summer day. The night would help to restore him, as would a new layer of his native earth in the soles of his Persian-style boots.

"Then what am I to do?" She did not expect an answer, and so was startled when Germain le-Comte spoke.

"If Plague were not abroad in the land, I would recommend that you ask the regional magistrate to offer a reward for her. You may want to authorize the huntsmen to search the woods for her again, with the incentive of gold if they find her." He slewed around in the high-canteled saddle. "I have no wish to distress you, but I doubt she will be found alive."

"I know," said Heugenet, and stared ahead into the vast darkness. She could not make herself think about what she would have to do next; her husband would have to return to Mon Gardien and the Bishop—who might not still be alive—would have to come to officiate at the obsequies of the Ducesse and recognize her investiture in the title. Dwelling on these possibilities gave her no pleasure, but they continued to occupy her thoughts as they went on through the night.

"What's the matter?" Germain le-Comte asked, the kindness in his voice once again; he had let his horse drop back so now they rode side by side.

"I was trying to think of everything I will have to do once . . . once the Ducesse is declared dead." She sighed. "I do not want to have all my time claimed by ceremonies, not now. Verviers has enough to contend with; no one wants more impositions, yet I am preparing for them. If the Great Dying were finally over, so that we would have no cause to fear gatherings, if the war between England and France were settled, it would not be a difficult thing to arrange the celebration. It is foolish to have great display when death is all around us." She glanced at him. "I have hoped my husband would remain at the Emperor's Court for the rest of the year."

"Heugenet, you—" He began only to be interrupted.

"In the last several days you have given me more happiness than I have known in all the rest of my life," she said directly. "I do not want to lose it so soon."

"And what of the risk?" Germain le-Comte asked. "We have lain to-

gether three times; if we do so another three times, you will be one of my
blood when you die, and you, too, will wander the world after death."

She crossed herself. "You've warned me. But look around you, Germain le-Comte. They say the Peste Maiden has Blood Roses strewn wherever she goes. To be assured that no illness could touch me, that would not
be unwelcome to me." Although she could not bring herself to look at
him, she did incline her head in his direction.

"Heugenet, think of what you are saying," he told her without rebuke.
"You have learned little about how I live, or how you would have to live if
you came to my life." His voice softened, and she could feel his compelling
gaze on her. "I will deny you nothing, only be certain it is what you want."

"I will consider everything you tell me," she said, adding, "And there is
Armand."

"In what sense?" Germain le-Comte was at once playful and cautious.

"He relies on you to tutor him, and he needs instruction." She realized
her argument was thin, and did what she could to reinforce it. "If you
leave, it will be months before someone qualified may be found to replace
you, and if the Blood Roses continue to bloom, we might never have a tutor
to take up Armand's education."

"You might also find that many good men who had pupils before are
now without a livelihood and would be eager to have such a student as Armand d'Ais." His horse began to move faster, aware that its stall was near.

"Half a league, then we are home," said Heugenet, letting her shoulders
sag for the first time that day. "I am hungry and too tired to eat."

"That is when you must have food," he said. "Otherwise you will weaken
yourself. It would not be wise to take such a chance."

"Strange advice, coming from you," she teased him. "I will take it, in any
case. I am sorry Perside is dead: no one has cooked as well as she."

"Marrow broth and new bread at least," he recommended. "There is no
art to marrow broth; a scullion could prepare it, or I could, for that matter. Your baxter is capable and you have not complained that her loaves are
poor."

"She does well enough, when her yeast is full-grown," Heugenet allowed, then tried to stretch her arms above her without tugging on the
reins. "I will probably be stiff for three days."

"I will give you a tincture to help ease your muscles," he offered. "If you
bathe, I have an unguent to put in the water as well. I will heat the bath-
house for you, if you like; none of the servants need be bothered with the
task."

A loud clank of a bell followed by a goat's bleat heralded their approach
to the village below Mon Gardien. These familiar sounds set off a volley of
barking from the peasants' dogs.

"They will know we are coming," said Heugenet, listening as the cacophony increased to include the cries of villagers.

"Something must have happened," said Germain le-Comte, who detected in the excitement of their arrival more than the usual reception given to arrivals after nightfall.

She, too, caught something in the welling sounds that was beyond the usual. "I think you are right," she said, and urged her reluctant mare to a jogging trot.

Germain le-Comte touched the hilt of the dagger he carried in his boot, ready to fend off any attack; he wished now he had his francisca tucked into his belt at the small of his back; his little throwing-axe had served him well many times. "Rein in," he told Heugenet. "In case there is trouble."

She began to ask what trouble there could be, but stopped herself before she spoke the words: trouble could be found anywhere in these times. She pulled in her mare, who was relieved to walk again, and peered at Germain le-Comte, trying to discern what he was doing. "What must I do?"

"Ride half a length behind me. We cannot be easily separated if you do that." He had lowered his voice so she could barely hear him over the sound of the hoofbeats and the clamor from the village; he shifted his seat, ready to control his horse with heels and knees if needed.

The noise grew louder and the excitement increased as villagers carrying torches came down the road toward them.

"What is going on?" Heugenet asked of the air; she was beginning to feel uneasy, recalling all the rumors of peasant uprisings that had been reported from France to the Lowlands.

"I don't know," Germain le-Comte said as he pulled his dagger from the top of his thick-heeled Persian boot.

The faces of the villagers, illuminated by the torches they carried, seemed to float forward on choppy black seas; most of them were shouting, their voices a mixed and incomprehensible babble until the bee-keeper roared out, "The Ducesse is dead!" At this announcement, the people surged forward, crying out Heugenet's name and calling on God to protect them all.

"Dead?" Heugenet repeated as the first of the villagers reached them. She rocked in the saddle as her mare shied away from the torches.

"Stand back!" Germain le-Comte's voice was not loud but it carried to every person in the crowd with indisputable authority. "Keep the torches away from the horses." Something in his demeanor subdued the villagers. "Now then," he went on. "One of you tell Lady Heugenet what has happened."

"Let Celine tell it; she found her," one of the men suggested; his suggestion found eager support from most of the rest.

Heugenet had calmed herself enough to deal with the crowd. "Yes; let Celine speak."

The young woman who spoke up was no more than fifteen; her first pregnancy was just beginning to show beneath her voluminous skirts, and she became flustered as she kept her eyes averted from Heugenet looming above her. "This afternoon I went into the forest," she said, doing her best to tell the story clearly. "I wanted to pick berries and most of the patches near the edge of the forest are empty now." She began to twist a bit of her skirt, screwing the fabric tight and then releasing it to twist it the other direction. "I went more than a league into the forest, into the defile beyond the three burned trunks?" The location was familiar enough to the villagers that many nodded in support of her description. "I knew there were many berry vines in the defile, and the animals do not eat them all." She looked away from Heugenet, out into the night. "I was in the defile before I noticed the smell. At first I thought a wolf or a wildcat had died; I paid no attention as I went about picking berries. Then I saw a bit of cloth snagged on the vines, and I knew." She crossed herself. "She must have been eating berries and got caught by the vines; she was deep in the thicket. Something had gnawed her feet and ankles and there were bugs everywhere."

"You need not go on," Heugenet said, trying to make this as much a condolence as an order.

But Celine was engrossed in her story and continued. "I saw the necklace and I knew it had to be the Ducesse. I hurried back to the village and summoned the woodsmen to help."

A man of middle years with few teeth remaining in his mouth, took up the story. "We followed Celine back to the defile and we cut the body out with our axes and brought it back to Mon Gardien. The heir has sent one of his men-at-arms for a priest to bury her."

The villagers crossed themselves; a few of them were weeping.

"What do we do now, Ducesse?" the woodsman asked.

Heugenet started at the unfamiliar title. She was so flustered that she tripped over her words of thanks and had to begin again. "You have done good service to d'Ais. You will be rewarded for what you have done. I ask you to pray for the soul of the Ducesse."

The uncertain movement among the crowd turned to milling; they were reluctant to leave Heugenet without escort. There were bits of prayers buzzing, and one of the youngsters began to cry.

"I think we had better lead them," said Germain le-Comte to Heugenet, nudging his horse with his knees.

"You're probably right," said Heugenet, thinking of Armand, and feeling proud of his decisiveness. "Take the lead, will you?"

"At your service, ma Ducesse," he said, bowing in the saddle as much as it would allow. He squeezed his calves and the horse responded, going forward in a gathered trot; the villagers parted to let him pass, Heugenet following after him.

As they started up the slope to Mon Gardien, Heugenet said, "I am sorry she is dead, but I wish she had waited a little longer to die."

"You will have much to do," Germain le-Comte said, watching the portcullis rising as they approached.

"So I will," she said. Everything she had considered on the ride from Sant-Amienne came back to haunt her; what had been theory now became reality, and she realized there would be more to do than she had first anticipated.

Armand was waiting in the main courtyard, his face unusually somber. "Thank God you are back," he said as Germain le-Comte dismounted and went to help Heugenet out of the saddle. "You will have to help me, and the Ducesse"—he glanced uneasily at his mother as he used the unfamiliar title—"prepare all the dispatches we must send."

"Of course," said Germain le-Comte as he handed the horses over to the groom. "I must see to my patients in the stable. Lady Heugenet is hungry, and you need not have everything accomplished at once."

"Germain le-Comte is right," said Heugenet. "I am famished. Come, Armand, there are things we must discuss privately. Leave Germain le-Comte to his duties in the stable while you and I arrange ourselves." She took her son by the shoulder and turned him away from Germain le-Comte. As she propelled the young man toward the keep, she managed one swift glance over her shoulder, her look beseeching him to understand.

Text of a letter from the Bishop of Cambrai to Armandal d'Ais, Duc de Verviers, at the Court of the Holy Roman Emperor.

To my most devout earthly son, my condolences accompany this missive upon the occasion of the death of your mother; rest assured that she has been welcomed in Heaven as the virtuous woman she was so well-reputed to be. Her earthly travail is over, and you may thank God for His Mercy.

God has called us all to redouble our efforts in these days, to show the strength of our faith and to conduct ourselves virtuously in hardship. Had I not been your Confessor, I would not so admonish you, but as God has advanced me in His Church through the tragedy of others, I must advise you to put yourself in God's Hands with a humble heart and an obedient soul.

I have sent messengers to Mon Gardien granting your wife, Heugenet de Brabant, the position and title of Ducesse which shall be officially confirmed by your own hands in ceremonies that are part of the d'Ais traditions. She may require the force of her position in these terrible times, which is why I have gone to these unusual lengths, making it possible for her to carry out her duties that must be dealt with while you are absent from Mon Gardien.

It is unfortunate that your heir is so young, for he will need his mother to act for him much of the time. I am therefore urging you to consider residing at Mon Gardien for a period of at least a year during which time you will instruct your heir in the execution of his position. I am aware that your oldest son did not live to occupy your place, and that you had hoped this boy would have a vocation for the Church. Now you can see God's Hand in this, for your son who is now your heir is unencumbered by obligations that would make it impossible for him to succeed you.

You will want to find a bride for your son Armand as soon as may be. There have been so many alterations in the alliances of great Houses that no one may think any contract secure without rigorous enforcement. You will arrange to bring her to Mon Gardien to live under the chaperonage of your wife, so that she will be well-schooled in her role as wife of the Duc de Verviers. If the times were less difficult, I would not be so stringent in my suggestions, but given that Blood Roses may take their toll of anyone at any time, I think it advisable for you to act in a timely manner, and do all that you may to insure the continuation of your House in spite of all the Great Dying may do.

It is said that Heugenet da Brabant is a woman of good sense, and one who is not easily led into feminine errors, for which you must be deeply grateful. Your wife is said to be one woman who is not turned by extravagance or flattery, who seeks no suitors for herself, and does not in any way bring dishonor to your name. If you will let her help in the choosing of a bride for your heir, I think you may look forward to a fruitful and appropriate union that will advance your ambitions and those of the House with which you ally your family.

I pray for wisdom for your House, and I pray that God will keep you safe from all the dangers of this world. I pray your wife will discharge her office in a worthy manner, and I pray that all of us will be united once again at the Throne of Glory in Paradise,

Eustace, Bishop of Cambrai
By my own hand

On the last day of August in the 1350th Year of Man's Salvation.

Amen

7

Gold coins glistened as they fell through Heugenet's fingers in a glorious stream; there were suggestions of features carved on them, and a faint sign of mintage, but nothing more distracted from the brilliant shine of the wonderful metal. They chimed musically as they dropped into the bushel basket where more of them were lying.

"How am I to thank you?" Heugenet asked Germain le-Comte as she looked from the gold to the black-clad man in front of the athanor.

"No thanks are necessary," he said, and smiled at her. "You will need the money in the days to come."

She sighed and let the rest of the coins fall into the basket at her feet. "With my husband's mother about to be put into her final grave, I fear you are right—that is, assuming there are enough foodstuffs to buy with this or any other payment, and means to house those who will come to see the Mass for her soul." Her sea-green eyes grew serious. "What am I to do, if Armandal demands that we honor her death with all the pomp to which she is entitled?"

"I doubt he will do that." His bluntness was mitigated by the warmth in his gaze. "You know as well as Armandal that most people are afraid to travel any distance for fear of passing through the miasma of the Great Dying. And the Blood Roses are everywhere; you cannot blame those who do not wish to attend one funeral at the risk of having their own."

"No. I can't." Heugenet glanced toward the window that glowed with the first light of morning. "I wish I could remain here all day long, but—" She shoved herself off her tall stool. "I must attend to the preparation of the tomb for the coffin of my husband's mother. I will be glad when the Mass is said at last. Not that it will be pleasant. You saw the condition her body was in when they brought it back, two days ago. She has been dead long enough that—" She stopped herself from saying anything more. "It will be difficult to convince the understewards to bring her up from her temporary grave."

"At least they are sending a priest from Sant-Amienne; that should ease the problem for you. The servants will do what he tells them to for the sake of their salvation." He came up behind her and laid his hands on her shoulders; his touch was calming and she welcomed it with a half-shrug to show how much she benefited from his attention.

"I want to have time with you, to lie with you." She leaned back against him, her eyes half-closed, and tried to forget everything that she had to do before sunset. "I didn't think I would miss the Ducesse, but I do. She was always—" She did not go on.

"You are Ducesse now," Germain le-Comte reminded her.

"Not entirely, not until Armandal arrives to set his seal upon my acquisition of the title." She moved away from him reluctantly, getting off the stool in a sinuous movement that put the basket of gold at her feet.

"You said you expect him in two or three days, did you not?" He wanted to find an excuse to keep her with him, knowing all the while that he should not.

"If he travels fast. Four is probably . . ." She did not finish her observation. "May God pardon me, but I cannot think of Armandal without comparing him to you, and finding him wanting." With a gesture of abandon, she went to him and walked into his arms. "Twice damned," she whispered before she kissed him.

Germain le-Comte held her for as long as he could, as aware as she that they would not have much time together in the coming days. Slowly he let her go. "You will have to be very careful; I don't want you to put yourself in harm's way."

"I won't do that," she said, glancing at the gold. "You said a bushel. I didn't believe you."

"Why not?" he challenged her gently. "Why should you doubt me?"

"I shouldn't," she said, her face somber. "Of all those I have known in my life, you have been the truest." She released him and backed away. "Will you carry that down? I don't think I can."

"Better send two servants to bear it," Germain le-Comte suggested. "You do not want anyone wondering about my strength, or believing that the gold is sham." He had learned this precaution long ago, and was not inclined to bring notice to himself or the gold he made.

"Armand told me he doubts you, that you can make gold. He will be surprised." She opened the door and dropped him a slight curtsy. "Thank you, Germain le-Comte, for your gift; I accept it on behalf of my husband and my son, and will praise you for your generosity."

Taking his tone from hers, Germain le-Comte bowed. "There is no call for gratitude or praise, Ducesse. I have repaid your hospitality in the way I presume is most appropriate."

There was silence between them; finally Heugenet said, "Well. I will send two servants for the gold. They will bear it to the strongroom and enter a counting of it in the muniment-room."

"As you wish," he answered, and watched as she closed the door. He listened to her steps, and when he was satisfied she was down the stairs, he followed her, going to his rooms to shave, and to put on his haincelin over his black chamise.

Armand was waiting for him in the room that was part library, part study; he was in full mourning, with red-and-black bands on his sleeves. "I heard about the gold."

"It will be in your strongroom shortly," said Germain le-Comte. He studied Armand briefly, thinking how quickly the lad was changing. In another year he would have a beard and his voice would have lost all its treble breaks. Now he was still young enough to have a touchy, brittle pride that made him difficult to teach, and more difficult to encourage.

"Why do you do this for us? Or is it for my mother? Payment for her kindness?" He leaned forward in his tall chair, trying to make an impression on Germain le-Comte; he offered no apology for the implication of his questions.

"I do it for your House as well as for your mother," Germain le-Comte answered smoothly; he had anticipated a confrontation of this sort for some time. "You have given me shelter when the world has provided none. I would be an ingrate, and worse, if I had it within my capabilities to relieve your distress and did not."

"Because you seek favor from my mother," said Armand.

"Rather because I hold her in high regard." He came closer to Armand. "If you have no compunction about shaming Heugenet, I do."

Armand colored to the roots of his hair. "I do not shame her—you do."

"Then you must suppose that the Devil has sent me to shake her resolution to virtue, for otherwise you must assume that she was made flawed." He maintained an affable expression although he was growing weary of the game.

"You have lured her, played on her weakness and seduced her as Eve was seduced, with promises of rewards beyond merit." His indignation increased as he spoke.

Germain le-Comte's answer was as mild as Armand's words were choleric. "You have proof of this, do you. You know I have betrayed your hospitality and exposed your mother to exile." He stood directly in front of his pupil. "I have never denied my fondness, nor has Heugenet. But I swear on my eternal soul that I have done nothing to disgrace Heugenet, and would defend her honor with my life."

"Only a noble may do that, not a bastard who has been a troubador, an alchemist, and who knows what else?" He had not learned how to sneer, but he did his best to show contempt with a haughty lift of his brows.

"You have rebuked me for supposed insults," Germain le-Comte said, wholly unflustered. "That will not save you from more Latin verbs and the geography of France and the Holy Roman Empire."

"I have just called you a reprobate, a whoremonger," said Armand, irritation increasing. "Have you no integrity, that you permit this?"

Germain le-Comte folded his arms and regarded Armand with indulgent exasperation. "As you have already pointed out, I am not your equal in rank, so I would have no right to issue any challenge to you, let alone any acceptable grounds. You are the son of the House that has given me patronage which I will not dishonor by so reprehensible an act as casting a gauntlet at one so much younger than I am, who is not known for his skill at arms."

"And you are, I suppose?" Armand goaded.

"Oh, yes. I am quite deadly," Germain le-Comte answered in such quiet calm that Armand became chilled by the tone of his voice. When neither had spoken for a little while, Germain le-Comte went and picked up a volume of Latin essays. "You have been reviewing these, haven't you? How far have you come with your translations?"

"It doesn't matter? I call you demeaning names and you do nothing?" Armand had half-risen from his tall chair.

"When you are my age, Armand, such calumny will not disturb you." He held out the book. "Show me how far you have gotten."

Armand seized the book and threw it across the room. *"That* for your Latin!"

Germain le-Comte went to retrieve the book, inspecting its parchment pages for tears or marring. "This book has not offended you; it deserves no punishment."

"And you are a coward who will not stand against me." His face was flushed and his breathing was becoming strident.

"That may well be," Germain le-Comte said briskly. "Where is your tincture? Have some in wine with honey or you will be coughing again." He went to the door and called for a servant, issuing a few terse orders. "The wine and honey will be brought shortly. Sit back and breathe slowly."

Armand crossed himself. "Sympathy from one such as you." He made a sound that was intended to be scoffing and turned out to be a high, hacking cough; at the sound he paled. "God, no."

"No," said Germain le-Comte with authority. "This is not the first touch of the Plague, it is only your old ailment, returning to wear you down." He strode to Armand. "You may not rely on me to conduct myself properly with the Ducesse, but you may have complete confidence in me in this regard: if you had contracted the disease, it would be in the smell of you, and your body would be hot with fever. Your heat comes from anger, which worsens your breathing. Now: where is your tincture? You should carry that vial upon you."

Galling as it was to show any faith in Germain le-Comte, Armand pulled his vial from his square sleeve and held it up. "Here it is."

"Drink half of it right now," Germain le-Comte said composedly. "Take the rest with the honey and wine. Your seizure will pass quickly."

Armand did his best to stifle the cough and ended up struggling to exhale. "What is this? What have I done that God visits this upon me?" He got his words out with difficulty, his face livid with spots in his cheeks.

"This affliction is an old one, and the cause is not found in God or the Devil, but in the strengths and weaknesses of the body," said Germain le-Comte. "It has been recorded through all time, and in all places. I have studied these things for most of my life," he replied, and was relieved to hear a scratch on the door. "This will be your wine and honey."

The servant held a tray with a tankard of wine and a pot containing a honeycomb. He gave it to Germain le-Comte after glancing uneasily into the room. Knowing he must not linger, he ducked his head and turned away as Germain le-Comte closed the door.

"You have them all fooled," Armand rasped.

"Perhaps. Let us deal with that later," Germain le-Comte came toward the young man; he put the tray down and lifted the honeycomb from its pot and over the tankard to let some of its contents run into the wine. "May I have the vial? I will make sure you have more of them in a day or two."

"After you make more gold for my mother?" Armand persisted, although his strident breathing was beginning to ease. He glared at Germain le-Comte, as if his recovery were an additional fault to hold against him.

As Germain le-Comte added the last of the vial's contents to the honied wine, he said, "No; I have done that already." He paused as he put the honeycomb back in the pot. "I am afraid I will still be in short supply of some medicaments." Most particularly, he was very low on syrup of poppies and would be unable to make more while he remained in these northerly climes. That caused him genuine concern, for his other anodynes had nowhere near the strength of the syrup of poppies, and were therefore not as useful in treating the severely injured.

"What is it?" Armand asked as he took the tankard Germain le-Comte held out to him. "Your face was troubled." He sounded more disturbed than accusing now.

"You need not concern yourself," said Germain le-Comte, shaking off his reflective mood and making himself give Armand his full attention; he handed the tankard to him. "I will make sure you have tincture enough to last for many years." As soon as he spoke, he realized he had said the wrong thing.

Gulping down one mouthful, he burst out, "You are going to leave, aren't you?" his voice rising.

"In time, I must," he said. "You cannot say you welcome me wholeheartedly—can you." He waited while Armand worked his answer through.

"If you would not . . . You have done the people of Mon Gardien much good, and I would be lax in my obligations to send away one who tends to their hurts and ailments so successfully. No barber has ever done so well, and the herb-woman is dead." He set the tankard down with care.

"A gracious compliment, to be sure," said Germain le-Comte with no attempt to disguise his irony. "It is for that reason that I am leaving many tinctures and unguents, with instructions to your mother in how to use them." He almost laughed at the smile that came over Armand's face.

"Oh!" he exclaimed. "You have been *teaching* her." His laughter was eloquent; he now had an acceptable reason for his mother to be so often in Germain le-Comte's company.

"In a manner of speaking," said Germain le-Comte.

"Of course," Armand said, taking on an air of shared confidence. "It isn't usual to teach women anything complicated. But you are right: since my mother is Ducesse now, she has responsibilities that are beyond the common ones." He glanced at the book in Germain le-Comte's hands. "I shouldn't have thrown that. As you said, the book has done nothing to offend me."

"Nor have I," Germain le-Comte reminded him. "Drink the rest of the honied wine and we will get on with our lessons."

"If you insist. But I will have clerks and others to read and write for me," Armand reminded him.

"Who will not always be loyal to you, or as well-educated as they say they are. If you read and write, you will know precisely what you are agreeing to, and how you are presenting the material you write. You need not depend on the probity of others; you will be able to manage your affairs privately, without others privy to them." He watched Armand finish the wine, and then said, "You will be easier in your mind, in the coming years, if you are able to be your own clerk."

Armand sighed. "No doubt," he said uncertainly.

"Then let us begin," Germain le-Comte said, opening the book to the middle pages where the essayist described the methods of procuring goods from the lands of the East. "Being here: *The people of Hind . . .*" As he looked at the page, he vividly recalled Dantinusha's small kingdom, and his sister, Padimiri, and his daughter, Tamasrajasi.

"*The people of Hind have . . . spices and . . . and . . .*" He glanced at Germain le-Comte, too proud to ask for help.

"Aromatic woods," Germain le-Comte supplied.

"*. . . aromatic woods in great quantity, which their merchants . . . carry with them . . . many leagues. The markets of Constantinople and . . .*" Again he stopped.

"Trebizond," said Germain le-Comte.

"*Trebizond . . .* Trebizond. Where is that?" Armand asked, his thoughts wandering as the wine did its work on him.

"On the southern shore at the end of the Black Sea. It is east of Constantinople." He pointed to the page. "Go on."

"*Merchants from Venice and Genoa bring these . . . these fine things to . . . European ports in the south from where they are carried to . . .*" His face paled. "That is where the Blood Roses came from, isn't it?"

"Yes," said Germain le-Comte.

"The heathens of the East sent it to bring about the destruction of the world!" he shouted, slamming the book closed.

"No, they did not," said Germain le-Comte. "They have suffered from it longer than you have; if it travels it is because it finds a means to travel, not because the people of the East have sent it here." He was about to open the book once again when a sound from the courtyard reached him.

"*Francois de Saint-Germain, Sieur Ragoczy!*" came the ragged shout from a ruined voice, accompanied by other cries and exclamations.

"What on earth—?" Armand said, his curiosity excited as the shout was repeated. "There is no one here . . ." Then he looked at his tutor, and crossed himself.

Germain le-Comte knew there was only one person in Verviers who would call him by that name; he rose heavily and gave a single nod. "I will attend to this."

" 'Sieur Ragoczy'?" Armand pursued. " 'Sieur'? A bastard a lord?"

"I'll explain later," said Germain le-Comte as he reached the door and hurried down the corridor to the stairs that led down to the ground floor. As he went, he saw servants beginning to stare and whisper. He emerged in the courtyard at a measured pace, aware that self-possession was crucial now. Ahead near the raised portcullis he saw a knot of servants and men-at-arms gathered around a figure in dirty white garments who continued to yell his abandoned name. As he approached a path opened before him.

"There!" Seur Jenfra pointed at him. "You execrable atrocity! You vile miscreant!"

Germain le-Comte halted and looked directly at her. "How have I offended you, Seur Jenfra, that you make such vituperations against me."

"I? Against you? You have—" She began to cough. "You have *destroyed* me!"

He kept his distance from her, but did not speak haughtily. "How can that be? If I have done anything deserving of your opprobrium, I ask you to tell me what it is and permit me to put it to rights once again: in the name of your father's memory and your vocation." With a respectful bow he waited for her to respond; he could see she was ill, from the glitter of her eyes to the shine of sweat on her skin.

"Put right? *Put right?*" She reached up and pulled down the front of her habit, exposing her flesh to the waist; red-black buboes swelled in her armpits and on her neck. "How will you put this right?"

Those who had been standing near her fell back in fear; even the men-at-arms moved away, praying for protection.

Seur Jenfra advanced on Germain le-Comte, her fervid eyes fixed on him. "For more than a year I tended the stricken, yet the Blood Roses could not touch me. God protected me from them as reward for my chastity. Then you came. *You!* I had forgot you, I was content! You polluted my dreams and perverted my prayers, and God has punished me for my perfidy." She reached him. "You have done this to me. My damnation is on your head." And she spat upon him.

An appalled wail went up from those who were watching, and a few of the servants began to run from the courtyard. One of the servants bolted for the stable, shouting that he would see if any of the injured Germain le-Comte had been treating now harbored Blood Roses.

Germain le-Comte closed his eyes a moment, then looked directly at Seur Jenfra. "I brought you no Blood Roses, Jenfra d'Ormonde. I swear on my life I did not."

"But you debauched me," she declared. "You insinuated yourself into my devotions, and for that I will die and burn in Hell." She began to weep in abject dejection. "I am dead already."

Knowing that there was nothing he could do that would stigmatize him more than Seur Jenfra had done, he went to her and carefully lifted the torn front of her tunic before putting his arm around her. "Seur Jenfra, I have done you no injury, I give you my Word." He knew he could not take her to the stable, or anywhere else inside the walls of Mon Gardien, so he gathered her into his arms and bore her unimpeded down the slope to the village and into the house of the swineherd who had died two months ago, where he could tend her for what little remained of her life: no one interfered and no one followed them.

It was after midnight when he returned to Mon Gardien, admitting himself by the rear gate so as to attract as little notice as possible. He had removed his haincelin while he treated Seur Jenfra and now had a rough smocked surtout of loose-weave wool over his black chamise. He made his way through the keep with a quiet that was almost stealth, and reached his rooms without causing alarm.

Heugenet was waiting for him; she met him with the passion of despair as she rushed into his arms, clinging to him as if to absorb his presence into her. When she spoke at last, she was tranquil. "Sieur Ragoczy. Everyone is talking about you."

"I am Germain le-Comte," he said, hoping to reassure her.

"And Sieur Ragoczy, and who knows what other names you have had." She was not angry, but her words were crisp, a concession to his alienness; she turned away from him, pacing the room.

"Many others," he told her.

She nodded. "And the nun?"

"She died quickly; Blood Roses can be fast. She used all her strength coming here." He paused. "I knew her father, in Provence; she was then as young as Armand is. I thought she died with him." He came up behind her, not touching her.

"And now?" She shivered as she asked, and crossed herself automatically.

"I buried her next to the village shrine," he said. "I put a cross on her grave."

She steeled herself for what she said next. "If the Blood Roses come here now, you will have to leave."

"Yes," he said, a world of loss in his voice. "I know."

Text of a letter from the Abbe Quantpris at Martelaunge to Heugenet, Ducesse de Verviers, at Mon Gardien; delivered by the man-at-arms Montcerry.

To the most noble Ducesse de Verviers, the condolences and prayers of the monks of Sant-Rohan at Martelaunge, and the assurances that God will watch over all those upon whom He lays His Hands most heavily.

There is no easy way to impart such news, and so I will not attempt to soften this terrible blow: I regret to tell you that your husband, Armandal d'Ais, Duc de Vervier has succumbed to a rotten limb which resulted from a broken ankle two days since. The injury was not thought to be mortal, or the Duc would not have left the Emperor's Court. I will tell you how it came about, as much as I know of it, for some of what I tell you is on the sworn testimony of his man-at-arms, who will add his mark to my signature at the end of this letter.

Four or five days before he left the Emperor's Court in Luxembourg, I am told your husband joined in the hunt for stags and boars. This was the specific pleasure of Carles himself, and Armandal d'Ais was honored to ac-company the Emperor on this occasion. Sometime during the hunt, your husband sustained a fall from his horse. It was not a serious fall, or so it seemed, although his ankle was injured: at the time there was no indication that the hurt was severe.

Upon receiving word from the Bishop of Cambrai that he was required at Mon Gardien, which occurred the next day or the day after, the Duc de Verviers arranged to take his leave of the Imperial Court, pleading for and obtaining the permission of the Emperor to depart betimes. This was fitting and the Emperor was inclined to grant leave to your husband. Armandal d'Ais acted promptly. His ankle was swollen and he occasionally had to lean on the arm of one of his men as he went about preparing to leave. He gave orders that Phetine, his mistress, was to come with him and remain at his side, which delayed their departure for one day while she made ready to travel.

With his men-at-arms around him and his entourage mounted or traveling in wagons, the Duc de Verviers left the Imperial Court six days ago, traveling on the high roads and making good speed. On the second day after leaving the Court, the Duc was taken with fever and was forced to ride in a wagon, for his ankle was then so swollen that he could not sit his horse. His mistress, Phetine, tended him devotedly for two days. It was she who finally insisted that they interrupt their journey to obtain some relief for the Duc, who was by then quite feverish and occasionally out of his senses. Some feared he had contracted Blood Roses, but there were none found on his flesh, and when wasps stung him, he did not blister and bruise as he would have if he suffered from Black Plague.

When the party arrived at Sant-Rohan, we took the Duc into our infirmary. We had to cut his boots and clothes off him, so hard-swollen had his leg become. When we examined his ankle, we saw that it was discolored and that red lines ran up his leg, which all Christians know is a mortal sign. Our monks bled him, but the humors had become too heated for bleeding to provide relief. Your husband bore his agony as a Christian, with prayerful acquiescence to the Will of God. His men-at-arms have declared that his body must be returned to the Imperial Court so that the Emperor Carles may recognize the Duc's son in his succession, and bury him with full honors appropriate to his House and his loyalty to the Emperor. We have today dispatched his men with his coffin, with Phetine accompanying him in your stead. Upon its arrival in Luxembourg, he will be given the rites to which he is entitled and the Dukedom will pass into the hands of your son. Until such dispatches arrive from the Imperial Court, this will afford temporary authority of succession to your son.

I will give this into the hands of Frer Adonais to carry to you with all seemly haste, with the instructions that he remain with you through your first year of grief, so that you will not lack for the counsel of one who was with your husband at the last. He will serve as the Duc's deputy in guiding the steps of his son as he assumes his position.

May God comfort you and give you to see His Face; may It shine upon you for all your days, and may the House of d'Ais endure until the end of time. This by my own hand,

Abbe Quantpris, Ambrosian
Sant-Rohan Monastery
The mark of Jean Montcerry, in witness

On the 11th day of September, the Feast of Sants Protus and Hyacinth, in the 1350th Year of Grace.

8

Black-and-red pennons hung over the entrance to Mon Gardien, in official recognition of the death of Armandal d'Ais; the brisk breeze, heralding the arrival of autumn, sent the pennons dancing. Frer Adonais, standing on the battlements above the pennons, shook his head at the display as if to condemn the wind for impiety. Below him in the courtyard, Heugenet stood in full mourning, her black veil hanging almost to her feet; Armand was next to her, the coronet of rank circling his brow decked with twined red-and-black ribbands.

"I don't like that Ambrosian," said the young Duc. "He is asking questions all the time."

"No doubt he was told to," said Heugenet with a slight shrug; she was still feeling somewhat dazed; ever since Montcerry had arrived with Frer Adonais bringing word of Armandal's death, she had found it difficult to concentrate. This day, three weeks after the news was delivered, she had to remind herself of what to call her son. At that recollection she once again found herself fretful of his safety, and worried about his future. "You are Duc. You can refuse to answer."

"He is very persistent. He is always coming where I do not expect him." He was unaware of the anxiety his complaint caused his mother. "When he came into the strong-room, I told him the gold Germain le-Comte made for us came from a secret treasury, brought back from the First Crusade, hidden by our forefather against a time of need or war." He made a gesture to show that he did not care whether or not Frer Adonais believed him. "He doesn't know about the jewels."

"Let us hope he never finds out. I will guard my tongue; you must do the same." She glanced about as Guillem approached, hand to his forelock. "What is it now?"

"What rooms are to be given to your younger sons when they return, Ducesse?" he asked hurriedly. "We do not know which to prepare."

Heugenet stopped herself from upbraiding the steward who was still getting used to his advancement; he knew nothing of the rivalry that could arise among noble brothers. "You will determine how best to accommodate them," she said.

Guillem nodded twice. "I will consider the question carefully," he said. "They will want to be accorded all courtesy due them."

"Then decide on that basis. The Duc has taken his suite of rooms, leaving many others at your disposal. I do not think we will have to house more than two dozen guests for Armand's investiture." She felt like a puppet controlled by skilled jongleurs, mouthing words that someone else spoke. Her head ached and she wished she could go inside and have Germain le-Comte rub an ointment on her temples to take away the pain; she wondered if Armand was as disoriented as she, or as fearful.

"Will I be allowed to command some of the villagers to assist me?" Guillem asked, glancing from Armand to Heugenet and back again, as if unsure of whose authority to solicit. "There are not many who have time to spare."

"If the villagers are willing," said Heugenet. "Those men that Germain le-Comte healed will surely help."

"You can tell them there will be recompense for their efforts: measures of wool and grain will be given to those who will come," said Armand, his head up to show he expected to have his rank honored by all those who worked for him, for all they were unused to it.

"There is not much to spare in the way of wool," said Guillem, then said, "Remi and the servants at the dowager's house could do some work, if you will order them."

Armand looked about as if waiting for someone to tell him what to do. When his mother said nothing, he sighed. "Yes. You are probably right. You and Remi may divide the duties between you while we have guests here."

Heugenet nodded absently. "Remi is a good man. He took great care of the old Ducesse while she lived." She folded her hands under her veil. "I will want to have our blankets inspected; they have been in trunks for a while, and some of them may be damaged." That much was certain, and she knew if she kept her mind on such ordinary tasks, she would feel less cast-adrift.

Guillem ducked his head at once. "Yes, and the bedding should be changed; there are mice in some of the mattresses."

"Then see that it is done," Armand declared. He rocked back on his heels in a display of confidence that no one believed. "They say there will be a harvest market at Laurentspont."

"If there is a market, we will go," said Guillem carefully. "We must also secure another cook, and scullions, if we are to feed so many."

"Yes," said Heugenet. "Be sure there will be gold for that." She considered a moment. "You will have Montcerry and Biebart to go with you."

Armand cleared his throat importantly. "What the Ducesse says is very true; I endorse her suggestion. Have Montcerry and Biebart accompany you and Remi. You will be safe with those men-at-arms to guard you. I will provide enough gold to allow you to remain at Laurentspont for the night so you need not fear having to travel when robbers are abroad."

"That is good of you, mon Duc," said Guillem, bowing almost double before backing away from mother and son as if they were royalty.

"Do you think we will find a good cook at last? All the good meat and fruits will mean nothing if they are prepared badly," Armand asked when Guillem was out of earshot.

"I hope so. We do not want anyone complaining that we slight our guests. If the Blood Roses are fading at last, we will have to show how we have recovered from our losses." Heugenet pressed her lips together to keep from weeping; she had done that once already today, and it was unseemly of her to behave like some peasant-woman. The worst part of it was that she did not comprehend why she should weep at all: her husband was dead and she would mourn him as custom required, but her grief was no greater for him than for many others who had died in the last two years. "I am going to the stable," she announced abruptly.

"Why?" Armand asked. "There are only two patients there. Germain le-Comte will take care of them."

"If we are going to expect their help when your brothers arrive, I had best alert them now," said Heugenet. "Do you think we do not need them?" It was less than the truth, but she could not explain why she had to have some time to herself.

Armand shrugged. "A carpenter and a goatherd," he said, dismissing them. "They are peasants and bound to our land."

"They have children and families, and we have need of servants," said Heugenet as she started toward the stable.

"Oh, very well," Armand called after her.

She reached the shadowed entrance to the stable before her tears caught up with her; she stepped into the first stall, crying wretchedly and silently, her bones seeming to go weak within her. Leaning against Germain le-Comte's donkey cart, she jammed her fist into her mouth to stop the wailing she dared not voice.

"Heugenet?" Germain le-Comte spoke her name softly as he came up to her. He had completed his inspection of his patients just before she had entered the stable and had seen her come into the stall; as much as he would have wanted to hold her, he was aware that they were observed and so he maintained his most courtly behavior. "Ma Ducesse, is there anything you require of me? You have only to name it."

She shook her head, trying to wave him away. Her hands tangled in her veil, making her want to shriek with vexation. "You shouldn't . . ."

He came to her side, his manner respectful and his speech correct;

only the warmth in his eyes revealed his emotion. "You have need of a composer, I see. If you will permit me, I will prepare a draught for you that will restore your serenity."

"And your other patients?" she asked, doing her best to make light of her despair. "Do they demand nothing more from you?"

"They will not need me again until evening." He made no attempt to touch her, but his words were almost a caress. "I am at your disposal until then. It would give me great satisfaction to be allowed to help you, ma Ducesse." He watched her shiver as she listened to him, and felt an answering thrill in himself.

"And I, too, would find that welcome." She daubed at her eyes with the hem of her veil. "I am so tired. It is because I am tired that so many things overset me."

Germain le-Comte nodded as if she had convinced him. "Then the composer will help you to rest. Come, ma Ducesse, let me take you back to the keep. You will want to have time for meditation and repose."

"I suppose I will," she said, looking at him with such yearning that he was glad they were not closely observed. "You are always kind to me."

"You need not wonder at it," said Germain le-Comte, bowing again. "You have had much to do in this last fortnight."

"There were constraints upon me before then." She held out her hand, although she knew it would be improper for him to take it. "So many things have happened: I thank God there have been no more Blood Roses since Seur Jenfra came here. She was so very ill I thought everyone would take it from her."

"That she was," said Germain le-Comte, thinking back to her last few hours of life; he had washed her face and tried to get her to drink water, but she was soon lost in a delirious half-sleep that faded into death as the light faded from the sky.

"You have said nothing about how she died," Heugenet said, her hands beginning to shake.

"No, I haven't," he agreed, escorting her out of the stable and across the side courtyard to the kitchen entrance to the keep.

"Was it very dreadful?" Before he answered, Heugenet went on. "I hope it was not, though it must have been. There has been so much death that I have to know."

"She was peaceful at the end," said Germain le-Comte as he stood aside to permit her to enter the keep ahead of him. "The Black Plague can be like that—making those who suffer from it restless and unable to keep still, during which time they are driven to acts that would exhaust anyone, and then lulling them with sleep." He had seen it before, in China, in the Roman Empire, in Persia, but he had not been able to reconcile himself to the ferocity of the disease; not even such a death as Seur Jenfra's seemed kind to him.

"That was merciful," said Heugenet; she rounded on him. "I am so afraid. Everywhere I look I see Death staring at me from the shadows. So many have died, and nothing stops it. Where there is death, there is also treachery. My son is Duc now, but if I should die before he comes of age, his brothers will claim his title, with their cousins to aid them. I know they will; they never expected Armand to have the title. Bernard was the heir and everyone accepted it. His brothers will not be content to have Armand in their father's place, for they think him a weakling who has no stomach for battle." This came out in a whispered rush. She looked about quickly to be sure they were not overheard. "You must promise to help me, Germain le-Comte."

"I have done so already," he said, wondering what she meant by her hushed outburst.

"Yes; yes. But promise again. *Promise,*" she murmured. A moment later she stepped back from him. "You will play for us tonight, but only songs that praise Our Lord. It is so soon after my husband's death that we must not have levity here."

"Certainly, ma Ducesse," said Germain le-Comte as Perinne, the cheese-maker, came through the kitchen and ducked her head respectfully.

"Where is the composer you said you had? I will be grateful for it." Heugenet's demand was sharp and she spoke loudly enough for anyone in the kitchen to hear.

"It is in my private study. I will bring it to you, ma Ducesse." He bowed again, and started away from her.

"Bring it to my music room. I will be there." She glanced at the carcass of a young sheep that was being rubbed with onions and rosemary. "When will the meal be ready?" she asked the two new scullions as Germain le-Comte went toward the servants' stairs, thinking that the sheep would not go far and that other fare would be required.

His composer was a tincture of mugwort and blessed thistle in spirits of wine; he took it from his red lacquer chest and poured some into a chalcedony cup; he added spring water to it and carried it down to the music room where he found Heugenet playing her regal and singing *"Doulce Sciencia en Marie."* He paused on the threshold so that she could finish the refrain, then entered the music room. "You should drink this, ma Ducesse."

She set the regal aside and took the cup. "This is a wonderful room; I have such happy memories of it." The expression in her eyes was eloquent, harking back to the day they had come there as lovers. "Music is a consolation."

"Yes, it is," said Germain le-Comte, half-closing the door. "I am concerned for you, Heugenet."

As she drank she watched him. "Must I take it all?" she asked when she lowered the cup. "It is . . . strange to the taste."

"You should drink it all," he said, and added softly, "I miss you."

Her eyes filled with tears again. "I am so *lonely,*" she whispered. "I wake in the night and there is only emptiness." She drank the rest of the liquid in the chalcedony cup. "It will be worse later, when you are gone."

"That will not be for a while yet," he said, aching to comfort her.

"Unless the Blood Roses come again; then you will have to go or be burned for a sorcerer: you said it yourself." She held up her hand to silence his protest. "The whole of Verviers has heard of what you have done, saying your powers are beyond nature. The servants talk of it openly, because too many of those you have treated have recovered; they say you are as much magician as troubador, and for that they are leery of you. If Seur Jenfra had not denounced you, it might be otherwise, but to have a nun accuse you as she did— I could not protect you if the Blood Roses came again."

"I would not ask it of you," he told her, his voice deep and gentle.

"And I will not watch them kill you. That would be more than I could bear." She held out her arms to him. "We are alone. No one will come."

He went and took her hands in his. "Frer Adonais is seeking to know all he can about this place. He has followed you, and he has followed me."

"And today he is following Armand." She tightened her grip on his hands. "Germain le-Comte, you need not dissemble—probably before winter comes you will be gone. I have known you would have to go for some days."

He could not deny it. "I do not want to leave you."

"But you are a troubador; troubadors travel. There have been the Blood Roses to account for your staying here. If there were not so much dying, your presence would have been remarked upon last spring. It doesn't matter that you have been teaching Armand, or that you have treated the sick and injured; now that there are fewer taken with Blood Roses, you cannot remain on that account." She had to stop, to steady the tremor in her voice. "Before you leave, there is one thing I beg you will do, if you love me. Give me your Word you will grant my request."

"If it is within my power, I will do it," he said, listening intently to any sounds from outside the door; he did not want a servant to stumble upon them now.

"It is within your power: I want you to make me what you are. Before you have to leave." She saw the shock in his eyes. "No, *listen* to me. You have warned me that I may become like you when I die, but that is not what I want, for my death may be long in coming, or so hideous that my survival would be untenable." Her voice was urgent as she picked up her portative organ and began to play it to cover what she said to him. "I have been thinking about this for some days, and it is finally clear to me: I must become a vampire now. Before anything else happens. I have considered everything you have told me, and I have decided that the only way I can preserve my son is to be what you are."

Germain le-Comte stared at her. "You do not know what you ask," he said softly.

"You have shown me how you live; you will teach me what I need to know and I will arrange it so that no one will notice." She played more loudly. "I am a widow now. If I choose to withdraw from the world and keep only to this place, no one will think it strange, not in these times. No one will fault me for devoting myself to my son."

"You do not know what you are asking," he repeated, shaking his head. "Give me back my promise, Heugenet," he pleaded. "You cannot know—"

"No, Germain le-Comte, I will not release you from your Word: I hold you to it," she said firmly. "If you refuse, I will despise you forever." She pounded out two dissonant chords. "You swore to grant my request."

"Yes," he said.

"And you will abide by your Word," she went on triumphantly.

"Yes," he said.

"We will hunt together, you and I, until I can do as I must on my own." She smiled with the same intensity that she had wept earlier. "That is why you must make me a vampire now, so that you will have time to teach me."

He said nothing for a short while. "Once you are like me, I will have to leave. In a castle and village like this one of my blood can survive without too much danger; in a city as many as two of us can find sustenance without attracting undue notice. We do not hunt, Heugenet; if you wish to live as anything but a monster, you must have no prey. That is why only one of us could live in Mon Gardien. One. But two vampires—in a place like this? I have curtailed my . . . feeding as much as I am able; you have provided what I have sought, and my native earth has done the rest. If there were two of us, we would be found out, and that would mean the True Death for us both."

"But we will have each other, at the first," she protested, unwilling to give up her vision.

He realized that his arguments were making no impression upon her. "Once you become like me," he said carefully, "you will have to find gratification elsewhere, as will I."

The music from her portative organ stopped. "What do you mean?"

"Those of us who have died and risen seek life, Heugenet. *Life.* It is the one thing we cannot give one another." He leaned toward her. "You would have to—"

She began playing again. "We have some time, no matter how you change me. It was you who told me that we change by our own volition, and now I believe you. I have chosen to die now, and to prepare for living as you live." As she picked out a martial melody, she said, "I cannot desert my son. There is only one way I can be sure I will not fail him."

Germain le-Comte considered her. "Very well. But I have one request to make: wait for three days to be sure this is what you want, for once you come to my life, you will have to live as those of my blood must; it will be too late to change your mind." He went down on his knee in front of her. "Heugenet, think of what you are asking. You have endured much, and your soul is volatile because of it. If this is truly what you want, your decision will not waver. When you come to my life, it will be for decades; surely taking three days to be certain of your intent is not so great a loss?"

"In three days I could be dead of Blood Roses," she said bluntly.

He shook his head. "You have no fever and—"

"But I could have it, if the miasma spreads to this place again," she insisted, her playing emphatic; then she sighed. "All right. Three days. At the end of that time you will bring me to your life."

"Unless you change your mind," he pointed out, his enigmatic gaze holding her entire attention.

"Three days," she repeated.

"And then I will have to leave you," he said, his voice sad for all his bluntness. "Shall I tell Armand I am going?"

Her fingers hesitated on the keys. "Let me," she said at last. "He will have many questions, and he will want you to stay." She played for a long moment while she pursued her own thoughts. "I will speak to him tomorrow, so he will not have too long to muster arguments against your going."

"If he should order me to stay, what then?" he asked, curious to hear how she would answer.

"You have said it yourself: troubadors and jongleurs swear fealty to no one. You may come and go as you like; you are no vassal, to be forever at the service of your lord," she said, her music more confident now. "He may not be pleased, but he will not compel you to remain."

Germain le-Comte rose from his knee. "There are preparations you will have to make," he warned her; he began to number them in his thoughts: her native earth, shoes with soles to contain it, bedding that was lined with it . . .

"You will tell me what they are," she informed him, concluding her playing with a flourish. "There. I am myself again. Your composer has calmed me: I am certain of my course."

"I hope you will have no cause to regret your decision," he said, and knew that she would not admit it if she had.

Text of a ruling from the Acting Magistrates of Marsailla, posted throughout the city, and copies supplied to the Papal Court at Avignon and the Imperial Court of Carles IV, at Luxembourg.

To the people of the City of Marsailla, these are the rulings of your Magistrates who serve as deputies to those lost in the Great Dying.

The drivers of the dead-carts will receive two golden crowns each, except for those who have been caught selling the goods from the houses of the dead: those said irreligious robbers will suffer hanging for their crimes, the sentence to be carried out on the city gallows.

Those merchants who have lost cargos due to the Blood Roses will be entitled to the sum of ten golden crowns for the purpose of purchasing more cargo in lieu of what was lost, said golden crowns to come from the sale of houses of the dead where there are no heirs to claim them, or where any heirs have fled the region. Said fugitive heirs will have until the second anniversary of this edict to put forth their claims, after which time the houses, lands, and moveables will be forfeit to the city and sold for the benefit of honest merchants.

Claims on the estates of deceased residents may be presented to the Magistrates, who are currently sitting at Aix-en-Provence; proof of claims will be judged by the Magistrates, whose decisions are final but for those of Carles IV, the Holy Roman Emperor, and Pope Clement VI.

Those who have lands or estates in Provence may apply to these Magistrates for verification of their claims, but the decision of these Magistrates must be upheld by higher authorities as well as by the Emperor and the Pope. Any estates having unresolved titles may, at the discretion of said Magistrates, be claimed in the name of the Emperor or the Pope. Such dispositions are final and may not be appealed for a period of five years.

Contracts of marriage where the wedding was not celebrated or the union unconsummated due to the flight or illness of one party or the other shall be declared null and void, unbinding on survivors or heirs; said contracts, if negotiated, must be submitted to these said Magistrates for verification and endorsement of terms. Should these said Magistrates find the contractual terms unsuitable, the said contracting parties will be required to submit more equitable provisions within a period of one year before the said contract will be recognized by these said Magistrates as valid.

Contracts of adoption shall be held to the same terms as those of marriage contracts stipulated above. Claims made against adoptive heirs for the sake of depriving entitled adoptive children of the inheritances to which they are entitled shall result in imprisonment of the perjurative claimant under conditions to be decided by these said Magistrates: pursuant to this provision, these said Magistrates sentence Josue Roebertis, currently of Trier, to five years of labor as an oarsman on a merchant's galley, for the crime of attempting to obtain for himself the estate of Hue d'Ormonde; the said estate is bequeathed by law to the adoptive son of Hue d'Ormonde, Hilaire, currently residing in Toulouse, a notary's apprentice. May this sentence serve as a warning to all who would deprive recognized heirs of their legacies.

Servants whose employers have fled or perished may claim up to a year's employment from the city of Marsailla, said employment to consist of cleaning, repairing, and restoring deserted houses to habitability. This said employment shall provide housing for the said servants while their labors are on-going in the said abandoned dwellings. These said servants may, upon the sale of the said dwelling, have first claim to continuing on as household servants for the new or returning occupant. All labor of said servants is to be regarded as full payment of any taxes levied against residents of Marsailla for the time the said servants are in the employ of the city and these said Magistrates.

Peasants who have brought goods to market in Marsailla are hereby excused from all market taxes for the period of one year, as an encouragement to return to the city's markets. Those craftsmen who have sold goods at the Marsailla markets are also excused from taxation on their goods for a period of one year. The sole exceptions shall be brewers and vintners, whose tuns shall be taxed at half the rate of former years, said taxes to be equally divided between the city's treasury and that of the Church.

Tradesmen of Marsailla, or those tradesmen who may come to Marsailla, will be excused from all civic taxes for a period of one year with the exception of shipwrights, who will be excused for two years. Tithes and other payments to the Church will be determined by His Holiness the Pope, and all men shall honor them or face expulsion from their Guilds. The shipwright, Simone d'Ostia, who has submitted a claim for extension of the said exemption for a period of three years in order to build a new wharf for ships as well as two ships specifically, will be excused his full taxation for two years; the third year his taxes will be levied at half the rate applied to foreign merchants at that time.

It is the decision of the Holy Roman Emperor and the Pope that where the holdings of nobles are left vacant, the Vidames of the same jurisdiction shall have primary claim on the said vacated holdings. Submission of such claims must be presented to these said Magistrates within the next two years; endorsement of the Pope and the Emperor will be required before the said vacated holdings will be assigned to any said Vidame claiming any said vacated land. In accordance with this provision, these said Magistrates have taken under consideration the application of Percevall, Vidame de Saunt Joachim, for title to the vacated estate Clair dela Luna of the late Francois de Saint-Germain, Sieur Ragoczy; the holding is near Orgon, not in Marsailla, but it is within the former jurisdiction of the Chief Magistrate of these said Magistrates and is being addressed as a means to put the process to the test of law. Proof of the death of the fugitive Francois de Saint-Germain having been secured by these said Magistrates, the petition of Percevall, Vidame de Saunt Joachim, is hereby accepted for adjudication.

In the case of any question of occupancy or taxation not covered in this edict, the said Magistrates will hear all petitions at Aix-en-Provence until such time as the Holy Roman Emperor orders the return of these said Magistrates to the city of Marsailla.

> *Eudoin Tissant, Chief Magistrate of Marsailla*
> *by the hand of Frer Placide, Dominican*

At Aix-en-Provence, in the Holy Roman Empire, on the 29th day of September, the Feast of Michael the Archangel, in the 1350th Year of Man's Salvation.

9

Caesar was shedding out his summer coat, his shaggy hair thickening in preparation for winter; he seemed to sense the coming departure, for he ate more greedily than usual, his nose deep in his manger filled with oat-hay. The sound of his chewing was loud in the stable.

In the next stall, Germain le-Comte finished stowing his chests and cases, securing a thick cloth atop them for additional protection. He had donned his troubador's motley once again; his grander clothing was packed away in a chest, the case containing his mandola atop it in the cart.

"So it will be tomorrow," said Armand, his young face set with disappointment as he strove to make the best of this unwanted farewell. "You need not sleep here in the stable tonight simply because all your goods are already on your cart."

"But I am leaving so early; before first light," said Germain le-Comte, who knew he would be gone by midnight.

"All those you've treated have left," he said, looking about at the empty stalls.

"You'll have more than three horses to house next year. It's just as well they've left," Germain le-Comte remarked.

"I wish you could stay for my investiture," said Armand, repeating his request for the ninth time that afternoon.

"You will have other musicians for that occasions, and players and jongleurs as well," said Germain le-Comte; he had not anticipated his sorrow at leaving this youngster. "You know enough Latin to study on your own."

Armand did his best to laugh. "I will not have a stringent master to keep me at my books."

"Then you must learn to master yourself," said Germain le-Comte. He reached over the stall wall and patted Caesar's shoulder. "He has had a long time to grow lazy, and we have over a hundred leagues to go." He was bound for Il Capolavoro at last; he hoped he would get there before snow blocked the mountain passes and kept him in the Duchy of Swabia for the winter.

"A hundred leagues," Armand marveled, the wistful light of adventure in his serious young face. "In all my life, I have not been so far."

"If you have gone to Sant-Amienne and Laurentspont thirty times between them, you have traveled a hundred leagues," Germain le-Comte pointed out.

"It's not the same," said Armand.

Germain le-Comte met the young man's eyes. "No; it is not." Then he clapped the Duc on the shoulder. "Come. It is time I took my leave of your household. They will all be asleep when I depart."

"Do you want them to honor you?" He was prepared to make an occasion out of this last appearance, no matter how irregular such distinction would be.

"Why?" Germain le-Comte asked. "If you do that you will fix my strangeness in their memories for years to come. Best they forget all but the troubador." He smiled at Armand. How few times he had had the luxury of leaving a place so cordially, Germain le-Comte thought. In his centuries of life he could count on the fingers of both hands the number of times he had been able to leave a place as welcome as when he came.

With a gesture of resignation, Armand squared his shoulders. "As you wish. Once I am invested, I will not be so willing to set aside all you have done." He went out into the light ahead of Germain le-Comte and squinted up at the sky where high, thin streamers of clouds spread in from the west. "You may have rain before you go too far."

"I have endured rain before," said Germain le-Comte quietly.

Armand indicated the men-at-arms gathered near the raised portcullis, Montcerry sporting the household badge of d'Ais on his surcote. "They know you have spared them all pain, and while they are no cowards, they are grateful for your skill."

Germain le-Comte inclined his head to the men-at-arms. "I am pleased I could be of use to them. It is not often men-at-arms are made better by ballades." The humor of his remark was weak, but Montcerry chuckled.

"A good ballade is no little thing," he said as he crossed himself. "God keep you, troubador," he said for all his men.

"And give you the victory in battle and honor for your Duc," Germain le-Comte finished for him.

"Amen to that," cried Montcerry, and signaled a ragged cheer from his men. "We will be glad to see you here again, troubador."

"I will leave by the garden gate so none of you will have to raise this noisy barrier," Germain le-Comte told the warders. "You may rest easy in the night."

"Make sure one of the scullions locks it after you," the senior warder told him.

"That I will," said Germain le-Comte, knowing it would be Heugenet who locked the gate when he had gone; he went on to the main door of the keep where Guillem and Remi were waiting. They tugged their forelocks to Armand and nodded to Germain le-Comte, who told them, "Take care of this fine place. You have heavy responsibilities put upon you."

"You left your tinctures and ointments; we will use them according to your instructions," said Remi. "May God speed you on your road, and may you take no Blood Roses from any village along your way."

"A most welcome sentiment," said Germain le-Comte, relieved that the sun was setting. "I will think of you all as I travel and will probably berate myself as a fool for leaving at least once a day." He smiled quickly.

"Then come again soon," said Remi. "With new songs."

Germain le-Comte cocked his head, unwilling to lie to the two stewards. He was preparing to go back to the stable when Heugenet came to the window of the room on the floor above and called down to him. He bowed at the sound of her voice.

"You have done d'Ais many kindnesses and we are grateful for them. You and yours may command d'Ais anything at any time as long as there are descendants of this House in the world. I will have this entered in the annals of the House, and a sign for your descendants to use: a vial and its purpose to d'Ais, and the subject of the Latin book you used for instruction, I think. That should be unlikely enough to make it impossible for an imposter to abuse your legacy." She tossed him a small purse filled with a dozen of the coins he had made for her. "To ease your travels, troubador."

He bowed to her again and noticed that Frer Adonais was standing behind her, watching everything that passed between them. "You reward me beyond my deserving," he said, following the ritual of leave-taking as if he were bound on a pilgrimage. He made a show of securing the purse to his belt. "I cannot lose it now."

"Then ready yourself for the road at first light," said Heugenet, dropping the shutter on the window for emphasis.

"There will be goose stuffed with apples tonight," said Armand. "It isn't fine fare, but better since Cadon arrived two days ago. You could join us, so we can drink your health, and to your journey."

"You will do that whether I am there or not: you know I dine privately," said Germain le-Comte, who had found Frer Adonais asking questions about him in the kitchen that morning and who was already beginning to have reservations about this mysterious troubador. "Cadon will do well in your kitchen; it was good of the Count of Hainaut to send him to you."

"The Count of Hainaut wants something from me," said Armand, his face darkening at the thought of the hidden motive in this gesture of goodwill. "I suppose most everyone who does something for me now will do it because he expects to receive some benefice in return."

"Do not be discouraged, Armand," said Germain le-Comte. "And trust those men whose motives link with yours; all men act from self-interest, although sometimes the self-interest is generous: if a man has nothing at stake, he will lack commitment." He had made his back to the stable door again. "I have waterskins to fill yet, and two sacks of grain for Caesar; we may have to travel far to find better fodder than grass for him, so . . ." He held up his small hands to show his labor was not complete.

"Of course," said Armand, looking down at the toes of his solers. "I have duties inside." He hitched up his shoulder. "I have your instructions for the tincture to end my coughing spasms, and I have the jug of the tincture you have made, which will serve my needs for some time to come: I am in your debt for that as well as so many other things."

"I am in yours for the haven you provided me," said Germain le-Comte. "There have been many who turned me away." He regarded Armand steadily. "Mon Duc, the world is not as it was before the Blood Roses came; do not waste your time trying to regain what was lost, for that can never happen, no matter what the Emperor declares or the Pope decrees."

Armand nodded twice. "I will not forget," he said, and waited for Germain le-Comte to bow to him before he sauntered back across the side courtyard to the keep; Germain le-Comte watched him go with regret that he would not see the man Armand would become.

By nightfall the waterskins were filled and tied to the donkey cart and the sacks of grain were in place. The grooms had fed the horses and left the stable for their supper and beer, and Germain le-Comte was alone with Caesar. He tugged a comb through the donkey's mane, then made a final check of his hooves. "You have forgotten what it is to travel at night, but you will remember," he promised the animal as he gave him a final pat. "I am going into the loft."

He had laid a blanket on the hay, still sweet and smelling of summer, and he stretched out to wait in this very protected place. Some while after he had climbed into the loft he heard raucous singing from the keep, and smiled. When that faded there were other sounds, of the guard being posted, of the slops being taken out the garden gate to the sty where the hogs were, of the last trips to the privy before Guillem secured the servants in the keep. As he listened he reminded himself that Heugenet might still have changed her mind; he would not let that decision trouble him, for he was still convinced that she would not be truly happy in his life. He had told her the day before that he would leave at midnight; he was reviewing the route he would take toward Trier when he heard one of the mares whicker as the tack-room door opened and Heugenet, Ducesse de Verviers, stepped into the main aisle of the stable, her hands held out to feel her way in the dark.

"Germain le-Comte," she whispered as if afraid she might receive no answer.

"The ladder is by Caesar's stall," he said as quietly as he could, his night-seeing eyes unhampered by the near-absence of light. "About twenty steps ahead and to the right." He went to hold his end of the ladder steady to help her climb to the loft.

"I have it," she said as she took hold of it; of necessity she continued to whisper. "I am coming up, Germain le-Comte."

"You need not rush; we have time," he assured her.

"How long will you need?" she asked as she made her way up the rungs, fussing with her skirts as she climbed. "Are you going to drain me of blood?"

He almost let go of the ladder. "What sort of monster do you take me for?" he demanded without raising his voice. "No. Certainly not. What made you think I would?"

"Frer Adonais: he warned of demons who drain Christians of their blood and their souls at the same time. He said when God lays His Hand so heavily on His children, the Devil comes also, to harvest those whose faith is weak." She was two rungs below the loft now and she stared into the darkness in an attempt to read his face; she was doing all that she could to control the fear the monk had inspired in her.

"If that is what you think I will do, why did you come?" His words were sharp but there was a sadness in them that banished her fear.

"Because I cannot believe you would betray me so," she answered.

"Thank God for small favors," he exclaimed sardonically.

"Frer Adonais said we must cast out Devils with the fires of Hell." She stepped into the loft. "My father used to have poachers drawn and quartered outside the church after Mass, and that was with the priests' blessings." Reaching for his hands, she steadied her nerve. "Is it wrong to die unblessed?"

"You will come to my life by moonrise, in the middle of the night: you may attend Mass at sunrise," he promised her. "If that is what you wish to do."

She drew him to her. "Yes." Her answer was soft but so filled with conviction that she trembled against him. "How will it happen?"

He faltered. "I have a soporific; when we have exchanged blood, you will drink it and sleep. When you wake you will be of my nature." He stroked her back. "If you have any doubts, Heugenet, do not undertake—"

"I have no doubts," she assured him, tugging on his arm in excitement. "I am ready."

"Then come with me," he said, helping her to find her way to the blanket. "We have a long time until midnight."

She had not worn a gorget or wimple. "You can bite me now, if you like," she told him as she ran her hand along her neck.

"By all the forgotten gods, Heugenet, what do you take me for?" There was more anguish than anger in his outburst. He waited until she regarded him with full attention; his voice was deep, penetrating, and gentle. "I am a vampire, not a ravening animal, as you should realize. What I seek in blood is the whole of you, and our touching. Tonight greater intimacy is wanted."

Chastened, she released him. "I . . . I didn't think," she whispered, her need to apologize making her hesitate as she went on. "I thought changing me to your life . . . it wasn't like taking a mistress, I assumed it was like getting an heir; that you would do the act with dispatch so that it would be over."

The enormity of her observation shook him to the core. "Heugenet, Heugenet," he murmured, all animosity gone as quickly as it had arisen. "This is our farewell to one another. What we have now must be enough to sustain the love that will be part of the bond of blood that will endure to the True Death itself." His lambent caress sharpened her desire for him as his arms enfolded her.

She pulled at his houppelande, a soft, urgent cry escaping her. As she pushed away from him, she began to wriggle out of her old cotehardie, finally casting the garment away from her. Standing in her chamise, she confronted him. "Well?"

His houppelande was half-unlaced as he smiled at her. "Would you like to do the rest?" he offered. Without speaking she closed the distance between them and reached for the laces. She worked them loose and began to remove it. She cursed once under her breath, and felt his small hand close on her wrist. "You need not rush, Heugenet. This is not a race."

"Then what is it?" She was stunned by her own audacity, and was about to ask his pardon for this lapse when he spoke.

"It is a transformation," he told her as he came up to her again. "I would like you to enjoy all that passes between us, so that when you remember this change, you will do so with happiness."

"If it comes from you, how could I not?" she asked, resting her head on his shoulder.

"It has happened before," he said, a hint of dryness in his tone: Csimenae and Nicoris came to mind, the old ache they evoked in him making him wince inwardly; he shook off their recalled presence.

"It cannot happen with me," she promised him as she caressed his face. "I know what you are giving me. I sought it."

"Yes," he murmured, her nearness filling his senses with her. He opened her lips with his own, hearing her pulse with his fingers as well as his ears. His hands slipped inside her chamise, persuasive and exciting in their explorations, touching everywhere reverently as if her flesh were holy.

She sighed as her anxiety finally ended; she closed her eyes and was caught in the sensual feast her body provided. Every tingle, every frisson, every eruption of pleasure she treasured as Germain le-Comte magnified her responses with the intensity of his esurience. She repeated his name, making a liturgy of it, enshrining him in her soul as she was brought to the brink of release; at the culmination of her rapture, he used the brooch from her chamise to nick the flesh just above his collarbone. As he bent his head to her neck, he pressed her mouth to his own wound and let their ecstasy carry them.

He came to himself sooner than she did; he luxuriated in the fulfillment that still echoed within him, his being still replete with her gratification. Kissing her brow, he reached out for his houppelande and carefully pulled the vial from the pocket high in the triangular sleeve. Then he lay still and waited for her to speak.

Her sigh was eloquent; she snuggled closer to his side and said, "Thank you thank you thank you." She traced the line of his brow with two fingers, fixing him in her memory. "I'm ready now."

For her sake, he reminded her that she did not have to die tonight. "After what we have done, you will come to my life when you die, no matter what," he said to her, stroking her shoulder as he spoke.

"No," she said. "I want to choose the time, and I want to be prepared. I'm ready." She held out a steady hand. "Give me the tincture."

He handed her the vial. "There is no pain in it, only sleep," he pledged to her.

"And your life when the moon rises," she said as she removed the stopper, sniffed, and drank. "It's a bit sour under the sweetness." When she handed the vial back to him, she kissed the corner of his mouth.

He eased her against his deep chest, her head tucked under his, one hand resting on her hair. "You will find you are stronger than you were; be careful how you use your strength, for people notice strength in women, and you will not want them questioning it; sunlight will burn you easily, and you will have to line the soles of your footwear with your native earth to be able to walk in the sun. The earth will have to be renewed after every new moon. You will line your mattress with your native earth as well, and the seats of your carriage, or traveling will be unpleasant and you will become severely nauseated crossing running water."

She murmured a few disjointed endearments and began to breathe more deeply.

His voice was soothing as he went on, "Anything that breaks the spine is harmful or fatal to us. Fire can kill us. A stake that breaks our backs can kill us. We cannot drown, but water will immobilize us until we are eaten or broken. Blood—any blood—will feed us; but nourishment comes from touching. We cannot starve but we will madden with hunger. Visiting people in sleep can provide sustenance, and it will suffice when other, more fulfilling contact is impossible, but eventually you will need the intimacy, the knowledge, the comprehension that comes from the knowledge of another."

Heugenet was asleep now, her body relaxed, her pulse slow and steady.

Patiently Germain le-Comte continued, "You will not need to sleep much when you are well-fed, but when you do, you will sleep in a stupor so profound that some may think you dead; have your servants know how to wake you, which can be done with bright light: it is unpleasant but it never fails. Because you will not sleep much, you will be able to go about the world when everyone else is abed. Then you will be able to deepen their slumber so you may find sustenance without risking discovery. To visit someone in sleep, wait until you are certain they cannot easily be roused, and speak to them softly. Tell them how pleasant their dream is, how it will bring them joy. When you taste their blood you will know their dream more than their totality, but you will satisfy your esurience. If the dreams are frightening or filled with grief, do not taste of the dreamer, for fear and loss are poor nourishment. If the dreams begin in sorrow and end in its alleviation, speak to the dreamer of anodyne things, to mitigate their suffering."

Her breathing faltered; the rhythm of her heart stumbled.

"Do not blame them for the brevity of their lives, Heugenet, cherish them for it." He kissed her hair as she died. "The moon will rise soon." He held her as her flesh began to cool.

Some time later she shook herself and pushed up from his supine form. "It did not work," she said, her disappointment showing in the droop of her shoulders.

He laid his hand over hers. "The moon has risen," he said softly.

She stared down at him, reading his features easily in the dark. "It isn't wise to have a light in here; you told me so yourself."

"There is only moonlight," he said. "Go to the loft-door if you doubt me." He moved so she could rise.

She shrugged but did as he suggested, frowning a little as she looked about for the lanthorn he must have concealed in the loft. The loft-door was ajar, letting in a wedge of moonlight, pale as water. For a short time Heugenet stood in its spill, her thoughts in confusion as she attempted to resolve what she saw with what she believed. Then she dropped to her knees and crossed herself. "I have done it," she cried out, then clapped her hand over her mouth.

Below her one of the mares whuffled, but there was no other indication she had been heard until Germain le-Comte came up behind her and laid his hands on her shoulders. "You are blood of my blood now, Heugenet. You and I are bound by it until the True Death."

She leaned back against him, feeling his strength for what seemed the first time. A cool wind plucked at her chamise but did not chill her. For an instant she was afraid, and then she chuckled. "It would be easy to forget all the ills of the world."

"Easy and foolish," Germain le-Comte said sharply. "They are many and we are few, and they loathe us."

"I never loathed you," she said, turning to look at him.

"No, but you did not know my true nature until you had some affection for me." He gave her a moment to consider this. "You will have to be careful; many eyes will be on you, and not all of them will be your friends."

"I know that," she said somberly. "The House of d'Ais has enemies."

He chose his next words carefully. "If you can find an ally, do not endanger him and yourself with bringing him to your life before he dies in his full time. I have warned you already: to have more than one vampire in a place like this is to bring about discovery and oppression. Be careful of how you bestow your love: you may knowingly love five or six times without risk to your lover, but then it is a certain thing that your lover will walk again after death. If that happens, prepare him for his life before he comes to it." He kissed the side of her face as she rested against him.

"I will remember," she vowed. "I will remember all." With that, she turned around to face him. "You must not linger."

"No," he agreed, and started away from the loft-door. "Be sure to brush all the hay off your clothing or your servants will wonder where you have been."

She picked up her cotehardie and slapped at it several times while she watched him pull on his houppelande and tighten the lacings. "You will not be back this way, will you?"

"Perhaps, in time," he said, deliberately evading her question.

"Germain le-Comte," she said reproachfully.

"All right: I will not return for at least half a century, and not as Germain le-Comte, troubador. Is that what you wanted to know?" He saw her nod. "If you live for many years, you will need to travel, too. Otherwise there will be questions."

"Oh, I've thought of that already. I am going to wear mourning from now on. The veil will hide my face and my relatives will not try to find a new husband for me." She held out her hands to him. "I am going to miss you more than life itself."

Though he did not take her hands, his chuckle was compassionate. "In time you may change your mind." He bent and picked up the blanket, folding it with care in spite of the hay clinging to it.

She stood still as he finished this task. Realizing he was about to leave, she said softly, "To think it was Blood Roses that brought you to me." Seeing the startled look in his eyes, she added, "I am thankful for that."

"For Blood Roses?" he asked, troubled by what she said.

"No; that you were with me when—" She ran a few steps to him to embrace him one last time; she could not bring herself to kiss him. They stood together for a short while, and then she stepped away. "It is time you were gone."

"Yes." He took her hands and kissed them. "Ma Ducesse."

"Go harness your donkey. I will wait until you leave." She began to pick bits of hay from her cotehardie. "Go."

He inclined his head before he went down the ladder. He haltered Caesar and led him out of his stall to be harnessed to the cart; he could feel Heugenet above him in the loft, as he knew he would feel her if he were in China and she remained at Mon Gardien. When the last buckle was fastened, he tied a long rope to the halter for a lead, then opened the stable-door. As he led Caesar out of the stable, he called up to Heugenet, "Lock the gate after me."

If there was an answer, he did not hear it; he glanced at the night-sky and the waning moon hanging a little way above the horizon. At the garden gate Caesar balked, as if aware that this departure was final. He resisted all coaxing, then, in the way of donkeys, moved at last as if it were his idea. Germain le-Comte led him down to the path that skirted the village, then on to the road, past the turning to Cascade-en-Foudre. The troubador set a steady pace, not too swift to be tiring but one that ate up distance, reaching the merchants' road to Trier before the night was over: he did not look back until he and Caesar had topped the rise, four leagues to the east of Mon Gardien, when the sky ahead of him was beginning to pale, when he knew the castle would be lost to sight.

Text of a letter from Frer Adonais to the Archbishop of Liege and Aachen.

To the most puissant Prince of the Church, Your Grace the Archbishop of Liege and Aachen, the obedient observations of your most humble servant, Frer Adonais, regarding the young Duc de Verviers, Armand d'Ais, and his mother, the Ducesse, in accordance with Your Grace's private instructions, and as a demonstration of my devotion to Your Grace's cause in the world.

I have been at Mon Gardien for a month now, and I have been at pains to discover all I might in regard to the ambitions of the new Duc, Armand d'Ais. I have found the young man to be of a secretive disposition; he prepares his own dispatches, not deigning to avail himself of my services as his clerk, and keeps all his records in the strong-room under lock. This may itself be significant, for it has been said that before Armand became his father's heir, Armandal intended this son for the Church and encouraged him to acquire those skills valued by the Church. I can inform you that Armand reads Latin essays and poetry for pleasure, or so he claims.

In regard to the Ducesse, she is thus far a model of fidelity; she has announced her intention to mourn her husband for the rest of her life, in spite of the fact that as the widow of a Duc she might reasonably expect to have suitors for her hand, her fortune, and her connections. I have lauded her pious intentions and cautioned her against the lack of steadiness of purpose that is forever the failing of women. If she is still professing such dedication in two years, I will own myself convinced of her faithfulness.

I have gone twice to Sant-Amienne to help in giving Christian comfort to those suffering from Blood Roses, and I am encouraged to report that the numbers of those coming to the nuns for care is waning. The Sisters themselves have remarked upon it, and have sung Psalms of thanksgiving for what they hope is their deliverance from the Great Dying. They have lost many of their own numbers to this great calamity, and it is their hope that they will see an end to it before the next Pascal Mass.

The men-at-arms at Mon Gardien are few in number; the Emperor has recalled four of the men to his service, leaving only a handful of soldiers to man this castle, and the forts of Verviers. It is my understanding that the men-at-arms have encouraged the young Duc to petition the Emperor for an increase in their numbers so that the castle and the forts may hold the frontier for the Emperor when the war between France and England is resumed; everyone here expects the English to attempt to secure Flanders and Brabant as a means of forcing the French to acquiesce to the English claims; in that case, Verviers becomes crucial in maintaining the Empire and therefore deserving of full garrison.

Since many of the servants here at Mon Gardien are new to their posts, I can learn little about how much the Great Dying has changed Verviers.

There is a new cook, and most of the scullions have been taken from the castle's village. It is an advancement for the scullions, but it means that their ties to the place are stronger than is their loyalty to the cook, and they do not gossip except among themselves. I have heard from Remi, who stewards the dowager's house, that the troubador who was here for some months had some skill at treating injuries and that some of the villagers think the troubador was a wizard come to care for them. I am attempting to remind them of God's Mercy so that they will cease to repeat stories about the troubador.

This castle, this Duchy, may be small, but, as you have shown me, its importance is very great. I am growing more aware of how well-founded your concerns are in regard to Verviers. The French would benefit from an alliance with Duc Armand, as would the Comte de Hainaut, or the Comte de Flanders, for many of the same reasons that Verviers is important to the English and to the Emperor. Those who have the ear of the Duc will be able to advise him in ways that could influence the course of nations for years to come.

You must see, Your Grace, how difficult it is going to be for me. If I cannot put my hands on the correspondence of the Duc, I am at a loss as to how I may discover his intentions in regard to his neighbors. He keeps his own counsel, which I take as the arrogance of his youth. His brothers may have reason to reprove him in future. I am striving to show the Duc how important your good opinion may be to his success in time to come. I have spoken to the Ducesse, but her understanding is not great, being that she is a woman and subject to the ills of her sex. I will persevere; I have been here only a short while, and work of this sort is done over time. I ask you to continue to rely on me; I am wholly committed to you, Your Grace, and to your cause.

Frer Adonais

By my own hand at Mon Gardien in the Duchy de Verviers on the 18th day of October in the 1350th Year of Grace.

EPILOGUE

*T*ext of a letter from Heugenet, Ducesse de Verviers at Mon Gardien, to Germain le-Comte, sent in care of Atta Olivia Clemens at her estate Sanza Pari near Rome.

To the troubador Germain le-Comte, or whatever name you are using now, the fond greetings of Heugenet, Ducesse de Verviers.

It has been thirty-eight years since I have seen you, and yet you remain as vivid to me today as you did all those years ago, when the Blood Roses bloomed for the first time. They have come twice since, as I suppose you must know, but not so severely as they did when you were here.

I am writing to tell you that my son, Armand, Duc de Verviers, has died, leaving his son Bernard to succeed him. His second wife, a daughter of the Duc de Brittanie, survives him, along with two other sons and four daughters, one of whom is married to the second son of the Comte d'Auvergne. You perceive we have increased our ties to France, and have been shown favor for it. Our garrison is secure and our lands are in good heart. So we have done well. As you can see, I have even learned to read and write: Armand taught me.

My long widowhood is about to come to an end. With Armand dead, my purpose is gone, and my age has become so remarkable that I cannot continue it much longer without very real risk of questions being asked that I cannot answer. I have considered your methods, but I dislike travel, and I do not want to spend decades in exile from Mon Gardien.

So I will end my life—your life. I have made all my arrangements. By the time this reaches Rome, I should be finally in my grave. If you come here again you will find me lying under the floor on the east side of the chapel. Do not think I do not value the gift you gave me all those years ago. I have thanked you every day since for your goodness to me, and your love. But I find I do not want to live in a world that has no place for me. Before that happens, I will take my leave on my terms, as I did when you made me one of your blood.

I wish I could console you, or comfort you, or ease your grief, but I know I cannot, for I know you. Surely that is the most generous of all the gifts you have given me, and the one for which I have no thanks sufficient to honor.

You said that our love would last until the True Death, but with all the love I still have for you, and the joy it has brought me, and still brings me as I remember it, I think it may continue beyond. For your sake, and mine, I pray it is true.

Heugenet

By my own hand on the 19th day of February in the 1388th Year of Grace, at Mon Gardien.